I'm so confused I might as well be drunk. 8/13/00
5:59 pm
-Slack

TWENTIETH CENTURY FOX PRESENTS A FIGMENT FILM

LEONARDO DiCAPRIO

"THE BEACH"

TILDA SWINTON VIRGINIE LEDOYEN GUILLAUME CANET AND ROBERT CARLYLE

CO-PRODUCER CALLUM McDOUGALL MUSIC BY ANGELO BADALAMENTI COSTUME DESIGNER RACHAEL FLEMING

EDITOR MASAHIRO HIRAKUBO PRODUCTION DESIGNER ANDREW McALPINE

CINEMATOGRAPHY DARIUS KHONDJI, A.S.C., A.F.C BASED UPON THE BOOK BY ALEX GARLAND SCREENPLAY BY JOHN HODGE

PRODUCED BY ANDREW MACDONALD DIRECTED BY DANNY BOYLE

"This exceptional first novel by twenty-six-year-old Alex Garland creates a picture of an ideal society gone awry . . . *The Beach* is very much a hallucinatory *Lord of the Flies* for twentysomethings. An action novel that provokes subtle responses, *The Beach* takes in ideas about man's inevitable progress from noble savage to social breakdown—the line of thought followed by Golding and by Aldous Huxley in *Island*—but it is also concerned with the related tradition of nature versus art."
—*Times Literary Supplement*

"Generation X has its first great novel. . . . May be the best novel written by anyone currently younger than thirty. . . . *Lord of the Flies* . . . *On the Road* . . . *Animal Farm* . . . *The Beach* can hang with those classics on a purely literary level and as a postmodern update of them."
—*The Oregonian* (Portland, OR)

"Remarkable . . . A classic story of generational envy and displacement. Much like the crystal-clear lagoon where it takes place, this astonishingly assured first novel is a smooth surface behind whose sunny scrim hides heaps of bad juju. . . . Echoing *Dog Soldiers* as much as *Lord of the Flies*, Garland discovers the hell lurking in heaven's tide pools while delivering as much karmic payback as anything since *Treasure Island*. Primitives vs. sophisticates, nature vs. culture, life vs. art—it's all here, in language whose gripping and deceptive simplicity masks something dreadful and true. Garland's timeless fluid sentences seem to seek the clarity that Hemingway sought, without descending into self-parody for an instant. . . . Garland's deceptively transparent book would have been just as momentous and refreshing if it had been written twenty years ago. Take it for what it is: a luminous voyage into the dark side of humanity's increasingly tenuous dreams of paradise."
—Salon.com

"Garland's provocative style—somewhere between Joseph Conrad, Bret Easton Ellis, and Stephen King—creates a modern-day Eden where Nintendo Game Boy, *Apocalypse Now*, and a drug-trafficking Thai militia blend seamlessly into the landscape."
—*Vogue*

"The novel's detailed account of their journey is not only suspenseful but surprisingly plausible. . . . Garland . . . has a clear, engaging storytelling style and a vivid imagination. Deftly, he uses real-life travel details—smells, optical effects, quirks of language, social rituals—to keep the reader's disbelief at bay. . . . His novel is a genuine page-turner, full of color and menace. . . . The final chapters are suitably nightmarish and exciting." —*The New York Times Book Review*

"*The Beach* makes for a relevant and fascinating read. . . . An excellent critique of the backpacker phenomenon—its nouveau colonialism and its tragically misdirected idealism."

—*Time Out*

"A mesmerizing first novel that manages to be many things at once: a smart look at a generation way beyond mere disillusionment, an anti-travelogue to the most exotic of locales, a study in small-group psychology, and a convincing profile in madness. All this, and the dynamics of a fast-paced thriller."

—*Kirkus Reviews* (starred review)

"Garland is a wonder; he's able to write unrelentingly suspenseful, downright hallucinatory action scenes, then balance them with passages of chillingly accurate psychology. His intensely imagined tale is, on one level, a brilliant update of *Lord of the Flies,* and on another, a wholly original and unsettling depiction of psyches shaped by the bewildering messages of Looney Tunes, *Apocalypse Now,* Nintendo, and the age-old cult of oblivion. *The Beach* has cult status scrawled all over it."

—*Booklist* (starred review)

"Alex Garland has given us a shrewd, subtle protest against the hipness of contemporary travel culture. *The Beach* is a suspenseful story about the heedlessness of youth in one of the most treacherous of psychological landscapes—paradise. Coolly observed, expertly told, *The Beach* has that rare power of seeming to have captured the sensibility of a generation."

—Darryl Pinckney, author of *High Cotton*

continued . . .

"Compelling and very contemporary . . . But what makes the book memorable, along with vivid writing and sometimes hair-raisingly tense episodes, is its cultural and social detail. . . . An impressive new writer has arrived."

—*Sunday Times* (London)

"A riveting read about disaffected twentysomethings searching for a real-life Eden as they backpack through the pop-culture wasteland of Asia." —*Details*

"Garland shows a precociously sure hand in this taut, exotic thriller." —*People*

"Amphetamine-paced . . . Richard's nicotine-fueled narrative of how the denizens of the beach see their comity shatter and break into factions is taut with suspense . . ."

—*Publishers Weekly*

"The storyline is winningly compulsive, the writing deceptively simple in this, frankly, brilliantly conceived first novel."

—Q *Magazine* (five-star review)

"Steeped in pop culture, hypnotically readable, the book is an impressive achievement for one so young." —*Mademoiselle*

"[W]onderful . . . [Garland] writes cannily of the doomed search for authenticity that's inherent in both postmodern youth and in travel itself. . . . *And* it's a ripping yarn."

—*Seattle Weekly*

"[G]ripping, intelligent and written with a discipline many young writers only grow into." —*New York Newsday*

THE BEACH

alex garland

riverhead books, *new york*

Riverhead Books
Published by The Berkley Publishing Group
A division of Penguin Putnam Inc.
375 Hudson Street
New York, New York 10014

Book design by Nicola Ferguson

First Riverhead hardcover edition: February 1997
First Riverhead trade paperback edition: February 1998
Riverhead trade paperback ISBN: 1-57322-797-8

The Penguin Putnam Inc. World Wide Web site address is
http://www.penguinputnam.com

The Library of Congress has catalogued the Riverhead hardcover edition as follows:

Garland, Alex.
The beach / Alex Garland.
p. cm.
ISBN 1-57322-048-5
I. Title
PR6057.A639B4 1997 96-25033 CIP
823′.914—dc20

Printed in the United States of America

25 24 23 22 21

for suzy

THE BEACH

boom-boom

Vietnam, me love you long time. All day, all night, me love you long time.

"Delta One-Niner, this is Alpha patrol. We are on the northeast face of hill Seven-Zero-Five and taking fire, I repeat, taking fire. Immediate air assistance required on the fucking double. Can you confirm?"

Radio static.

"I say again, this is Alpha patrol and we are taking fire. Immediate air assistance required. Can you confirm? We are taking fire. Please confirm. We are— Incoming, incoming!"

Boom.

". . . Medic!"

Dropping acid on the Mekong Delta, smoking grass through a rifle barrel, flying on a helicopter with opera blasting out of loudspeakers, tracer fire and paddy field scenery, the smell of napalm in the morning.

Long time.

Yea, though I walk through the valley of death I will fear no evil, for my name is Richard. I was born in 1974.

bangkok

6:07 pm

I am chewing on a whole pack of Trident like Elliot bet Rizzo he couldn't do nearly a year ago. I am strung tight.

bitch

The first I heard of the beach was in Bangkok, on the Ko Sanh Road. The Ko Sanh Road was backpacker land. Almost all the buildings had been converted to guest houses, there were long-distance telephone booths with air-con, the cafés showed brand-new Hollywood films on video, and you couldn't walk ten feet without passing a bootleg tape stall. The main function of the street was as a decompression chamber for those about to leave or enter Thailand; a halfway house between the East and the West.

I'd landed at Bangkok in the late afternoon, and by the time I got to Ko Sanh it was dark. My taxi driver winked and told me that at one end of the street was a police station, so I asked him to drop me off at the other end. I wasn't planning on crime but I wanted to oblige his conspiratorial charm. Not that it made much difference at which end one stayed, because the police obviously weren't active. I caught the smell of grass as soon as I got out of the cab, and half the travelers weaving past me were stoned.

The driver left me outside a guest house with an eating area open to the street. As I studied it, checking the clientele to gauge what kind of place it was, a thin man at the table nearest me leaned over and touched my arm. I glanced down. He was, I guessed, one of the heroin hippies that float around India and Thailand. He'd probably come to Asia ten years ago and turned an occasional dabble into an addiction. His skin was old, though I'd have believed he was in his thirties. The way he was looking at me, I had the feeling I was being sized up as someone to rip off.

"What?" I said warily.

He pulled an expression of surprise and held up the palms of his hands. Then he curled his finger and thumb into the O-shaped perfection sign, and pointed into the guest house.

"It's a good place?"

He nodded.

I looked again at the people around the tables. They were mostly young and friendly-looking, some watching the TV and some chattering over their dinner.

"Okay." I smiled at him in case he wasn't a heroin addict but just a friendly mute. "I'm sold."

He returned the smile and turned back to the video screen.

Quarter of an hour later I was settling into a room that was a little larger than a double bed. I can be accurate about it because there was a double bed in the room, and on each of its four sides there was a foot of space. My bag could just slide into the gap.

One wall was concrete—the side of the building. The others were Formica and bare. They moved when I touched them. I had the feeling that if I leaned against one it would fall over and maybe hit another, and all the walls of the neighboring rooms would collapse like dominoes. Just short of the ceiling, the walls stopped, and across the space was a strip of metal mosquito netting. The netting almost upheld the illusion of being in a confined, personal area, until I lay down on my bed. As soon as I relaxed, I began to hear cockroaches scuttling around in the other rooms.

At my head end I had a French couple in their late teens—a beautiful, slim girl with a suitably handsome boy attached. They'd been leaving their room as I got to mine and we exchanged nods as we passed in the corridor. The other end was empty. Through the netting I could see that the light was off, and anyway, if it had been occupied I would have heard the person breathing. It was the last room on the corridor, so I presumed it faced the street and had a window.

On the ceiling was a fan, strong enough on full setting to stir the air. For a while I did nothing but lie on the bed and look up at it. It was calming, following the revolutions, and with the mixture of heat and soft breeze, I felt I could drift to sleep. That suited me. West to east is the worst for jet lag, and I wanted to fall into the right sleeping pattern on the first night.

I switched off the light. Enough of a glow from the corridor outside came through for me to still see the fan. Soon I was asleep.

Once or twice I was aware of people in the corridor, and I thought I heard the French couple coming back, then leaving again. But the noises never woke me fully and I was always able to slip back into the dream I'd been having before. Until I heard the man's footsteps. They were different, too creepy to doze through. They had no rhythm or weight and dragged on the floor.

A muttered stream of English swearwords floated into my room as he jiggled the padlock on his door. Then there was a loud sigh, the lock opened with a click, and his light came on. The mosquito netting cast a patterned shadow on my ceiling.

Frowning, I looked at my watch. It was two in the morning—late afternoon, English time. I wondered if I might get back to sleep.

The man slumped onto his bed, giving the wall between us an alarming shake. He coughed awhile, then I heard the crackle of a joint being rolled. Soon there was blue smoke caught in the light, rolling through the netting.

Aside from the occasional deep exhalation, he was silent. I drifted back to sleep, almost.

"Bitch," said a voice. I opened my eyes.

"Fucking bitch. We're both as good as . . ."

The voice paused for a coughing fit.

"Dead."

I was wide awake now, so I sat up in bed.

"Cancer in the corals, blue water, my bitch. Fucking Christ, did me in," the man continued.

He had an accent but at first my sleep-fogged head couldn't place it.

"Bitch," he said again, spitting out the word.

A Scottish accent. Beach.

There was a scrabbling sound on the wall. For a moment I thought he might be trying to push it over, and I had a vision of myself being sandwiched between the Formica board and the bed. Then his head appeared through the mosquito netting, silhouetted, facing me.

"Hey," he said.

I didn't move. I was sure he couldn't see into my room.

"Hey. I know you're listening. In there, I know you're awake."

He lifted up a finger and gave the netting an exploratory poke. It popped away from where it was stapled to the Formica. His hand stuck through.

"Here."

A glowing red object sailed through the darkness, landing on the bed in a little shower of sparks. The joint he'd been smoking. I grabbed it to stop it from burning the sheets.

"Yeah," said the man, and laughed quietly. "Got you now. I saw you take the butt."

For a few seconds I couldn't get a handle on the situation. I kept thinking—what if I actually had been asleep? The sheets might have caught fire. I might have burned to death. The panic flipped into anger, but I suppressed it. The man was way too much of a random element for me to lose my temper. I could still only see his head and that was backlit, in shadow.

Holding up the joint, I asked, "Do you want this back?"

"You were listening," he replied, ignoring me. "Heard me talking about the beach."

". . . You've got a loud voice."

"Tell me what you heard."

"I didn't hear anything."

". . . Heard nothing?"

He paused for a moment, then pressed his face into the netting. "You're lying."

"No. I was asleep. You just woke me up . . . when you threw this joint at me."

"You were *listening,*" he hissed.

"I don't care if you don't believe me."

"I don't believe you."

"Well . . . I don't care . . . Look." I stood on the bed so our heads were at the same level, and held up the joint to the hole he'd made. "If you want this, take it. All I want is to go to sleep."

As I lifted my hand he pulled back, moving out of the shadow. His face was flat like a boxer's, the nose busted too many times to have any form, and his lower jaw was too large for the top half of his skull. It would have been threatening if not for the body it was attached to. The large jaw tapered into a neck so thin it seemed incredible that it supported his head, and his T-shirt hung slackly on coat hanger shoulders.

Past him I saw into his room. There was a window, as I'd assumed, but he'd taped it up with pages from a newspaper. Apart from that it was bare.

His hand reached through the gap and plucked the butt from my fingers.

"Okay," I said, thinking I'd gained some kind of control. "Now leave me alone."

"No," he replied flatly.

". . . No?"

"No."

"Why not? What do you . . . Do you want something?"

"Yep." He grinned. "I want lots. And that's why"—again he pushed his face into the netting—"I won't leave you alone."

But as soon as he said it he seemed to change his mind. He ducked out of sight, obscured by the angle of the wall. I stayed standing for a couple of seconds, confused but wanting to reinforce my authority—like it wasn't me stepping down, just him. Then I heard him relight his joint. I let that mark the end of it and lay back down on the bed.

Even after he'd switched his light off, twenty or so minutes later, I still couldn't get back to sleep. I was too keyed up, too much stuff was running through my head. Beaches and bitches, exhaustion; jumpy with adrenaline. Perhaps, given an hour of silence, I might have relaxed, but soon after the man's light went out the French couple came back to their room and started having sex.

It was impossible, hearing their panting and feeling the vibrations of their shifting bed, not to visualize them. The brief glimpse of the girl's face I'd caught in the corridor was stuck in my head. An exquisite face. Dark skin and dark hair, brown eyes. Full lips.

After they'd finished I had a powerful urge for a cigarette, empathy maybe, but I stopped myself. I knew that if I did they'd hear me rustling the packet or lighting the match. The illusion of their privacy would be broken.

Instead I concentrated on lying as still as I could, for as long as I could. It turned out I could do it for quite a long while.

geography

6:14 pm

The Ko Sanh Road woke early. At five, muffled car horns began sounding off from the street outside, Bangkok's version of the dawn chorus. Then the water pipes under the floor started to rattle as the guest house staff took their showers. I could hear their conversations, the plaintive sound of Thai rising above the splashing water.

Lying on my bed, listening to the morning noises, I felt the tension of the previous night become unreal and distant. Although I couldn't understand what the staff were saying to each other, their chattering and occasional laughter conveyed a sense of normality. They were doing what they did every morning, their thoughts only connected to routine. I imagined they might be discussing who would go for kitchen supplies in the market that day or who would be sweeping the halls.

Around five-thirty a few door bolts clicked open as the early-bird travelers emerged and the die-hard partygoers from Patpong returned. Two German girls clattered up the wooden stairs at the far end of my corridor, apparently wearing clogs. I realized that the dreamless snatches of sleep I'd managed were finished, so I decided to have a cigarette, the one I'd denied myself a few hours before.

The early-morning smoke was a tonic. I gazed upward, an empty matchbox for an ashtray balanced on my stomach, and every puff I blew into the ceiling fan lifted my spirits a little higher. Before long my mind turned to thoughts of food. I left my room to see if there was any breakfast to be had in the eating area downstairs.

There were already a few travelers at the tables, dozily sipping glasses of black coffee. One of them, still sitting in the same chair as yesterday evening, was the helpful mute/heroin addict. He'd been there all night, judging by his glazed stare. As I sat down I gave him a friendly smile and he tilted his head in reply.

I began studying the menu, a once white sheet of paper with such an extensive list of dishes that I felt making a choice was beyond my ability. Then I was distracted by a delicious smell. A kitchen boy had wandered over with a tray of fruit pancakes. He distributed them to a group of Americans, cutting off a good-natured argument about train times to Chiang Mai.

One of them noticed me eyeing their food and he pointed at his plate. "Banana pancakes," he said. "The business."

I nodded. "They smell pretty good."

"Taste better. English?"

"Uh-huh."

"Been here long?"

"Since yesterday evening. You?"

"A week," he replied, and popped a piece of pancake in his mouth, looking away as he did so. I guessed that signaled the end of the exchange.

The kitchen boy came over to my table and stood there, gazing at me expectantly through sleepy eyes.

"One banana pancake, please," I said, obliged into making a snap decision.

"You wan' order one banan' pancake?"

"Please."

"You wan' order drink?"

"Uh, a Coke. No, a Sprite."

"You wan' one banan' pancake, one Spri'."

"Please."

He strolled back toward the kitchen, and a sudden warm swell of happiness washed over me. The sun was bright on the road outside. A man was setting up his stall on the pavement, arranging bootleg tapes into rows. Next to him a small girl sliced pineapples, cutting the tough skin into neat, spiraling designs. Behind her an even smaller girl used a rag to keep the flies at bay.

I lit my second cigarette of the day, not wanting it, just feeling it was the right thing to do.

The French girl appeared without her boyfriend and without any shoes. Her legs were brown and slim, her skirt short. She padded delicately through the café. We all watched her. The heroin mute, the group of Americans, the Thai kitchen boys. We all saw the way she moved her hips to slide between the tables, and the silver bracelets on her wrists. When her eyes glanced around the room we looked away, and when she turned to the street we looked back.

After breakfast I decided to have a wander around Bangkok, or at the very least, the streets around Ko Sanh. I paid for my food and headed for my room to get some more cash, thinking I might need to get a taxi somewhere.

There was an old woman at the top of the stairs, cleaning the windows with a mop. Water was pouring off the glass and down to the floor. The lady herself was completely soaked, and as the mop lurched around the windows it skimmed dangerously close to a bare light bulb hanging from the ceiling.

"Excuse me," I said, checking I wasn't about to be included in the puddle of potential death that was expanding on the floor. She turned around. "That light is dangerous with the water."

"Yes," she replied. Her teeth were either black and rotten or as yellow as mustard, and it looked like she had a mouth full of wasps. "Hot-hot." She deliberately brushed the light bulb with the edge of her mop. Water boiled angrily on the bulb and a curl of steam rose up to the ceiling.

I shuddered. "Careful! The electricity could kill you."

6:19 too much chewing gum can give a stomach ache

"Hot."

"Yes but . . ." I paused, seeing that I was onto a nonstarter language-wise, then decided to soldier on.

I glanced around. We were the only two people on the landing.

"Okay, look."

I began a short mime of mopping down the windows before sticking my imaginary mop into the light. Then I began jerking around, electrocuted.

She placed a shriveled hand on my arm to stop my convulsions.

"Hey, man," she drawled in a voice too high-pitched to describe as mellow. "It cool."

I raised my eyebrows, not sure I'd heard her words correctly.

"Chill," she added. "No worry."

"Right," I said, trying to accept the union of Thai crone and hippy jargon with grace. She'd clearly been working on the Ko Sanh Road a long time. Feeling chided, I started walking down the corridor to my room. "Hey," she called after me. "Le'er for you, man."

I stopped. "A what?"

"Le'er."

". . . Letter?"

"*Le'er!* On you *door!*"

I nodded my thanks, wondering how she knew which was my room, and continued down the corridor. Sure enough, taped to my door was an envelope. On it was written, "Here is a map," in labored joined-up writing. I was still so surprised at the old woman's strange vocabulary that I took the letter in my stride.

The woman watched me from down the corridor, leaning on her mop. I held up the envelope. "Got it. Thanks. Do you know who it's from?"

She frowned, not understanding the question.

"Did you see anybody put this here?"

I started another little mime and she shook her head.

"Well, anyway, thanks."

"No worry," she said, and returned to her windows.

A couple of minutes later I was sitting on my bed with the ceiling fan chilling the back of my neck and the map in my hands. Beside me the empty envelope rustled under the breeze. Outside the old woman clanked up the stairs with her mop and bucket to the next level.

The map was beautifully colored in. The islands' perimeters were drawn in green ink, and little blue pencil waves bobbed in the sea. A compass sat in the top right-hand corner, carefully segmented into sixteen points, each with an arrow tip and appropriate bearing. At the top of the map it read, "Gulf of Thailand," in thick red marker. A thinner red pen had been used for the island names.

It was so carefully drawn that I had to smile. It reminded me of geography homework and tracing paper. A brief memory surfaced of my teacher handing out exercise books and sarcastic quips.

"So who's it from?" I muttered, and checked the envelope once more for an accompanying note of explanation. It was empty.

Then on one of a cluster of small islands I noticed a black mark. An X mark. I looked closer. Written underneath in tiny letters was the word "Beach."

I wasn't sure exactly what I was going to say to him. I was curious, partly, just wanting to know what the deal was with this beach of his. Also I was pissed off. It seemed like the guy was set on invading my holiday, freaking me out by hissing through the mosquito netting in the middle of the night and leaving strange maps for me to find.

His door was unlocked, the padlock missing. I listened outside a minute before knocking, and when I did the door swung open.

In spite of the newspaper pages stuck over the windows, there was enough light coming in for me to see. The man was lying on the bed, looking up at the ceiling. I think he'd slit his wrists. Or it could have been his neck. In the gloom, with so much blood splashed about, it was hard to tell what he'd slit. But I knew he'd done the cutting. There was a knife in his hand.

I stood still, gazing at the body for a couple of moments. Then I went to get help.

etienne

The policeman was perspiring, but not with the heat. The air-con in the room made it like a fridge. It was more to do with the exertion of speaking English. When he came to a difficult word or complicated sentence his brow would crease into a hundred lines. Then little beads of sweat would pop up like opals on his brown skin.

"But Mis'er Duck no you frien'," he said.

I shook my head. "I'd never met him before last night. And listen. The Duck name, it's not real. It's a joke name."

"Jo' name?" said the policeman.

"Not a true name." I pointed to where he'd written the name in his notebook. "Daffy Duck is a cartoon character."

"Ca'oon?"

"Yes."

"Mis'er Duck is Ca'oon?"

"Like Bugs Bunny. Uh, Mickey Mouse."

"Oh," said the policeman. "So, he give false name to gues' house."

"Definitely."

The policeman wiped his shirtsleeve over his face. Sweat sprinkled over his notebook, blurring the ink. He frowned and new droplets replaced the ones he'd just swept away.

"Now I wan' ask you abou' scene of crime."

"Okay."

"You en'er Mis'er Duck room, because wha'?"

I'd worked this out on the walk down the Ko Sanh Road to the police station.

"Because he'd been keeping me awake last night and I wanted to tell him not to do it again."

"Ah. Las' nigh' Mis'er Duck make a noise."

"Right."

"And wha' you fin' in room, hah?"

"Nothing. I just saw him dead and went to tell the guest house manager."

"Mis'er Duck already dead? How you know abou' tha'?"

"I didn't. I just thought he was. There was a lot of blood."

The policeman nodded sagely, then leaned back on his chair.

"I think you angry abou' so much noise las' nigh', hah?"

"Sure."

"How angry with Mis'er Duck?"

I held up my hands. "I spent the whole morning in the restaurant eating breakfast. From six until nine. A lot of people saw me there."

"Maybe he die before six."

I shrugged. I wasn't worried. There was a clear image in my head of the low light coming through the newspapered windows and the sparkling highlights on Mister Duck. The blood had been pretty wet.

The policeman sighed. "Okay," he said. "You tell me again abou' las' nigh'."

Why didn't I mention the map? Because I didn't want to get involved in some foreign police investigation and I didn't want my holiday fucked up. Also I didn't care much about the guy's death. I saw it as, well . . . Thailand's an exotic country with drugs and AIDS and a bit of danger, and if Daffy Duck got too caught up, then it was his lookout.

I didn't get the impression that the policeman cared much about the whole thing either. After another thirty minutes of ruthless interrogation ("Can you ve'ify you eat banan' pancake?") he let me go, asking me not to leave Ko Sanh within twenty-four hours.

The French girl's boyfriend was sitting on the steps of the police station with his face angled up toward the sun. Obviously he'd been brought in for questioning too. He glanced around as I walked down the steps, maybe thinking I was the girl, then turned back.

Normally I'd have taken that as a sign someone doesn't want to chat. I do a lot of my traveling alone, so sometimes I get starved of conversation and company. It makes me alert to body language, because even if I'm feeling a bit lonely I don't want to inflict myself on a person who isn't interested. But this time I ignored the sign. Despite my not wanting to get involved with the police, the death had made for an unusual start to the day and I had the urge to talk about it.

I sat down right beside him so he couldn't avoid me. As it turned out I'd read the sign wrong anyway. He was very friendly.

"Hi," I said. "Speak English? Uh, *je parle français un petit peu mais malheureusement je suis pas très bon.*"

He laughed. "I speak English," he replied in a gently accented voice.

"You're here about that guy who died, huh?"

"Yes. I heard you were the one to find him."

Fame.

"Yep," I replied, pulling my cigarettes out of my pocket. "Found him this morning."

"It must have been bad for you."

"It was okay. Do you smoke?"

"No thank you."

I lit up.

"So I'm Richard," I said, exhaling.

"Etienne," said Etienne, and we shook hands.

Last night I'd put him at eighteen or so, but in the daylight he looked older. Twenty or twenty-one. He had a Mediterranean look about him—short dark hair and a slim build. I could see him in a few years' time, a couple of stone heavier, a glass of Ricard in one hand and a *boule* in the other.

"This is so weird," I said. "I only got to Thailand last night. I wanted to relax in Bangkok, if that's possible, and instead I got this."

"Oh, we have been here already four weeks, and it is weird for us, too."

"Well yeah, I suppose someone dying is always a bit strange. So where've you been for the last month? Not only Bangkok, surely."

"No, no." Etienne shook his head vigorously. "A few days in Bangkok is enough. We have been north."

"Chiang Rai?"

"Yes, we went on a trek. We rafted on a river. Very boring, no?" He sighed and leaned backward, resting his back on the stone step behind him.

"Boring?"

Etienne smiled. "Raft, trek. I want to do something different, and everybody wants to do something different. But we all do the same thing. There is no . . . ah . . ."

"Adventure."

"I think it is why we come here." He pointed around the corner of the police station, toward the Ko Sanh Road. "We come for an adventure, but we find this."

"Disappointing."

"Yes."

Etienne paused for a moment, frowning slightly; then he said, "This man who died. He was very strange. We would hear him late at night. He would talk and shout . . . The walls are so thin."

To my irritation I blushed, remembering the sound of Etienne and his girlfriend having sex. I took a deep drag on my cigarette and looked down at the steps we were sitting on. "Are they?" I said. "I was so tired last night I slept . . ."

"Yes. Sometimes we do not return to the guest house until late so he will already be asleep."

"It won't be a problem anymore."

"Often we could not understand him. I know he talked English, because I would recognize some words, but . . . it was not easy."

"It wasn't easy for me either. He was Scottish. Strong accent."

"Oh . . . You heard him last night?"

Now it was Etienne's turn to go red while I concentrated on my cigarette. My embarrassment was compounded by his. It was odd, but if his girlfriend had been ugly, then I'd only have been amused, but because she was so attractive it almost felt as if I'd had some kind of affair with her. Which of course I had. A mental affair.

We blushed at each other until the awkward silence became too oppressive.

"Yes," I said, far too loudly. "He had a thick Scottish accent."

"Ah," replied Etienne, also a little firmly. "Now I understand."

He stroked his chin thoughtfully as though he were

smoothing down a beard, although I could see from his light stubble that he was a long way from being able to grow one. Then he said, "He would talk about a beach."

He looked straight at me as he said it. He was watching my face for a reaction—it was obvious. I nodded to make him continue.

"He would talk about it all night. I would lie on my bed awake, because I could not sleep with his shouting, and I would try to follow his words. Like a puzzle." Etienne laughed. "Fokkin' bitch," he said, approximating the man's voice pretty well. "It took me three nights to understand it was a beach. Just like a puzzle."

I took another drag on my cigarette, leaving a pause in the conversation, letting Etienne fill it.

"I like puzzles," he said, but not really to me. Then he let the silence grow.

A trip to India, seventeen years old, more dope than sense, me and one friend decided to take about an eighth of hash on a flight from Srinagar to Delhi. We each made our own plans as to how to take it. I wrapped mine up in plastic, swathed it in masking tape and deodorant to mask the smell, and tucked it into a bottle of malaria pills. The precautions were probably unnecessary. The customs officers were unlikely to be too interested in internal flights, but I did it anyway.

When we got to the airport I was shit scared. I mean I was *shit scared*—eyes popping, shaking, sweating like a pig. But in spite of my fear, I did the most extraordinary thing. I told a complete stranger, a guy I met in the waiting lounge, that I had some dope hidden in my backpack. It wasn't even like he'd winkled the information out of me. I volunteered it. I made the conversation move onto the subject of drugs, and then confessed that I was a smuggler.

I don't know why I did it. I knew it was a fantastically stupid thing to do, but I went right ahead and did it anyway. I simply needed to tell someone what I was doing.

"I know where the beach is," I said.

Etienne raised his eyebrows.

"I've got a map."

"A map of the beach?"

"The dead guy drew it for me. I found it stuck to my door this morning. It shows where the beach is, how to get there. I've got it in my room."

Etienne whistled. "You told the police?"

"Nope."

"Perhaps it is important. Maybe it is something to do with why he . . ."

"Maybe it is." I flicked away my cigarette. "But I don't want to get involved. Maybe they'd think I knew him or something, but I didn't. I never met him before last night."

"A map," said Etienne quietly.

"Cool, huh?"

Etienne stood up suddenly. "Can I see it? Would you mind?"

"Uh, not really," I replied. "But aren't you waiting for . . ."

"My girlfriend? Françoise? She knows the way back to the guest house. No, I would like to see the map." He rested a hand lightly on my shoulder. "If I may."

I was surprised by the intimacy of the gesture; my shoulder twitched and the hand dropped. "Yeah, sure," I said. "Let's go."

mute

We didn't talk as we walked down the Ko Sanh Road toward the guest house. There was no point. Dodging through the hundreds of travelers made it impossible to have a conversation. Passing the bootleg tape stalls, moving through the music zones, picking up the walking pace for one beat, slowing it for another. Credence Clearwater told us to run through the jungle, as if we needed to be told. A Techno beat pumped out of fuzzy speakers, then Jimi Hendrix.

Platoon. Jimi Hendrix, dope, and rifle barrels.

I looked for the smell of grass to complete the connection, and found it through the stench of a hot gutter and sticky tarmac. I think it came from above—a balcony full of braided hair and dirty T-shirts, leaning on the guardrail, enjoying the scene below.

A brown hand flashed out and caught hold of me. A Thai trader sitting by his stall, a slim man with acne scars, was gripping my arm. I looked toward Etienne. He hadn't seen, was still walking down the road. I lost him behind bobbing heads and tanned necks.

The man began stroking my forearm with his free hand, smoothly and swiftly, not loosening his grip. I frowned and tried to pull away. He pulled me back, taking my hand toward his thigh. My fingers clenched to a fist and my knuckles pressed against his skin. People pushed past me on the pavement, knocking me with their shoulders. One caught my eye and smiled. The man stopped stroking my arm and started stroking my leg.

I looked at him. His face was passive and unreadable and his gaze was leveled at my waist. He gave my leg a final caress, turning his wrist so his thumb slipped briefly under the material of my shorts. Then he released my arm, patted me on the behind, and turned back to his stall.

I jogged after Etienne—he was standing on the pavement twenty yards ahead with his hands on his hips. As I approached he raised his eyebrows. I frowned and we continued walking.

At the guest house the silent heroin addict sat in his usual seat. When he saw us he drew a line with his finger over each wrist. "Sad, huh?" I tried to say, but my lips were sticky and barely opened. The sound that came from my throat was a sigh.

françoise

Etienne gazed at the map for five minutes without speaking. Then he said, "Wait," and darted out of my room. I heard him rummaging around next door, then he came back holding a guidebook. "There." He pointed to an open page. "These are the islands in the map. A National Marine Park west of Koh Samui and Koh Phangan."

"Koh Samui?"

"Yes. Look. All the islands have protection. Tourists cannot visit, you see?"

I couldn't. The guidebook was written in French, but I nodded anyway.

Etienne paused, reading, then continued. "Ah. Tourists can go to . . ." He took the map and pointed to one of the bigger islands in the small archipelago, three islands down from where X marked the beach. "This one. Koh Angthong. Tourists can go to Koh Angthong on a special guided tour from Koh Samui, but . . . but they can only stay one night. And they cannot leave the island."

"So this beach is in a National Park?"

"Yes."

"How are people supposed to get there?"

"They cannot get there. It is a National Park."

I leaned back on the bed and lit a cigarette. "That's settled then. The map is bullshit."

Etienne shook his head. "No. Not bullshit. Really, why did the man give it to you? He went to so much trouble. See the little waves."

"He called himself Daffy Duck. He was mad."

"I do not think so. Listen." Etienne picked up his guidebook and began a halting translation. "The most adventurous travelers are . . . exploring the islands beyond Koh Samui to find . . . to find, ah, tranquillity, and Koh Phangan is a favorite . . . destination. But even Koh Phangan is . . ." He paused. "Okay, Richard. This says travelers try new islands beyond Koh Phangan, because Koh Phangan is now the same as Koh Samui."

"The same?"

"Spoiled. Too many tourists. But look, this book is three years old. Now maybe some travelers feel these islands past Koh Phangan are also spoiled. So they find a completely new island, in the National Park."

"But they aren't allowed in the National Park."

Etienne raised his eyes to the ceiling. "Exactly! This is why they go there. Because there will be no other tourists."

"The Thai authorities would just get rid of them."

"Look how many islands are there. How could they be found? Maybe if they hear a boat they can hide, and the only way to find them is if you know they are there—and we do. We have this." He slid the map across the bed at me. "You know, Richard, I think I want to find this beach."

I smiled.

"Really," said Etienne. "You can believe me. I do."

I did believe him. He had a look in his eye that I recognized. In my early adolescence I went through a stage of mild delinquency, along with two of my friends, Sean and Danny. During the early hours of the morning, weekends only because we had school to think of, we would patrol the streets around our area, smashing things. "Hot Bottle" was the favorite game. It involved stealing empty milk bottles from people's doorsteps. We would throw the bottles high into the air and try to catch them. Most of the fun came when bottles were dropped, seeing the silvery explosion of glass, feeling the shards flick against our jeans. Running from the scene of the crime was an extra kick, ideally with the shouts of enraged adults ringing in our ears.

The look I recognized in Etienne's eyes came from one particular experience when we graduated from smashing milk bottles to smashing a car. We'd been sitting in my kitchen, playfully discussing the idea, when Sean said, "Let's just do it." He said it casually, but his eyes said he was serious. Through them I could see he'd already moved beyond thoughts of practicality and consequence, and was hearing the sound of the windshield folding in.

Etienne, I imagined, was hearing the sound of the surf on this hidden beach, or hiding from the Marine Park wardens as he made his way to the island. The effect on me was the same as when Sean said, "Let's just do it." Abstract thoughts suddenly flipped into thoughts about reality. Following the path of the map had become something that could happen.

"I think," I said, "we could probably hire a fisherman to take us to the island."

Etienne nodded. "Yes. It might be difficult to get there, but not impossible."

"We'd have to go to Koh Samui first."

"Or Koh Phangan."

"Or maybe we could even do it from Surat Thani."

"Or Koh Angthong."

"We'd have to ask around a little . . ."

"But there would be someone to take us."

"Yes . . ."

At that moment Françoise appeared, having returned from the police station.

If Etienne was the one who turned the idea of finding the beach into a possibility, it was Françoise who made it happen. The odd thing was, she did it almost accidentally, simply by taking for granted that we were going to try.

I didn't want to seem impressed by her prettiness, so when she stuck her head round the door, I looked up, said "Hi," then went back to studying the map.

Etienne shifted over on my bed and patted the space he had made. Françoise stayed in the doorway. "I did not wait for you," he said, presumably speaking in English for my sake. "I met Richard." She didn't follow the language lead and began rattling away in French. I couldn't follow their conversation past recognizing the odd word, including my own name, but the speed and forcefulness of the exchange made me think that either she was pissed off that he'd left without her, or she was just keen to fill him in on what happened at the police station.

After some minutes the tone of their voices relaxed. Then Françoise said in English, "May I have a cigarette, Richard?"

"Sure." I gave her one and held out a light. As she cupped her hands to cover the flame from the ceiling fan, I noticed a tiny dolphin tattoo half hidden beneath her watch strap. It seemed like a strange place for a tattoo and I nearly commented on it, but to do so seemed too familiar. Scars and tattoos. You need to know someone fairly well before asking questions.

"So what is this map from the dead man?" Françoise asked.

"I found it on my door this morning," I started to explain, but she cut me off.

"Yes, Etienne has told me already. I want to see it."

I passed the map to her and Etienne pointed out the beach.

"Oh," she said. "Near Koh Samui."

Etienne nodded enthusiastically. "Yes. Just a little ride on a boat. Maybe first to Koh Angthong, because the tourists can go there for one day."

Françoise put her finger on the X-marked island. "How can we know what we will find here?"

"We can't," I replied.

"And if there is nothing, how do we get back to Koh Samui?"

"We get back to Koh Angthong," said Etienne. "We wait for a tourist boat. We say we were lost. It doesn't matter."

Françoise took a delicate puff on her cigarette, barely taking the smoke into her lungs. "I see . . . Yes . . . When are we leaving?"

I looked at Etienne and he looked back at me.

"I am tired of Bangkok," Françoise continued. "We can get the night train south tonight."

"Well, uh," I stammered, thrown by the speed at which events were developing. "The thing is, we've got to wait a bit. This guy who committed suicide . . . I'm not supposed to leave the guest house for twenty-four hours."

Françoise sighed. "Go to the police station and explain you have to leave. They have your passport number, yes?"

"Yeah, but . . ."

"So they will let you go."

She stubbed out her cigarette on the floor as if to say, end of discussion. Which it was.

local color

That afternoon I went back to the police station, and as Françoise predicted I didn't get any hassle. The detailed excuse I'd worked out, about how I had to meet a friend at Surat Thani, was brushed aside. Their only concern was that Mister Duck had been without ID, so they didn't know which embassy to inform. I said I'd thought he was Scottish, and they were pleased about that.

As I walked back to the guest house, I found myself thinking what would happen to Mister Duck's body. Amidst all the business of the map, I'd forgotten that someone had actually died. Without ID, the police would have nowhere to send him. Perhaps he'd lie in a Bangkok deep freeze for a year or two, or perhaps he'd be incinerated. An image came into my head of his mother back in Europe, unaware that she was just about to start several dark months of trying to find out why her son had stopped contacting her. It seemed wrong that I could have such an important piece of information while she remained ignorant. If she existed.

These thoughts unsettled me. I decided not to continue directly to the guest house, where Etienne and Françoise would be wanting to talk about the beach and the map. I felt like a bit of time alone. We'd arranged to catch the eight-thirty train south, so there was no need for me to get back for at least two hours.

I took a left off the Ko Sanh Road, went down an alley, ducked under the scaffolding of a half-finished building, and came out on a busy main street. I suddenly found myself surrounded by Thais. I'd half forgotten which country I was in, stuck in backpacker land, and it took me a few minutes to adjust to the change.

Before long I came to a low bridge over a canal. It was hardly picturesque but I stopped there to find my reflection and follow the swirls of petrol color. Along the canal banks, squatters' shacks leaned dangerously. The sun, hazy throughout the morning, now shone hard and hot. Around the shacks a gang of kids cooled off, dive-bombing each other and playing splashing games.

One of them noticed me. I suppose that a pale face would once have had some interest for him, but not now. He held my gaze for a few seconds, either insolent or bored, then leapt into the black water. He achieved an ambitious somersault and his friends shouted their appreciation.

When the kid surfaced, he looked at me again, treading water. The motion of his arms cleared a circle in the floating litter. Shredded polystyrene that, for a moment, looked like soapsuds.

I tugged at the back of my shirt. Sweat was making it stick to my skin.

All in all, I probably walked two miles from the Ko Sanh Road. After the canal, I ate some noodle soup from a roadside stall, wove through some traffic jams, passed by a couple of small temples that were tucked discreetly between stained concrete buildings. Not sights that made me regret leaving Bangkok so soon. I'm not much for sight-seeing, anyway. If I'd stayed a few more days, I doubt I'd have explored any further than the strip joints in Patpong.

Eventually I'd wandered so far I didn't have a clue how to get back to the guest house, so I caught a *tuk-tuk.* In a way it was the best part of the excursion, chugging along in a haze of blue exhaust fumes, spotting the kind of details you miss when you're on foot. Can't think what they are now. I just remember that the ride was more interesting than the walk.

Etienne and Françoise were in the eating area, their bags beside them.

"Hey," said Etienne. "We thought you had changed your mind."

I said I hadn't and he looked relieved.

"So maybe you should pack soon. I think we should arrive early for the train."

I went upstairs to get my bag. On the landing of my level I passed the heroin mute on his way down. A double surprise, partly to see him moved from his usual seat and partly because it turned out he wasn't mute after all.

"You off?" he said as we neared each other.

I nodded.

"Heading for white sands and blue water?"

"Uh-huh."

"Well, have a safe trip."

"I'll try."

He smiled. "Of course you'll *try* to have a safe trip. I'm saying, actually have one."

it's life, jim, but not as we know it

We took the night train south from Bangkok, first-class. In first class you get a waiter come to your table, a cheap meal of good food, and an hour later the table is flipped up to reveal spotless bunk beds. At Surat Thani we got off the train and took a bus to Donsak. From there we caught the Songserm ferry, straight to the pier at Na Thon.

That was how we got to Koh Samui.

I only felt able to relax once I'd shut the curtains on my bunk bed and cut myself off from the rest of the train. More to the point, cut myself off from Etienne and Françoise. Things had been awkward since leaving the guest house. It wasn't that they were getting on my nerves, just that the reality of our undertaking was sinking in. Also, I was remembering that we were virtual strangers—something I'd forgotten in the excitement of our quick decision. I'm sure they were feeling the same, which is why their attempts at conversation were as limited as mine.

I lay on my back with my hands behind my head, content in the knowledge that the muffled sound of the wheels on the tracks and the rocking movement of the carriage would soon send me to sleep.

While I waited, I studied the clever design of my bunk. The carriage had been dimmed, but enough light came through the gap around my curtain for me to see. There was a whole array of useful pouches and compartments which I'd done my best to employ. My T-shirt and trousers were tucked into a little box at my foot end, and I'd put my shoes in an elastic net above my waist. Above my head was an adjustable reading lamp, switched off, but beside it a tiny red bulb gave a reassuring glow.

As I became sleepy I started to fantasize. I imagined the train was a spaceship and I was en route to some distant planet.

I don't know if I'm alone in doing this kind of thing. It isn't something I've ever talked about. The fact is, I've never grown out of playing pretend, and so far there are no signs that I ever will. I have one quite carefully worked-out night-time fantasy that I'm in a kind of high-tech race. The race takes place over several days, even a week, and is nonstop. While I sleep my vehicle continues on autopilot, speeding me toward the finish line. The autopilot thing is the rationalization of how I can be in bed while I'm having the fantasy. Making it work in such a logical way is important—it would be no good fantasizing that the race was in a Formula One car, because how could I go to sleep in that? Get real.

Sometimes I'm winning the race, other times I'm losing. But on those occasions I also fantasize that I have a little trick up my sleeve. A shortcut perhaps, or just a reliance on my ability to take corners quicker than the other competitors. Either way, I fall asleep quietly confident.

I think the catalyst for this particular fantasy was the little red bulb beside the reading lamp. As everyone knows, spaceships aren't spaceships without little red bulbs. Everything else—the clever compartments, the rushing noise of the train's engine/warp drive, the sense of adventure—was a happy complement.

By the time I fell asleep, my scanners were detecting life forms on the surface of a distant planet. Could have been Jupiter. It had the same kind of cloud patterns, like a tie-dye T-shirt.

The warm security of my spaceship capsule slipped away. I was back on my bed on the Ko Sanh Road, looking up at the ceiling fan. A mosquito was buzzing in the room. I couldn't see it but its wings pulsed like a helicopter when it flew near. Sitting beside me was Mister Duck, the sheets around him red and wet.

"Would you sort this out for me, Rich?" Mister Duck said, passing me a half-rolled joint. "I can't do it. My hands are too sticky. The rizla . . . The rizla keeps falling apart."

He laughed apologetically as I took the joint.

"It's my wrists. Slit them all over and now they won't stop bleeding." He lifted up his arm and a squirt of blood arced across the Formica wall. "See what I mean? What a fucking mess."

I rolled the joint but didn't lick it. On the strip of gum was a red fingerprint.

"Oh. You don't want to worry about that, Rich. I'm clean." Mister Duck looked down at his sodden clothes. "Well, not clean . . ."

I licked the rizla.

"So spark it up. I'll only make it wet."

He held out a light and I sat up on the bed. My weight sank the mattress and a stream of blood ran down the slope, soaking into my shorts.

"Now how's that? Hits the fucking spot, huh? But you want to try it through a rifle barrel. That's a serious hit, Rich."

"Blow my mind."

"Yeah," said Mister Duck. "That's the boy. That's the kid . . ."

He lay back on the bed with his hands above his head, wrists facing upward. I took another drag. Blood ran along the blades of the fan and fell around me like rain.

Koh Samui

The journey from the train station at Surat Thani to Koh Samui passed in a sleep-fogged blur. I vaguely remember following Etienne and Françoise onto the bus to Donsak, and my only memory of the ferry ride is of Etienne shouting in my ear over the noise of the boat's engines. "There, Richard!" he yelled, pointing toward the horizon. "That's the Marine Park!" A cluster of blue-green shapes was just visible in the distance. I nodded obligingly. I was more interested in finding a soft spot on my backpack to use as a pillow.

Our Jeep from the Koh Samui port to the Chaweng beach resort was a big open-top Isuzu. On the left the sea lay blue between rows of coconut palms, and on the right a jungle-covered slope rose steeply. Ten travelers sat behind the driver's cabin, our bags clamped between our knees, our heads rolling with the corners. One had a baseball bat resting against his shoulder, another held a camera on his lap. Brown faces flashed past us through the green.

"Delta One-Niner," I muttered, "this is Alpha patrol."

The Jeep left us outside a decent-looking bunch of beach huts, but backpacker protocol demanded we check out the competition. After half an hour of slogging across the hot sand, we returned to the huts we'd first seen.

Private showers, a bedside fan, a nice restaurant that looked onto the sea. Our huts faced each other over a gravel path lined with flowers. It was *très beau*, Françoise said with a happy sigh, and I agreed.

The first thing I did after shutting the door behind me was to go to the bathroom mirror and examine my face. I hadn't seen my reflection for a couple of days and wanted to check that I was looking okay.

It was a bit of a shock. Having been around lots of tanned skin, I'd somehow assumed I was also tanned, but the ghost in the mirror corrected me. My whiteness was accentuated by my stubble, which, like my hair, is jet-black. UV deprivation aside, I was in bad need of a shower. My T-shirt had the salty stiffness of material that has been sweated in, sun-dried, then sweated in again. I decided to head straight to the beach for a swim. I could kill two birds with one stone—soak up a few rays and get clean.

Chaweng was a travel brochure photo. Hammocks slung in the shade of curving palm trees, sand too bright to look at, Jet Skis tracing white patterns like jet planes in a clear sky. I ran down to the surf, partly because the sand was so hot and partly because I always run into the sea. When the water began to drag on my legs I jumped up and the momentum somersaulted me forward. I landed on my back and sank to the bottom, exhaling. On the seabed I let myself rest, head tilted slightly forward to keep the air trapped in my nose, and listened to the soft clicks and rushes of underwater noise.

I'd been splashing around in the water for fifteen minutes or so when Etienne came down to join me. He also ran across the sand and somersaulted into the sea, but then he leapt up with a yelp.

"What's up?" I called.

Etienne shook his head, pushing backward through the water away from where he'd landed. "This! This animal! This . . . fish!"

I began wading toward him. "What fish?"

"I do not know the English. Aaah! Aaah! There are more! Aaah! Stinging!"

"Oh," I said as I reached him. "Jellyfish. Great!"

I was pleased to see the pale shapes, floating in the water like drops of silvery oil. I loved their straightforward weirdness, the strange area they occupied between plant and animal life.

I learned an interesting thing about jellyfish from a Filipino guy. He was one of the only people my age on an island where I'd once stayed, so we became pals. We spent many happy weeks together playing Frisbee on the beach, then diving into the South China Sea. He taught me that if you pick up a jellyfish with the palm of your hand, you don't get hurt—although then you had to be careful to scrub your hands, because if you rubbed your eyes or scratched your back the poison would lift off and sting like mad. We used to have jellyfish fights, hurling the tennis-ball-sized globs at each other. On a calm day you could skim them over the sea like flat pebbles, although if you chucked them too hard they tended to explode. He also told me that you can eat them raw, like sushi. He was right. Literally speaking, you can, as long as you don't mind a few days of stomach cramps and vomiting.

I looked at the jellyfish around us. They looked the same as the ones in the Philippines, so I decided it was worth the risk. The gamble paid off. Etienne's eyes opened wide as I plucked one of the quivering blobs from the sea.

"Mon Dieu!" he exclaimed.

I smiled. I didn't realize French people actually said *"Mon Dieu."* I always thought it was the same thing as English people supposedly saying "what" at the end of every sentence.

"It is not hurting, Richard?"

"Nope. It's about how you hold it, like stinging nettles. You try."

I held out the jellyfish.

"No, I do not want to."

"It's fine. Go on."

"Really?"

"Yeah, sure. Hold your hands like mine."

I slid the jellyfish into his cupped hands.

"Oooh," he said, a big grin spreading over his face.

"But you can only touch it with your palms. If you touch it anywhere else it'll sting."

"Only the palm? Why is that?"

I shrugged. "Don't know. That's the rule."

"I think maybe the skin is more thick there."

"Maybe." I picked another one out of the water. "They're weird, aren't they? Look, you can see right through them. They don't have any brains."

Etienne nodded enthusiastically.

We peered at our jellyfish in silence for a few moments, then I noticed Françoise. She was on the beach, walking toward the water in a one-piece white swimsuit. She saw us and waved. As her arm lifted, her swimsuit drew tightly over her chest and shadows from the one o'clock sun defined her breasts, the dip under the rib cage, a groove of muscle down her stomach.

I glanced at Etienne. He was still examining his jellyfish, pulling its tentacles outward from the bell so it sat on his palm like a glass flower. Perhaps familiarity had blunted him to Françoise's beauty.

When she reached us she was unimpressed by our catch. "I do not like them," she said curtly. "Will you come for a swim?"

I pointed at the chest-deep water, shoulder-deep for Françoise. "We are swimming, aren't we?"

"No," said Etienne, finally looking up. "She means a swim." He gestured to the open sea. "Out there."

---

41 the beach

We played a game as we swam out. Every thirty feet we would each dive to the bottom and return with a handful of sand.

I found the game strangely unpleasant. A meter below the surface, the warmth of the tropical sea would turn cold, so abruptly that by treading water one could pinpoint the dividing line. Diving down, the chill would start at the fingertips, then swiftly envelop the length of the body.

The further we swam, the blacker and finer the sand became. Soon the water at the bottom became too dark for me to see in, and I could only kick out blindly with my legs, arms outstretched, until my hands sank into the silt.

I began dreading the cold area. I would hurry to catch my fistful, pushing up hard from the seabed though my lungs were still full of air. During the times I waited at the surface, while Etienne or Françoise swam down, I would keep my legs bunched up beneath me, using my arms to stay afloat.

"How far out do we go?" I said when the sunbathers on the beach behind us had turned into ants.

Etienne smiled. "You would like to go back now? Are you tired? We can go back."

Françoise held up her hand clear of the water and unclenched her fingers. A lump of sand rolled out and dropped into the sea, where it sank, leaving a cloudy trail behind. "You are tired, Richard?" she said, eyebrows arched.

"I'm fine," I replied. "Let's swim further."

suckered

At five that afternoon the temperature cooled, the sky turned black, and it rained. Unexpectedly, loudly—heavy droplets, cratering and recratering the beach. I sat on the small porch outside my hut and watched a miniature Sea of Tranquillity form in the sand. Across the way Etienne appeared briefly, snatching the swimming shorts he'd left out to dry. He called something to me but it was lost in a roll of thunder; then he ducked back inside.

I had a tiny lizard on my hand. It was about three inches long, with enormous eyes and translucent skin. The lizard had been sitting on my cigarette packet for ten minutes and when I'd got bored with watching it, waiting for a tongue to lash out and lasso a fly, I'd reached out and picked it up. Instead of wriggling away, as I'd expected, the lizard had casually rearranged itself on my hand. Surprised by its audacity, I let it sit there—even though it meant keeping my hand in an unnatural position, palm facing upward, which made my arm ache.

My attention was distracted by two guys running up the beach, whooping and shouting as they came. As they reached my hut they turned off the beach and leapt athletically onto the porch next to mine.

"Man!" whooped one of them, white-blond with a goatee.

"That's some fuckin' storm!" replied the other, yellow-blond and clean-shaven. "Whoop!"

"Americans," I whispered to the lizard.

They rattled at their door, then ran back into the rain toward the beach restaurant, weaving around, trying to dodge the rain. A couple of minutes later they came speeding back. Again they rattled at their door—then white-blond saw me, apparently for the first time. "Lost our fuckin' key!" he said, and jabbed a thumb toward the restaurant. "They lost theirs too! Can't get in!"

"Stuck out here!" said yellow-blond. "In the rain!"

I nodded. "Bad luck. Where did you lose it?"

White-blond shrugged. "Miles down the fuckin' beach, man! Miles and miles!" Then he walked up to the wooden guardrail that separated our two porches and peered over. "What you got in your hand there?" he asked.

I held up the lizard.

"Wow! Is it, like, dead?"

"Nope."

"Excellent! Hey, can I come over? You know, meet the neighbors!"

"Sure."

"You want to smoke a joint?"

"Sure."

"Excellent!"

The two of them vaulted over the guardrail and introduced themselves. White-blond was Sammy, yellow-blond was Zeph.

"Zeph's a strange name, right?" said Zeph as he shook my left hand, not wanting to disturb the lizard. "Can you guess what it's short for?"

"Zephania," I answered confidently.

"Wrong, dude! It isn't short for anything! I was christened Zeph, and everyone thinks it's short for Zephania, but it isn't! Cool, huh?"

"Definitely."

Sammy started rolling up, pulling the dope and papers out of a waterproof plastic bag in his pocket. "You're English, huh?" he said as he flattened out a rizla with his fingers. "English people always put tobacco in joints. You see, we never do. Are you addicted to smoking?"

"Afraid so," I replied.

"I'm not. But if I put tobacco in joints I would be. I smoke all day, like that song. How's that song go, Zeph?"

Zeph started singing a lyric that said, "Don't bogart that joint, my friend," but Sammy cut him off.

"No, dude. The other one."

"What, 'I smoke two joints in the morning'? That one?"

"Yeah."

Zeph cleared his throat. "Uh, it goes, 'I smoke two joints in the morning, and I smoke two joints at night, and I smoke two joints in the afternoon, and then I feel all right . . .' And then it goes, 'I smoke two joints in times of peace, and two in times of war. I smoke two joints before I smoke two joints, then I smoke two more.' I can't remember the rest." He shook his head.

"No matter, dude," said Sammy. "You get the idea, Ricardo? I smoke a lot."

"Sounds like it."

"Uh-huh."

Sammy had finished rolling the joint while Zeph had been singing. He lit it up and passed it straight to me. "That's another thing about English dudes," he wheezed, smoke coming out of his mouth in short bursts. "You hang on to the joint for ages. Us Americans take a toke or two and pass it on."

"It's true," I replied, sucking in.

I was going to apologize for the poor manners of my countrymen but I collapsed into a coughing fit.

"Rickster!" said Zeph, patting me on the back. "You gotta cough to get off."

A couple of seconds later a blistering bolt of lightning crackled over the sea. After it was gone, Sammy said in an awestruck voice, "Most totally excellent, dude!" Zeph quickly followed it up with, "Like, utterly outrageous, compadre!"

I opened my mouth, then hesitated. "Excellent, dude," I muttered thoughtfully.

"Most excellent," Sammy repeated.

I groaned.

"A problem, Ricardo?"

"You're winding me up."

Sammy and Zeph looked at each other, then at me.

"Winding you up?"

"Having me on."

Sammy frowned. "Speak in English, my man."

"This . . . Keanu Reeves thing. It's a joke, right? You don't really talk like that . . . do you?"

There was a brief silence, then Zeph swore. "We're rumbled, Sammy."

"Yeah," Sammy replied. "We overplayed our hand."

They were Harvard students. Sammy was studying law, Zeph was studying Afro-American literature. Their surf act was a reaction to the condescending Europeans they kept meeting in Asia. "It's a protest against bigotry," Zeph explained, pulling knots out of his tangled blond locks. "Europeans think all Americans are stupid, so we act stupid to confirm your prejudices. Then we reveal ourselves as intelligent, and by doing so, subvert the prejudice more effectively than an immediate barrage of intellect—which only causes confusion and, ultimately, resentment."

"Really?" I said, genuinely impressed. "That's so elaborate."

Zeph laughed. "No, not really. We just do it for fun."

They had other acts they liked to do. Zeph's favorite was the surf dude, but Sammy had another—he called it the nigger-lover. As its name implies, it was a bit more risqué than the surf dude.

"One time I got punched doing the nigger-lover," Sammy said, as he began to roll another joint. "Knocked flat on my fuckin' back."

I wasn't at all surprised. The act involved Sammy starting

violent arguments with total strangers, insisting that because there's a country in Africa called Niger, all people from Niger were niggers—regardless of whether they were black or white.

"Aren't they called Nigerians?" I asked, bristling slightly, despite knowing I was being suckered.

Sammy shook his head. "That's what everyone says, but I don't think so. Think about it. Nigeria is right below Niger. They border each other, so if they were both called Nigerians it would cause chaos."

"Well, I still doubt they're called niggers."

"Oh, sure. Me too. I only say it to make a point. . . . Fuck knows what the point is, but . . ." He drew on the joint and passed it on. "It's like my granddad taught me. He was a colonel in the U.S. Marines. Sammy, he'd say, the ends *always* justify the means. And you know what, Richard? He was right."

I was about to disagree, but I realized he was winding me up again. Instead I replied, "You can't make an omelette without breaking some eggs."

Sammy smiled and turned to look at the sea.

"That's the boy," I thought I heard him say.

Lightning silhouetted the line of palm trees on the beach into a line of claws with pencil arms. The lizard scuttled out of my hand, startled by the flash.

"That's the kid."

I frowned. "Sorry? What was that?"

He turned back, also frowning, but with the smile still not faded from his lips. "What was what?"

"Didn't you just say something?"

"Nope."

I looked at Zeph. "Didn't you hear him say something?"

Zeph shrugged. "I was watching the lightning."

"Oh."

Just the dope talking, I guessed.

The rain continued as night fell. Etienne and Françoise stayed in their hut, and Zeph, Sammy, and I stayed on the porch until we were too stoned to do anything but sit in silence, passing the odd comment between us if there was an impressive roll of thunder.

An hour or two after dark a tiny Thai woman came over to our porch from the restaurant, almost hidden under a giant beach parasol. She looked at the dope paraphernalia strewn about us with a wan smile, then handed Zeph a spare key to their room. I took that as my cue to crawl into bed. As I said good night, Sammy croaked, "Hey, nice meeting you. Catch you tomorrow, dude."

He seemed to say it without a trace of irony. I couldn't work out whether it was a continuation of his surfer joke, or the grass had regressed his Harvard mind. It seemed too complicated to ask, so I said, "Sure," and shut the door behind me.

At around three in the morning I woke up for a short while, dry-mouthed, still high, and listened. I could hear cicadas and waves sucking down the beach. The storm had blown itself out.

spaced invaders

The next morning the sky was still clouded over. As I walked out onto the porch, scattered with rain-soaked joint butts, I had the bizarre sensation that I was back in England. There was a slight chill in the air and I could smell wet earth and leaves. Rubbing the sleep from my eyes, I padded over the cool sand to Etienne and Françoise's hut. There was no answer from their door, so I tried the restaurant and found them eating breakfast. I ordered a mango salad, thinking an exotic taste might compensate for the feeling of being in England, and sat down with them.

"Who did you meet last night?" said Etienne as I pulled up a chair. "We saw you talking outside your room."

"We watched you from our window," Françoise added.

I pulled out a cigarette to kill time before breakfast arrived. "I met a couple of Americans. Zeph and Sammy."

Françoise nodded. "Did you tell them about our beach?"

"No." I lit up. "I didn't."

"You shouldn't tell people about our beach."

"I didn't tell them."

"It should be a secret."

I exhaled strongly. "And that's why I didn't tell them, Françoise."

Etienne interrupted. "She was worried you might have . . ." The sentence trailed off into a nervous smile.

"It didn't even cross my mind," I replied irritably, and stubbed out my cigarette hard. It was tasting like shit.

When the mango salad arrived I made an effort to relax. I told them about how the Americans had fooled me with their surfer act. Françoise thought the story was extremely funny. Her laughter partially diffused the tension and we began making plans for the day ahead.

We decided that we had to hire a boat. The normal tour agencies wouldn't do because they'd be too organized and we doubted we'd be able to slip away from their supervision. Instead we would need to find a fisherman who was unaware of or unconcerned about the rules concerning tourists in the Marine Park.

After breakfast we split up to optimize our chances. I went north, toward Koh Matlang, and the other two went south, aiming for a small town we'd passed on the Jeep ride. Our rendezvous was in three hours' time, back at our huts.

The sun came out as I set off down Chaweng, but it did little to improve my mood. Flies buzzed around my head, smelling the sweat, and the walking became increasingly laborious as the night's rain dried off the sand.

I began counting the guest houses I passed along the shoreline. After twenty minutes I'd counted seventeen, and they were still showing no signs of thinning out. If anything, the palm trees were more cluttered with Ray-Bans and concrete patios than before.

In 1984 I sat in my living room, playing on my Atari, and listened to the baby-sitter talk about Koh Samui. As I mopped the screen clear of space invaders, names and places stuck in my head.

Pattaya was a hellhole. Chiang Mai was rainy and cold. Koh Samui was hot and beautiful. Koh Samui was where she had stayed with her boyfriend for five months, hanging out on the beach and doing strange things she was both reluctant and keen to talk about.

Exams out of the way, my friends and I scattered ourselves around the globe. The next August we started coming back, and I learned that my baby-sitter's paradise was yesterday's news. Koh Phangan, the next island along, was Thailand's new Mecca.

A few years later, as I checked my passport and confirmed my flight to Bangkok, a friend telephoned with advice. "Give Koh Phangan a miss, Rich," she said. "Hat Rin's a long way past its sell-by date. They do printed flyers for the full-moon parties. Koh Tao. That's where it's at."

After an hour of walking I gave up trying to find a fisherman. The only Thais I met were selling gemstones and baseball caps. By the time I got back to my beach hut I was exhausted, sunburned, and pissed off. I went straight to the restaurant and bought a packet of cigarettes. Then I chain-smoked in the shade of a palm tree, looking out for Etienne and Françoise, hoping they'd had better luck.

tv heaven

Thais, or Southeast Asians in general, make eerily convincing transvestites. Their slight builds and smooth faces are a recipe for success.

I saw a particularly stunning transvestite as I waited under the palm tree. His silicon breasts were perfectly formed and he had hips to die for. The only thing to betray his gender was his gold lamé dress—a bit too showy to be worn by a Thai girl on a stroll down Chaweng.

He was carrying a backgammon set under his arm, and as he slunk past he asked if I wanted to play a game.

"No thanks," I replied with neurotic haste.

"Why?" he wanted to know. "I think maybe you afrai' I win."

I nodded.

"Okay. Maybe you wan' to play in bed?" He tugged at the long slit up the side of his dress, revealing fabulous legs. "Maybe in bed I le' you win . . ."

"No thanks," I said again, blushing slightly.

He shrugged and continued walking along the beach. A

couple of beach huts down someone took him up on the backgammon offer. Curious, I tried to see who, but they were blocked by the trunk of a leaning coconut tree. A few minutes later I looked back and he was gone. I guessed he'd found his punter.

Etienne appeared not long after, beaming.

"Hey, Richard," he said. "Did you see the girl walking this way?"

"With a lamé dress?"

"Yes! My God, she was so beautiful!"

"She was."

"Anyway, Richard. Come to the restaurant." He reached out a hand and hauled me up. "I think we have a boat to take us into the Marine Park."

The man was a Thai version of a spiv. Instead of being lean and weasel-like, with a pencil mustache and a flash suit, he was short, fat, and wore drainpipe marbled jeans tucked into giant Reebok trainers.

"Tha' can be arrange'," he said, quoting from the universal phrase book of the entrepreneur. "Of course, yes." He grinned and made an expansive gesture with his arms. Gold sparkled in his mouth. "No' difficul' for me to do tha'."

Etienne nodded. So far he'd done all the bargaining, which was fine as far as I was concerned. I don't like dealing with money transactions in poor countries. I get confused between feeling that I shouldn't haggle with poverty and hating getting ripped off.

"Actually, my frien', your gui'book is no' correc'. You can stay Koh Angthong one nigh', two nigh'—is okay. Bu' this island you can only stay one nigh'." He took Etienne's book and laid a chubby finger on an island close to Angthong.

Etienne looked at me and winked. From my memory of

Mister Duck's map, which was back in the beach hut, our island was the next one along.

"Okay," said Etienne, and lowered his voice conspiratorially, even though there was no one around the restaurant to hear. "This is the island we want to see. But we want to stay more than one night. That is possible?"

The spiv furtively looked over his shoulder at the empty tables.

"Yes," he whispered, leaning forward, then looked around again. "Bu' is mo' money, you un'erstan'."

The deal was eventually struck at 1,450 baht, diligently knocked down from 2,000 by Etienne. At six the next morning we were to meet the spiv in the restaurant and he would take us to his boat. Only then would we pay him the money, a point Etienne wisely insisted upon, and he would take us to the island. Three nights later he would come back to pick us up—our contingency plan in case we got stuck there.

That left us with only a couple of problems.

If we successfully made it to the next island along, we would be missing when the spiv came to collect us. To deal with this, Etienne invented a story about some other friends we were going to meet there, so we might come back early—no cause for alarm.

Another difficulty was how to get from the drop-off island to the beach island. We could have asked the boat to take us directly there, but not knowing exactly what we were going to find on the beach, we didn't want to blunder in on a motorboat. Anyway, as the beach island was out of bounds to tourists, we thought it better to start from one where technically we were allowed to stay—if only for one night.

Etienne and Françoise seemed far less concerned about this last step of the journey than I was. They had a simple solution—we would swim. By examining Mister Duck's map and the map in their guidebook, they'd decided that the islands were roughly a kilometer apart. According to them, that was a manageable distance. I wasn't so confident, and remembered the diving game from the day before. The tide had pulled us a long way down Chaweng beach as we swam. If the same thing happened between the islands, the length of the swim could effectively double as we corrected and recorrected our course.

The final problem was what we would do with our bags. Again, Etienne and Françoise had worked out a solution. Apparently they'd done a lot of planning last night while I was getting stoned. Later that day, sitting in the shallows with the wash collecting sand around our feet, they explained.

"The backpacks will not be a problem, Richard," said Françoise. "Actually, maybe they will help us to swim."

I raised my eyebrows. "How's that?"

"We need some plastic bags," said Etienne. "If we have some plastic bags we can tie them so water does not enter. Then . . . they float. The air inside."

"Uh-huh. You think it'll work?"

Etienne shrugged. "I think it will. I saw it on television."

"On TV?"

"It was the A-Team."

"The A-Team? Oh, that's great. We'll be fine, then."

I lay back in the water, propping myself up on my elbows.

"I think you are very lucky to have met us, Richard." Etienne laughed. "I think without us you could not reach this beach."

"Yes," Françoise said. "But also we are lucky to meet him."

"Oh of course. Without your map we could not find the beach either."

Françoise frowned, then smiled at me. "Etienne! We are lucky to meet him anyway."

I smiled back, noticing as I did so that the bad mood I'd been carrying all morning had completely lifted. "We're all lucky," I said happily.

Etienne nodded. "Yes. We are."

We sat in silence for a few minutes, basking in our luckiness. Then I stood up, clapping my hands together. "Right. Why don't we go for a long swim now? It could be a practice."

"It is a very good idea, Richard," Etienne replied, also standing. "Come on, Françoise."

She shook her head and pouted. "I think I will stay in the sun. I shall watch you two strong men from here. I will see who can swim the furthest."

Doubt flickered in my mind. I looked at her, trying to see if her words were as loaded as they appeared. She was watching Etienne as he made his way into the sea, giving nothing away.

That's it then, I thought. Just wishful thinking.

But I failed to convince myself. As I waded after Etienne, I couldn't help wondering if Françoise's eyes were now on my back. Just before the water became deep enough to swim I needed to know, and glanced behind me. She had moved up the beach to dry sand and was lying on her front, facing the land.

Just wishful thinking after all.

eden

Sunset was spectacular. Red sky gently faded to deep blue, where a few bright stars already shone, and orange light threw elastic shadows down the beach as people strolled back to their huts.

I was stoned. I'd been dozing on the sand with Françoise and Etienne, recovering from our epic swim, when Sammy and Zeph had turned up with half an ounce of grass wrapped in newspaper. They'd spent the day at Lamai hunting for their lost room key and found it hanging on a piece of driftwood, stuck in the sand. They'd bought the grass to celebrate.

"Someone must have put it there knowing we'd come looking," Zeph had said as he sat down beside us. "Isn't that such a decent thing to do?"

"Maybe it was a stupid thing to do," Françoise replied. "Someone could have taken this key and robbed your room."

"Well, uh, yeah, I suppose." Then he'd looked at Françoise, obviously taking her in for the first time, and given his head a little shake. I think he was clearing a mental image that had just appeared. "No, definitely. You're right."

The sun had begun its rapid descent to the horizon line as the grass began to take hold. Now we all sat, watching the colors in the sky as intently as if we were watching television.

"Hey," said Sammy loudly, breaking us out of our reverie. "Has anyone ever noticed that if you look up at the sky, you can start to see animals and faces in the clouds?"

Etienne looked round. "Have we ever noticed?" he said.

"Yeah," Sammy continued. "It's amazing. Hey, there's a little duck right above us, and that one looks like a man with a huge nose."

"Actually, I have noticed this since I was a small child."

"A small child?"

"Yes. Certainly."

Sammy whistled. "Shit. I only just noticed it. Mind you, that's mainly to do with where I grew up."

"Oh?" said Etienne.

"See, I grew up in Idaho."

"Ah . . ." Etienne nodded. Then he looked confused. "Yes, Idaho. I have heard of Idaho, but . . ."

"Well, you know about Idaho, huh? There's no clouds in Idaho."

"No clouds?"

"Sure. Chicago, the windy city. Idaho, the cloudless state. Some weird weather thing to do with atmospheric pressure, I don't know."

"There are no clouds at all?"

"Not one." Sammy sat up on the sand. "I can remember the first time I saw a cloud. It was in upstate New York, the summer of '79. I saw this vast fluffy thing in the sky, and I reached and tried to grab it . . . but it was too high." Sammy smiled sadly. "I turned to my mom and said, 'Why can't I have the cotton candy, Mommy? Why?' " Sammy choked and looked away. "I'm sorry. It's just a stupid memory."

Zeph leaned over and patted him on the back. "Hey, man," he murmured, just loud enough to hear. "It's okay. Let it out. We're all friends here."

"Yes," said Etienne. "We don't mind. Of course, everybody has a sad memory."

Sammy spun around, his face all screwed up. "You, Etienne? You have a sad memory too?"

"Oh yes. I used to have a little red bicycle, but it was stolen by some thieves."

Sammy's expression darkened. "The bicycle thieves? They stole your little red bike?"

"Yes. I was seven."

"Seven!" Sammy shouted and thumped the ground with his fist, spraying everyone with sand. "Jesus! That makes me so fucking mad!"

There was a shocked silence. Then Sammy grabbed the rizlas and started furiously rolling up, and Zeph changed the topic of conversation.

The outburst was probably a clever move. Etienne's response had been so charming that it would have been cruel to reveal the truth. Sammy's only way out was to follow the bluff to its natural conclusion.

By the time we'd smoked the joint, the sun had almost disappeared. Just the slightest curve of yellow shimmered over the sea. A slight breeze picked up, sending a few loose rizlas skimming along the sand. With the breeze came the smell of cooking, lemongrass and fried shellfish, from the restaurant behind us.

"I'm hungry," I muttered.

"Smells good, huh?" said Zeph. "I could do with a big plate of chicken noodles."

"Or dog noodles," said Sammy. He turned to Françoise. "We had dog noodles in Chiang Mai. Tasted like chicken. All those things, dog, lizard, frog, snake. They always taste like chicken."

"How about rat?" I asked.

"Uh-huh, rat too. Distinctly chickenlike."

Zeph picked up a handful of sand and let it run through his fingers, trailing patterns between his legs. Then he coughed, almost in a formal way, as if he wanted everyone to pay attention. "Hey," he said. "Do you know about Kentucky Fried Rat?"

I frowned. It sounded like another wind-up, and I felt that if Etienne was going to fall for it in the same kind of way, I might start crying. I still had a picture in my head of his concerned face as he explained about his little red bike.

"No. What is it?" I said warily.

"It's one of those stories that gets around."

"Urban myths," said Sammy. "Like someone got a small bone stuck in his throat. Then he got it analyzed and it was a rat bone."

"Yeah, and the guy it happened to was a friend's aunt's cousin. It never happened to the person you're talking to."

"Oh," I said. "I know."

"Right. So there's a Kentucky Fried Rat doing the rounds at the moment. You heard it?"

I shook my head.

"About a beach. This amazing beach hidden somewhere, but no one knows where it is."

I turned my head away. Down by the sea a Thai boy was playing with a piece of coconut husk, keeping it in the air using his knees and the sides of his feet. He timed a flick badly and the husk flew into the water. For a few moments he stood there with his hands on his hips, perhaps wondering if it was worth getting wet to retrieve it. Then he started jogging up the sand toward the guest house.

"No," I said. "I haven't heard about that. Fill us in."

"Okay," said Zeph. "I'll paint you a picture." He lay back on the sand. "Close your eyes and think about a lagoon."

Think about a lagoon, hidden from the sea and passing boats by a high curving wall of rock. Then imagine white sands and coral gardens never damaged by dynamite fishing or trawling nets. Freshwater falls scatter the island, surrounded by jungle—not the forests of inland Thailand, but jungle. Canopies three levels deep, plants untouched for a thousand years, strangely colored birds and monkeys in the trees.

On the white sands, fishing in the coral gardens, a select community of travelers pass the months. They leave if they want to, they return, the beach never changes.

"Select?" I asked quietly, as if talking through a dream. Zeph's vision had entirely consumed me.

"Select," he replied. "Word of mouth passes on the location to a lucky few."

"It's paradise," Sammy murmured. "It's Eden."

"Eden," Zeph agreed, "is how it sounds."

Françoise was completely thrown by hearing that Sammy

and Zeph also knew about the beach. She couldn't have acted more suspicious if she'd tried.

She stood up suddenly. "Now then," she said, dusting sand off her legs. "We leave early tomorrow morning for, ah, for Koh Phangan. So I think we shall go to bed now. Etienne? Richard? Come."

"Huh?" I said, disoriented as the image of the beach splintered. "Françoise, it's seven-thirty in the evening."

"We leave early in the morning," she repeated.

"But . . . I haven't eaten any dinner. I'm starving."

"Good. So we shall eat now. Good night, Sammy and Zeph," she said, before I could ask them to join us. "It was very nice meeting you. And really, your beach, what a silly story." She laughed gaily.

Etienne sat upright, looking at her as if she'd lost her mind, but she ignored his appalled expression and began marching toward the restaurant.

"Look," I said to Sammy and Zeph. "I think she's . . . If you want to eat with us . . ."

"Yes," said Etienne. "You are very welcome. Please."

"It's cool," Sammy replied, smiling slightly. "We'll hang out here a bit longer. But listen, have a good time in Koh Phangan. Are you coming back this way?"

I nodded.

"Okay, so we'll catch up later on. We're here for a while. A week at least."

We all shook hands, then Etienne and I followed after Françoise.

Dinner was laden with heavy silences, sometimes broken by a terse exchange in French. But Françoise knew she'd acted foolishly and was apologetic as we said good night.

"I do not know," she explained. "I was suddenly frightened they would want to come with us. Zeph made it sound so . . . I only want it to be us . . ." She frowned, frustrated by her inability to express herself. "Do you think they have realized we know about the beach?"

I shrugged. "Hard to say. Everyone was pretty stoned."

Etienne nodded. "Yes," he said, and put his arm around her shoulder. "Everyone was stoned. We should not worry."

It took me a long time to get to sleep that night. It wasn't just because I was anxious about what might happen tomorrow, although that was part of it. I was also troubled by the hurried way I'd said good-bye to Zeph and Sammy. I'd enjoyed their company and knew it was unlikely I'd find them again, if I did come back to Koh Samui. Our parting had been too quick and awkward, too confused by dope and secrets. I felt there was something I'd left unsaid.

a safe bet

I wouldn't call it a dream. Nothing with Mister Duck was like a dream. In this case, it was more like a movie. Or news footage, swaying on a hand-held camera.

Mister Duck was sprinting toward me across the embassy lawn, his wrists still freshly slit, blood looping out from the cuts as he pumped his arms. I was reeling from the noise of the screaming crowds and helicopters, watching a snowfall of shredded files. Classified snow, swirling in the backdraft from the rotor blades, settling on the manicured grass.

"Born twenty years too late?" shouted Mister Duck, belting past me and flipping into a cartwheel. "Fuck that!" His blood echoed the movement, briefly hanging in the air like the trace from a firework.

"See up there!"

I looked where he pointed. A hovering insect shape was lifting off the roof with people clinging to the landing skids. It dipped as it pulled away, struggling with the heavy load, and clipped a tree outside the embassy walls.

I shouted with excitement.

"That's the boy!" Mister Duck yelled, ruffling my hair with a wet hand, soaking the collar of my shirt. "That's the kid!"

"Do we get to escape from the embassy roof?" I yelled back. "I always wanted to do that!"

"Escape from the embassy roof?"

"Do we get to?"

"You bet," he laughed. "You fucking bet."

leaving

I drew quickly, sweating despite the early-morning chill. There wasn't time to take the same kind of care over the map as Mister Duck. The islands were rough circles, the curving shoreline of Thailand a series of jagged lines, and there were only three labels. Koh Samui, Koh Angthong, and Eden.

At the bottom of the page I wrote, "Wait on Chaweng for three days. If we haven't come back by then it means we made it to the beach. See you there? Richard."

I crept outside. A light already shone in Françoise and Etienne's hut. Shivering, I stole along the porch and slipped the map under Zeph and Sammy's door. Then I collected my bag, locked up my room, and went to the restaurant to wait for the others.

The Thai boy who'd been kicking the coconut husk was sweeping the floor. As I arrived he glanced outside, to check it was as early as he thought it was.

"You wan' banan' pancake?" he asked cautiously.

I shook my head. "No thanks. But I would like to buy four hundred cigarettes."

getting there

littering

The spiv's motorboat was painted white down to the watermark strip, and below that it was yellow—or yellow when it lifted clear of the sea, pale green when it sank back down. At one time his boat must have been red. The white was blistered or scraped away in places, leaving crimson streaks that looked like cuts. That, with the rolling movement and growling engine, was enough to make me feel the boat was alive. It knew which way I expected it to lurch and routinely surprised me.

Beside us, where the water was disturbed, the morning sun played tricks in the sea. Gold shapes like a shoal of fish spun beneath the surface, matching our speed. I reached down and trailed my hand, catching a fish on my palm. It swam there, flickering over my life line, until I balled my fist. The fish slipped out and swam on my closed fingers.

"You should not look down," said Françoise, leaning over from the other side of the boat. "If you look down, you will feel sick. Watch the island. The island does not move."

I looked where she pointed. Strangely, Koh Samui seemed miles behind us but the drop-off island still appeared as distant as it had an hour ago.

"I'm not feeling sick," I said, and sank my head back over the side.

Hypnotized by the gold fish, I didn't move again until the water turned blue and I saw a coral bed loom beneath me. The spiv cut the engine. I put a hand up to my ears, surprised by the silence, half thinking I might have gone deaf. "Now you pay," said the spiv reassuringly, and we slid toward the shore.

The sand was more gray than white and strewn with dried seaweed, laid out in overlapping arcs by the tide. I sat on the trunk of a fallen coconut tree, watching our ride chug into the distance. Soon it was hard to find, a white speck occasionally appearing on the ridge of a high swell. When five minutes passed without a sighting I realized that it had gone and our isolation was complete.

A few meters away, Etienne and Françoise leaned against their rucksacks. Etienne was studying the maps, working out which of the several islands near us we had to swim to. He didn't need my help, so I called to him that I was going to take a walk. I'd never been on a real desert island before—a deserted desert island—and I felt I ought to explore.

"Where?" he said, looking up and squinting against the sun.

"Just around. I won't be long."

"Half an hour?"

"An hour."

"Yes, but we should leave after lunch. We should not spend the night here."

I waved in reply, already walking away from them.

I stuck to the coast for half a mile, looking for a place to turn inland, and eventually found a bush whose canopy made a dark tunnel into the treeline. Through it I could see green leaves and sunlight, so I crawled inside, brushing spiderwebs from my face. I came out into a glade of waist-high ferns. Above me was a circle of sky, broken by a branch that jutted out like the hand of a clock. On the far side of the glade the forest began again, but my impulse to continue was checked by a fear of getting lost. The tunnel I'd crawled through was harder to make out from this end, disguised by the tall grasses, and I could only orientate myself by the sound of breaking waves. I gave up my token exploration and waded through the ferns to the middle of the glade. Then I sat down and smoked a cigarette.

Thinking about Thailand tends to make me angry, and until I started writing this book, I tried not to do it. I preferred it to stay tucked away in the back of my mind. But I do think about Thailand sometimes. Usually late at night, when I've been awake long enough to see the curtain patterns through the darkness and the shapes of the books on my shelves.

At those times I make an effort to remember sitting in the glade with the shadow of the clock-hand branch lying across the ferns, smoking my cigarette. I choose this moment because it was the last time I could pinpoint that I was me being myself. Being normal, with nothing much going through my head apart from how pretty the island was, and how quiet.

It isn't that from then on every second in Thailand was bad. Good things happened. Loads of good things. And mundane things, too: washing my face in the morning, swimming, fixing some food, whatever. But in retrospect, all those instances are colored by what was going on around them. Sometimes it feels to me that I walked into the glade and lit the cigarette, and someone else came along and finished it. Finished it, stubbed it out, flicked it into the bushes, then went to find Etienne and Françoise. It's a cop-out, because it's another thing that distances me from what happened, but that's how it feels.

This other person did things I wouldn't do. It wasn't just our morals that were at odds, there were little character differences, too. The cigarette butt—the other guy flicked it into the bushes. I'd have done something else. Buried it maybe. I hate littering, let alone littering in a protected Marine park.

It's hard to explain. I don't believe in possession or the

supernatural. I know that in real terms it was me who flicked the cigarette butt.

Fuck it.

I've been relying on an idea that these things would become clear to me as I wrote them down, but it isn't turning out that way.

When I got back to the beach, I found Etienne crouched over a little Calor gas camping stove. Laid out beside him were three piles of Magi-Noodle packets—yellow, brown, and pink.

"Great," I said. "I'm starving. What's on the menu?"

"You may have chicken, beef, or . . ." He held up a pink packet. "What is this?"

"Shrimp. I'll go for chicken."

Etienne smiled. "Me also. And we can have chocolate for dessert. You have it?"

"Sure." I unclipped my rucksack and pulled out three bars. The ones closest to the top had melted and remolded themselves around the shape of my water bottle, but the foil hadn't split.

"Did you find anything interesting on your walk?" asked Etienne, cutting open one of the yellow packs with a penknife.

"Nothing in particular. I stuck to the coastline mainly." I looked around. "Where's Françoise? Isn't she eating with us?"

"She has already eaten." He pointed down the beach. "She went to see if it is a big swim to our island."

"You worked out which one it is?"

"I think so. I'm not sure. There are many differences between the map in my guidebook and your friend's map."

"Which one did you go for?"

"Your friend."

I nodded. "Good choice."

"I hope so," said Etienne, hooking a noodle from the boiling water with his penknife. It hung limply on the blade. "Okay. We can eat now."

thai-die

Françoise said it was one kilometer away and Etienne said two. I can't judge distances over water, but I said one and a half. Mainly it just looked like a long swim.

The island across the sea was wide, with tall peaks at each end that were joined by a pass about half their height. I guessed it had once been two volcanoes, close enough together to be connected by their lava flow. Whatever its origins, it was at least five times the size of the one we were on, and gaps in the green showed rock faces which I hoped we wouldn't need to climb.

"Are you sure we can do this?" I said, more to myself than anyone else.

"We can," said Françoise.

"We can try," Etienne corrected, and went to get the backpack he'd prepared with plastic garbage bag liners, bought from the restaurant that morning.

The A-Team: a television series that was a hit when I was around fourteen years old. They were B. A. Barracus, "Faceman," Murdock, and "Hannibal"—four Vietnam veterans accused of a crime they didn't commit, who now worked as mercenaries, taking on the bad guys the law couldn't touch.

They let us down. For a moment it had looked as if Etienne's contraption would float. It dipped underwater and held its level, the top quarter bobbing above the surface like an iceberg. But then the bags collapsed and the pack sank like a stone. Three other attempts failed in exactly the same way.

"This will never work," said Françoise, who had rolled her swimming costume down to her waist to get an even tan and was not catching my eye.

"There's no way," I agreed. "The rucksacks are far too heavy. You know, we really should have tried this out on Koh Samui."

"Yes," Etienne sighed. "I do know."

We stood in the water, silently considering the situation. Then Françoise said, "Okay. We take one plastic bag each. We only take some important things."

I shook my head. "I don't want to do that. I need my rucksack."

"What choice? We give up?"

"Well . . ."

"We need some food, some clothes, only for three days. Then if we do not find the beach, we swim back and wait for the boat."

"Passports, tickets, traveler's checks, cash, malaria pills."

"There is no malaria here," said Etienne.

"Anyway," Françoise added. "We do not need a passport to go to this island." She smiled and absently brushed a hand between her breasts. "Come on, Richard. We are too close, huh?"

I frowned, not understanding, a list of possibilities appearing in my mind.

"Too close to give up."

"Oh," I said. "Yes. I suppose we are."

We hid our rucksacks under a thick patch of shrubs near a distinctive palm tree—it had two trunks growing from a single stem. In my garbage bag I packed puri-tabs, the chocolate, spare shorts, a T-shirt, Converse shoes, Mister Duck's map, my water bottle, and two hundred cigarettes. I wanted to take all four hundred, but there wasn't room. We also had to leave the Calor gas stove. It meant that we'd have to eat cold noodles, soaked long enough to make them soft, but at least we wouldn't starve. And I left the malaria pills, too.

After tying the bags with as many knots as the plastic would allow and then sealing them again inside a second one, we tested their seaworthiness. Without the weight of the rucksacks they floated better than we could have hoped. They were even strong enough to lean on, so we only had to swim with our legs.

At a quarter to four we waded into the sea, finally ready to leave. "Maybe more than one kilometer," I heard Françoise say behind me. Etienne said something in reply, but it was lost as a wave broke.

The swim passed in stages. At first we were full of confidence, chatting as we found a kicking rhythm and making jokes about sharks. Then, as our legs began to ache and the water no longer felt cold enough to cool us down, we stopped talking. By this time, as on the boat ride from Koh Samui, the beach behind us seemed as far away as the island ahead. The jokes about sharks became fears, and I started to doubt that I had the strength to finish the swim. We were about halfway between the two points. Not being able to finish the swim would mean dying.

If Etienne and Françoise were also worried they didn't show it. In any case, it wasn't like there was anything we could do to make things easier. We'd put ourselves into the situation. All we could do was deal with it.

And then, strangely, things did become easier. Although my legs still ached like crazy, they'd developed a kind of reflex kick, something like a heartbeat. It kept me moving and allowed my mind to drift beyond the pain. One idea that kept me distracted for ages was composing the newspaper headlines that would inform people back home of my fate. "Young Adventurers in Thai-Die Death Swim—Europe Mourns," covered the necessary angles. Writing my obituary was harder, as I'd never done anything of much importance, but my funeral was a pleasant surprise. I drafted some good speeches, and a lot of people came to hear them.

I'd moved on to thinking that I should try to pass my driving test if I got back to England, when I saw driftwood on the beach ahead and realized we were nearly there. We'd been careful to stick together over most of the swim, but in the last hundred meters Etienne pulled away. When he reached the beach he did a cartwheel, achieved with a last reserve of energy, because then he collapsed and didn't move again until I joined him.

"Show me the map," he said, trying to sit up.

"Etienne," I replied between gasps for breath, and pushed him back down. "We've done enough. We're staying here tonight."

"But the beach may be close, no? Maybe it is only a short way down the island."

"Enough."

"But—"

"Shh."

I lay down, pressing the side of my face into the wet sand, my gasps becoming sighs as the aching drained from my muscles. Etienne had a strand of seaweed caught in his hair, a single green dreadlock. "What is this?" he muttered, tugging at it weakly. Down by the sea Françoise splashed out of the water, dragging her bag behind her.

"I hope this beach exists," she said as she flopped beside us. "I am not sure I can do the swim again." I was too exhausted to agree.

all these things

There are one hundred glow-stars on my bedroom ceiling. I've got crescent moons, gibbous moons, planets with Saturn's rings, accurate constellations, meteor showers, and a whirlpool galaxy with a flying saucer caught in its tail. They were given to me by a girlfriend who was surprised that I often lay awake after she went to sleep. She discovered it one night when she woke to go to the bathroom, and bought me the glow-stars the next day.

Glow-stars are strange. They make the ceiling disappear.

"Look," Françoise whispered, keeping her voice low so Etienne wouldn't wake. "Do you see?"

I followed the path of her arm, past the delicate wrist, up her finger to the million flecks of light. "I don't," I whispered back. "Where?"

"There . . . Moving. You can see the bright one?"

"Uh-huh."

"Now look down, then left, and . . ."

"Got it. Amazing . . ."

A satellite, reflecting what—the moon or earth? Sliding quickly and smoothly through the stars, tonight its orbit passing the Gulf of Thailand, and maybe later the skies of Dakar or Oxford.

Etienne stirred and turned in his sleep, rustling the plastic bag he'd stretched out beneath him on the sand. In the forest behind us some hidden night bird chattered briefly.

"Hey," I whispered, propping myself up on my elbows. "Do you want me to tell you something funny?"

"What about?"

"Infinity. But it isn't that complicated. I mean, you don't need a degree in—"

Françoise waved a hand in the air, tracing a red pattern with the tip of her cigarette.

"Is that a yes?" I whispered.

"Yes."

"Okay." I coughed quietly. "If you accept that the universe is infinite, then that means there's an infinite amount of chances for things to happen, right?"

She nodded and sucked on the red coal floating by her fingertips.

"Well, if there's an infinite amount of chances for something to happen, then eventually it will happen—no matter how small the likelihood."

"Ah."

"That means somewhere in space there's another planet that, by an incredible series of coincidences, developed exactly the same way as ours. Right down to the smallest detail."

"Is there?"

"Definitely. And there's another which is exactly the same, except that palm tree over there is two feet to the right. And there's another where the tree is two feet to the left. In fact, there're infinite planets with infinite variations on that tree alone . . ."

Silence. I wondered if she was asleep. "So how about that?" I prompted.

"Interesting," she whispered. "In these planets, everything that can happen will happen."

"Exactly."

"Then in one planet, maybe I am a movie star."

"There's no maybe about it. You live in Beverly Hills and swept last year's Oscars."

"That's good."

"Yeah, but don't forget, somewhere else your film was a flop."

"Oh?"

"It bombed. The critics turned on you, the studio lost a fortune, and you got into booze and Valium. It was pretty ugly."

Françoise rolled on to her side and looked at me. "Tell me about some other worlds," she whispered. In the moonlight her teeth flashed silver as she smiled.

"Well," I replied. "That's a lot to tell."

Etienne stirred and turned over again.

I leaned over and kissed Françoise. She pulled away, or laughed, or shook her head, or closed her eyes and kissed me back. Etienne woke, clasping his mouth in disbelief. Etienne slept. I slept while Françoise kissed Etienne.

Light-years above our garbage bag beds and the steady rush of the surf, all these things happened.

After Françoise had shut her eyes and her breathing had eased into a sleeping rhythm, I crept off my plastic sheet and walked down to the sea. I stood in the shallows, slowly sinking as the tide pulled away the sand around my feet. The lights of Koh Samui glowed on the horizon like a trace of sunset. The spread of stars stretched as far as my ceiling back home.

in country

We set off immediately after breakfast: half a bar of chocolate each and cold noodles, soaked in most of the water from our canteens. There wasn't any point in hanging around. We needed to find a freshwater source, and according to Mister Duck's map, the beach was on the other side of the island.

At first we walked along the beach, hoping to circle the coast, but the sand soon turned to jagged rocks, which turned to impassable cliffs and gorges. Then we tried the other end, wasting precious time while the sun rose in the sky, and found the same barrier. We were left with no choice but to try inland. The pass between the peaks was the obvious goal, so we slung our plastic bags over our shoulders and picked our way into the jungle.

The first two or three hundred meters from the shore were the hardest. The spaces between the palm trees were covered in strange rambling bushes with tiny leaves that sliced like razors, and the only way past them was to push through. But as we got further inland and the ground began to rise, the palms became less common than another kind of tree—trees like rusted, ivy-choked space rockets, with ten-foot roots that fanned from the trunk like stabilizer fins. With less sunlight coming through the canopy, the vegetation on the forest floor thinned out. Occasionally we were stopped by a dense spray of bamboo, but a short search would find an animal track or a path cleared by a fallen branch.

After Zeph's description of the jungle, with Jurassic plants and strangely colored birds, I was vaguely disappointed by the reality. In many ways I felt like I was walking through an English forest, I'd just shrunk to a tenth of my normal size.

But there were some things that felt suitably exotic. Several times we saw tiny brown monkeys scurrying up the trees, Tarzan-style lianas hung above us like stalactites, and there was the water—it dripped on our necks, flattened our hair, and stuck our T-shirts to our chests. There was so much of it that our half-empty canteens stopped being a worry. Standing under a branch and giving it a shake provided a couple of good gulps, as well as a quick shower. The irony of having kept my clothes dry during the swim, only to have them soaked when we turned inland, didn't escape me.

After two hours of walking we found ourselves at the bottom of a particularly steep stretch of slope. We had to pull ourselves up on the tough fern stems to keep from slipping down on the mud and dead leaves. Etienne was the first to get to the top and he disappeared over the ridge, then reappeared a few seconds later, beckoning enthusiastically.

"Hurry up!" he called. "Really, it is amazing!"

"What is it?" I called back, but he'd disappeared again.

I redoubled my efforts, leaving Françoise behind.

The slope led to a soccer-field-sized shelf on the mountainside, so flat and neat that it seemed unnatural in the tangle of the surrounding jungle. Above us the slope rose again to what appeared to be a second shelf, and above that it continued straight up to the pass.

Etienne had gone further into the plateau and was standing in some bushy plants, gazing around with his hands on his hips.

"What do you think?" he said. I looked behind me. Far below I could see the beach we had come from, the island where our hidden rucksacks lay, and the many other islands beyond it.

"I didn't know the Marine Park was this big," I replied.

"Yes. Very big. But that is not what I mean."

I turned back to the plateau, putting a cigarette in my mouth. Then, as I patted down my pockets looking for my lighter, I noticed something strange. All the plants in the plateau looked vaguely familiar.

"Wow," I said, and the cigarette dropped from my lips, forgotten.

"Yes."

". . . Dope?"

Etienne grinned. "Have you ever seen so much?"

"Never . . ." I pulled a few leaves from the nearest bush and rubbed them in my hands.

Etienne waded further into the plateau. "We should pick some, Richard," he said. "We can dry it in the sun and . . ." Then he stopped. "Wait a moment, there is something funny here."

"What?"

"Well, it is just so . . . These plants . . ." He crouched down, then looked round at me quickly. His lips had begun to curve into a smile, but his eyes were wide and I could literally see color draining from his face. "This is a field," he said.

I froze. "A field?"

"Yes. Look at the plants."

"But it can't be a field. I mean, these islands are . . ."

"The plants are in rows."

"Rows . . ."

We stared at each other. "Jesus Christ," I said slowly. "Then we're in deep shit."

Etienne started running back toward me.

"Françoise?"

"She's . . ." My mind was filling with too many thoughts to answer the question. "Coming," I eventually replied, but he had already passed me and was crouching over the slope.

"She's not there!"

"But she was just behind me." I jogged to the ridge and looked over. "Maybe she slipped."

Etienne stood up. "I will go down. You look here."

"Yes . . . Right."

He began slithering down the mud, then I saw the yellow flash of her T-shirt in some trees further along the edge of the plateau. Etienne had already slid halfway down the slope and I threw a pebble at him to get his attention. He swore and began making his way back up.

Françoise had come out into the plateau, tucking her T-shirt into her shorts. "I needed the bathroom," she called.

I waved my hands frantically, mouthing at her to keep her voice down. She cupped a hand by her ear. "What? Hey! I have seen some people further up the mountain. They are coming this way. Maybe they are from the beach, no?"

Hearing her, Etienne called from down the slope, "Richard! Make her be quiet!"

I sprinted toward her. "What are you doing?" she asked, and then I'd reached her and was pushing her to the ground.

"Shut up!" I said, clamping my hand to her mouth.

She tried to squirm out of my grip and I pressed harder, bending her head back on her shoulders. "This is a dope field," I hissed, carefully enunciating each word. "Do you understand?"

Her eyes bulged wide and she started snorting through her nose. "Do you understand?" I hissed again. "It's a fucking field."

Then Etienne was behind me, pulling at my arms. I dropped Françoise, and for a reason I still don't understand, I lunged for his neck. He twisted behind me and wrapped his arms around my chest.

I tried to struggle but he was too strong. "You idiot! Let me go! There are people coming!"

"Where are the people?"

"On the mountain," Françoise whispered, rubbing her mouth. "Higher."

He looked up to the second plateau. "I can't see anyone," he said, easing his hold on me. "Listen. What is that?"

We all went silent but I couldn't hear anything except blood pounding in my ears.

"Voices," said Etienne quietly. "You can hear it?"

I strained to listen again. This time I found it, distant but getting clearer.

"It's Thai."

I choked. "Fuck! We've got to run!" I clambered to my feet but Etienne dragged me back down.

"Richard," he said, and through my fear some part of me registered surprise at the calm expression on his face. "If we run we will be seen."

"So what do we do?"

He pointed to a dark copse. "We hide in there."

Lying flat against the earth, peering through the mesh of leaves, we waited for the people to appear.

At first it seemed that they would pass us out of sight, but then a branch cracked and a man stepped into the field, close to where Etienne and I had been standing a few minutes before. He was young, maybe twenty, with a kick-boxer's build. His chest was bare and etched with muscle, and he wore military trousers—dark green and baggy with pouches sewn into the legs. In his hand was a long machete. Slung over his shoulder was an automatic rifle.

I could feel Françoise's body pressed against mine—she was trembling. I looked round, somehow thinking I might calm her, but I could feel the tightness in my face. She stared at me, eyebrows raised as if she wanted me to explain. I shook my head helplessly.

A second man appeared, older, also armed. They stopped

and exchanged a few words. Though they stood more than twenty meters away, the curious looping sound of their language carried perfectly over the distance. Then another man called out from within the jungle and they set off again, vanishing over the ridge, down the slope we'd originally come from.

Two or three minutes after their singsong chatter had faded away, Françoise suddenly burst into tears. Then Etienne started crying too. He lay on his back and covered his eyes, his hands bunched into fists.

I watched the two of them blankly. I felt in limbo. The shock of discovering the fields and the tension while we'd been hiding had left me empty. I just kneeled on the ground, sweat running from my hairline and down the side of my face, and thought of nothing.

Finally I managed to gather my wits. "Okay," I said. "Etienne was right. They didn't know we were here, but they might find out soon." I reached for my bag. "We've got to leave."

Françoise sat up, wiping her eyes on her mud-streaked T-shirt. "Yes," she muttered. "Come, Etienne."

Etienne nodded. "Richard," he said firmly. "I do not want to die here."

I opened my mouth to speak but couldn't think what to say.

"I do not want to die here," he repeated. "You must get us out."

falling down

I must get them out? Me? I couldn't believe my ears. He'd been the one who'd kept his head when the dope guards were coming. I'd lost my shit. I felt like saying, "*You* fucking get us out!"

But just by looking at him I could tell he wasn't about to take control of the situation. And neither was Françoise. She was gazing at me with the same scared, expectant expression as Etienne.

So, not having a choice, I ended up being the one who made the decision to go on. In one direction there were gunmen, walking along the tracks we had ignorantly assumed were made by animals. Perhaps they were even on the way to the beach and might find a chocolate wrapper or footprints that would betray our presence. In the other direction we didn't know what we might find. Maybe more fields, maybe more gunmen, maybe a beach full of Westerners, and maybe nothing at all.

Better the devil you know is a cliché I now despise. Hidden in the bushes, shivering with fright, I learned that if the devil you know is the guard of a drug plantation, then all other devils pale in comparison.

I have almost no recollection of the few hours after we left the plateau. I think I was concentrating so hard on the immediate that my mind couldn't afford space for anything else. Maybe to have a memory, you need time for reflection, however brief, just to let the memory find a place to settle.

What I do have is a couple of snapshot images: the view from the pass looking back on the dope fields below us, and a more surreal one—surreal because it's a sight I could never have seen, but if I close my eyes I can see it as clearly as I can see any image in my mind.

It's the three of us making our way down the mountain on the far side of the pass. I'm looking from behind, so I can only see our backs, and the image is elevated slightly as if I'm standing further up the slope. We don't have our garbage bags. My arms are empty and outstretched, like I'm trying to steady myself, and Etienne is holding one of Françoise's hands.

The other strange thing is that beyond us I can see the lagoon and a white smear of sand over the treetops. But that isn't possible. We never saw the lagoon until we reached the waterfall.

It was the height of a four-story building—the kind of height that I hate to stand upright near. To gauge the drop I had to crawl to the cliff edge on my belly, afraid that the sense of balance which allows me to stand on a chair would desert me and I would lunge drunkenly forward to my death.

On either side the cliff continued, eventually curving around into the sea, then, unbroken, rejoining the land on the far side. It was as if a giant circle had been cut out of the island to enclose the lagoon in a wall of rock—just as Zeph had described. From where we sat, we could see that the sea-locked cliffs were no more than twenty meters thick, but a passing boat could never guess what lay behind them. They would only see a continuous jungle-topped coastline. The lagoon was presumably supplied by underwater caves and channels.

The falls dropped into a pool from which a quick-flowing stream ran into the trees. The highest trees were more than equal to our height. If they'd been a little closer to the precipice, we could have used them to get down—and getting down was the big problem. The drop was too sheer and too far to consider climbing.

"What do you think?" I said, crawling back from the cliff edge toward Etienne and Françoise.

"What do *you* think?" Etienne replied, apparently not yet ready to let control pass from my hands.

I sighed. "I think we've definitely found the right place. It's where Mister Duck's map says it is, and it fits Zeph's description perfectly."

"So near and so far."

"So near and yet so far," I corrected vacantly. "That's about it."

Françoise stood up and stared over the lagoon toward the seaward rock face. "Perhaps we should walk around there," she suggested. "It may be easier to climb."

"It's higher than here. You can see where the land rises."

"We could jump into the sea. It is not too high to jump."

"We'd never clear the rocks."

She looked irritated and tired. "Okay, Richard, but there must be a way down, no? If people go to this beach, there must be a way."

"If people go to this beach," I echoed. We hadn't seen any sign that people were down there. I'd been carrying an idea that when we reached the beach we'd see groups of friendly travelers with sun-kissed faces, hanging out, coral-diving, playing Frisbee. All that stuff. As it was, from what we could see the beach looked beautiful but completely deserted.

"Maybe we can jump from this waterfall," said Etienne. "It is not so high as the cliff in the sea."

I thought for a moment. "Possibly," I replied, and rubbed my eyes. The adrenaline that had kept me going over the pass had faded and now I was exhausted; so exhausted I couldn't even feel relief at having found the beach. I was also dying for a cigarette. I'd thought of lighting up several times but was still too jumpy about who might smell the smoke.

Françoise seemed to read my mind. "If you want a cigarette, you should have one," she said, smiling. I think it was the first time one of us had smiled since leaving the plateau. "We saw no fields on this side of the pass."

"Yes," Etienne added. "And maybe it can help . . . The nicotine . . . It helps."

"Good point."

I lit up and crawled back to the cliff edge.

If, I reasoned, the waterfall had been pounding down into the pool below for a thousand years, then it was likely that a basin had been eroded into the rock. A basin deep enough to accommodate my leaping into it. But if the island had been created relatively recently, maybe the result of volcanic activity two hundred years ago, then there might not have been time for a deep enough pool to have formed.

"But what do I know?" I said, exhaling slowly, and Françoise looked up to see if I was talking to her.

The pebbles in the water were smooth. The trees below were tall and old.

"Okay," I whispered.

I stood up cautiously, one foot an inch from the cliff, the other set back at a stabilizing angle. A memory appeared of making Airfix airplanes, filling them with cotton wool, covering them in lighter fuel, setting fire to them, and dropping them from the top window of my house.

"Are you jumping?" called Etienne nervously.

"Just taking a better look."

As the planes fell they would arc outward, then appear to curve back toward the wall. The point where they landed, exploding into sticky burning pieces, always seemed to be nearer to the edge of the house than I expected. The distance was difficult to judge; the model planes always needed a harder shove than seemed necessary if they were to clear the doorstep, as well as the head of anyone coming to investigate the patches of flame around the yard.

I was turning this memory over when something happened. An overwhelming sensation washed over me, almost boredom, a strange listlessness. I was suddenly sick of how difficult this journey had become. There was too much effort, too many shocks and dilemmas to dissect. And this sickness had an effect. For a vital few seconds it liberated me from a fear of consequences. I'd had enough. I just wanted it over with.

So near and so far.

"So jump," I heard my voice say.

I paused, wondering if I'd heard myself correctly, and then I did. I jumped.

Everything happened as things are supposed to happen while one falls. I had time to think. Stupid things flashed through my head, such as how my cat slipped off the kitchen table one time and landed on its head, and how once I misjudged a dive from a springboard and the water felt like wood—not concrete or metal but wood.

Then I hit the pool. My T-shirt shot up my chest and jammed under my neck and seconds later I bobbed to the surface. The basin was so deep I never even touched the bottom.

"Ha!" I shouted, thrashing the water around me with my arms, not caring who might hear. "I'm alive!"

I looked up and saw Etienne's and Françoise's heads poking over the cliff.

"You are okay?" called Etienne.

"I'm fine! I'm brilliant!" Then I felt something in my hand. I was still holding my cigarette—the tobacco part had been torn away but the brown filter sat in my palm, soggy and nicotine stained. I started laughing. "Fucking brilliant! Chuck down the bags!"

I sat on the pool's grassy shore, my feet dangling in the water, and waited for Etienne and Françoise to jump. Etienne was having some difficulty psyching himself up, and Françoise didn't want to jump first and leave him up there on his own.

The man appeared just as I was lighting another cigarette to make up for the one I'd ruined. He walked out of the trees a few meters away from me. If it hadn't been for his features and his full beard I could hardly have told he was a Caucasian. His skin was as dark as an Asian's, although a slightly bronze color hinted it had once been white. All he had on was a pair of tattered blue shorts and a necklace made of seashells. With the beard it was hard to tell his age, but I didn't think he was much older than me.

"Hey," he said, cocking his head to one side. "Pretty quick, for an FNG. You did the jump in twenty-three minutes." His accent was English and regionless. "It took me over an hour, but I was alone, so it was harder."

fng

I covered my eyes with an arm and lay back. Over the sound of the waterfall, Etienne's disembodied voice called to me, saying he was about to jump. From his angle, he wouldn't have been able to see the man. I didn't bother to answer him.

"You okay?" I heard the man ask, and the grass rustled as

he took a few steps toward me. "I'm sorry, I should have . . . You must be really freaked out."

Freaked out? I thought. "Not really. I feel quite relaxed."

Extremely relaxed. Floaty. Between my fingers I could feel the cigarette warming my skin, burning closer to my hand.

"Who are you calling an FNG?" I murmured.

A shadow passed across my face as the man bent over to check that I hadn't fainted. "Did you say something?"

"Yeah. I did."

Etienne shrieked as he fell, and the noise of his splash merged into the pounding of the water, and the pounding of the water sounded like the pounding of a helicopter.

"I said, who are you calling an FNG?"

The man paused. "You've been here before? I don't recognize you."

I smiled. "Sure I've been here before," I replied. "In my dreams."

Fragging. Bagging. Klicks. Grunts. Gooks. Charlie. MIA. KIA. LZ. DMZ. FNG.

FNG. Someone who's just starting his first tour in Vietnam. A Fucking New Guy.

Where do I learn these things?

I saw *84 Charlie Mopic* in 1989. I saw *Platoon* in 1986. My friend Tom said, "Rich, you want to see *Platoon?*" "Okay," I said, and he grinned. "Then you'd better find someone to go with." He was always making jokes like that—it was as natural to him as breathing. We went to see it that night at the Swiss Cottage Odeon, screen one, 1986.

In 1991, standing in an airport lounge, looking for something to pass the hours over a long flight to Jakarta. "Eric Van Lustbader?" suggested Sean, and I shook my head. I'd seen Michael Herr sending dispatches. The hours flew by.

Fucking New Guy? Yea, though I walk through the valley of death I will fear no evil, for I am the evilest motherfucker in the valley.

New to what?

We followed the man through the trees. Sometimes we crossed the stream from the pool as it meandered through the jungle, and sometimes we passed glades—one with a smoldering campfire and charred fish heads strewn around it.

We didn't talk much as we walked. The only thing that the man would tell us was his name—Jed. The rest of our questions he waved aside. "Simpler to deal with the talking at the camp," he explained. "We've got as many questions for you as you've got for us."

At first glance the camp was close to how I'd imagined it might be. There was a large dusty clearing surrounded by the rocket ship trees and dotted with makeshift bamboo huts. A few canvas tents looked incongruous, but otherwise it was very like a kind of Southeast Asian village I'd seen many times before. At the far end was a larger construction, a long-house, and beside it the stream from the waterfall reemerged, bending around to run along the edge of the clearing. From the straightness of its banks, it had obviously been deliberately diverted.

It was only after taking all this in that I noticed there was something strange about the light. The forest had been both dark and bright by turns, but here everything was lit in an unchanging twilight, more like dusk than midday. I looked up, following the trunk of one of the giant trees. The height of the tree alone was breathtaking, accentuated by the fact that the lower branches had been cut away, so it was possible to appreciate its size. Higher up the branches began to grow again, curving upward across the clearing like gables until they joined with the branches from the other side. But their point of joining seemed too dense and thick, and as I looked harder I began to see that they were coiled around each other, intertwining to form a cavernous ceiling of wood and leaves, hanging with the stalactite vines that now became magically appropriate.

"Camouflage," said Jed, behind me. "We don't want to be seen from the air. Planes sometimes fly over. Not often, but sometimes." He pointed upward. "Originally the branches were tied together with ropes but now they just grow that way. Every so often we have to cut them back a bit, or it gets too gloomy. Impressive, huh?"

"Stunning," I agreed, and was so captivated by this sight that I didn't even register that people had begun to emerge from the longhouse and were walking across the clearing toward us. Three people to be exact. Two women and a man.

"Sal, Cassie, and Bugs," said one of the women as they reached us. "I'm Sal, but don't try to remember our names." She smiled warmly. "You'll only get confused when you meet the others, and you'll learn them all eventually."

I'm not likely to forget Bugs, I thought to myself, just managing to suppress a laugh. I frowned and put a hand up to my temples. Since I'd jumped off the waterfall my head had been feeling increasingly light. Now it had started to feel like it might float off my shoulders.

Françoise stepped up to the woman and said, "Françoise, Etienne, and Richard."

"You're French! Lovely! We've only got one other French person here."

"Richard is English." Françoise gestured to me and I tried to nod politely, but I overran the motion forward and the nod turned into a little bow.

"Lovely!" exclaimed the woman again, watching me curiously out of the corner of her eye. ". . . Well, let's get you some food, because I know you're all hungry." She turned to the man. "Bugs, you want to fix some stew? Then we can all have a good long chat and get to know each other. Does that sound good?"

"It sounds great, Sal," I said loudly. "You know, you're quite right. I do feel hungry." The laugh I'd suppressed before suddenly worked its way out. "We've only eaten these cold Magi-Noodles and chocolate. We couldn't take the Calor gas stove . . . Etienne's stove . . . And . . ."

Jed lunged to catch me as I fainted, but too late. His alarmed face spun out of view as I toppled backward. The last thing I saw was a blue pinprick of sky through the canopy ceiling, before darkness rushed in and engulfed it.

batman

I waited patiently for Mister Duck to show up. I knew he was near, because in the candlelight I could see blood scattered in the dust around my bed and there was a red handprint on the sheets. I guessed he was in the shadows at the other end of the longhouse, waiting to loom out and surprise me. But he was the one who was going to be surprised. This time I was expecting him.

Minutes passed. I sweated and sighed. Wax ran down the candle, balling in the dust. A lizard fell from a beam above and landed between my legs.

The lizard from the rainstorm, come back to visit me.

"Aah," I said. "Hello there." I reached to pick him up but he wriggled free, leaving a centimeter of pink tail behind.

One of Mister Duck's games.

I swore and held up the tail, and it flopped around on my palm. "Very clever, Duck. Don't know what it means, but it's very clever." I sank back on the pillow. "Hey, Duck! That's the kid, huh? That's the boy!"

"Who are you talking to?" said a sleepy voice from deep in the shadows.

I sat up again. "That you, Duck? You sound different."

". . . It's Bugs."

"Bugs. I remember. Hey, let me guess. Bugs Bunny, right?"

There was a long pause. "Yes," said the voice. "That is right."

I scratched my head. Sticky clumps were matted into my hair. "Yeah, thought so. So you've taken over from Duck now. Who's next?" I giggled. "Road Runner?"

Two people muttered in the darkness.

"Porky Pig? Yosemite Sam? No, wait, I've got it . . . Wile E. Coyote. It's Wile E. Coyote, isn't it?"

In the orange candlelight I saw a movement down the longhouse, a figure padding toward me. As it moved closer I recognized the slim shape.

"Françoise! Hey, Françoise, this is a better dream than the last one."

"Shh," she whispered, kneeling beside me, her long white T-shirt drawing up around her thighs. "You are not dreaming."

I shook my head. "No, Françoise, I am. Trust me. Look at the blood on the floor. That's Mister Duck, from his wrists. They never stop bleeding. You should have seen what happened to my room in Bangkok."

She looked around, then back at me. "The blood is from your head, Richard."

"But . . ."

"You hurt it when you fell."

". . . Mister Duck."

"Shh. There are people asleep in here. Please."

I lay back, feeling puzzled, and she rested her hand on my forehead.

"You have a little temperature. Do you think you can go back to sleep?"

". . . I don't know."

"Will you try?"

". . . Okay."

She tucked the sheets over my shoulders, smiling slightly. "There now. Close your eyes."

I closed them.

The pillow shifted as she leaned over. She kissed me gently on the cheek.

"I am dreaming," I murmured as her footsteps padded away down the longhouse. "I knew it."

Mister Duck hung above me like a wingless bat, his legs gripping the beam, the curve under his rib cage stretched into a grotesque cavity, his swinging arms dripping steadily.

"I knew it," I said. "I knew you were near." A pulse of blood splashed onto my chest. "Cold like a fucking reptile."

Mister Duck scowled. "It's as hot as yours. It's only cold because of the fever. And you should put the covers back. You'll catch your death."

"Too hot."

"Mmm. Too hot, too cold . . ."

I wiped my mouth with a wet hand. "Is it malaria?"

"Malaria? Nervous exhaustion, more like."

"So how come Françoise doesn't have it?"

"She wasn't as nervous as you." His outsized jaw jutted out and split his face into a mischievous grin. "She's been very attentive, you know. Very attentive indeed. Checked on you twice when you were asleep."

"I am asleep."

"Sure . . . Fast asleep."

The candle flame faltered as melting wax began to flood

the wick. Cicadas chirped outside. Blood like icy water dripped, made me shiver and twist the sheets.

"What was the deal with the lizard, Duck?"

"Lizard?"

"It ran away. In the rainstorm I could hold it in my hand. But here it ran away."

"I seem to remember it running in the rainstorm, Rich."

"I held it in my hand."

"Is that what you remember, Rich?"

The pool of wax grew too large for the candle to contain. Suddenly it drained away and the wick flared brightly, throwing a crisp shadow on the longhouse ceiling. A silhouette. A wingless bat with hanging claws and pencil arms.

"Lightning," I whispered.

The jaw jutted out. "That's the boy . . ."

"Fuck . . ."

". . . That's the kid."

". . . you."

Minutes passed.

talk

Late morning, I reckoned. Only from the heat. In the darkness of the longhouse and the steady glow of the candle, there was nothing else to reveal the time.

A Buddha sat cross-legged at the foot of my bed, palms resting flat on ocher knees. An unusual Buddha, female, with an American accent, heavy breasts clearly outlined through a saffron T-shirt, and long hair tied back from her perfectly round face. Around her neck was a necklace of seashells. Beside her, incense sticks burned, sending tiny spirals of perfumed smoke up to the ceiling.

"Finish it, Richard," said the Buddha, looking pointedly at the bowl I held in my hands—half a freshly cut coconut, now nearly drained of a sugary fish soup. "Finish all of it."

I lifted the bowl to my mouth, and the smell of the incense mixed with the fish and sweetness.

I put it down again. "I can't, Sal."

"You must, Richard."

"I'll throw up."

"Richard, you must."

She had the American habit of frequently using one's name. It had the strange effect of being both disarmingly familiar and unnaturally forced.

"Honestly. I can't."

"It's good for you."

"I've finished most of it. Look."

I held up the bowl for her to see and we stared at each other across my bloodstained sheets.

"Okay," she sighed. "I guess that'll have to do." Then she folded her arms and narrowed her eyes and said, "Richard, we need to talk."

We were alone. Occasionally people would enter and leave but I never saw them. I'd hear the door at the far end of the longhouse bang open and a small rectangle of light would hover in the darkness until the door swung shut.

When I reached the part about finding Mister Duck's body, Sal looked sad. It wasn't a strong reaction; her eyebrows flicked downward and her lower lip tensed. I guessed she'd already heard about Duck's death from Etienne and Françoise, so the news wasn't as shocking as it could have been. Her reaction was pretty hard to read. It seemed more directed at me than anything else, like she was sorry that I'd had to witness something so horrible.

Aside from that one moment, Sal made no other signs. She didn't interrupt me, frown, smile, or nod. She just sat in her lotus position, motionless, and listened. At first her blankness was disconcerting and I paused after key events to give her time to comment, but she'd only wait for me to continue. Soon I found myself slipping into a stream of consciousness, talking to her as if she were a tape recorder or a priest.

Very like a priest. I began to feel as if I was in confession, describing my panic on the plateau with embarrassment and trying to justify why I'd lied to the Thai police; and the silent way she absorbed these things was like absolution. I even made an obscure reference to my attraction to Françoise, just to get it off my chest. Probably too oblique for her to pick up, but the intention was there.

The only thing I held back was that I'd given two other people directions to the island. I knew I should tell her about Zeph and Sammy, but I also thought she might be pissed off if she knew I'd spread their secret. Better to wait until I knew more about the setup on the island.

I also didn't tell her about my dreams with Mister Duck, but that was different. There wasn't any reason why I should.

I punctuated the end of the story, leading right up to the point where I'd walked into the camp and collapsed, by leaning out of bed and pulling the carton of two hundred cigarettes out of my plastic bag. Sal smiled and the confessional atmosphere was broken, abruptly flipped back to the semi-familiarity of before.

"Hey," she said, stretching out the word in her North American drawl. "You sure came prepared."

"Mmm," I replied, all I could say as I sucked the candle flame onto the tip. "I'm the addict's addict."

She laughed. "I see that."

"You want one?"

"No thanks. I'd really better not."

"Giving up?"

"Given up. You should try too, Richard. It's easy to give up here."

I took a few quick drags without inhaling, to burn the waxy taste out of the cigarette. "I'll give up when I'm thirty or something. When I have kids."

Sal shrugged. "Whatever," she said, smiling, then brushed a finger over each eyebrow, smoothing out the sweat. "Well, Richard, it sounds like you had quite an adventure getting here. In normal circumstances, new guests are brought here under supervision. Your circumstances were very unusual."

I waited for her to elaborate but she didn't. Instead she uncrossed her legs as if she was about to leave.

"Uh, now can I ask you some questions, Sal?" I said quickly.

Her eyes flicked down to her wrist. She wasn't wearing any watch; it was a motion of pure instinct.

"I have some things to do, Richard."

"Please, Sal. There's so much I've got to ask you."

"Sure there is, but you'll learn everything in time. There's no particular hurry."

"Just a few questions."

She crossed her legs again. "Five minutes."

"Okay, uh, well, first I'd just like to know something about the setup. I mean, what is this place?"

"It's a beach resort."

I frowned. "A beach resort?"

"A place to come to for vacations."

I frowned harder. By the look in Sal's eyes, I could see she found my expression amusing.

"Holidays?" I tried to say, but the word caught in my throat. It seemed so belittling. I had ambiguous feelings about the differences between tourists and travelers—the problem being that the more I traveled, the smaller the differences became. But the one difference I could still latch onto was that tourists went on holidays while travelers did something else. They *traveled.*

"What did you think this place was?" Sal asked.

"I don't know. I didn't think anything really." I exhaled slowly. "But I certainly didn't think of a beach resort."

She waved a chubby hand in the air. "Okay. I'm kind of teasing you, Richard. Of course this is more than a beach resort. But at the same time, it is just a beach resort. We come here to relax by a beautiful beach, but it isn't a beach resort because we're trying to get away from beach resorts. Or we're trying to make a place that won't turn into a beach resort. See?"

"No."

Sal shrugged. "You will see, Richard. It's not so complicated."

Actually, I did see what she meant but I didn't want to admit it. I wanted her to describe Zeph's island commune of free spirits. A holiday resort seemed like a poor reward for the difficulties we'd had to overcome, and a rush of bitterness ran through me as I remembered the swim and the terror of hiding on the plateau.

"Don't look so disappointed, Richard."

"No, I'm not . . . I'm . . ."

Sal reached over and squeezed my hand. "After a little while you'll see that this is a wonderful place, as long as you appreciate it for what it is."

I nodded. "I'm sorry, Sal. I didn't mean to look disappointed. I'm not disappointed. I mean, this longhouse and the trees outside . . . It's all amazing." I laughed. "It's silly really. I think I was expecting an . . . an ideology or something. A purpose."

I paused while I finished the cigarette. Sal made no movement to leave. "How about the gunmen in the dope fields?" I asked, conscientiously tucking the dead butt back into the packet. "Are they anything to do with you?"

Sal shook her head.

"They're drug lords?"

"I think drug lords is a bit dramatic. I have a feeling the fields are owned by ex-fishermen from Koh Samui, but I could be wrong. They turned up a couple of years ago and pretty much took over that half of the island. We can't go there now."

"How do they get around the Marine Park authorities?"

"Same as us. They keep quiet. And half of the wardens are probably in on it, so they make sure the tourist boats don't come near."

"But they know you're here."

"Of course, but there isn't much they can do. It's not like they can report us. If we got raided, then they'd get raided too."

"So there's no trouble between you?"

Sal's hand flicked to the seashell necklace around her neck. "They stick to their half. We stick to ours," she said briskly, then suddenly stood up, patting the dust from her skirt with pointless attention. "Enough talk, Richard. I really do have to go now and you're still running a fever. You need some rest."

I didn't bother protesting and Sal began walking away, her T-shirt catching the candlelight a little longer than her skin and skirt.

"One more question," I called after her, and she looked round. "The man in Bangkok. You knew him?"

"Yes," she said quietly, then she began walking again.

"Who was he?"

"He was a friend."

"He lived here?"

"He was a friend," she repeated.

"But . . . Okay, just one more question."

Sal didn't stop, and now only her saffron T-shirt was visible, bobbing in the darkness.

"One more!"

"What?" her voice floated back.

"Where's the toilet?"

"Outside, second hut down by the edge of the camp."

The bright sliver of light through the longhouse door slid back to blackness.

exploring

The toilet, a small bamboo hut on the edge of the clearing, was a good example of how well the camp had been organized. Inside the hut was a low bench with a football-sized hole, through which I could see running water—a tributary from the diverted waterfall stream. There was a second hole cut into the roof, to let in what little light filtered past the canopy ceiling.

All in all, it was a lot more agreeable than many of the bathrooms one finds outside the Westernized world. There wasn't, however, any toilet paper. Not a surprise in itself, but I'd thought there might be some leaves or something. Instead, by the water channel, there was a plastic pitcher.

You find plastic pitchers all around provincial Asia and their purpose has confounded me for years. I refuse to believe that Asians wipe themselves with their hands—it's a ridiculous idea—but aside from washing digits, I can't see what other use the pitcher has. I'm sure they don't splash themselves down. Apart from being ineffective it would make an incredible mess, and they emerge from their ablutions as dry as a bone.

Of the various mysteries of the Orient this should be the easiest to unravel, but the subject matter appears to be veiled in a conspiracy of silence. A Manilan friend once came with me on a trip to a small island off the coast of Luzon. One day I found him standing on a mud dike, peering into the mangrove swamps with obvious concern. When I asked him what the matter was he blushed furiously, which made his brown skin go almost purple, and pointed to some bits of toilet paper that were floating in the water. The tide was leading the toilet paper toward some houses, and this prospect had thrown him into a panic. Not for reasons of hygiene but because it would betray his Western toilet habits—habits the locals would find unacceptably disgusting. In his shame, he was considering wading into the swamps to hoick the pieces out and hide them elsewhere.

We managed to solve the problem by bombarding the water with stones until the paper shredded or sank. As we slunk away from the scene of the crime I asked him to describe the locals' acceptable alternative, but he refused to tell me. He just hinted darkly that I'd find it as disgusting as they found our way. This was as close as I ever got to finding out the truth.

Luckily I only needed to piss, so I was spared having to experiment. When the time came for solids, I decided, I'd slip into the jungle.

I left the toilet and began walking back across the clearing. I was still feeling slightly feverish but I didn't want to spend any more hours breathing stuffy air and watching flickering candle flames. Instead I continued past the longhouse, thinking I might explore. I also hoped that I might find Etienne and Françoise, who'd been missing since I woke up. I imagined they were exploring too.

I counted nine tents in the clearing and five huts, not including the longhouse. The tents were only used for sleeping—inside the flaps I could see backpacks and clothes, and in one I even saw a Nintendo Game Boy—but the huts all seemed to have functional uses. Apart from the toilet, there was a kitchen and a washing area, also fed by tributaries. The other huts were for storage. One contained carpentry tools and another some boxes of tinned food. It made me wonder how long the camp had existed. Sal had said that the dope fields had appeared a couple of years ago, which implied that the travelers had been around for some time before that.

Tents, tools, tinned food, Nintendo. The more I saw, the more I marveled. It wasn't just how organized the camp was, it was *how* it had been organized. None of the huts looked newer than the others. The tents' guylines were held with rocks, and the rocks were molded into the ground. Nothing seemed random, everything seemed calculated: designed as opposed to evolved.

As I wandered around the clearing, peering through tent flaps and studying the canopy ceiling until my neck ached, my sense of awe was only matched by a sense of frustration. Questions kept appearing in my mind, and each question raised another. It was clear that, at some point, the people who'd set up the camp had needed a boat. This suggested the help of Thais, which in turn suggested a certain kind of Thai. A Koh Samui spiv might bend the rules to let backpackers stay on a Marine Park island for a few nights, but it was harder to imagine them ferrying crates of food and carpentry tools.

I also found it strange that the camp was so deserted. It apparently supported a large number of people, and a couple of times I thought I heard voices nearby, but no one ever appeared.

After a while, the quietness and occasional distant voices

began to get to me. At first I just felt a little lonely and sorry for myself. I didn't think Sal should have left me on my own, especially when I was ill and new to the camp. And Etienne and Françoise were supposed to be my friends. Shouldn't friends have hung around to make sure I was okay?

But soon loneliness turned into paranoia. I found that I was starting when I heard jungle noises, my shuffling footsteps in the dirt sounded oddly loud, and I caught myself acting with an affected casualness, aimed at the eyes I suspected were watching me from the trees. Even the absence of Etienne and Françoise became a reason to worry.

Maybe it was partly to do with my fever, or maybe it was a normal reaction under abnormal circumstances. Either way, the eerie quietness was freaking me out. I decided I had to get out of the clearing. I went back to the longhouse to pick up my cigarettes and some shoes, but when I saw the long avenue of shadow that lay between the door and my candlelit bed, I changed my mind.

There were several paths that ran from the clearing. I chose the nearest.

By good luck, the path I chose led directly to the beach. The sand was too hot for bare feet, so I jogged down to the water's edge, and after making a mental note of where I'd come out of the jungle, I flipped a mental coin and took a left.

Getting out from the claustrophobic cavern of trees calmed me. There was plenty to distract me as I walked through the shallows.

From the waterfall, I'd seen the vast circle of granite cliffs as a barrier to getting down, but now they were a barrier to getting back up. A prison could hardly have been built with more formidable walls, although it was hard to think of such a place as prisonlike. Aside from the lagoon's beauty, there was a sense that the cliffs were protective—the walls of an inverse castle, sunk instead of raised. Sal hadn't given me the impression of being very threatened by the dope farmers, but the knowledge that the cliffs lay between me and them was still comforting.

The lagoon itself was almost perfectly divided between land and sea. I estimated its diameter at a mile, though I wouldn't rely on the accuracy of this guess. Now, nearer to the seaward cliffs than on the waterfall, I could make out features in the rock face I hadn't seen before. Along the watermark were black hollows and caves. They looked as if they penetrated the cliff deeply—perhaps deeply enough to provide a passage for a small boat. The sea itself was punctuated by protruding boulders, slick where the waves lapped against them, flattened into slabs by centuries of tropical rain.

I'd walked a few hundred meters down the beach when I noticed some shapes splashing around one of the larger boulders, Bizarrely, my first thought was that they were seals, until I realized there couldn't possibly be seals in Thailand. Then, looking harder, I realized they were people. At last I'd found someone.

I checked the urge to call out, for no particular reason other than a vague instinct to be cautious. Instead I jogged back over the sand to the treeline, where I could sit in the shade and wait until the swimmers returned. There I found footprints, T-shirts, and to my delight, an open packet of Marlboros. After a millisecond of debate I stole one.

Contented for the moment, I blew smoke rings into the still air, discovering that when they floated over the beach they would rise quickly and, without dissipating, drift into the overhanging palm leaves. It took me several baffled puffs to work out that it was due to heat rising from the sunbaked sand.

The swimmers were less confusing. They were spearfishing. Every so often they'd all get out of the sea and gaze intently at the water around them, spears poised. Then they'd all throw their spears at once, dive back in, splash around a bit, and repeat the process. They seemed to catch a lot of fish.

exocet

Neutralized by wet hair and dark skin, each of the six swimmers looked like a carbon copy of the others. I didn't recognize Etienne and Françoise until they'd crossed the hot sands and were laying out their catch on the grass.

Something made me hesitate before I stepped out from behind the treeline. Seeing my two traveling companions on such friendly terms with the other swimmers felt strange. They were all laughing and calling each other by name. It made me realize how much I'd been left out by sleeping through the first night and day in the camp. And then, when I did step out, none of the group noticed me. I had to stand there a few moments, a grin frozen on my face, waiting for one of them to look up.

Eventually, not knowing what else to do, I coughed. Six heads turned in unison.

"Hi," I said uncertainly. There was a silence. Françoise was frowning slightly, as if she couldn't quite place me. Then Etienne's face split into a huge smile.

"Richard! You are better!" He bounded over and embraced me. "Everybody," he said, tightly gripping me with one wet arm and making an expansive gesture with the other. "This is our friend who was sick."

"Hi, Richard," the swimmers chorused.

"Hi . . ."

Etienne hugged me again. "I am so happy you are better!"

"I'm happy too."

I looked over Etienne's shoulder at Françoise. She was still standing with the group and I smiled at her. She returned the smile but in a lopsided way. Or a knowing way. I suddenly wondered what kinds of things I might have blurted out to her in my delirious state.

As if to panic me further she walked over and lightly brushed a hand against my arm. "It is good to see you better, Richard," she said flatly; then as I opened my mouth to reply she turned away.

"I caught a fish!" said Etienne. "This is my first time fishing, and I caught a big fish!" He pointed to the catch. "You see this big blue fish?"

"Uh-huh," I replied, only half listening as cold thoughts flooded my head.

"Mine!"

I was introduced to the other swimmers.

Moshe was a tall Israeli with an earsplitting laugh. He used it in the same way as a madman uses a gun, spraying it around with bewildering randomness. Hearing the laugh made me blink instinctively, like hearing a hammer pound on brick or metal. Our conversation was impeded by having to watch him through the strobe effect of my convulsing eyes.

Then there were two haughty Yugoslavian girls whose names I could never pronounce and certainly never spell, and who made a big deal about being from Sarejevo. They said, "We are from Sarejevo," then paused meaningfully like they expected me to faint or congratulate them.

And there was Gregorio. Gregorio I warmed to at once.

He had a kind face and a soft Latin lisp, and when we were introduced he said, "I am very pleathed to meet you." Then he dried his hand on his T-shirt before offering it to shake, adding, "We are all very pleathed to meet you."

I can't remember one thing about what Etienne said to me as we walked back along the shallows. I remember he was talking about what I'd missed while I was asleep, and I have a vision of the way he cradled his catch, smothering his brown chest with silver scales, but everything else is a blank. It's a measure of how disturbed I was by what I might have said to Françoise.

I realized I had to find out the truth or it would drive me crazy. Françoise was walking a few paces behind the group, so I lagged behind Etienne, pretending to find an interesting seashell. But as soon as I did so, she picked up her pace. Then when I caught up with her she seemed to deliberately drop behind again.

Seemed. It was impossible for me to tell. When she slowed she was apparently distracted by something in the trees, but that might have been no more real than my interesting seashell.

It was enough for me. By now I felt sure my suspicions were correct and, rational or otherwise, I decided I had to clear the air without any delay.

When I lagged behind the next time, I caught her by the arm.

"Françoise," I asked, trying to find the right balance between firm and casual, "is there something funny going on?"

"Funny?" she replied, wide-eyed. "Oh, well, everything here is so strange. Of course, I am not used to it yet."

"No, I didn't mean here. . . . Look, maybe it's just me, but it feels like there's something funny going on between us."

"Us?"

"Me and you," I said, and instantly began to blush. I coughed and pointed my head at the ground. "I thought that, while I was ill, maybe I said something that . . ."

"Oh." She looked at me. "What are you afraid you said?"

"I don't know what I said. I'm asking you."

"Yes. And I am asking what you are afraid you said."

Fuck, I thought. Rewind.

"Nothing. I'm not afraid I said anything."

"So . . . ?"

"So I don't know. I just thought you were acting funny. It's just me. Forget it."

Françoise stopped. "Okay," she said. The rest of the group began drawing away from us. "Let me say it, Richard. You are worried you said you loved me, yes?"

"What?" I exclaimed, momentarily thrown by her Exocet-like bluntness. Then I gathered my wits and lowered my voice. "Jesus Christ, Françoise! Of course not!"

"Richard . . ."

"I mean, that's a ridiculous idea."

"Richard, please. It is not ridiculous. It was what you were afraid of."

"No. Not at all. I was . . ."

"Richard!"

I paused. She was staring straight at me. "Yes," I said slowly. "It's what I was afraid of."

She sighed.

"Françoise," I began, but she interrupted me.

"It does not matter, Richard. You had this fever, and in a fever people can say strange things, no? Things they do not mean. So you are afraid you said something strange. It means nothing. I understand."

"You aren't angry?"

"Of course not."

"And . . . did I say anything? Anything like that?"

"No."

"Really?"

She looked away. "Yes, really. You are very sweet to worry, but it is nothing. Do not think of this again." Then she pointed to the others, who were now fifty feet down the beach. "Come. We should go."

"Okay," I said quietly.

"Okay."

We caught up with the group, neither of us talking. Françoise walked up to Etienne and started chatting with him in French, and I walked a little aside from the others. As we neared the turning to the campsite, Gregorio sidled over.

"You feel like the new boy in school?"

"Oh, uh . . . Yeah. A bit."

"These first days are difficult, of course, but do not worry. You will find friends quickly, Richard."

I smiled. The way he emphasized the "you" made it sound personal, like he thought there was something particular about me that would make it easy to find friends. I knew it was just the way he spoke English, but it made me feel better all the same.

game over, man

While we'd been on the beach, the camp had filled up with people. I could see Bugs and Sal by the entrance to the longhouse, talking to a group who all carried ropes. A fat guy was busy gutting fish outside the kitchen hut, stacking the hollowed bodies on broad leaves and emptying the innards into a blood-smeared plastic bucket. Beside him a girl blew on a wood fire and fed the flames with kindling.

The center of the clearing seemed like a focus point. Most of the people were there, just milling around and chatting. At the furthest end a girl was carefully laying wet clothes over tent guylines.

Gregorio was right. I did feel like the new boy in school. I scanned the clearing as if it were the playground on my first day's lunch break, wondering what divisions and hierarchies would have to be learned, and which of the thirty or so faces would end up as friends.

One face stuck out. It belonged to a black guy sitting alone, his back against a storeroom hut. He looked around twenty, he had a shaved head, and his eyes were fixed intently on a small gray box in his hands—the Nintendo Game Boy I'd spotted earlier.

Etienne and Françoise followed Moshe to deposit their catch with the fish gutters. I nearly trailed after them. The schoolyard atmosphere was telling me to stick with the people I knew, but then I looked back at the Nintendo guy. His face suddenly screwed up and over the murmur of talking I heard him hiss, "Game Over."

I began walking toward him.

I once read that the most widely understood word in the whole world is "okay," followed by "Coke," as in cola. I think they should do the survey again, this time checking for "Game Over."

Game Over is my favorite thing about playing video games. Actually, I should qualify that. It's the split second before Game Over that's my favorite thing.

Streetfighter Two—an oldie but goldie—with my friend Leo controlling Ryu. Ryu's his preferred character because he's a good all-rounder—great defensive moves, pretty quick, and once he's on an offensive roll he's unstoppable. My brother Theo's controlling Blanka. Blanka's faster than Ryu, but he's only really good on attack. The way to win with Blanka is to get in the other player's face and just never let up. Flying kick, leg sweep, spin attack, head bite. Daze them into submission.

Both players are down to the end of their energy bars. One more hit and they're down, so they're both being cagey. They're hanging back at opposite ends of the screen, waiting for the other guy to make the first move. Leo takes the initiative. He sends off a fireball to force Theo into blocking, then jumps in with a flying kick to knock Blanka's green head off. But as he's moving through the air he hears a soft tapping. Theo's tapping the punch button on his control pad. He's charging up an electricity defense so when Ryu's foot makes contact with Blanka's head it's going to be Ryu who gets KO'd with 10,000 volts charging through his system.

This is the split second before Game Over.

Leo's heard the noise. He knows he's fucked. He has time to blurt, "I'm toast," before Ryu is lit up and thrown backward across the screen, flashing like a Christmas tree, a charred skeleton. Toast.

The split second is the moment you comprehend you're just about to die. Different people react to it in different ways. Some swear and rage. Some sigh or gasp. Some scream. I've heard a lot of screams over the twelve years I've been addicted to video games.

I'm sure that this moment provides a rare insight into the way people react just before they really do die. The game taps into something pure and beyond affectations. As Leo hears the tapping he blurts, "I'm toast." He says it quickly, with resignation and understanding. If he were driving down the highway and saw a car spinning into his path I think he'd react in the same way.

Personally, I'm a rager. I fling my joypad across the floor, clench my eyes shut, throw back my head, and yell abuse at anything within abusing distance.

A few years ago I had a game called Alien 3. It had a great feature. When you ran out of lives you'd get a photo-realistic picture of the Alien with saliva dripping from its jaws, and a digitized voice would bleat, "Game Over, man!"

I really used to love that.

"Hi," I said.

The guy looked up. "Hi."

"How many lines did you make?"

"One-four-four."

"Uh-huh. Pretty good."

"I can do one-seven-seven."

"One-seven-seven?"

He nodded. "How about you?"

"Uh, about a hundred and fifty is my best."

He nodded again. "You're one of the three FNGs, huh?"

"Yep."

"Where are you from?"

"London."

"Me too. Want a game?"

"Sure."

"Okay." He gestured to the dirt. "Pull up a chair."

beach life

assimilation, rice

A few years ago I was going through the process of splitting up with my first serious girlfriend. She went away to Greece for the summer and when she came back she'd had a holiday romance with some Belgian guy. As if that wasn't bad enough, it seemed that the guy in question was going to show up in London sometime over the next few weeks. After three hellish days and nights, I realized that I was dangerously close to losing my head. I biked over to my dad's flat and emotionally blackmailed him into lending me enough cash to leave the country.

On that trip I learned something very important. Escape through travel works. Almost from the moment I boarded my flight, life in England became meaningless. Seat belt signs lit up, problems switched off. Broken armrests took precedence over broken hearts. By the time the plane was airborne I'd forgotten England even existed.

After that first day, wandering around the clearing, I didn't really question a single thing about the beach.

The rice: Over thirty people, two meals every day, eating rice. Rice paddies need acres of flat, irrigated land which we simply didn't have, so I knew we couldn't be growing it. If the situation hadn't come up with the Rice Run, I might never have known where it all came from. Unremarked, I would have let it pass.

Assimilation: From day one we were working, everybody

knew our names, we had beds allocated in the longhouse. I felt like I'd been living there all my life.

It was the same thing that had happened on the airplane; my memory began shutting down. Koh Samui became a hazy, dreamlike place, and Bangkok became little more than a familiar word. On the third or fourth day I remember thinking that Zeph and Sammy might turn up soon, and wondering how people would react. Then I realized I couldn't quite recall Zeph's and Sammy's faces. A couple of days later I'd forgotten they might be coming at all.

There's this saying: In an all-blue world, color doesn't exist. It makes a lot of sense to me. If something seems strange, you question it, but if the outside world is too distant to use as a comparison, then nothing seems strange.

Why would I question it, anyway? Assimilating myself was the most natural thing in the world. I'd been doing it ever since I became a traveler. Another saying: When in Rome, do as the Romans. In the traveler's ten commandments, that's commandment number one. You don't march into Hindu temples and start saying, "Why are you worshiping a cow?" You look around, take on board, adjust, accept.

Assimilation and rice. These were just things to accept—new aspects of a new life.

But even now, I'm not asking the right questions.

It doesn't matter why I found it so easy to assimilate myself into the beach life. The question is why the beach life found it so easy to assimilate me.

Over the first two or three weeks there was a song that I couldn't get out of my head. Actually it wasn't even a song. It was just a couple of lines from a song. And I don't know the song's name but I suspect it's called "Street Life," because the only lyric I could remember went, "Street life, it's the only life I know, street life, dah dah-dah dah dah dah dah-da-

dah." Except the way I sang it went, "beach life," instead of, "street life," and all I could do was repeat that little bit over and over.

It used to drive Keaty crazy. He'd say, "Richard, you've got to stop singing that fucking song," and I'd have to shrug and say, "Keaty, I can't get it out of my head." Then I'd make an effort not to sing it for a while, but without meaning to I'd start again a couple of hours later. I'd only realize I'd started again when Keaty would smack his forehead and hiss, "I asked you not to fucking sing it! *Jesus*, Richard!" Then I'd have to shrug again. Eventually I got Keaty singing it too, and when I pointed this out he said, "Aaargh!" and wouldn't let me play on his Nintendo for the rest of the day.

night, jim-bob

I quickly fell into a routine.

I'd wake around seven, seven-thirty, then head straight down to the beach with Etienne and Keaty. Usually Françoise wouldn't swim because it was too much hassle getting the salt out of her long hair every day, but sometimes she would. Then we'd go back to the camp and rinse off in the shower hut.

Breakfast was at eight. Every morning the kitchen crew would boil up a load of rice and it was up to the individual to sort out anything else. Most had their rice plain but a few made the effort to boil up some fish or vegetables. I never bothered. For the first three days we mixed in our Magi-

Noodles for a bit of flavor, but when the Magi-Noodles ran out we settled for the rice.

After breakfast people would begin to disperse. Mornings were for working and everybody had their job to do. By nine the camp was always empty.

There were four main areas of work: fishing, gardening, cooking, and carpentry.

Etienne, Françoise, and I were on the fishing detail. Before we'd arrived there'd been two fishing groups, but we made it three. Gregorio and us made up one group, Moshe and the two Yugoslavian girls made up another, and a bunch of Swedish guys were the third. They were very serious about their fishing and every day they'd swim through the cliff caves to the open sea. Sometimes they'd come back with fish as big as your leg and everybody would make a fuss over them.

Workwise, I felt pretty lucky. If it hadn't been for Etienne and Françoise volunteering to go fishing on that first day, we wouldn't have met Gregorio, and I might have ended up on the gardening detail. Keaty was on the gardening detail and complained about it all the time. He had to work over half an hour from the clearing, up by the waterfall. The head gardener was Jean, a farmer's son from southwestern France who pronounced his name like he was clearing his throat, and he ran his garden with an iron fist. The problem was, once you'd taken on a job it was pretty hard to change. It wasn't like there were rules, but everybody worked in groups, so if you changed jobs you had to leave one group and break into another.

If I hadn't been a fisher, I probably would have tried to get in with the carpenters. Kitchen duties didn't appeal at all. Aside from the hellish chore of cooking dinner for thirty people every day, the three cooks all carried a lingering odor of fish innards. The head cook, whose nickname was Unhygienix, had his own private store of soap in his tent. He seemed to get through a bar a week, but it didn't do any good.

The carpenters were run by Bugs. Bugs was Sal's boyfriend, and he was a carpenter by trade. He'd been responsible for the longhouse and all the huts, and he'd had the idea of tying the branches together to make the canopy ceiling. From the way people treated him, it was obvious that Bugs was much respected. It was partly that everybody relied on the things he made, but it was also because he was Sal's boyfriend.

If there was a leader, it was Sal. When she talked, people listened. She spent her days wandering around the lagoon, checking on the different work details and making sure things were running smoothly. At first she devoted a lot of time to making sure we were settling in okay. She often joined us when we swam down to the boulders, but after the first week she seemed satisfied and we rarely saw her during the work period.

The only person who didn't have a clear working detail was Jed. He spent his days alone and was usually the first person to leave in the mornings and the last person to come back. Keaty said that Jed spent a lot of time near the waterfall and above the cliffs. Every now and then he would disappear and spend the night somewhere on the island. When he turned up again he usually had fresh grass, clearly taken from the dope fields.

Around two-thirty, people would start drifting back to camp. The kitchen crew and the fishers would always be first so the food could be prepared. Then the garden detail would arrive with their vegetables and fruit, and by three the clearing would be full again.

Breakfast and dinner were the only meals of the day. We didn't really need more. Dinner was at four o'clock and usually people went to bed about nine. There wasn't much to be done after dark, apart from get stoned. Nighttime campfires weren't allowed because fires were too conspicuous to low planes, even through the canopy ceiling. There were a lot of low planes around, flying to and from the airstrip on Koh Samui.

Apart from those with tents, everybody slept in the longhouse. It took me a while to get used to sleeping with twenty-one other people, but soon I started to enjoy it. There was a strong sense of closeness which Keaty and the others with tents missed out on. There was also the ritual. It didn't happen every night, but it happened often, and every time it made me smile.

The origin of the ritual was *The Waltons* TV series. At the end of each episode you'd see a shot of the Waltons' house and hear all of them saying good night to each other.

The way it worked in the longhouse was like this.

Just as people were drifting off, a sleepy voice from somewhere in the darkness would say, "Night, Jim-Bob." Then there'd be a short pause while we waited for the cue to be picked up, and eventually you'd hear someone say, "Night, Jesse," or "Sal," or "Gregorio," or "Bugs," or anyone they felt like saying good night to. Then the named person would have to say good night to someone different, and it would go around the whole longhouse until everyone had been mentioned.

Anybody could start the game off and there was no order to the names called out. When there were only a few names left it got difficult remembering which people had been mentioned and which hadn't, but that was part of the game. If you screwed it up, then there'd be loud tuts and exaggerated sighs until you got it right.

Although the ritual was sort of taking the piss, in another way it wasn't. No one's name was ever passed over and right from the first time, Etienne, Françoise, and I were included.

The nicest thing was when you heard your name but

couldn't recognize the voice. I always found it comforting that someone unexpected would think to choose me. I'd fall asleep wondering who it could have been, and who I'd choose the next time.

negative

On the morning of my fourth Sunday, all the camp was down on the beach. Nobody worked on Sundays.

The tide was out, so there was forty feet of sand between the treeline and the sea. Sal had organized a huge game of soccer and just about everyone was taking part, but not me and Keaty. We were sitting out on one of the boulders, listening to the shouts of the players drifting over the water. Along with video games and movies, an indifference to soccer was something we shared.

A flash of silver slipped past my feet. "Gotcha," I muttered, flicking an imaginary spear at the fish, and Keaty scowled.

"Easy life," he said.

"Fishing?"

"Fishing."

I nodded. Fishing was easy. I'd had the idea that as a city-softened Westerner I wouldn't be able to manage such ancient skills, but actually it was as simple as anything. All you had to do was stand on a rock, wait until a fish swam by, then skewer it. The only trick was in snapping the wrist, the same as throwing a Frisbee. That way it spun in the water and didn't lose momentum.

Keaty ran a hand backward over his head. He hadn't shaved it since I'd arrived and now his scalp was covered in a few weeks' worth of stubble.

"I'll tell you what it is," he said.

"Mmm?"

"It's the heat. Fishing you can cool off anytime, but in the garden you just bake."

"How about the waterfall?"

"Ten minutes away. You go there, swim, and by the time you get back you're hot again."

"Have you talked to Sal?"

"Yesterday. She said I can transfer if I find someone to swap with, but who wants to work on the garden detail?"

"Jean does."

"Yeah. Jean does." Keaty sighed. "Jean de fucking Florette."

"Jean le Frogette," I said, and he laughed.

A cheer erupted from the beach. Etienne appeared to have scored a goal. He was running around in circles with his hands in the air and Bugs, captain of the other side, was yelling at his goalkeeper. Up by the trees I could see Françoise. She was sitting with a small group of spectators, applauding.

I stood up. "Feel like a swim?"

"Sure."

"We could swim over to the corals. I haven't really checked them out yet. I've been meaning to."

"Great, but let's get Greg's mask first. There's no point swimming to the corals without the mask."

I glanced back to the beach. The game had started again. Bugs had the ball and was weaving down the sand, looking to make up the deficit, and Etienne was hot on his tail.

"You want to get it? I'll wait here."

"Okay."

Keaty dived off the boulder. For a few strokes he stayed underwater, and I followed his shape along the seabed until he was lost from view. He finally resurfaced an impressive distance away.

"I'll get some grass, too," he called.

I gave him the thumbs-up and he ducked back under again.

I turned away from the beach, toward the seaward cliffs. I was looking for a split in the rock face that Gregorio had pointed out a few days before. According to him, the most spectacular of the coral gardens lay in the waters directly beneath it.

At first I was confused. I was sure I was looking in the right place. Gregorio had indicated the split by making me follow a line of boulders that stretched across the lagoon like stepping stones. The boulders were still there, but the fissure had vanished.

Then I found it. Gregorio had shown me the spot in late afternoon. The cliffs had been in full shadow, and the split had been dark. But now, caught in the low morning sun, the jagged edge of the fissure glowed white against the black granite.

"Like a negative," I said out loud, smiling at my mistake.

corals

Under the weight of two grapefruit-sized stones, I drifted down to the seabed and sat, cross-legged, on the sand. Then I rested the stones on my lap so I wouldn't float back up again.

Around me were banks of coral: brightly colored pagodas, melted and sprawling in the hot tropical waters. In the recesses of their fans, something recoiled at my presence. It was almost imperceptible—a slight ripple of light spreading across the colors. I gazed harder, trying to pinpoint the strange effect, but once the change had happened the corals looked no different from before.

A strange creature was lying in front of me. A name popped into my head—sea cucumber—but only because I'd heard that such things existed. It could have been a sea marrow for all I knew. The creature was just over a foot in length and about the thickness of my forearm, and at the end nearest to me it had a nest of tiny tentacles. Using a snapped finger from one of the coral fans, I gave it an exploratory poke. The cucumber didn't move or flinch, so, emboldened, I touched it with my own finger. It was the softest thing I'd ever felt. Only the barest sensation of resistance was offered by the silky flesh, and I pulled back for fear of tearing its skin.

Curiouser and curiouser, I thought, smiling. Holding my breath was getting me high. From the blood humming in my ears and the mounting pressure in my lungs, I guessed I had less than twenty seconds of air remaining.

I looked up. Six or seven feet above me, perched on an overhanging rock shelf, I could see Keaty's disembodied legs. He was swinging them gently, like a kid on a high chair, and had attracted the attention of a little blue fish. The fish was mainly interested in his ankles. Every time they swung near, it would dart forward as if to take a bite, but stop abruptly an inch or so away. Then, as his ankles swung back, the fish would flick its fins and retreat, perhaps cursing itself for its lack of courage.

A cold trickle of water eased past the hollow of my temples. With my head pointed upward, the trapped air was pulling the mask away from my face. I looked down quickly, pushing at the glass to reestablish the seal, but it was no use. Too much water had worked its way in. I rolled the stones off my lap and let myself float back to the surface.

On impulse, I nipped Keaty's ankle as I passed it by, using my bunched fingernails like a row of teeth.

"What did you do that for?"

I rubbed at the itch from where the mask had been gripping my face. Keaty was rubbing his ankle.

"There was this little fish," I began, then started laughing.

"What little fish?"

"It wanted to bite you but didn't have the nerve."

Keaty shook his head. "I thought it was a shark."

"There's sharks here?"

"Millions." He jabbed a finger at the cliffs behind him, indicating the open sea, then shook his head again. "You made me jump."

"Sorry."

I hauled myself out of the water and sat next to Keaty on the rock shelf. "It's amazing down there. It would be so good to have Aqua-Lungs or something. A minute isn't really long enough."

"Or a hosepipe," Keaty said. He pulled a plastic film carton from his pocket. Inside were loose rizlas and grass. "I went to Ujung Kulon two years ago. You been there?"

"Charita."

"Well, in Ujung Kulon there were some corals and these guys there used a hosepipe. You could stay under for a while, but you couldn't really move around. Still . . ."

"I don't suppose we've got a hosepipe here?"

"Nope."

I waited while Keaty finished rolling the joint.

". . . So you've done a lot of traveling."

"Sure. Thailand, Indonesia, Mexico, Guatemala, Colombia, Turkey, India, and Nepal. Oh, also Pakistan. Sort of. I was in Karachi for three days on a stopover. You count that?"

"Uh-uh."

"Me neither. How about you?"

I shrugged. "I've never done any of the Americas stuff, nor Africa. Just around Asia really. Europe too, I suppose. How about Europe? Does Europe count?"

"Not if you won't count Karachi." He lit up. "Got a favorite?"

I thought for a couple of moments. "It's a toss-up between Indonesia and the Philippines."

"And your worst?"

"Probably China. I had a lousy time in China. I went for five days without talking to one person except when I ordered food in restaurants. Terrible food too."

Keaty laughed. "My worst was Turkey. I was supposed to stay for two months but I left after two weeks."

"And the best?"

Keaty looked around, inhaling deeply, then passed me the joint. "Thailand. This place, I mean. It isn't really Thailand, considering there's no Thais, but . . . yeah. This place."

"This place is unique. . . . How long have you been here?"

"Two years. Just over. I met Sal in Chiang Rai and we got friendly. Hiked around a bit. Then she told me about this place and took me along."

I flicked the dead joint butt into the water. "Tell me about Daffy. No one talks about him."

"Yeah. People were shocked when they heard." Keaty scratched at his stubble thoughtfully. "I'm not a good person to ask. I barely knew the guy. He was a bit distant, to me anyway. I mean, I knew who he was, but we didn't talk much."

"So who was he?"

"Are you kidding?"

"No. Like I said, nobody mentions him, so . . ."

Keaty frowned. "You haven't seen the tree yet? The tree by the waterfall?"

"I don't think so."

"Shit! You don't know anything, do you, Rich? You've been here, what? A month?"

"Just over."

"Man." Keaty smiled. "I'll take you to the tree tomorrow. Then you'll see."

"How about now?"

"I want to swim. Especially now I'm stoned. And it's my turn with the mask."

"I'd really like to . . ."

Keaty slipped into the water. "Tomorrow. What's the hurry? You waited four weeks." He snapped the strap tight over the back of his head and ducked under, end of discussion.

"Okay," I said to the flat water, allowing dope and beach life to cloud my curiosity. "Tomorrow then."

On my next turn with Gregorio's mask I looked out for any shifting colors in the corals, but the strange effect refused to repeat itself. The coral-dwellers were still hidden in their pagoda homes. Either that, or my presence no longer scared them.

bugged

That night, just as the light was starting to fade, we were given our seashell necklaces. It wasn't a big deal, no ceremony or anything. Sal and Bugs just wandered over to where we were sitting and handed them over. Still, it was quite a big deal for me. However friendly everyone was, being the only ones without necklaces drew attention to our new-arrival status. Now that we'd got them, it was like our acceptance had been made official.

"Which is for me?" said Françoise, carefully examining each one in turn.

"Whichever you like, Françoise," Sal replied.

"I think I will have this one. I like this color on the big shell." She looked at me and Etienne, challenging us to make a rival claim.

"Which do you want, Etienne?" I said.

"You."

"I don't mind."

"I also do not mind."

"So . . ."

We shrugged at each other and laughed. Then Sal leaned forward and plucked the two remaining necklaces from Françoise's hands. "Here," she said, and made the choice for us. They were both much the same, but mine had a centerpiece, the snapped arm of a red starfish.

I slipped it over my head. "Well, thanks a lot, Sal."

"Thank Bugs. He made yours."

"Okay. Thanks, Bugs. It's a really nice necklace."

He nodded, accepting the compliment silently, then began walking back across the clearing to the longhouse.

I couldn't make up my mind about Bugs. It was weird, because he was exactly the kind of guy I felt I ought to like, almost out of obligation. He was broader and more muscular than me; as head of the carpentry detail, he had obvious skills; I also suspected he was pretty intelligent. This was harder to gauge because he didn't speak much, but when he did speak it seemed to be things worth saying. But despite all these fine characteristics, there was something about him that left me a little cold.

One example was the way he accepted my thanks for the necklace. His silent nod belonged in Clint Eastwood land; it didn't feel like it had a place in the real world. Another time we were going to eat some soup. Gregorio said he was going to wait until the soup cooled down—it was bubbling and still over the flame. Bugs immediately made a point of taking a spoonful straight from the saucepan. He didn't say anything, just took the spoonful. It was such a small thing that repeating it now, I'm almost embarrassed by how petty it sounds.

Maybe this stands up to repeating. On the Monday of my second week, I saw Bugs struggling to fit a swinging door on the entrance to one of the storeroom huts. He was having trouble because he only had two hands, and he needed three: two to keep the door in place and a third to hammer a peg into the hinge. I watched him for a while, wondering whether to offer any help, and as I began walking over, the hammer slipped from his grip. Instinctively, he moved to catch it and the door also fell, bashing against his leg.

"Shit," I said, breaking into a jog. "You okay?"

Bugs glanced down. Blood was dripping from a nasty graze on his shins. "I'm fine," he said, then bent to pick up his hammer.

"Do you need a hand holding the door?"

Bugs shook his head.

I went back to where I'd been sitting, slicing the tops off bamboo sticks to make spears for fishing, and about five minutes later I misjudged a swipe and cut open my thumb.

"Ow!" I shouted.

Bugs didn't look round, and as Françoise ran over, her face even prettier for being alarmed, I could sense his satisfaction—stoically tapping the peg into place while blood collected in dusty pools around his feet.

"That really hurt," I said when Françoise reached me, and made sure I said it loud enough for Bugs to hear.

While I'm on a roll, I might as well add that there was one more thing that bothered me about Bugs. His name.

The way I saw it, calling himself Bugs was like, "I'm taciturn and stoical, but I don't take myself too seriously! I call myself Bugs Bunny!" As with my other gripes, it wasn't a reason to dislike him; it was just something that grated. The whole point was that Bugs took himself extremely seriously.

Over the two weeks I was getting to know Bugs, I spent some time wondering where his name had come from. If, like Sal, he'd been American, I could have imagined that Bugs Bunny was how he'd been christened. No disrespect to Americans—they just come up with some odd names. But Bugs was South African, and I couldn't see Warner Brothers as having that strong an influence over Pretoria. Then again, I once met a South African called Goose, so you never know.

Anyway. Back to the night I received my necklace.

"Night, Jim-Bob."

Silence . . . Panic.

Had I said it loudly enough? Was there a rule of etiquette

that I hadn't picked up on? Getting the necklace had given me the courage, but maybe only group leaders were allowed to start it off, or people who'd been coming to the beach more than three years. . . .

My heart began to pound. Sweat sprung. Well, that's it, I thought to myself. It's all over. I'll leave tomorrow morning before dawn. I'll just have to swim the twenty miles back to Koh Samui, and I'll probably be eaten by sharks, but that's okay. I deserve it. I—

"Night, Ella," said a dozy voice in the darkness.

I froze.

"Night, Jesse," said another.

"Night, Sal."

"Night, Moshe."

"Night, Cassie."

"Night, Greg."

"Night . . ."

zero

Colorwise, progress was good. The sky had been mainly cloudy over the first few days, and by the time it had cleared I had enough of a base tan to avoid burning. Now I was getting close to my darkest shade. I peeked under the waistband of my shorts to check I was as dark as I hoped.

"Wow," I said, seeing the creamy skin beneath.

Etienne looked round. He was sitting by the edge of the boulder, cooling his legs in the water. His tan was rich and golden, I noticed enviously. I never went golden. At best I went the color of a recently plowed field. Walnut brown, I would sometimes describe it, but much more like earth.

"What is it?"

"Just my tan. I'm getting dark."

Etienne nodded, tugging absently at his necklace. "I thought maybe you were thinking of this place."

"The beach?"

"You said, 'Wow,' so I thought you were thinking how good it is here."

"Oh, well, I often think that . . . I mean, it was worth the trouble, wasn't it? That swim, and the dope fields."

"Worth the trouble."

"You fish, swim, eat, laze around, and everyone's so friendly. It's such simple stuff, but . . . If I could stop the world and restart life, put the clock back, I think I'd restart it like this. For everyone." I shook my head to stop myself rambling. "You know what I mean."

"All these thoughts are the same as mine."

"They are?"

"Of course. The same as everybody's."

I stood up and gazed around me. Gregorio and Françoise were climbing out of the water a few boulders over, and past them, near the sea-locked cliffs, three dots of color described Moshe and the two Yugoslavians. From the land I could hear a steady tapping—Bugs and the carpenters working on some new project—and walking along the beach, I could see a single figure. Ella, I thought, until I squinted against the bright white sands and recognized Sal.

I remembered the way Sal had teased me to realign my expectations. "You'll see that this is a wonderful place, as long as you appreciate it for what it is," she'd said. I pushed my shoulders back and closed my eyes against the hot sun, and thought how right she was.

I was broken out of my reverie by a sudden cold splash of water against my legs. I opened my eyes and looked down. It was the fish in the bucket, getting close to the split second before Game Over. I watched them for a while, impressed by their tenacity. It often surprised me how long it took for fish to die. Even speared right through their bodies, they still flapped about for as long as an hour, working up a bloody lather in the water around them.

"How many do we have?" said Etienne.

"Seven. A couple are big ones. That's enough, isn't it?"

Etienne shrugged. "If Gregorio and Françoise also have seven, it is enough."

"They'll have seven at least." I checked my watch. It was exactly midday. "I think I might go back early today. I'm meeting up with Keaty and he's going to show me this tree."

"Tree?"

"Some tree by the waterfall. Want to come? We could leave the bucket here."

He shook his head and pointed to Gregorio and Françoise. Gregorio had his mask pushed up onto his forehead. "I want to see the corals. They sound very beautiful."

"Yeah, they are. Maybe I'll come and find you after this tree thing."

"Good."

"Tell the others for me."

"Yes."

I dived into the water, shooting down at a steep angle, then leveling out to skim over the seabed. The salt stung my eyes but I kept them open. Even without Gregorio's mask, the blurred colors and scattering fish were a sight to see.

There were two ways I could get to the garden. The first was the direct route that Keaty walked every morning. It was the quickest way, but I'd only done it a couple of times, and that was with Keaty. I knew if I tried to do it alone I'd only get lost; once you were in the jungle, there wasn't much to orientate yourself by, apart from distinctive trees and plants. Instead I chose the second route, which was to follow the waterfall stream to its source. Once there, I could turn left and walk along the base of the cliff, which eventually led to the garden.

After about ten minutes of walking I began to empathize with Keaty's complaints about his work detail. Without a sea breeze or cool water, the heat was incredible. By the time I reached the waterfall my whole body was prickling with sweat.

Since arriving at the beach, I'd only been to the waterfall a couple of times, and never on my own. It was partly because I had no reason to go there, but also, I now understood, because the area made me feel uneasy. It represented a link between the lagoon and the outside world, the world I'd all but forgotten, and as I stood by the pool I realized that I didn't want to be reminded. Looking up through the fine mist of water vapor I could see the spot where I'd crouched before jumping. The memories it brought back were uncomfortable. I didn't even pause to cool my face. I found the path that led toward the garden and headed straight down it.

Quarter of an hour later I found Keaty on the outskirts of the vegetable patch, disconsolately poking at weeds with a Bugs-made trowel.

"Hey," he said, perking up. "What are you doing down here?"

"You were going to show me a tree. I got off work early."

"Right. I forgot." He looked over to where Jean was growling at one of the other gardeners. "Jean!"

Jean looked round.

"Gottataketimeoff."

"Heugh?" Jean replied.

"Backlaterifthere'stimeokay?"

Keaty waved and Jean waved back uncertainly. Then Keaty propelled me out of the garden. "If you talk quickly he can't understand," he explained. "Otherwise he would have tried to make you wait until the detail stopped work."

"Smart."

"Uh-huh."

It was a rocket ship tree about twenty meters to the right of the pool. I'd noticed it before when I'd been wondering how to get down from the waterfall. Some of its branches grew near to the cliff, and I'd considered an Indiana Jones–style leap into its lower canopy. Standing at its base, I was glad I'd had the sense not to try. I'd have jumped onto a deceptively thin layer of leaves and fallen forty feet to the ground.

It was, like all the other rocket ship trees, an impressive sight, but that wasn't why Keaty had brought me to see it. He'd brought me to see the markings cut into one of its twelve-foot stabilizer fins. Three names and four numbers. Bugs, Sylvester, and Daffy. The numbers were all zeros.

"Sylvester?"

"Salvester."

I shook my head. "Sal."

"I tawt I taw a puddy," said Keaty.

"So they were the first?"

"The first—1989. The three of them hired a boat from Koh Phangan."

"They knew about this place already, or . . ."

"Depends who you talk to. Bugs said he'd heard about a hidden lagoon from some fisherman on Koh Phalui, but Daffy used to say they were just island-hopping. Found the place by chance."

"Chance."

"But all the camp and stuff. That didn't start until '90. They spent the second half of '89 doing the Goa thing, then came back to Koh Phangan for the new year."

"And what, Koh Phangan was on the way out?"

Keaty nodded. "Well on the way. That's when it clicked. The thing was, those three had been going to Koh Samui since it was a secret, so when they saw Koh Phangan had maybe a year left . . ."

"A year left at best. I heard by '91 it was already fucked up."

"Right, so they'd seen it all before. Especially Daffy. Daffy was completely obsessed. You know he wouldn't ever go to Indonesia?"

"I don't know anything about Daffy."

"Boycotted because of Bali. He went there only once in the late eighties and wouldn't ever go back. Used to talk all the time about how sick it made him."

We sat down with our backs against the slab of root and shared a cigarette.

"I mean," said Keaty, exhaling hard, "you've got to hand it to them."

"Definitely."

"They really knew what they were doing. Most things were set up by the time Sal took me here, which was . . . uh . . . '93. The longhouse was up and the ceiling was sorted out."

"Two years."

"Uh-huh." He passed me the cigarette.

"So when you came, were there this many people?"

Keaty paused. "Well . . . Pretty much . . ."

I looked at him, sensing that he was being cagey. "How do you mean, pretty much?"

". . . Everyone apart from the Swedes."

"In two years, the only new people were the Swedes?"

". . . And Jed. The Swedes and Jed."

"That's not many. Well-kept secret."

"Mmm."

I stubbed out the cigarette. "And the zeros. What are they about?"

Keaty smiled. "That was Daffy's idea. It's a date."

"A date? The date of what?"

"The date they first arrived."

"I thought that was '89."

"It was." Keaty stood up and patted the stabilizer fin. "But Daffy used to call it year zero."

revelations

Set up in Bali, Koh Phangan, Koh Tao, Boracay, and the hordes are bound to follow. There's no way you can keep it out of the Lonely Planet, and once that happens it's countdown to doomsday. But set up in a Marine park, where you aren't even supposed to be . . .

The more I thought about it, the more the idea grew on me. Not just a Marine park but a Marine park in Thailand. Of all places, backpacker central, land of the beaten track. The only thing sweeter than the irony was the logic. The Philippines is an archipelago of seven thousand islands, but even in that huge fractured landscape, an equivalent secret would be impossible to contain. But with the legions of travelers passing through Bangkok and the southern islands, who'd notice when a few slipped away?

Strangely, the thing that least intrigued me was how they'd actually managed to get it all done. I suppose I sort of knew. If I'd learned one thing from traveling, it was that the way to get things done was to go ahead and do them. Don't talk about going to Borneo. Book a ticket, get a visa, pack a bag, and it just happens.

From Keaty's few words, I pictured the scene. January 1990, maybe New Year's Eve, Koh Phangan, maybe Hadrin. Daffy, Bugs, and Sal, talking as the sun comes up. Sal's found a boat to hire or even buy, Bugs has some tools in his backpack, Daffy's got a sack of rice and thirty packs of Magi-Noodles. Perhaps bars of chocolate have melted and molded around the shape of his water bottle.

By seven that morning they're walking down the beach. Behind them they can hear the rumble of a portable generator through the thump of a sound system. They don't look back, they just push off from the sand and head for the hidden paradise they found a year before.

As I walked back toward the camp, on the way to find Etienne at the coral garden, I found myself almost hoping for another meeting with Mister Duck. I wanted to shake him by the hand.

I never did find Etienne and Françoise. I bumped into Gregorio on the beach. He was carrying our catch back to camp, and when I told him I was going to the corals, he looked doubtful.

"I think you should wait," he said. "Wait for . . . maybe one hour."

"How come?"

"Etienne and Françoise . . ."

"They're having sex?"

"Well . . . I do not know, but . . ."

"Uh-huh. An hour, you reckon?"

"Oh . . ." Gregorio smiled awkwardly. "Maybe I am too generous to Etienne."

I shook my head, remembering my first night in Bangkok.

"No," I replied, irritated to hear a sudden tightness in my voice. "Spot on, I'd say."

So I went back to the camp with Gregorio.

There was nothing much to do there except compare fish sizes with the other details. The three Swedes, as usual, had caught the biggest and were swaggering about, telling the cooks about their fishing technique. I got pretty pissed off listening to them, but even more annoying were the images of Françoise and Etienne that kept popping into my head. Eventually, craving something to occupy my mind, I went to Keaty's tent and dug out his Nintendo.

Most bosses have a pattern; crack the pattern, kill the boss. A typical pattern is illustrated by Dr. Robotnik during his first incarnation in Sonic One, Megadrive version, Greenhills Zone. As he descends from the top of the screen, you jump at him from the left platform. Then, as he starts swinging toward you, you duck under and jump at him from the right. As he swings back, you repeat the process in reverse until, eight hits later, he explodes and runs away.

That's an easy boss. Others require much more manual dexterity and effort. The last boss on Teken 2, for example, is a relentless fist-swinging nightmare.

The boss that distracted me from Etienne and Françoise was none other than Wario, nemesis of Mario. The problem was that to reach him, I had to struggle through several tortuous stages. By the time I arrived at his lair I'd taken too many hits and had lost the vital power-ups I needed to finish him off.

Every now and then, Unhygienix would take a break from cooking and wander over to inspect my progress. He and Keaty were the only two people in the camp who'd ever completed the game. He'd say things like, "Don'ta pausa on thata platforma." (I'm abandoning his Italian accent from now on.)

I'd scowl in frustration. "If I don't pause I get spiked by the falling block."

"Si. So you jump more quickly. Like this."

He'd take the Game Boy, guiding Mario with amazing skill considering the size of his fat hands, and show me how the trick was done. Then he'd wander back to his cooking, fingers drumming a rhythm on his giant belly. The Game Boy was always slippery after he'd used it, and smelled of fish, but I considered that a fair price to pay for his expertise.

It took an hour and a half, but eventually I was able to reach Wario with a full complement of power-ups. Finally I could start trying to crack his pattern. Or so I thought, because at that moment the monochrome screen began fading away.

"Evereadys!" I yelped.

Keaty, who'd returned from the garden while I'd been playing, poked his head out of his tent.

"That was the last batch, Rich."

"There's none left?"

"None at all."

"But I've nearly cracked Wario!"

"Well . . ." He shrugged apologetically. "Leave it alone awhile. If you turn it off for twenty minutes you might get another five minutes' playing time."

I groaned. Five minutes wasn't nearly enough.

It was a bitter blow, running out of batteries. I could live without completing the Mario game, but Tetris was another matter entirely. Since Keaty had told me his record of 177 lines, I'd been trying hard to beat him. The closest I'd made was 161 but I was improving every day.

"This is ridiculous," I said. "Walkmans. What about them?"

Keaty sighed. "Forget Walkmans."

"Why?"

"Give, and gifts will be given to you, for whatever measure you deal out to others will be dealt to you in return."

I paused for a moment. "What?"

"I went to church every Sunday until I was fifteen."

"You're quoting the Bible?"

"Luke, six, thirty-eight."

I shook my head incredulously. "What's the bloody Bible got to do with anything?"

"There's only five people with Walkmans in the camp, and I've refused all of them batteries in the past."

"Then we're fucked."

"Mmm," Keaty agreed. "Looks like it."

invisible wires

But, as fate turned out, we weren't fucked. Help ar-rived from an unexpected source.

We went over to the cooking hut to tell Unhygienix about the batteries, and as I began to explain he turned from the fire, his face an angry red and shining with sweat. I took an instinctive step backward, amazed he was taking the news so hard.

"Batteries?" he said, in an alarmingly quiet voice.

"Uh . . . yes . . ."

"What about the rice?"

"The rice?"

Unhygienix began swiftly marching to one of the storeroom huts, so we followed behind.

"There!"

We looked inside. I could see three empty canvas sacks and two more, full.

"What's the problem?" said Keaty.

Unhygienix tore open the top of the nearest full sack and rice poured out, black and green, puffed up into fat clods of fungus, completely rotten.

"Jesus," I muttered, covering my nose and mouth to block the appalling smell. "That's horrible."

Unhygienix pointed to the roof.

"It leaked?"

He nodded, too furious to speak. Then marched back to his cooking.

"Well," said Keaty as we walked back to his tent. "It isn't all bad news about the rice. You should be glad, Rich."

"How's that?"

"No more rice means a Rice Run. Now we get some new batteries."

Keaty lay on his back, smoking one of my cigarettes. I was down to one hundred, but seeing as I'd finished up his Evereadys, I couldn't really refuse him.

"I think," he said, "there's two main reasons people don't like doing the Rice Run. Number one, it's a complete hassle. Number two, it means visiting the world."

"The world?"

"The world. It's another Daffy thing. The world is everything outside the beach."

I smiled. I knew exactly where Daffy had picked up the term; the same place I had. Keaty noticed and propped himself up on his elbows. "What's so funny?"

"Nothing. Just . . . The GIs used that word in the same way, to describe America . . . I don't know. I just thought it was funny."

Keaty nodded slowly. "Hysterical."

"So what happens on the Rice Run?"

"A couple of people take the boat and head for Koh Phangan. Then they pick up some rice, and head back here."

"We've got a boat?"

"Of course. Not all of us are such good swimmers as you, Rich."

"I didn't realize . . . I didn't think about that . . . Well, a quick trip to Koh Phangan doesn't sound too bad."

"Yeah." Now Keaty was grinning. "But you haven't seen the boat yet."

An hour later the entire camp sat in a circle, all except Etienne and Françoise, who still weren't back from the corals. The news about the rice had been spread quickly, and Sal had called a meeting.

Keaty nudged me while we waited for the talking to start. "I bet you Jed volunteers," he whispered.

"Jed?"

"He loves taking on missions. Just watch him."

I was about to reply when Sal clapped her hands and stood up. "Okay," she said briskly. "As everyone knows, we've got a problem."

"Too fuckin' right," drawled an Australian voice from the other side of the circle.

"We thought we had another seven weeks of rice, but it turns out we've only got enough for two days. Now, this isn't a major catastrophe, nobody's going to be starving to death, but it is a minor one." Sal paused. "Well, you know what's coming. We need to go on a Rice Run."

Several people booed, mainly, I guessed, out of a sense of duty.

"So . . . who's volunteering?"

Jed's hand shot up.

"What did I tell you?" hissed Keaty.

"Thank you, Jed. So okay . . . that's one . . . Who else?"

Sal scanned the faces, most of which had noticeably downcast eyes. "Come on . . . We all know Jed can't do it alone . . ."

Just as when I jumped from the waterfall, I only really realized what I was doing after I'd started doing it. An invisible wire seemed to have attached itself to my wrist and was pulling it upward.

Sal noticed, then glanced at Bugs. Out of the corner of my eye I saw him shrug. "Are you volunteering too, Richard?"

"Yeah," I answered, still a little surprised to find that I was. "I mean . . . Yeah. I'm volunteering."

Sal smiled. "Good. That's settled then. You'll leave tomorrow morning."

There wasn't much preparation to be done. All we needed was money and the clothes on our backs, and Sal produced the money. I spent the rest of the afternoon fielding Keaty's accusations about my sanity.

Etienne and Françoise finally returned from the corals as it was getting dark. They were also surprised I'd volunteered.

"I hope you are not bored with life here," Françoise said as we chatted outside the longhouse entrance.

I laughed. "No way. I just thought it might be interesting. Anyway, I haven't seen Koh Phangan yet."

"Good. It would be sad to be bored of Eden, no? If you are bored of Eden, what is left?"

"Eden?"

"Yes, you remember. Zeph called this place Eden."

"Zeph . . ." I frowned, because, of course, I hadn't remembered. "Yeah, that's right . . . he did."

'toon time

I stared hard at the water. I needed to stare hard. The image under the surface kept shifting and I had to concentrate to work out what I was seeing.

One moment I was looking at coral. Red corals with curving white fingers. The next moment I was looking at bare ribs poking out of bloody corpses. Ten or twenty ruined bodies, or as many bodies as there were coral beds.

"Rorschach," said Mister Duck.

"Mmm."

"Is it a cloud of butterflies? Is it a bed of flowers? No. It's a pile of dead Cambodians." He laughed quietly. "That's a test I don't see you passing."

"I don't see you passing it either."

"Well said, Rich. A salient point."

Mister Duck looked down at his wrists. Large black scabs had formed around his hands and lower arms. It seemed he'd finally stopped bleeding.

"I tell you, Rich," he said. "Getting these bastards to close up has been a nightmare. . . . A total fucking nightmare, I'm not kidding."

"How did you do it?"

"Well, I tied a cloth around the top of each arm, really tight, and that slowed the blood enough to let me clot. Clever, huh?"

"That's the boy . . ." I began, seeing my chance, but he interrupted me.

"All right, Rich. That'll do." He rocked on his heels like a kid with some good news to tell. "So, ah . . . do you want to know why I did it?"

"Healed the cut?"

"Yes."

"Okay."

Mister Duck smiled proudly. "I did it because you wanted to shake me by the hand."

I raised my eyebrows.

"Remember? You were walking back from the carved tree and you decided you wanted to shake me by the hand. So I said to myself, I'm not going to let Rich shake my hand if I'm bleeding all over the place! No fucking way!" He emphasized his words with a jabbing finger. "Rich is going to get a clean hand to shake! A dry hand! The kind of hand he deserves!"

I wondered how to respond. Actually, I'd completely forgotten about shaking his hand and wasn't even sure I still wanted to.

"Well . . ."

"Put it there, Rich!" A darkly stained palm shot out.

"I . . ."

"Come on, Rich! You wouldn't refuse to shake a guy's hand, would you?"

He was right. I never could turn down an extended hand, even from enemies. "No. Of course not . . ." I replied, and added, "Daffy," as an afterthought.

I reached out.

His wrists exploded. They burst apart into two red fountains, spraying like high-pressure garden hoses, soaking me and blinding me, filling my mouth.

"Stop it!" I yelled, spitting and spinning away from the jets.

"I can't, Rich!"

"Just fucking stop it!"

"I—!"

"Jesus!"

"Wait! Wait, wait . . . They're getting back to normal . . ."

The sound of the fountains dropped away to a steady splashing. Cautiously I looked around. Mister Duck was standing with his hands on his hips, still bleeding profusely; examining the mess and shaking his head.

"Christ," he mumbled. "How awkward."

I stared at him incredulously.

"Really, Rich, I can't apologize enough."

"You stupid bastard! You knew that was going to happen!"

"No . . . Well, yes, but . . ."

"You fucking planned it!"

"It was supposed to be a joke."

"A jo—" I hesitated. The taste of iron and salt in my mouth was making me feel sick. "Idiot!"

Mister Duck's shoulders slumped. "I'm really sorry," he said unhappily. "Maybe it wasn't a very good joke. . . . Perhaps I'd better go." Then he walked past me and straight off the edge of the rock shelf, but instead of falling the few feet down to the water, he simply hovered in midair.

"Could you just answer one thing, Rich?"

"What?" I snapped.

"Who are you planning to bring back?"

"Back from where?"

"The world. Aren't you and Jed . . ."

Mister Duck paused, suddenly frowning. Then he looked down at the empty space beneath him as if noticing it for the first time.

"Oh damn," he groaned, and dropped like a stone.

I looked over the shelf. When the ripples cleared, the water was cloudy and I couldn't make him out. I waited awhile, watching to see if he'd resurface, but he never did.

the rice run

jed

Jed wouldn't let me wake Etienne and Françoise. They'd asked me to say good-bye before I left, but Jed shook his head and said, "Unnecessary." I stood over their sleeping bodies, wondering what he meant. He'd woken me five minutes earlier by putting his hand over my mouth and whispering, "Shh," so close to my ear that his beard had brushed my cheek. I'd thought that had been pretty unnecessary myself.

I thought his knife was unnecessary too. It appeared as we stood on the beach, getting ready for the swim to the seaward cliffs, a green handled lock-knife with a Teflon-coated blade.

"What's that for?" I asked.

"It's a tool," he replied, matter of factly. Then he winked and added, "Sinister, huh?" before wading into the water with the knife between his teeth.

Until the Rice Run, Jed was a mystery to me. The most time we'd ever spent together had been on my first day, when he escorted us from the waterfall. After that we'd had almost no contact. Sometimes I saw him in the evenings—never earlier because he returned to the camp so late—and small talk had always been the extent of our conversations. Normally, small talk is enough for me to form an opinion of someone. I make quick judgments, often completely wrong, and then stick by them rigidly. But with Jed I'd made an exception and kept an open mind. This was mainly due to conflicting accounts about his character. Unhygienix liked him, and Keaty thought he was an idiot.

"We were sitting on the beach," Keaty had once said, his forehead creased up with irritation, "and there was this noise from the jungle. A coconut falling off a tree or something. A crack. So Jed suddenly stiffened up and did this little glance over his shoulder, like he was some finely tuned commando. Like he couldn't help his own reflexes."

I nodded. "He wanted you to notice."

"Exactly. He wanted us to notice how fucking alert he is." Keaty laughed and shook his head, then launched into a familiar diatribe about what crap it was to work in the garden.

But Unhygienix liked Jed. Sometimes I'd need the toilet late at night and found them still awake, sitting by the kitchen hut, getting stoned on grass nicked from the dope plantations. And if Unhygienix liked Jed, he couldn't be all bad.

There were three caves that led into the seaward cliffs. One was at the base of the jagged fissure, by the coral gardens, another was maybe two hundred meters to the right of the fissure, and the last was maybe fifty meters to the left. That was the one we swam for.

It was a good swim. The water was cool and cleared the morning haze out of my head. I spent most of the time underwater, watching fish scatter, wondering which ones might end up as today's lunch. It was strange that there were always so many fish in the lagoon. We must have been pulling out thirty a day, but the numbers never seemed to go down.

Dawn was breaking by the time we reached the cave. We couldn't see the sun yet—the east was blocked by the cliffs as they curved around to rejoin the island—but the sky was bright.

"You know this place?" Jed asked.

"I've seen it while I've been working."

"But you've never been through."

"No. I went up to the coral gardens once and saw the cave there . . . beneath the fissure."

"But you've never been through," he repeated.

"No."

He looked disapproving. "You should have. Golden rule, first thing to do when you arrive someplace is find out how you can get out again. These caves are the only ways out of the lagoon."

I shrugged. "Oh . . . So is that how you get above the waterfall?"

"See here." He walked into the entrance of the cave and pointed directly upward. Bizarrely, in the blackness, I could see a fist-sized circle of blue, and as my eyes adjusted to the light I made out a rope, hanging the length of the shaft.

"It's a chimney. You can climb it without the rope, but the rope makes it easier."

"And then you can walk around the cliff tops, back to the island."

"Exactly. Want to try?"

"Sure," I said quickly. I had the idea he was testing me.

Jed raised his eyebrows. "Uh-huh. An adventurous type. I had you down for something else."

That annoyed me. "I found this place, and what's the big deal about climbing up the—"

He cut me off. "Maybe this place found you," he said, looking at me out of the corner of his eye. Then suddenly he smiled. "I'm taking the piss, Richard. Sorry. Anyway, we don't have time now. The journey will take four hours at least."

I checked my watch. It was almost seven. "So our ETA is eleven hundred hours."

"Eleven hundred hours . . ." He chuckled and patted me on the arm, lapsing into an American accent. "ETAs, FNGs. You're my kinda guy."

Keaty had met Sal and Bugs in Chiang Rai. They'd gone on an illegal trek together over the Burmese border, and after the trek was over, Sal had asked him if he was interested in being taken to paradise.

Gregorio had met Daffy in Sumatra. Gregorio had been beaten up and robbed, and when Daffy found him he was trying to hitch his way to Jakarta so he could contact the Spanish embassy. Daffy had offered him cash to get to Java. Gregorio had been reluctant to accept, because he could see Daffy was short of money himself. Daffy had said, "Fuck Java," and told him about the beach.

Sal had been on an eighteen-hour bus ride with Ella. Ella had a portable backgammon set.

Daffy had heard Cassie asking for a job in a Patpong bar.

Unhygienix had cooked Bugs a six-course meal on a houseboat in Srinagar, starting with hot coconut soup and ending with a mango split.

Moshe had caught a Manilan pickpocket trying to razor Daffy's backpack.

Bugs had worked with Jean, grape picking in Blenheim, New Zealand.

Jed . . .

Jed had just turned up. Jumped from the waterfall, walked into the camp with a canvas overnight bag and a soaking-wet bushel of grass under his arm.

Keaty said the camp had been thrown into instant panic. Was he alone, how had he learned about the beach, were there more with him, more coming? Everyone ran around going crazy; then Sal, Bugs, and Daffy turned up. They took him into the longhouse to talk while everyone waited outside. People heard Daffy shouting and Bugs trying to calm him down.

The cliffs were about twenty meters thick, but you couldn't see through them to the open sea because, not far in, the roof of the cave dropped below the water level. I wasn't happy about swimming into the blackness but Jed assured me the roof rose up again quickly. "It's a piece of piss," he said. "You're up again before you know it."

"Really?"

"Yeah. It's low tide, so we only have to swim half the cave. When it's high tide you have to swim the whole cave in one go, and even that's easy." Then he took a deep breath and slipped under, leaving me alone.

I waited a minute, treading water and listening to my splashes echo round the walls. My feet and shins were cold, kicking in the chilled area, reminding me of the diving game on Koh Samui. "Put me down as the adventurous type," I said loudly. It was supposed to be a joke, something to give me courage, and in a way I suppose it worked. The echo spooked me so much that the inky water seemed less scary than hanging around.

Jed had worked on an official work detail, carpentry, for only six days. Then he'd been taken off and started doing his "missions crap," as Keaty put it, above the waterfall.

People talked about it at first. They thought he ought to be working and were irritated that Sal, Bugs, and Daffy refused to explain why he was allowed to do his own thing. But time passed, and as Jed's face became more familiar they stopped asking questions. The main thing was that no other travelers appeared immediately after him, which had been everyone's fear, and he brought in a steady supply of grass, previously a luxury in short supply.

Keaty had a theory. Because Jed hadn't been recruited he

was an unknown quantity, and therefore, if he decided to leave, a danger to the camp's secrecy. So when Sal had realized that Jed was the type who was into missions, she created one just to keep him happy.

Personally, I thought the theory was unlikely. Whatever Jed was doing, it was what Sal wanted him to be doing. Diplomacy wouldn't have entered into it.

Unusually for me, I kept my eyes shut as I swam, feeling my way along the cave roof with outstretched hands and only using my legs for propulsion. I guessed that each kick made a meter and carefully counted my strokes to give me a sense of distance. After I'd counted ten I began to feel worried. An ache was building in my lungs and Jed had been adamant that the underwater passage was no more than a forty-second swim. At fifteen I realized I had to make a decision about whether to turn back. I gave myself a limit of three more kicks; then my fingertips broke surface.

I knew there was something wrong as soon as I took a breath. The air was foul. So bad that even though I was bursting for oxygen, I could only manage short breaths before I started gagging. Instinctively, pointlessly, I looked around me, but the absence of light was so absolute that I couldn't see my fingers an inch from my face.

"Jed!" I called.

Not even an echo.

I reached up and my hand sank deep into something wet, with freezing tendrils that clung to my skin. A jolt of adrenaline rushed through my body and I snatched my hand back.

"It's seaweed," I whispered after my heart had stopped smashing into my eardrums. Seaweed, coating the rock, absorbing the noise.

I gagged again. Then I retched, pushing up a mouthful of vomit.

"Jed . . ."

self-help

Once I'd started, I kept throwing up for several minutes. Every time my stomach contracted I couldn't help doubling up and I'd vomit with my head underwater, then have to straighten up quickly to snatch a breath before the next heave. The vomiting finally stopped, although it took three dry retches before my stomach would concede it was empty. Then I was left floating in blackness and amino acids, wondering what the fuck I should do next.

My first thought was that I should continue down the passage—I was assuming that I'd surfaced too soon, tricked by an air pocket left over from some extra-low tide. But that was easier said than done. While I'd been throwing up I'd twisted and turned twenty times and was now completely disoriented. That led me to my second thought: that I should work out the dimensions of the air pocket. This, at least, was something I could accomplish. Steeling myself, I reached up again and pushed my hand into the seaweed. I flinched but this time I didn't pull my hand back, and through the slimy growth I felt rock an arm's length above my head.

Several fumbling minutes later I'd created a good mental image of my surroundings. The pocket was about two meters wide and three meters long. On one side there was a narrow shelf, big enough to sit on, and everywhere else the walls curved straight down from the ceiling and ran into the water. There, the mental image began to fall apart. By groping around with my hands and feet, I seemed to find four passages leading into the rock, but it was hard to judge underwater. There could even have been more.

It was a grim discovery. If there'd been only two passages, then whichever direction I chose to swim, I'd come up in either the lagoon or the ocean. But these other passages could lead to nowhere. I could find myself swimming into a maze.

"Two out of four," I heard myself muttering. "One in two. Fifty-fifty." But it didn't matter how I put it. The odds sounded bad.

The alternative was to stay put and hope Jed came to find me, but it wasn't very appealing. I felt like I'd lose the plot if I waited in the pitch blackness, swimming around in my own sick, and I hadn't the faintest how long it would be before I started breathing carbon dioxide. This was an idea I found particularly frightening. I could see myself huddled up on the small rock shelf, gradually succumbing to a sinister sleepiness.

For a minute I stayed relatively still, treading water and going over my options. Then I started to panic. I splashed around wildly, bumping into the walls, choking, whimpering. I snatched at the seaweed above my head and pulled it down in great clumps. I lashed out, smashed my elbow on the rock shelf, felt my skin tear and hot blood run over my arm. I shouted, "Help."

"Help."

My voice sounded pathetic, like I was crying. It was a shocking noise and it jolted me into a second of silence. A second later, my fear was swamped by a sudden tidal wave of disgust. Ignoring the foul taste, I took a huge gulp of air and ducked underwater. I didn't count the strokes this time, or worry about feeling my way. I took whichever of the four passages I found first and swam as hard as I could.

the list

I was in a bad way. My legs and hands were knock-ing painfully against the passage walls and there was a pressure deep inside my chest, something the size of a grapefruit trying to drive itself upward through my neck. After perhaps fifty seconds I began to see red through the darkness. It means I'm dying, I thought as the color grew brighter and the grapefruit reached my Adam's apple. In the middle of the redness a spot of light started to form. It was yellow, but I expected it to turn white. I was remembering a TV program about how dying people see light at the end of tunnels as their brain cells shut down. Suddenly resigned, I felt my kicks grow weaker. My powerful breaststroke became an erratic underwater doggy paddle. When I felt rock scraping along the length of my stomach I realized I was no longer aware if I was facing up or down.

To say that this pissed me off sounds flippant, but that's the best way I can describe it. I think that a part of my mind, however bewildered, resented being wrong about the split-second theory in video games. I wasn't raging or fighting in the way I'd always imagined I would. I was just fading away. The resentment provided a new burst of energy, and with it came the realization that the redness might not be death after all. It might be light. Sunlight, passing through the water and the lids of my tightly shut eyes. Drawing from my last reserve of strength, I forced myself to make one more hard kick.

I came straight up into brightness and fresh air. I blinked the glare out of my eyes, gasping like a speared fish, and slowly Jed came into focus. He was sitting on a rock. Beside him was a long boat, painted the same blue green as the sea.

"Hey," he said, not looking round. "You took your time."

I couldn't answer at first because I was hyperventilating.

"What were you doing back there? You've been ages."

"Drowning," I finally managed to say.

"Yeah? You know anything about engines? I've tried to get this going but I can't."

I splashed over to him and tried to haul myself onto the rock, but I was too weak and I slipped back into the water. "Didn't you hear me?" I panted.

"Sure." He started absently running the blade of his knife against his beard, as if he were shaving. "Now, I know it's got enough gas because the tank's full, and I know the Swedes said they had it running the other day."

"Jed! I got stuck in some air pocket with more exits than . . ." I couldn't think of anything famous with a large number of exits. "I nearly drowned!"

For the first time Jed looked at me. "An air pocket?" he said, lowering the knife. "Are you sure?"

"Of course I'm fucking sure!"

"Where?"

"I don't know, do I? Somewhere . . . in there." I turned back to the black entrance of the cave and shivered.

Jed frowned. "Well . . . that's pretty weird. I've been through there a hundred times and I've never found any air pocket."

"You think I'm lying?"

"No. . . . And there were several exits?"

"Four at least. I could feel them and I didn't know which one I should take. It was a fucking nightmare."

"So you must have strayed down a split off the main passage. Shit, Richard, I'm sorry. I honestly didn't know that could happen. I must have been through there so many times that I automatically follow the same route." He tutted. "But it's amazing. Everybody on the beach has swum through that cave and no one's ever got lost."

I sighed. "That's my fucking luck."

"Bad luck all right." He held out a hand and pulled me onto the rock.

"I might have died."

Jed nodded. "You might have. I'm sorry."

A voice in my head was telling me that I ought to lose my temper, but there didn't seem anything to lose my temper at. Instead I lay back and looked up at the clouds. A silver speck was threading a vapor trail across the sky and I imagined people inside peering out of the windows, watching the Gulf of Thailand unfold, wondering what things could be happening on the islands beneath them. One or two of them, I was sure, must be looking at my island.

They'd never have guessed what was happening in a million years. Thinking this, I managed a dizzy smile.

Jed brought me back to earth by saying, "You smell of sick."

"I've been swimming in the stuff," I replied.

"Your elbow's bleeding too."

I glanced down and at once my arm began to sting.

"Jesus. I'm a wreck."

"No." Jed shook his head. "It's the boat that's the wreck."

The boat was twenty feet long and four feet wide, with a single bamboo outrigger on the right-hand side. On the left side it was lying flat against the rocks, tied up, protected by a line of buffers made of tightly rolled palm leaves. It was also protected, and hidden, by the mini-harbor formed by the entrance to the cave.

Inside the boat were some of the Swedes' fishing implements. Their spears were cut longer than ours and they had a landing net, I noticed enviously. Not that we needed a landing net inside the lagoon, but it would have been nice to have one all the same. They had lines and hooks, too, which explained why they always caught the biggest fish.

Despite what Jed had said, I took to the boat immediately. I liked its Southeast Asian shape, the painted flourishes on its prow, the strong odor of grease and salt-soaked wood. Most of all I liked the fact that all this stuff was familiar to me, remembered from other island trips in other places. I felt pleased to have a store of memories which enabled me to feel nostalgic about such exotic things.

Collecting memories, or experiences, was my primary goal when I first started traveling. I went about it in the same way as a stamp collector goes about collecting stamps, carrying around with me a mental list of all the things I had yet to see or do. Most of the list was pretty banal. I wanted to see the Taj Mahal, Borobudur, the Rice Terraces in Banave, Angkor Wat. Less banal, or maybe more so, was that I wanted to witness extreme poverty. I saw it as a necessary experience for anyone who wanted to appear worldly and interesting.

Of course witnessing poverty was the first to be ticked off the list. Then I had to graduate to the more obscure stuff. Being in a riot was something I pursued with a truly obsessive zeal, along with being tear-gassed and hearing gunshots fired in anger.

Another list item was having a brush with my own death. In Hong Kong, aged eighteen, I'd met an old Asia hand who'd told me a story about having being held up at gunpoint in Vietnam. The story ended with him having the gun shoved in his chest and being told he was going to be shot. "The funny thing about facing death," he'd said, "is that you find you aren't afraid. If anything, you're calm. Alert, naturally, but calm."

I'd nodded vigorously. I wasn't agreeing with him out of personal experience. I was just too thrilled to do anything but move my head.

The dope fields had fitted neatly into this category of the list, and so did the air pocket. The only downside was that I wasn't able to claim being alert (naturally) but calm, which was a line I fully intended to use one day.

Twenty minutes later I was ready to get going.

"Right," I said, sitting up. "Let's start up the engine."

"The engine's fucked. You can't start it. I think we might have to go back and get the Swedes to sort it out."

"Sure I can start it. I've been on this kind of banka loads of times."

Jed looked doubtful but gestured for me to give it a try.

I crawled into the boat and slid down to the stern end, and to my great delight I recognized the engine type. It was started like a lawn mower, by winding a rope around a flywheel and giving it a hard tug. A closer look revealed a knot at one end of the rope and a groove in the wheel for it to fit into.

"I've tried that fifty times," Jed muttered as I put the knot in place.

"It's in the wrist," I replied with deliberate cheerfulness. "You have to start slowly, then snap it back."

"Uh-huh?"

When I was ready to pull I gave the engine a last cursory check. I wasn't looking for anything in particular but I wanted to give the impression that I was, and my shallowness paid off. Almost obscured by layers of grease and dirt was a small metal switch with "on/off" written beneath it. I glanced backward over my shoulder and discreetly flicked it to the correct setting.

"Here we go!" I shouted, and gave the rope a yank. Without even a splutter the engine roared into life.

westmoreland

When we finally set out, noisily chugging away from the mini-harbor in a cloud of petrol fumes, I was keen to get to Koh Phangan. Although I'd been told it was past its best, Hadrin still had a somewhat legendary reputation. As with Patpong Road or the opium treks in the Golden Triangle, I wanted to know what all the fuss was about. I was also pleased to be doing something important for the beach. I knew that Sal appreciated my volunteering for such an obviously unpopular task, and I felt like I was involved in something serious and worthwhile.

But an hour later, as the shape of Koh Phangan was forming on the horizon, I began to feel anxious. It was the same feeling I'd had under the waterfall. I was suddenly aware that encountering the world would bring back all the things I'd been doing such a good job of forgetting. I wasn't exactly sure what those things were, because I'd forgotten them, but I was pretty convinced that I didn't want to be reminded. Also, although we couldn't really talk over the noise of the engine, I sensed Jed was thinking along the same lines. He was sitting as rigidly as the choppy motion of the boat would allow, one hand gripping the tiller, keeping his eyes absolutely fixed on the island ahead.

I reached into my shorts pocket for a cigarette. I'd taken a new packet—hoping the seal would keep them waterproof—and matches. They were in the plastic film carton that Keaty used to keep his rizlas dry. "This is the most precious possession I have," he'd said before handing it over. "Guard it with your life." "Count on it," I'd replied earnestly, imagining a three-hour boat trip without nicotine.

Lighting up turned into a bit of a drama because the matches were a crappy Thai brand and they splintered if you pushed them too hard. The first three broke and the next four blew out in the wind. I'd only taken ten in the film can and was beginning to lose my cool when I finally managed to get the cigarette lit. Jed lit one too, off the end of mine; then we both went back to gazing at Koh Phangan. Between the blue and the green I could now make out a strip of white sand.

To avoid thinking about the world, I started thinking about Françoise.

A few days earlier, near the coral garden, Etienne and I had been having a diving competition to see who could make the smallest splash. When we asked Françoise to judge it, she watched us both and then shrugged, saying, "You are both very good." Etienne looked surprised. "Yes," he said impatiently. "But who is better?" Françoise shrugged again. "What shall I say?" She laughed. "Really. You are both as good as the other." Then she gave us both a little kiss on the cheek.

Her reaction had surprised me, too. The truth is, Etienne was a much better diver than I was. I knew that without a shadow of a doubt. He could do effortless backward dives, swan dives, jackknifes, weird twists without names, all sorts of things. I, however, could only manage a backward dive with a violent jerk that usually flipped me right back onto my feet. As for who could make the smallest splash, Etienne entered the water as straight as a bamboo spear. I didn't need to see myself to know that I was more like a tree trunk, branches and all.

So when Françoise said that we were both as good as the other, she was lying. A funny sort of lie. Not malicious, apparently diplomatic, but vaguely puzzling in a way I found hard to pin down.

"West . . . more . . . land . . ." I heard over the noise of the engine. Jed was calling to me, snapping me out of my daydreaming.

I looked round and cupped my hand to my ear. "What?" I yelled.

"I'm heading west! There's more open beach to land! Less beach huts!"

I gave him the thumbs-up and turned back to the prow. While I'd been thinking about Françoise, Koh Phangan had got much closer. I could now see the trunks and leaves of the coconut trees, and the midday shadows beneath them.

reentry

A hundred or so meters from the shore, Jed cut the engine so we could paddle the rest of the way in. The idea was to look like day-trippers, but we needn't have bothered. The stretch of beach we landed on was empty apart from a few beat-up old beach huts, and they looked like no one had stayed in them for quite a while.

We jumped out and waded to the sand, dragging the boat by the outrigger. "Are we going to leave the boat here?" I asked when we were clear of the water.

"No, we'll have to hide it." Jed pointed to the treeline. "Maybe up there. Go and check it out. Make sure this area is as empty as it seems."

"Okay."

I started jogging up the beach, then slowed to a walk almost immediately. My sense of balance still thought I was at sea and I was swaying drunkenly from side to side. It passed quickly, but for a couple of minutes I actually had to concentrate to keep from falling over.

Not far from where we'd landed I found two palms that were far enough apart to let the outrigger through and close enough together to look inconspicuous. Between them was a bush with a large canopy that would cover the boat completely, especially with the help of a few well-placed branches, and the nearest of the ramshackle beach huts was a good fifty meters away.

"Here seems fine," I called to Jed.

"Right. Give us a hand then."

Everything would have been much easier if there'd been a third person to help us. With the weight of the engine, it took both of us to lift the stern—we had to keep the propeller up to stop it from getting damaged—so the front end kept sliding away from us. It was hard enough on the sand, but getting it over the small grass verge was a nightmare. We had to shunt it in short backbreaking bursts, none of which seemed to move it more than a foot.

"Bloody hell," I panted, after the boat had swiveled away from the treeline for the twentieth time. "Is it always this hard?"

"Is what always this hard?"

"Rice Running."

"Of course," Jed replied, smoothing the sweat out of his beard. A stream of oily drops ran down his wrist and dripped off his elbow. "Why do you think nobody wants to do it?"

Eventually we managed to maneuver the boat between the trees and under the bush. After we'd knocked up some camouflage, there was no way anyone would have spotted it unless they were going out of their way to look. We were even worried that we'd have trouble finding it again ourselves, so we marked the spot by pushing a forked stick into the sand.

We were completely exhausted, but there were two consolations. One was that it would be easier getting the boat back to the water, because it would be downhill and the ocean made for a bigger target than the space between two palm trees. The other was that we could treat ourselves to a big meal as soon as we got to Hadrin.

We set off in high spirits, discussing which soft drinks we were going to order and whether Sprite had the edge on Coke. Jed noticed the couple first, but we were already a fair distance from the boat, so we didn't worry too much. As we passed them I looked straight at their faces, not for any reason except to be ready with a smile if they said hello.

They didn't. They kept their eyes pointed at the ground, and by their expressions I could see they were putting the same concentration into walking as I had earlier.

"Did you see them?" I said when they were out of earshot. "Wasted by lunchtime."

"Liquid lunch."

"Powdered lunch."

Jed nodded, then hawked up and spat on the sand. "Fucking freaks."

An hour later we were walking past rows of busy beach huts and weaving between sunbathers and Frisbee games. I was surprised that people weren't taking more notice of us. Everyone looked so strange to me that I couldn't believe I didn't look equally strange to them.

"Let's eat," said Jed when we were about halfway down Hadrin, so we walked into the nearest café and sat down. Jed looked over the menu while I continued to marvel at our surroundings. The concrete under my toes felt particularly weird, as did the plastic chair. It was just a standard chair—the same kind as I used to have at school; curved seat with a hole in the back, V-shaped metal legs—but I found it bizarrely uncomfortable. I couldn't work out the right way to sit on it: either I was slithering down or I was perched on the edge.

"How the hell do you do this?" I muttered.

Jed looked up from the menu.

"I can't seem to sit . . ."

He started laughing. "Does your head in, doesn't it? All this."

"It sure does."

"What about your reflection?"

". . . How do you mean?"

"When was the last time you saw your reflection?"

I shrugged. There was a makeup mirror outside near the shower hut which the men used for shaving, but it only showed a tiny area of your face at any one time. Apart from that, I hadn't seen myself since Koh Samui.

"There's a sink and mirror over there. Go and have a look. You'll get a real shock."

I frowned, suddenly worried. "Why? Has something happened to my face?"

"No. Just go and have a look. You'll see."

Shock was right. The person who gazed back at me over the sink was a stranger. My skin was darker than I'd imagined it could possibly get, my black hair had been sun-bleached almost brown and matted into curls, and my teeth were so white they seemed to jump out of my face. I also looked old—twenty-six or twenty-seven—and there were some freckles on my nose. The freckles were a particular shock. I never get freckles.

I stared at my reflection for five minutes at least, transfixed. I could have stared for an hour if Jed hadn't called me back to order some food.

"What did you think?" he asked as I wandered back to the table, grinning like an idiot.

"Really weird. Why don't you have a look too? It's great."

"No. . . . I haven't seen myself for six months now. I'm saving up to completely freak myself out."

"Six months!"

"Uh-huh. Maybe more." He tossed me the menu. "Come on. What'll it be? I'm starving."

I glanced down the enormous list, pausing on banana pancakes but thinking the better of it.

"I believe I'd like a couple of cheeseburgers."

"Cheeseburgers. Anything else?"

"Uh . . . okay. Spicy chicken noodles too. We're in Thailand, after all."

Jed stood up, glancing over his shoulder toward the sunbathers on the beach. "I'll take your word for it," he said dryly, then went to place our order.

While we waited for our food we watched TV. There was a video at the far end of the café and it was playing *Schindler's List*. Schindler was on a horse watching the ghettos being emptied, and he'd noticed a little girl in a red coat.

"How about that coat?" Jed asked, sipping his Coke.

I sipped my Sprite. "What about it?"

"Do you reckon they painted it on the film with a brush?"

"On each frame? Like animation?"

"Yeah."

"No way. They would have done it with a computer, like *Jurassic Park*."

"Oh . . ." Jed drained the bottle and smacked his lips. "It's the real thing."

I frowned. *"Schindler's List?"*

"No, you jerk. Coke."

The food must have taken ages, because by the time it

arrived, Schindler was looking at the red coat again. If you've seen the film you'll know that's an hour after he first sees it, if not more. Luckily I discovered that the café had an old Space Invaders machine, so for me the waiting wasn't so bad.

Kampuchea

Jed gave me a choice. I could go with him to sort out the rice or I could stay on the beach and meet him later. He didn't really need my help so I decided to stay. In any case, I had my own shopping to do. I wanted to restock my supply of cigarettes and get more batteries for Keaty's Game Boy.

In one of the other Hadrin cafés I found a shop—or a glass counter with a few goods beneath it—and after buying the batteries and cigarettes it turned out I still had plenty of money left to get a few presents.

First of all I bought some soap for Unhygienix. This was tricky because they had several varieties, some Western, some Thai, but none of them the brand I'd seen Unhygienix using. I rummaged through the bars for a while before finding one called Luxume. It said it was "luxuriant yet perfumed." The "yet" turned my head and the "perfumed" clinched it, since I knew how important this was to him.

Then I bought a load of razors, which I thought I'd share with Etienne, Gregorio, and Keaty. Then I bought a tube of Colgate for Françoise. Nobody used toothpaste on the beach; there were ten toothbrushes, which were shared by everyone, although many couldn't be bothered and just chewed a twig each morning. Françoise didn't mind sharing a toothbrush but she did miss the toothpaste, so I knew she'd appreciate the gift.

The next purchase was several packets of boiled sweets—I didn't want anybody to go empty-handed—and finally I bought a pair of shorts. Mine were getting ragged and I couldn't see them lasting more than a month or two.

With my shopping done I had nothing left to do. I had another Sprite, which didn't last long, so I decided to pass time by walking the length of Hadrin. After only a few hundred meters I gave up. There was nothing much to see apart from beach huts. Instead I sat on the sand and paddled my feet in the water, imagining the warm reactions I'd get when I handed out my presents. I envisaged an *Asterix*-style scene, returning from the adventure to a huge feast. We'd have to do without wild boars and Gaulish wine, but we'd have plenty of dope and more rice than you could shake a stick at.

"Saigon," said a male voice, and broke me straight out of my daydreaming. "Mad."

"Sounds it," said another voice, female.

"We were there two months. The place is like Bangkok ten fuckin' years ago. Probably better."

I looked round and saw four sunbathers. Two girls, English, and two boys, Australians. All of them were talking very loudly; so loudly it was like their conversation was aimed more at passersby than each other.

"Yeah, but if Saigon was mad, then Kampuchea was fuckin' unreal." This was the second Aussie speaking—a skinny guy with very cropped hair, long sideburns, and a tiny patch of beard on his chin.

"We were there for six weeks. Would have stayed longer but we ran out of cash. Had to get back to Thailand to pick up a fuckin' wire."

"Good scene," the first agreed. "Could have stayed six months."

"Could have stayed six years."

I looked back into the sea. It was a familiar enough exchange, I thought to myself, and not worth tuning in to. But then I found that I couldn't tune it out. It wasn't the volume of their chattering; I was intrigued that the guy had been talking about Kampuchea. I wondered if this was the new term for Cambodia.

Without thinking it over any more than that, I leaned toward them. "Hey," I said. "Out of interest, why do you call Cambodia Kampuchea?"

All four faces looked at me.

"I mean," I continued, "it's Cambodia, right?"

The second Aussie shook his head, not like he was disagreeing with me; like he was trying to figure out who I was.

"It's Cambodia, right?" I repeated, in case he hadn't heard me.

"Kampuchea. I've just been there."

I got up and walked over. "But called Kampuchea by who?"

"Cambodians."

"Not Kampucheans, then."

He frowned. "What?"

"I'm just interested to hear how you picked up the word Kampuchea."

"Mate," the first Aussie interrupted, "why does it matter what we call Kampuchea?"

"It isn't that it matters. I was just interested because I thought Kampuchea was a Khmer Rouge name. I mean, I'm probably wrong. Maybe it's just the old-fashioned name for Cambodia, but . . ."

The sentence trailed off. I was suddenly aware that all four of them were looking at me as though they thought I was insane. I smiled uncertainly. "It isn't a big deal . . . I was interested, that's all. . . . Kampuchea . . . It sounded strange . . ."

Silence.

I began to feel myself blushing. I knew I'd made some kind of faux pas but I didn't know what it might be. With my smile getting increasingly desperate, I tried to explain myself better, but my confusion and nervousness only made things worse. "I was just sitting over there and you said 'Kampuchea,' which I thought was a Khmer Rouge name, but you also used the old name of Ho Chi Minh City . . . Saigon . . . Not that I'm making a parallel between the VC and the Khmer Rouge, obviously . . . but . . ."

"So what?"

This was a fair point. I considered it for a couple of seconds, then said, "So nothing, I guess . . ."

"Then why are you bothering us, mate?"

I couldn't think what to say. I shrugged awkwardly and turned to walk back to my shopping bag, and behind me I heard one of them mutter, "Another fuckin' spacehead. Can't move for them, man." The comment made my ears burn and the tips of my fingers tingle. I hadn't had that feeling since I was a little kid.

When I sat back down I felt terrible. My good mood was completely gone. I couldn't understand what I'd said that was so wrong. All I'd been doing was joining in their conversation, which didn't seem like such a terrible thing to do. It was the beach and the world, I decided coldly. My beach, where you could walk into a conversation at any time between anybody, and the world, where you couldn't.

A few minutes later I got up to go. I'd noticed that their talking was quieter, and I had the miserable feeling that they were talking about me. I found a suitably secluded palm tree a short way up the beach and settled beneath it. I'd arranged to meet Jed at seven, back at the café where we'd eaten lunch, so I still had a few hours to kill. Too many hours. The wait was beginning to feel like it might be an ordeal.

I chain-smoked two and a half cigarettes. I wanted to chain-smoke three, or even more, but the third gave me a five-minute coughing fit. Reluctantly I stubbed it out and pushed it into the sand.

My embarrassment had turned quickly to anger. Before, I'd been looking at Hadrin with a detached curiosity, and now I was looking at it with hatred. I could sense shit all around me, Thais smiling like sharks and careless hedonism, too diligently pursued to ring true. Most of all, I could pick up the scent of decay. It hung over Hadrin like the sand flies that hung over the sunbathers, zoning in on the smell of sweat and sweet tanning lotion. The serious travelers had already moved on to the next island in the chain, the intermediary travelers were wondering where all the life had gone, and the tourist hordes were ready to descend on their freshly beaten track.

For the first time I understood the true preciousness of our hidden beach. To imagine Hadrin's fate unfolding in the lagoon made my blood run cold. I began scanning the dark bodies that lounged around me as if I were photographing the enemy, familiarizing myself with the images, filing them away. Occasionally couples walked near me and I caught snatches of their conversations. I must have heard twenty different accents and languages. Most I didn't understand, but they all sounded like threats.

Time dragged with only these thoughts for company, so when my eyes grew heavy I let them close. The heat and the day's early start had caught up with me. An afternoon siesta would be a welcome retreat.

blame

The music started up at eight, which was lucky or I might have slept until midnight. Up and down the beach, four or five different sound systems blasted out, each with its own agenda. I could only hear two clearly, the ones on either side of me, but all the bass lines seemed to be vibrating through my head. Swearing and rubbing the daze out of my eyes, I jumped up and ran back down the beach to the café.

The café was now packed with people but I spotted Jed immediately. He was at the same table we'd sat at earlier. He had a bottle of beer in his hands and was looking extremely pissed off.

"Where the fuck have you been?" he said angrily when I sat down beside him. "I've been waiting."

"I'm sorry," I replied. "I fell asleep . . . I've had a bad day."

"You did, huh? Well, I'll just bet it wasn't a patch on mine."

"Why, what happened? Didn't you get the rice?"

"I got the rice, Richard. Don't worry about that."

I looked at him hard. There was a worrying note of menace in his voice. "What then?"

"You tell me."

"Tell you . . . ?"

"About two Yanks."

"Two Yanks?"

Jed took a huge gulp of beer. "Two Yanks I heard talking about a place called Eden in the Marine Park."

". . . Oh shit."

"They know you, Richard. They used your name. And

they've got a map." He squeezed his eyes shut like he was fighting to keep control of his temper. "A fucking map, Richard! They were showing it to some Germans! And who knows who else has seen it."

I shook my head. I was feeling dazed. "I'd forgotten . . . I'd . . ."

"Who are they?"

"Jed, wait. You don't understand. I didn't tell them about the beach. They told me. They already knew about it."

He put his bottle on the table with a thump. *"Who are they!"*

". . . Zeph and Sammy. I met them on Koh Samui."

"Go on."

"They were just these two guys in the hut next to mine. We spent some time together, and the night before we were going to leave for Angthong, they started talking about the beach."

"Unprompted?"

"Yes! Of course!"

"So you drew them a map."

"No! I didn't say a thing, Jed! None of us did."

"Then where did the map come from?"

"The next morning . . . I drew it and pushed it under their door . . ." I pulled out a cigarette and tried to light it. My hands shook badly and it took me three attempts.

"Why?"

"I was worried!"

"You just drew them the map? They didn't even ask for it!"

"I didn't know if the beach really existed. We could have been aiming at nowhere. I had to tell someone where we were going in case something went wrong."

"What could go wrong?"

"I don't know! We didn't know anything! I just didn't

want us disappearing with nobody knowing where we'd gone!"

Jed put his head in his hands. "This could be bad, Richard."

"We could have disappeared into the Marine Park and no one would have . . ."

He nodded slowly. "I understand that."

We sat in silence for several minutes, Jed staring at the table and me looking anywhere but at him. Over by the Space Invaders machine a tubby black girl with cornrows was trying to hit the last invader. It was moving so fast it was a blur. She missed it on every pass, and just before it reached the bottom line she turned away, disgusted. The sound of talking and music was too loud for me to hear her exploding spaceship, but I saw it on her face.

Eventually Jed lifted up his head. "These two Yanks. Do you think they'll make the trip?"

". . . They might do, Jed. I don't know them well enough."

"*Fuck*. This could be so bad." Then suddenly he reached over and laid his hand on my forearm. "Listen," he said. "Are you blaming yourself?"

I nodded.

"Don't. I'm serious. Whatever happens with these Yanks, it isn't your fault. If I'd been in your shoes I might have done the same thing."

"How do you mean, 'whatever happens'?" I said warily.

"I mean . . . I mean whatever happens I don't want you to blame yourself. It's important, Richard. If you really want someone to blame, blame Daffy." He sighed deeply. "Or me."

"You?"

"Me."

I opened my mouth to ask him to explain, but he held up a hand. "There's no point talking about it."

"Okay," I said quietly.

"Look, we might not even have a problem. In a few weeks the Yanks will probably be flying off home and the map should go with them. Even if they stay in Thailand there's a good chance they won't bother trying to reach us. They seemed like a couple of airheads, and the trip isn't easy."

"I hope you're right," I said hollowly, remembering how skilled they were at their surfer act.

"Hoping's about all we can do. That and wait . . ." He finished his beer. "We've got to get the rice back to the boat tonight because I don't want to be carrying those sacks in broad daylight. Are you ready to go?"

"Yes."

He stood up. "Good. Then let's get to it."

Around the back of the café was a thin passage between two beach huts, and under a tarpaulin were our rice sacks. We put them on the tarpaulin so we could drag them along the sand, and, holding a corner each, we set off on the long trek back to the boat.

Just after leaving Hadrin, we had a fag break and ate a few of the boiled sweets from my bag of presents.

"I'm sorry if I flew off at you," Jed said as I passed him the packet.

"It's all right."

"No. I'm sorry. You didn't deserve it."

I shrugged. I felt like I did.

"I didn't ask you why your day was so bad."

"Oh. It's nothing . . . It was just Hadrin. The place, or the people . . . They gave me the creeps."

"Me too. Fucked up, isn't it?"

"Fucked up . . . Yeah. It is."

"Richard?"

"Yes?"

"When we get back to the camp, don't mention this thing with the Yanks."

"But . . ."

"Sal and Bugs. I don't think they'll understand."

I looked at him but he was busy trying to get the wrapper off one of the sweets.

"If you think that's the right thing to do."

"Yeah. I do."

It took us another three hours to get back to the marker. The forked stick showed up clearly in the bright moonlight, and we left the sacks beside it. Then I went to check on the boat while Jed moved the sacks off the tarpaulin and spread it across the sand. It was pitch-black under the bushes but I could feel the curved prow. That was enough for me. As long as we had our means of escape, I could relax.

Jed was already asleep by the time I got back to the marker. I lay beside him and looked at the stars, remembering the way I'd looked at the stars with Françoise. Somewhere amongst them was a parallel world where I'd kept the map to myself, I thought, and wished it could have been this one.

through early-morning fog i see

Mister Duck sat in his box room on the Ko Sanh Road. He'd pulled back one of the newspapers that covered the window and was peering down to the street. Behind him, strewn across his bed, were colored pencils. Obviously the ones he'd used to draw the map. The map was nowhere in sight, so maybe he'd already tacked it to my door.

I saw that his shoulders were shaking.

"Mister Duck?" I said cautiously.

He turned, scanned the room with a puzzled frown, then spotted me through the strip of mosquito netting.

"Rich . . . Hi."

"Hi. Are you all right?"

"No." A tear rolled down his grubby cheek. "I'm going to kill myself pretty soon. I'm feeling really bad."

". . . I'm sorry. Is there anything I can do?"

He sighed. "Thank you, Rich. You're a good friend, but it's too late now. I've been in a Bangkok morgue for the last eleven weeks."

"There's no one to collect you?"

"No one. The Thai police contacted the British embassy. They found my parents in Glasgow but my folks didn't want to come out here to sign the release papers. They don't care about me." Another tear trickled out. "Their only son."

"But that's awful."

"And I'm going to be incinerated in another four weeks if no one signs my release papers. The embassy won't cover the cost of returning my body."

"You . . . wanted to be buried."

"I don't mind being incinerated, but if my parents won't come to collect me, then I don't want to be sent. I'd rather have my ashes left out here." Mister Duck's voice began to crack. "A small ceremony, nothing fancy, and my ashes scattered into the South China Sea." Then he collapsed into uncontrollable sobbing.

I pressed my face and hands against the netting. I wished I were in the room with him. "Hey, come on, Mister Duck. It isn't so bad."

He shook his head angrily, and through his sobbing I noticed he'd started to sing the theme song from *M*A*S*H.*

I waited until he'd finished, not knowing where to look; then I said, "You've got a good voice," mainly because I didn't know what else to say.

He shrugged, wiping his face with his filthy T-shirt. His face ended up dirtier than it had been before. "It's a small voice but it can carry a tune."

"No, Mister Duck. It's a good voice . . . I always liked *M*A*S*H.*"

He appeared to brighten up slightly. "So did I. The helicopters at the beginning."

"The helicopters were great."

"It was about Vietnam. Did you know that, Rich?"

"Korea, wasn't it?"

"Vietnam. Korea was the excuse."

"Oh . . ."

Mister Duck turned back to peek between the newspapers again. He didn't seem like he was about to speak, so to keep the conversation going, I asked him what he was looking at.

"Nothing," he replied softly. "A *tuk-tuk* driver asleep in his cab . . . A stray dog sifting through litter . . . You take these things for granted when you're alive, Rich, but when they're the last things you're ever going to see . . ." His voice began to quaver again and he bunched up his fists. "It's time I got this over with."

". . . Killing yourself?"

"Yes," he said. Then he said it again, more firmly. "Yes."

He walked briskly over to the bed, sat down, and pulled a knife from under the pillow.

"Don't, Mister Duck! Don't do it!"

"My mind's made up."

"There's time to change your mind!"

"I won't turn back now."

"Mister Duck!" I cried out feebly.

Too late. He'd already started to cut.

I didn't watch him die because I thought it would be disrespectful, but I checked on him five minutes later to see how he was getting on. He was still alive, jerking around on the sheets and spraying the walls. I waited another fifteen minutes before checking again, wanting to be sure. This time he was still, lying in the position I'd first found him. His torso was twisted so that his legs were off the edge of the bed—a detail I hadn't noticed previously. Maybe he'd tried to stand up just before he died.

"I'll sort your ashes out, Mister Duck," I whispered through the netting. "You don't have to worry about that."

messed up

I woke up at the first glimmer of dawn. The sun was still under the horizon and the beach was lit with a strange blue light, both dark and bright at the same time. It was very beautiful and calm. Even the waves seemed to be breaking more quietly than usual.

I didn't wake Jed because I like being awake when other people are asleep. It makes me feel like pottering around, fixing breakfast if there's anything to be fixed, and in this case, wandering aimlessly up the shore. While I walked I looked out for pretty shells. The necklace that Bugs had made me was okay, but many of the shells were a bit drab. I got the feeling that he hadn't been too bothered to make them nice. Even Françoise's necklace, which was the best of the three, wasn't as good as most of the others in the camp. It didn't take long before I'd worked up a collection and was having to make hard choices about which shells to discard. The prettiest I found was flecked with blue, red, and green—the back of a tiny crab. I decided that this would make the centerpiece of my new necklace and looked forward to restringing it when I got home.

I found the couple lying fast asleep on the grass verge, about two hundred meters further on from where we'd hidden the boat. It was the same couple that Jed and I had passed yesterday. My first instinct was to turn back, but curiosity stopped me. They'd chosen an oddly remote beach hut to stay in, miles from Hadrin, and I was intrigued to see what kind of people they were. I pocketed my shells and padded across the sand toward them.

Now that I had a chance to see the couple from close up, they made an ugly sight. The girl had nasty sores around her mouth and was covered in fat black mosquitoes. At least thirty or forty were clustered on her legs and arms, and when I waved my hand over them they didn't budge an inch. There were no mosquitoes on the guy. "No surprise," I thought, because he wouldn't have made much of a meal. Judging by his height, I reckoned he should have been eleven stone, but he couldn't have weighed more than eight. His body was like an anatomical diagram. Every bone was clearly visible, as was every pitiful muscle. Beside him was a pill bottle, marked with the address of some dubious pharmacy in Surat Thani. I checked inside but it was empty.

I'd been studying the guy for a while before I noticed that his eyes were slightly open. Just little slits, easy to miss at first glance. I waited to see him blink. He didn't, or didn't seem to, so I waited to see him breathe. He didn't do that, either. Then I bent down and touched his chest. He was warm enough, but the air was pretty warm too, so that didn't mean anything. I pressed my hand down harder. My fingers sank deeply between his ribs and the skin moved slackly against the bone. No pulse. I started counting, carefully marking the seconds with elephants, and by the time I reached sixty I knew he was dead.

I frowned and looked around me. Apart from the silhouette of Jed and the rice sacks, the beach was completely deserted. Then I looked back at the girl. I knew she was alive because of the mosquitoes, and anyway, her chest was rising and falling.

This unsettled me. I wasn't bothered about the guy, because he'd come to Thailand and messed up, so that was his lookout. But the girl was another matter entirely. As soon as her opiate slumber wore off she'd wake up to an empty beach and a corpse. I thought that would be a terrible thing to happen, and seeing as I'd been the one to find her, I felt I had some responsibility for her. I lit up a cigarette and wondered how I might help.

Waking the girl up was out of the question. Even if I managed to bring her round, she'd only freak out. Then the authorities on Koh Phangan would get involved and it would be a disaster. Another option was to wake Jed up and ask his advice, but I decided against it. I knew what he'd say. He'd say it was none of our business and we should leave the couple as we found them, and I already knew I didn't want to do that.

Eventually I hit on a good idea. I would drag the guy's body away to the bushes and hide it. Then, when she woke up, she'd just think he'd gone for a walk. After a day or so she'd realize he was missing and might worry about what had happened to him, but at least she wouldn't know he was dead. By that time he would probably have been eaten by ants and beetles, and no one but me would be any the wiser.

I busied myself with the task at hand, keeping half an eye on my watch. Jed would be awake soon and then it would be time to leave.

"Jed!" I said softly.

He stirred and waved a hand over his face, like he was brushing away a fly.

"Jed! Wake up!"

"What?" he mumbled.

"We should go. It's getting light."

He sat up and looked up at the sky. The sun was fully above the horizon line. "Shit, yeah, we should. Overslept. Sorry. Let's get cracking."

When we were halfway between Koh Phangan and our island I told him what had happened with the corpse and how I'd dealt with it.

"Jesus fucking Christ, Richard!" he shouted—only because the engine was so loud. "What the flying fuck did you do that for?"

"Well, what should I have done?"

"You should have left him there, you bloody idiot! What did it have to do with us? Nothing!"

"I knew you'd say that," I said happily. "I knew it."

prisoners of the sun

bible bashing

No one was even slightly interested. A few asked, "How was it?" out of politeness, but as soon as I began to answer, their eyes glazed over or their attention became diverted by something over my shoulder.

At first I found this attitude pretty frustrating. I wanted to talk at length about how fucked up Koh Phangan was, and the frustration was compounded by the unenthusiastic response I got when I handed out my little presents. Françoise took one taste of the toothpaste and spat it out, saying, "Ugh, I did not remember the way it burns," and Keaty said I shouldn't have bought Thai-brand batteries because they run out so fast. The only person who seemed at all grateful was Unhygienix. He went straight off for a shower after I gave him the bars, and later he gave me a glowing report on the thick lather they produced.

But my frustration only lasted while Koh Phangan was fresh in my mind, which wasn't long. Just as when I'd first arrived at the beach, my memory began to shut itself down. Steadily, quickly, so that within a week nothing much existed beyond the lagoon and its circle of protective cliffs. Nothing except the world, that is, and that had returned to its previous condition, a name to something faceless and indistinct.

My worries about Zeph and Sammy were the last things to go. As late as the fifth night I was kept awake fretting about what plans they and the mysterious Germans might be making. But it became hard to maintain that level of worry as the days passed, and still no one had turned up. Having said that, the day after the fretful fifth night I did ask Jed whether he'd also been thinking about the Zeph and Sammy problem, and he made a seesaw motion with his hands. "I've been thinking about it a little," he said. "But I think we're okay."

"You do?" I replied, already sensing the weight of the problem lifting.

"Yeah. Those two were on the pilgrim's route. They had guidebook written all over them. If not, like I already said, we'll deal with it when it happens." He pulled a knot of hair out of his beard. "You know, Richard, one of these days I'm going to find one of those Lonely Planet writers and I'm going to ask him, what's so fucking lonely about the Ko Sanh Road?"

I smiled. "Just before you punch his lights out, right?"

The smile wasn't returned.

jaws one

A few weeks after the Rice Run, I woke up to the noise of rain on the longhouse roof. It had rained only three or four times since I'd arrived at the beach, and those had just been showers. This was a tropical storm, even heavier than the one on Koh Samui.

A few of us huddled around the longhouse entrance, looking out across the clearing. The canopy ceiling was channeling the water into thick streams that dropped like lasers and cut muddy holes into the earth. Keaty was standing under one of them, his top half obscured by the silver umbrella that exploded off his head. I only recognized him from his black legs and the faint sound of his laughter. Bugs was also standing outside. He had his head tilted so that one cheek was angled upward, his arms were held slightly away from his body, and his palms were ready to catch the rain.

"Thinks he's Christ," muttered a voice behind me. I turned around and saw Jesse, a compact New Zealander who worked in the garden detail with Keaty. Jesse was one of the people I'd never had much cause to speak to, but I'd always suspected that he'd been the one to pick up my first Jim-Bob cue.

I looked back at Bugs and smiled, because there *was* something piously Christlike about his pose. Either the pose or the beatific expression on his face.

"Know what I mean?" Jesse said.

I smiled.

"Maybe the carpentry's gone to his head," said Cassie, who was also standing near, and we all chuckled. I would have added something but Jesse nudged me. Sal had emerged from the far end of the longhouse and was walking toward us. Gregorio was beside her, looking a little hassled.

"What's the delay?" asked Sal as she approached.

Nobody answered her, so I said, "Delay about what?"

"Fishing, gardening, work."

Jesse shrugged. "Not much gardening to be done in the rain, Sal."

"The plants can be protected, Jesse. You can rig up a shelter."

"Plants need rain."

"They don't need rain like this."

Jesse shrugged again.

"And you, Richard? What will we eat with your rice if you don't go fishing?"

"I was waiting for Greg."

"Greg's ready now."

"Yes," said Gregorio, and Etienne and Françoise also appeared. "We are ready now."

We jogged down to the beach, sliding around in the mud. I don't know why we were jogging because we were soaked within seconds, and in any case, we were going to spend the next three hours in the sea. I suppose there was a general feeling that we wanted to get the fishing done as quickly as possible.

While we jogged, I thought over the brief exchange under the longhouse entrance. I'd never mentioned the way Bugs irritated me, not even to Keaty. It hadn't seemed like a wise idea, considering Bugs's standing in the camp, and my criticisms seemed so petty. But from the way Jesse and Cassie had been talking, I began to wonder if others felt the same way. Although they hadn't said anything nasty they'd certainly been taking the piss, and until that moment it hadn't occurred to me that people took the piss out of Bugs.

The thing that most struck me was the way they'd hushed up when Sal came over. If not for that, the joking would have seemed far less telling. As it was, I felt like I'd witnessed some kind of division—however slight—and had possibly been included in it. I wondered if I ought to find out more about Jesse and Cassie, if only to get to know them better. I'd have asked Gregorio but I knew I'd get a uselessly diplomatic answer. Keaty or Jed were the ones to talk to.

The sea was covered in a thick low mist of vaporized raindrops. Under the shelter of a palm tree, we leaned against our spears and shook our heads.

"This is too stupid," said Françoise. "We cannot kill fish if we do not see them."

Etienne grunted his agreement. "We cannot even see the water."

"Yes, we use the mask," Gregorio replied, holding it up, and I groaned.

"Is that what you normally do when it rains?"

"Of course."

"But that means only one person can fish at a time. It's going to take forever."

"It will take a long time, Richard."

"How about Moshe and the Yugoslavian girls, and the Swedes? They don't have masks."

"They will try to catch fish but they will kill only a few. . . . When it rains like this, we can get very hungry on the beach."

"And if it rains for five days?" said Françoise. "It can rain for five days, no?"

Gregorio shrugged and glanced at the sky. From the look of it, the rain wouldn't ease up for at least another twenty-four hours. "We can get very hungry on the beach," he repeated, and dug his spear further into the wet earth.

We lapsed into silence, each of us apparently waiting for someone else to take the first go on the mask. I wanted to stand under the palm tree all day, ignoring the enormity of the work ahead, because as soon as the work was begun we'd all be committed to finishing it.

Five minutes passed, then another five, and then Etienne slung his spear over his shoulder.

"No," I said, sighing. "I'll go first."

"Are you sure, Richard? We can throw a coin."

"You've got a coin?"

Etienne smiled. "We can throw . . . the mask. Facedown, I will go first."

"I don't mind going first."

"Okay," he said, patting my arm. "So I shall go next."

"Okay."

Gregorio passed me the mask and I set off for the water. "Swim deeply and look under the boulders," he called after me. "The fish will be hiding."

It was a buzz swimming through the thick vapor. I couldn't wear the mask because the spray was too dense to let me breathe through my mouth, which meant I was constantly blinking to clear the water from my eyes. With nothing to see but a blurred foot of sea on either side of me, and each breath requiring a manageable amount of labor, I felt agreeably cocooned by a mildly dangerous world.

I stopped at the first boulder I came to. It was one of the smaller ones, sixty or so meters from the shore. We rarely used it as there was only room for one person to sit on it at a time, but seeing as I was alone it didn't make much difference. When I stood up my top half cleared the layer of mist. Etienne was standing on the sand, holding his hands like a peaked cap to ward off the rain. I waved my spear in the air and he spotted me, then turned to walk back to the treeline.

The first thing I needed to do was to find a heavy stone so I could rest on the bottom with a decent lungful of air. I put on the mask and slipped into the water, kicking out for the sea floor. The light was dark gray, deadened by the black sky and the mist, but the visibility was good. There weren't, however, any fish to be seen. Not even the clouds of tiny fry that usually wheeled around the corals.

I took my time hunting for the stone, making myself move slowly. If there were any fish around I didn't want to scare them off. Eventually I spotted a stone that looked like the right size and weight. I'd run out of air by that time, so I stuck my spear beside it, to make it easy to find again, and rose up to the surface.

On the way back down a few milkfish appeared, coming to inspect the new arrival to their storm shelter. I settled at the bottom with the stone on my lap and waited for their curiosity to bring them within range.

I saw the shark on my third dive. I'd just killed my first milkfish, so it must have been attracted by the smell of the blood. It wasn't much of a shark, about a foot longer than my leg and much the same width, but it gave me a hell of a shock. I didn't know what to do. Despite its small size it made me nervous, but I didn't want to swim back with only one fish. I'd have to explain why I'd given up so soon, and it would also be embarrassing if the shark was seen later. It was probably only a baby.

I decided I'd have to resurface and hang around on the boulder, hoping it would go away. I did this and spent the next ten minutes shivering in the mist and rain, crouched down because I didn't want the others to see that I wasn't fishing. Every so often I peered underwater to check if it was still there. It always was, circling slowly near the spot where I'd been sitting, watching me—I reckoned—with its inky eyes.

A brilliant idea coincided with a blistering peal of thunder. I put my milkfish, which was still in the twitching stage of death, on the tip of my spear. Then I rolled onto my front so I could dip my head and arms into the water, and held the spear ahead of me. The shark responded at once, breaking out of its leisured pace with a crisp snap of its tail. It headed toward me at an angle that would have carried it past the boulder, but six feet away it turned abruptly and lunged at the milkfish.

Out of sheer instinct I pulled the spear back. The lunge had been so quick and threatening that my reflexes had gotten the better of my common sense. The shark whipped past me and vanished behind a bank of corals. It didn't reappear within ten seconds, so I pulled myself out of the water to get some air.

I swore at myself, took a few deep breaths, then dipped back in.

The next time the shark appeared, it was more cautious, swimming near but showing little interest. The milkfish was dead by now and floating limply, so I tried jerking the spear to approximate life. The shark's enthusiasm was revived. Again it began its angled approach, but this time I took care to tense my arms. As it lunged, I pushed. The point of the spear caught momentarily on its teeth or gums, then sank into its mouth.

With a mighty wrench I pulled myself upward, stupidly thinking I'd hoist the shark onto the boulder behind me, but the spear simply snapped. I looked blankly at my broken spear for a couple of seconds, then shoved myself completely off the rock.

Underwater, the grayness was already hanging with curiously static strings of blood. Close by, the shark wildly thrashed and twisted, champing at the splintered bamboo between its teeth, sometimes diving directly downward and ramming its snout on the seabed.

Watching it, I realized I'd never killed anything as large before, or anything that fought so violently for its survival. As if to complement my thought, the shark increased the intensity of its thrashing so that it became obscured behind a cloud of disturbed sand and shredded seaweed. Occasionally, like in a comic book fight, its tail or head would appear out of the cloud before darting back inside again. The sight made me grin and salt water eased through the sides of my mouth. I resurfaced. I needed to spit and I needed some air. Then, with no intention of going near it while it was in that frantic state, I floated facedown and waited for it to die.

hi, man

I don't keep a travel diary. I did keep a travel diary once, and it was a big mistake. All I remember of that trip is what I bothered to write down. Everything else slipped away, as if my mind felt jilted by my reliance on pen and paper. For exactly the same reason, I don't travel with a camera. My holiday becomes the snapshots, and anything I forget to record is lost. Apart from that, photographs never seem to be very evocative. When I look through the albums of old traveling companions I'm always surprised by how little I'm reminded of the trip.

If only there was a camera that captured smell. Smells are far more vivid than images. I've often been walking in London on a hot day, caught the smell of hot refuse or melting tarmac, and suddenly been transported to a Delhi side street. Likewise, if I'm walking past a fishmonger I think instantly of Unhygienix, and if I smell sweat and cut grass (the lawn kind) I think of Keaty. I doubt either of them would appreciate being remembered in such a way, especially Unhygienix, but that's how it is.

All that said, I wish there'd been someone with a camera when I sauntered out of the mist with a dead shark over my shoulder. I must have looked so cool.

That afternoon, I was the toast of the camp. The shark was grilled and cut into strips so everyone would get a proper taste, and Keaty made me stand up and repeat my story to the whole camp. When I got to the part about the shark's first lunge, everyone gasped like they were watching fireworks, and when I told how I tensed my arms for the death blow, everyone cheered.

For the remainder of that day and night I had people constantly coming up to me to give their congratulations. Jed was the nicest. He walked over to where I was smoking with Etienne, Françoise, and Keaty, and said, "Well done, Richard. That was really something. I think we ought to rename you Tarzan." That made Keaty giggle like crazy, mainly because he was so stoned, so Jed sat down with us and we all got wasted together.

It was doubly nice because Keaty and Jed got on so well. After the Rice Run I'd been trying to persuade Keaty that Jed was okay, and now I felt like I'd had some success. It also turned out they had something in common, one of those weird coincidences that could easily never have been realized. Six years ago they'd both stayed at the same guest house in Yogyakarta, on the very same night. They were able to work this out because on that night the guest house had mysteriously burned down—or not so mysteriously, as it turned out. Keaty had been tripping and the mosquitoes in his room were driving him mad. Knowing that mosquitoes were driven away by smoke, he lit a small fire, and the next thing he knew, the room was completely ablaze. Jed explained that he'd had to escape the guest house by jumping from a third-story window and that all his money had been burned, and Keaty apologized, and everyone rolled around laughing.

If there was a sour note to the evening, it was Bugs, but ironically even that turned out okay. He came over while we were in the middle of another laughing fit, this one about the moment when Etienne had realized we were standing in a dope field.

"Hi, man," he said, flicking his head back to clear the hair from his eyes.

At first I didn't answer, because I was out of breath, and then I said, "What?" It wasn't a good choice of words. I'd honestly meant it in a friendly way, but it came out sounding like a confrontation.

If Bugs was taken aback he didn't show it—then again, he wouldn't have.

"I just came over to say congratulations. About the shark."

"Oh, yeah. Thanks. I . . . uh . . . I'm glad I caught it . . ." Again, my stoned head seemed to be putting the most inappropriate words into my mouth. "I've never caught a shark before."

"We're all glad you caught it. . . . Actually, I've caught a shark before."

"Oh?" I said, now trying extremely hard to concentrate on what I was saying. "Really? That's amazing. . . . You should certainly . . . uh . . . certainly tell us about it."

"Certainly," Keaty echoed, then coughed in a way that sounded suspiciously like a suppressed giggle.

Bugs paused. "It was in Australia."

"Australia . . . Gosh."

"Must be about five years ago now."

"Five years? Was it as long ago as that . . . uh . . ."

"A tiger shark, twelve-footer."

"How very . . . huge."

Suddenly Keaty dissolved into hysterics, and he set off Jed, who set off the others.

Bugs smiled thinly. "Maybe I'll save it for another time."

"It sounds like a great story," I managed to say before he turned to go. Then Keaty gasped, "Certainly," and I collapsed as well.

"My God, Richard," said Françoise a couple of minutes later. Her face was shining from tears. "What were you saying to Bugs? Everything you said . . ."

"Was wrong. I know. I couldn't help it."

Etienne nudged me. "You do not like Bugs, huh?"

"It isn't that. I'm just wasted. I'm not thinking straight."

"That's bullshit, Rich," said Keaty, grinning slyly.

Jed nodded. "Admit it. I've seen the way you look at him."

There was a silence while everyone looked at me, waiting for an answer. Eventually I shrugged. "All right then, you've got me. I think he's a prat."

This time we laughed so long and so helplessly that people started peering at us to find out what was going on.

cab!

"Night, Jim-Bob," said a voice. Bugs's voice, loud and firm.

"Night, Rich," came the immediate reply—hard to recognize, but I guessed Moshe.

I grinned at the darkness. I knew Bugs had been pissed off by the way we'd laughed at him, and knew this was his way of regaining—what? Authority or respect. And now his cue had been chucked directly back to me, the person who had caused the laughter. That must have grated.

My grin widened and I let the silence hang for a few seconds, then I said, " 'Night, Jesse."

Jesse passed it to Ella, who passed it to an Aussie carpenter, who passed it to one of the Yugoslavian girls, and I tuned out the rest of the game.

There was a question that needed answering, I realized as I lay awake that night and listened to the laser beams hammering on the longhouse roof. Why did Bugs get on my nerves so much? Because he really did. I hadn't even realized how much until Jed had made me admit it.

I mean, it wasn't like he'd done anything bad to me or said anything rude. In fact I barely ever talked to him. Not *talk* talked. Our exchanges were all about work, arranging the carpentry detail to knock up some new spears, passing on a message from Gregorio or Unhygienix, stuff like that.

To answer the question I made a mental list of all the things he'd done to piss me off. There'd been his stupid stoicism when he hurt his leg, the thing with the soup, his almost wacky name. He also had an irritating competitive streak. If you'd watched the sun rise over Borobudur, he'd tell you that you should have seen the sun set, or if you knew of a good place to eat in Singapore, he'd know of one better. Or if you'd caught a shark with your bare hands . . .

I decided to deny him the chance to talk me through his tiger shark experience.

But anyway, these weren't big enough reasons. There had to be something else.

"Just a hunch then," I muttered, and rolled over to go to sleep, but it didn't satisfy me as an answer.

It would have been useful if Mister Duck had dropped by that night, because I could have asked him to fill me in more about Bugs's character. Unfortunately he didn't. He was a bit like taxis in that respect. Taxis and night buses.

seeing red

The rain continued to pour all through that week and half the next, but in the early hours of a Thursday morning it stopped. Everyone was relieved, and no one more than the fishing details. Sitting on the seabed for one-minute bursts, occasionally spotting a fish and usually missing it, had gotten old pretty fast. When we woke to see that the blue skies were back, we couldn't get down to the water quick enough. Something of a killing frenzy ensued—we caught our entire quota within an hour and a half—and after that, the only thing left to kill was time.

Gregorio and Etienne swam off to the coral gardens, and Françoise and I swam back to the beach to sunbathe. We lay in silence at first, me watching how much sweat could collect in my belly button before it spilled out, and Françoise on her front, sifting sand through her fingers. A few meters away, in the shade of the trees, our catch splashed in their buckets. Considering its source, the sound was strangely soothing. It complemented the moment—the sea breeze and the sunshine—and I missed it when the fish were all dead.

Not long after the last splash Françoise sat up, twisting gracefully out of her recline so that she was kneeling with her hands on her hips and her slim brown legs tucked neatly to the side. Then she rolled the top of her swimsuit down to her waist and stretched her arms up toward the blue sky. She held that pose for several seconds before relaxing again and dropping her hands into her lap.

Without thinking I sighed, and Françoise glanced at me. "What is the matter?" she said.

I blinked. "Nothing."

"You sighed."

"Oh . . . I was just thinking"—my mind ran through a quick list of options: the return of the sunshine, the stillness of the lagoon, the whiteness of the sand—"how easy it would be to stay here."

"Ah yes." Françoise nodded. "To stay on the beach forever. Very easy . . ."

I paused for a moment, then sat up too, spilling my sweat reservoir into the waistband of my shorts. "Do you ever think about home?"

"Paris?"

"Paris, family, friends . . . All that."

"Uh . . . no, Richard. I do not."

"I don't either. But don't you think that's a bit strange? I mean, I've got a whole life back in England that I can hardly remember, let alone miss. I haven't telephoned or written to my parents since arriving in Thailand, and I suppose I know they'll be worried about me, but I don't feel the urge to do anything about it. When I was in Koh Phangan, it didn't even cross my mind . . . Don't you think that's strange?"

"Parents . . ." Françoise frowned as if she were struggling to remember the word. "Yes, it is strange, but . . ."

"When did *you* last contact them?"

"I do not know. . . . It was . . . That road. The road we met you."

"Ko Sanh."

"I called them from there . . ."

"Three months ago."

"Three months . . . Yes . . ."

We both lay back down on the hot sand. The mention of our parents was slightly disquieting and neither of us wanted to dwell on the subject.

But I did find it interesting that I wasn't the only one to experience the amnesiac effect of the beach. I wondered where the effect came from, and whether it was to do with the beach itself or the people on it. It suddenly occurred to me that I knew nothing about the past lives of my companions, except their place of origin. I'd spent countless hours talking to Keaty, and the only thing I knew about his background was that he used to go to Sunday school. I didn't know if he had brothers or sisters, or what his parents did, or which area of London he grew up in. We might have had a thousand shared experiences that we'd never made an effort to uncover.

The only talking topic that stretched beyond the circle of cliffs was travel. That was something we talked about a lot.

Even now, I can still reel off the list of countries that my friends had visited. In a way it wasn't so surprising, considering that (apart from our ages) an interest in travel was the only thing we all had in common. And actually, travel conversation was a pretty good substitute for conversation about home. You could tell plenty about someone from the places they'd chosen to visit, and which of those places were their favorites.

Unhygienix, for example, reserved his deepest affection for Kenya, which somehow complemented his taciturn nature. It was easy to imagine him on safari, quietly absorbing the vastness of the landscape around him. Keaty, livelier and more prone to enthusiastic outbursts, was much more suited to Thailand. Etienne had an unfulfilled yearning to go to Bhutan, quietly good-natured fellow that he was, and Sal often talked about Ladakh—the northern province of India, laid-back in some ways and hard-edged in others. I knew my affection for the Philippines was equally as telling: a democracy on paper, apparently well ordered, regularly subverted by irrational chaos. A place where I'd felt instantly at home.

Amongst some of the others, Greg went for gentle southern India, Françoise for beautiful Indonesia. Moshe for Borneo (which I took as connected to the junglelike growth of his body hair), and the two Yugoslavian girls chose their own country, appropriately nationalistic and off the wall. Daffy, I didn't need to be told, would have chosen Vietnam.

Of course, I know that there's an element of pop psychology about how much you can read into people's favorite travel locations. You can choose which aspects of a nation's character you want to accept or ignore. In the case of Keaty, I chose liveliness and enthusiasm because mercenary and calculating didn't fit the bill, and in the case of Françoise I ignored dictatorship and mass murder in East Timor. But nonetheless, I have faith in the principle.

"I'm going to take the catch back," I said, standing up.

Françoise pushed herself up on to her elbows. "Now?"

"Unhygienix might be ready."

"He will not be ready."

"Well, no . . . but I fancy a walk. You want to come?"

"Where will you go?"

"Uh, don't know. I was thinking about heading for the waterfall or into the jungle somewhere . . . maybe to find that pool."

"No, I think I will stay here. Or maybe I will swim to the corals."

"Okay."

I walked to the buckets, and as I bent to lift them up I saw my face reflected in the bloody water. I paused to study myself, almost a silhouette with two bright eyes, and then I heard Françoise padding over the beach toward me. Her dark face appeared behind my shoulders and I felt her hand on my back.

"You do not want to come to the corals?"

"No." My fingers squeezed around the handles but I didn't straighten, knowing that if I did her hand would drop. "I'd rather go for a walk. . . . Are you sure you don't want to come?"

"Yes." Her red reflection shrugged. "It is too hot to walk today."

I didn't reply, and a couple of seconds later I heard her footsteps padding back across the sand. When I looked around she was wading into the water. I watched her until the water reached her torso, then started the walk back to camp.

naturism

Facing in the direction of the mainland, the jungle to the left was familiar because the carpentry detail used it for their lumber. The area was crisscrossed with paths, some of which led to Jean's garden and the waterfall, some of which led down to the beach. To the right, however, the jungle was still virgin, so this was the direction I chose to explore.

The only path that led into it stopped after fifty meters. It had originally been cleared because a freshwater pool lay further along, and Sal had thought it could be converted as a larger substitute for the shower hut. The idea was abandoned when Cassie discovered that monkeys used the pool for drinking, and now the path was only used by people who, like me, were uncomfortable with the plastic pitcher option in the toilet. Judging from the faces I'd passed on the path, I'd say that accounted for at least three quarters of the camp. It was used commonly enough to have acquired a nickname—the Khyber Pass—and the regular tramping of our feet kept the weeds under control.

It took me half an hour to find my way to the pool, which turned out to be a slight disappointment. As I picked my way through the undergrowth, I'd been imagining a cool glade where I could bathe whilst watching monkeys swinging in the trees. Instead I found a muddy puddle and a cloud of flies. Flies that bit, I should add. I stayed by the pool for less than a minute. Then I pressed on into the jungle with the sound of primate laughter ringing in my ears.

Apart from the sharp grasses that occasionally nicked my legs, the walking wasn't taxing. Weeks without shoes had hardened the soles of my feet and left them almost numb. A few days before, I'd pulled a thorn from my heel, half a centimeter long. Its base had been covered in a crust of dirt and I guessed I'd been strolling around with it for quite some time, never feeling a thing.

The hardest part about walking was that my progress was so slow. I was constantly detouring around thickets and bamboo clusters, and I was never completely sure about which direction I was heading. This didn't worry me too much, because I was sure that sooner or later I'd reach the beach or the wall of cliffs. Unfortunately my confidence also meant I didn't make an effort to remember my route, so when I came across the papaya orchard, over an hour later, I didn't have a clue as to how I could ever find it again.

I call it an orchard for want of a better word. The papayas were random in size and spacing, so they hadn't been planted. Possibly the soil in that patch was particularly suitable or the limited room on the forest floor had kept them all together. Whatever, they made a wonderful sight. Much of the fruit was ripe, bright orange and as big as marrows, and the air was filled with sweetness.

I pulled one down with an easy twist of the stalk and split it open on a tree trunk. The fluorescent flesh tasted like melon and perfume—not, perhaps, as nice as it sounds, but pretty good all the same. Then I pulled out the joint I'd rolled before leaving the camp, found a clear area to sit, and settled down to watch smoke collect beneath the papaya leaves.

After a while, monkeys began to appear. I couldn't name their species but they were small and brown, with long tails and oddly catlike faces. At first they kept their distance. They didn't study me or register my presence in any way, beyond giving me a wide berth. But then a mother monkey with a tiny baby clinging to her stomach ambled over and took a piece of papaya from my hand. I hadn't even been holding it out to her—I'd been saving it until I finished the joint—but clearly she had other ideas. She casually helped herself, and I was too surprised to do anything but gape.

It didn't take long before another monkey followed the mother monkey's cue. Then another, and another. Within a couple of minutes the papaya was being pulled out of my hands as quickly as I could tear it from the fruit. My body was covered in sticky juice, my eyes were watering because I didn't have time to pull the joint from my lips, and little black fingers were pawing at me from all directions. Eventually all of them managed to get a chunk, and I was left sitting cross-legged in a sea of munching monkeys. I felt like David Attenborough.

It was the distinctive sound of falling water that finally led me out of the jungle. I heard it fifteen minutes after leaving the orchard, and then it was just a matter of zoning in on the noise.

I came out by the carved tree and immediately dived into the waterfall pool, keen to wash the sweat and papaya juice off my body. It was only when I came up that I realized I wasn't alone. Sal and Bugs were kissing, naked, in the penumbra of the spray.

Damn, I thought, and was about to swim discreetly back to the bank when Sal noticed me.

"Richard?"

"Hi, Sal. Sorry. I didn't see you there."

Bugs looked at me and smirked. It seemed to me that he was saying my apology was prurient. Gauche next to his relaxed but frank sexuality. The prick. I held his gaze and his smile twisted into an inane sneer, the expression he should have started with.

"Don't be silly, Richard," Sal said, detaching herself from Bugs's embrace. "Where have you come from?"

"I went for a walk down the Khyber Pass and found a bunch of papaya trees, then ended up here."

"Papayas? How many?"

"Oh, loads."

"You should tell Jean, Richard. He's always interested in that sort of thing."

I shrugged. "The problem is, I doubt I could find them again. It's hard to keep your bearings in there."

Bugs revived the sneer. "It takes practice."

"Practice with a compass."

Smirk. "I spend so much time in the trees, I suppose I've got an instinct . . . almost animal, man . . ." He pushed his wet hair back with both hands. "Maybe I'll find them tomorrow."

"Good luck." I turned to go, adding, "Don't get lost," quietly.

I ducked under and swam back to the shore, surfacing only when the water was too shallow to cover me. But I hadn't escaped quite yet.

"Richard," Sal called as I hauled myself out. "Hang on."

I looked round.

"Are you heading back to the camp?"

"I was going to."

"Well . . . wait." She began to swim over, looking slightly like a turtle with her chin jutting up clear of the water. I waited until she reached me.

"Will you walk with me to the garden? I've got to go down there and Bugs has to go to the longhouse. I'd like some company, and we haven't talked for a while."

I nodded. "Okay, sure."

"Good."

She smiled and went to get her clothes.

the good news

The walking pace Sal set was slow. Sometimes she paused to look at flowers or to pull a weed from the path. Sometimes she stopped for no apparent reason, aimlessly drawing dust circles with her toes.

"Richard," she began, "I want to tell you how pleased we all are that you found our secret beach."

"Thanks, Sal," I replied, already understanding that this conversation had a point beyond a casual chat.

"Can I be blunt, Richard? When you three arrived, we were all a little worried. Perhaps you can understand why . . ."

"Of course."

"But you all fitted in so *well*. You really entered into the spirit of what we have here, better than we could have hoped . . . You mustn't think we didn't appreciate you doing the Rice Run, Richard, and catching that lovely shark."

"Oh, well." I tried to look modest. "The shark was a fluke."

"Garbage, Richard. The shark gave everyone something to feel good about, and morale does get low during rainstorms. I still feel a little guilty about the way I spoke to you that wet morning, but sometimes I need to be . . . pushy. I don't consider myself to be the leader here, but . . ."

"We all understand that."

"Thank you, Richard."

"And you *are* the leader really, Sal."

"Oh, maybe in some ways I am. Reluctantly." She laughed. "People come to me with their problems and I try to sort them out . . . Keaty, for example. I know you and Keaty are close, so I presume you know about his problem."

"He wants to leave the garden detail."

"That's right. Such a headache. It isn't easy moving people around. Someone has to provide the space before he can move, and the fishing detail is already full. . . . He wants the fishing detail, you know."

"Uh-huh."

"For months now I've been telling him it isn't possible. You see, he was about to start fishing when your little group arrived. He was terribly disappointed, Richard, but he took it very well. Others might have . . . I don't know . . . held it against you."

"Sure. Three people turning up out of the blue, taking his job."

"Exactly, Richard. I was so grateful to him, and so pleased when you became friends. I was only sorry I couldn't do anything to improve his situation . . ." A weed caught Sal's eye and she pulled it out, tutting at its stubborn grip on the dirt. "But my hands were tied without a vacancy in the fishing detail. And now I've realized that one isn't going to appear unless I make it. . . ."

I gulped. "Uh, no one wants to move, I suppose. What about one of the Swedes?"

"One of the Swedes?" Sal chuckled. "You couldn't break up their trio without a gun, and even then you'd have a job. No, they're together to the death. The Three Blond Musketeers."

"Moshe?"

"Mmm . . . I don't think I'd want him to move. He's rather good with those Yugoslavian girls."

"Who then?" I asked, and obviously failed to keep a note of anxiousness out of my voice.

"Yes, Richard. I'm sorry. I don't have a choice."

I groaned. "Oh no, Sal. Please, I really don't want to move. I love the fishing detail, and I'm good at it."

"I *know* you are, Richard. I *know*. But do try to see it from my position. Keaty needs to move out of the garden, I can't separate Etienne and Françoise, Gregorio has been fishing for two years, the Yugoslavians . . ." Sal shook her head. "Well I shouldn't really tell you this, Richard, but they haven't the wit to do anything else. Jean can't bear them and they could never cope with carpentry. I regret bringing them here at all. I'm a pushover for refugees. . . . Truly, Richard, if I had a choice . . ."

"Yeah," I muttered.

". . . And it isn't like I'm going to put you in the garden detail."

I paused. "You aren't?"

"God, no. I don't think I'd be able to do that after the things Keaty must have been telling you."

A terrible thought crossed my mind. Given a choice between the garden detail and working with Bugs in carpentry, I'd have taken Jean's iron discipline anytime. "Well," I began to say, not bothering to disguise my nervousness. "He hasn't said that much . . ."

"I'm sure he's said plenty, Richard. No need to be diplomatic."

"No, Sal, honestly . . ."

She waved her hand. "It doesn't matter anyway. You won't be working in the garden detail . . ."

I closed my eyes, waiting for my sentence.

". . . you'll be working with Jed."

I opened my eyes again. *"Jed?"*

"Yes. He wants a partner on his excursions, and he suggested you."

"Wow," I said, genuinely. It had never occurred to me that Jed might want someone with him. Although we'd become friendly, he still struck me as a loner.

"I know, he never seemed the team type," Sal continued, apparently reading my mind. "I was just as surprised. You must have made a good impression on the Rice Run."

"But what does Jed need help with? Doesn't he just . . . steal grass?"

"He does that, yes, but other things besides. He'll explain."

". . . I see."

Sal beamed. "Richard, I'm so glad we've sorted it all out. I've been worried about telling you this for days . . . Now then, all that remains is to find Keaty. Would you like to give him the good news or shall I?"

ich bin ein beacher

When we reached the garden, Jean told us that Keaty had already started out back to the camp, so I jogged off to catch up to him and Sal stayed behind, explaining to Jean that he'd have to make do with one less worker.

I found Keaty a few hundred meters down the track, and when I told him the news he was very sympathetic, despite the fact that it was good news for him.

"I feel shit about this, Rich," he said after I'd finished explaining. "I didn't mean for Sal to take you off fishing, I swear."

I nodded. "My guess is, it has more to do with Jed than you. You've been asking to leave the garden detail since I got here, and it's only now that something's happened."

"Maybe . . . You're pissed off, right?"

". . . Well . . ."

"I'm sorry."

"No, it isn't your fault. It's just bad . . . luck. Or something. But not your fault."

"Well, I hope not, Rich . . . and I'm sorry anyway."

We walked in silence for a few moments, then Keaty said, "Do you know why Jed's suddenly decided he needs help?"

"I don't even know what he needs help with. We still don't know what he does up there."

"At least now we'll find out."

"I will, you mean. If I were to tell you what goes on I'd have to kill you straight after."

Keaty smiled. "You know what? I bet you're secretly pleased about all this. I bet you're looking forward to prowling around up there."

I shrugged. "Ask not what your beach can do for you."

"That's the spirit."

"Yeah . . ." I paused. "I suppose if I've got to leave the fishing detail, then I'd rather I was working with Jed than anyone else."

"Uh-huh. I wouldn't wish the garden detail on you."

"And the other option was carpentry. For a moment I thought that's what Sal was suggesting and I nearly had a fucking heart attack. I got this sudden flash of working with Bugs all day, so when Sal said it was with Jed . . . I don't know . . . I had to feel relieved."

"If you say so, Rich."

"I think I do."

We turned a corner on the path and saw the longhouse through the trees. There were figures around the kitchen hut, so I guessed the other fishers were back with their catch. I couldn't see any of my detail. They probably weren't back from the corals yet.

Just as we were about to enter the clearing, someone behind us called our names. We both turned round and saw Jesse jogging along the track with a bag of vegetables from the garden.

"Hey, man," he said to Keaty as he reached us. "Hear you're leaving the Jar Dan." It took me a couple of seconds to translate his Kiwi accent to *jardin*.

"Yep. I'm moved to the fishing."

"I heard, you lucky bastard." Jesse looked at me. "Not you though, mate. You must be pissed off, losing that cushy number. You'll be sweating with us now."

"I'm not going to the garden."

Jesse grinned. "Carpentry! With Jesus!"

"No. Jed."

"Jed?"

"Uh-huh."

"Blow me. What's all that about? Not enough weed to go round?"

"Maybe. I'll find out soon, anyway."

"Yeah . . . You will." He nodded thoughtfully, then he patted Keaty on the back. "You'll be all right, anyhow. Get to watch Françoise swimming all day. I could do with a bit of that."

Keaty shot me a quick glance, which puzzled me, and said, "Watch it, Jesse. You don't want Cassie to hear you."

Jesse laughed. "Too right. Skin me alive." He winked at no one in particular, then looked into the clearing. "So. Looks like the cooks have got food on the way. Better get the veg down there."

"Sure," said Keaty, and Jesse jogged off. Keaty watched him go, then turned to me. "He's the one person I'll really miss from the garden detail."

"Seems like a decent guy."

"He is. You'd like him and Cassie a lot. Especially as they aren't exactly Bugs's biggest fans."

"Oh?"

"I used to bitch about Jean being a tough boss, but Bugs . . . he drives Cassie nuts."

"I'd picked up on that before."

". . . I guess you'll miss working with your detail too."

"Mmm." I took a deep breath and exhaled slowly. Probably too deeply and too slowly, because I noticed Keaty giving me another curious glance. "I'm sure I will."

dislocation

It was a long walk from where I entered the clearing to where Etienne, Françoise, and Gregorio stood talking. I had plenty of time to think about how much the change of work detail would affect my life on the beach. Mainly I thought in rapid slide-show images, different shots of the four of us chatting and having fun: diving off our favorite fishing boulder, taking bets on who would catch the biggest fish, swimming for spears that had missed their mark or found their mark, or reenacting throws that were comically bad. The image I lingered on the longest was, unsurprisingly, of Françoise. Françoise as an Amazon, frozen with a spear poised above her head, concentrating fiercely on the shapes beneath the water. Even now it's a picture I can clearly recall.

It seemed to me, as I got nearer, that they must have heard the news. They paused in their conversation and all turned, watching me with quiet and serious expressions. But it was simply that they'd read the look on my face. That and my posture, and the speed I was walking. If someone walks unhurriedly toward you, head bowed, you have to know that something's up.

There was a strange moment when I reached them. They remained silent, waiting for me to speak, but I felt like I'd already been isolated from their group. It reminded me of the first morning after my fever, discovering that Etienne and Françoise had made themselves a part of the new world while I had been asleep. When no words came I frowned and put a hand on the back of my neck, then shrugged helplessly.

"What is it, Richard?" said Etienne apprehensively. "There is something the matter?"

I nodded.

"What? Tell us."

". . . I'm off the fishing detail."

"Off?"

"Moving to another detail. Sal . . . She just told me."

Françoise gasped. "But why? How can she do that?"

"Something to do with Jed. He needs a work partner. Keaty's going to replace me."

Gregorio shook his head. "But wait, Richard. You do not want to move, yes?"

"I like the fishing detail . . ."

"Then okay. You will stay. I will find Sal and talk to her now." Then he marched off toward the longhouse.

"Gregorio will stop this," said Etienne a few moments later. "Do not worry, Richard. You will not have to move."

"You will not have to move," Françoise echoed. "We are a good team, Richard. Of course you will stay with us."

I nodded, pleased by my friends' display of solidarity, but at the same time I was entirely unconvinced. I knew that Sal's decision would be final, and, as if to force the point home, the sound of her low voice began to drift across the clearing, telling Gregorio that this was the only way it could be.

Although I was feeling sorry for myself, unsure of the sudden way in which things had developed, as the day went on I felt more sorry for Keaty. After Gregorio's failure to change Sal's mind, the four of us spent the rest of the afternoon sitting in a circle, getting stoned and bitching about the way things had turned out. Keaty, however, sat by the entrance of his tent. He was apparently engrossed in his Game Boy, but he looked miserable. I think he felt responsible for everything, and it must have been depressing to feel that his new workmates were so unhappy with the circumstances of his arrival.

Eventually, Keaty's obvious discomfort became intolerable. Sensing that the onus was on me, I called over to him and suggested he join us. He sheepishly put down his Nintendo and came over, immediately launching into an apology for the situation he felt he'd caused. All of us protested at once but it did nothing to cheer him up. He also told us that he'd spoken to Sal himself, insisting that he didn't mind remaining in the garden detail, to no effect. This, at least, provided a topic of discussion that didn't make Keaty's discomfort any more acute, because it raised the underlying reason for the job switch.

"Perhaps," Françoise said, "there is something happening on the island. Something to do with the drug farmers."

Keaty muttered his agreement, but Gregorio looked doubtful. "So maybe the Thais are putting new fields on this side of the island. It would be a problem, but why would Jed need a partner? If he had ten or fifty partners, he could not stop them. There is no difference."

"Is there ever any talking with the Thais?" Etienne asked.

Gregorio shook his head. "Daffy spoke to them when they first came, but he is the only one. He said they knew we were here already, and they were not interested in us if we did not move from the lagoon. Since then, nothing."

"Maybe they've got pissed off with Jed nicking grass," I suggested.

"Yes, but it is the same thing. If they are angry or not angry, what difference if Jed has a partner?"

"So what else could it be?"

Gregorio looked down at his hands, then back at me. "I do not know, Richard . . . I really do not know."

—

We continued chatting until late evening, but only going round in circles. Without Jed or Sal, there was no way our questions could be answered, but Jed was still absent by the time we went to bed, and no one felt like talking to Sal.

It took me over two hours to get to sleep that night, and the thoughts that kept me awake were as unusual as the rest of the day had been. For the first time since arriving on the beach, I started thinking about home. Almost, in fact, wishing I could return. Not to leave the beach permanently; just to contact a few important people and let them know I was still alive and okay. My family particularly, and a few of my friends.

I suppose it may have had as much to do with my earlier conversation with Françoise as with the subsequent unsettling events. The mention of parents had hovered in the back of my mind, reluctant to fall under the beach's amnesiac spell.

the decisive moment

"Hi," said a voice, and I turned round. A small boy was standing in the gateway of the house behind me. He grinned and marched over the pavement. "Would you like a drink?"

I looked at him blankly. Mister Duck was fair-haired and close to tubby as a child. It surprised me that this well-fed kid would become the scrawny figure I'd meet on the Ko Sanh Road.

"That is you, isn't it?" I said, to make certain.

"It's me." His chubby arms stretched out and clapped me on the shoulders. "Would you like a drink?"

"Well . . ." I rubbed my throat. "What have you got?"

"Orange squash or water."

"Orange squash is good."

"Okay. Wait here."

Mister Duck went inside the house, waddling slightly as he walked. I wondered if that was where his nickname had originally come from. A minute later he came back out, holding a cup in both hands.

"I'm afraid it's not really very cold. It takes ages for the tap to run cold."

"That's okay."

He gave me the cup and watched me closely while I drank it.

"Is it all right? Maybe I should've put some ice in it."

"It's very nice."

"I can get some ice for you."

"No." I drained the remainder. "It was just right."

"Great!" He smiled radiantly. "You want to see my room?"

Mister Duck's bedroom was a lot like mine had been: clothes in heaps, dog-eared posters on the walls, duvet scrunched up at the bottom of the mattress, battered matchbox cars on the shelves, marbles and toy soldiers everywhere else. The main difference was that I'd shared my room with my younger brother, so the mess was doubled.

In the middle of the floor was a collapsed pile of Tintin and Asterix books.

"Shit," I said admiringly, as I spotted them. "That's a good collection."

Mister Duck's eyes opened wide, then he ran to his bedroom door and peered nervously out. "Richard," he hissed, turning back to me with a sternly raised finger, "you mustn't say that!"

". . . Shit?"

His tiny face went bright red and he waved his arms. "Shh! Someone will hear you!"

"But . . ."

"No buts!" He dropped his voice to a whisper. "Swearing carries a twopence fine in this house!"

"Oh . . . right. I won't swear anymore."

"Good," he said gravely. "I should ask you for some money, but you didn't know the rule, so we'll leave it at that."

"Thanks . . ." I walked over to the pile of books and picked one up—*Cigars of the Pharaoh*. "So you like Tintin, huh?"

"I *love* Tintin! Do you? I've got every Tintin book except one."

"I've got every Tintin book except none."

"Including *The Blue Lotus?*"

"Only in French."

"Exactly! That's why I haven't got it. It really annoys me."

"You should get someone to talk you through it. My mum went through it with me. It's pretty good."

Mister Duck shrugged. "My mum can't speak French."

"Oh."

"So which is your favorite one?"

"Hmm. Tricky question." I thought for a couple of seconds. "It isn't *Tintin in America*."

"No. And it isn't *The Castafiore Emerald*."

"No way. It might be *Tintin in Tibet* . . . or *The Crab with the Golden Claws*. I can't decide."

"Do you want to know what my favorite is?"

"Sure."

"Prisoners of the Sun."

I nodded. "That's a good choice."

"Yes. Would you like to know another book I like?"

"Okay."

Mister Duck walked over to his bed and crouched down, feeling around underneath. Then he dragged out a large hard-back, coffee table size. Its cover was plain red and stamped with gold-leaf writing. It read: *Time. A Decade in Photographs: 1960–1970.*

"This book is my dad's," he said airily, squatting down and beckoning me to sit beside him. "I'm not even supposed to have it in my room. You know what?"

"What."

"In this book"—he paused for dramatic effect—"there's a picture of a girl."

I snorted. "Big deal."

"A naked girl!"

"Naked?"

"Uh-huh. You want to see it?"

"Sure."

"Okay . . . hold on." Mister Duck started flicking through the pages. "It's somewhere near the middle . . . Ah! Here it is!"

I pulled the book onto my lap.

The girl was indeed naked, and aged between ten and twelve, I guessed. She was running down a country road.

Mister Duck leaned over and put his mouth to my ear. "You can see *everything*!" he whispered excitedly.

"You certainly can," I agreed.

"Everything! All her bits!" He started giggling and rolled forward with his hands over his mouth. "Everything!"

"Yes," I said, but I was suddenly feeling uncertain. There was something puzzling about the photo.

I noticed the fields that surrounded the country road; they were strangely flat and alien. Then I noticed the collection of indistinct buildings behind the girl, either out of focus or made fuzzy through clouds of smoke. And the girl was upset, holding her arms away from her sides. Other kids ran beside her. A few soldiers, apparently indifferent, watched them as they passed.

I frowned. My gaze flicked quickly from the girl to the soldiers, back to the girl again. It was as if my eyes had become confused, unsure of where to settle. I wasn't even sure what they were settling on.

"Fuck," I muttered, and shut the book with a snap.

Mister Duck sat up. "I'm sorry, Rich," he said. "But I've already warned you once about swearing. This time it's going to cost you."

in country

aspect one

Jed's eyes were a little wider apart than mine, so it took some adjustment before I was seeing one crisp circle instead of two hazy ones. Then I had to scan slowly across the sea, steadying myself on my elbows as the tiniest movement sent the image a mile off track. It took me several seconds to find the strip of sand and line of green palms, but once there, I located the five familiar figures almost immediately. They were in the same place they'd been yesterday morning, and nearly every morning for the past nine days. The only exception had been four days ago when the beach was completely empty. That had caused us a bit of concern, until they reappeared from the treeline a couple of hours later.

"They're still there," I said.

"Up to anything?"

"Uh-uh."

"Just lying there."

"Looks like one is standing, but he isn't moving."

"And you can count all five."

I paused. "Five, yeah. They're all there."

"Good." Jed coughed quietly into his hand. We had to be careful about noise, this close to the dope fields, and we couldn't smoke either, which didn't do much for my nerves.

My first day with Jed had started off badly. I'd woken up in a shit mood, the previous night's dream still clinging to me, faintly depressed about leaving the fishing detail. But as soon as he'd explained about the people, I'd understood. Then I'd been thrown into a panic, saying, "It's the worst-case scenario," over and over like a mantra, while Jed patiently waited for me to calm down. It took some time but eventually I stopped jittering long enough for him to get a word in edgeways, and I was able to take in the exact nature of the situation.

The good news was that Sal still didn't know about my indiscretion with the map. Jed had only told her that we had new guests on the neighboring island, but not that they might have a connection with me. As far as Sal was concerned, the reason I was working with Jed was because he'd gotten fed up with being alone and wanted a partner. The other good news was that the people had been hanging around on the island for two days before Sal had agreed to move me. So if they were aiming for our beach, they were obviously finding it difficult to reach us.

On the downside, we had to assume that the people *were* aiming for the beach. We also had to assume that two of them were Zeph and Sammy, and the other three were the Germans that Jed had seen on Koh Phangan. We couldn't be sure about this because the people were too small to make out clearly, even to see a flash of blond hair, but it seemed likely.

I'd spent the rest of that day in a state of shock, sitting with Jed's binoculars clamped to my face, convinced—every time one of them appeared to move—that they were about to start swimming toward us. But they didn't. In fact they barely budged from their patch of sand, occasionally taking a brief dip or disappearing into the jungle for a couple of hours. After three or four similar days had passed, my initial level of panic became impossible to sustain. It faded, mellowing into anxiousness, finally settling as a generalized tension. With the tension I was able to think more clearly and, in a manner of speaking, relax. That was when the other aspects of my new detail begin to emerge.

The first was getting to know Jed. We spent every hour

until nightfall sitting on a rocky outcrop at the highest point of our island, and aside from the spying, all we could do was talk. Mostly we talked about plan B, which was what we were going to do when they finally got here. The only problem with plan B was that, like most plan B's, it didn't exist. We had several options but could never agree on which one to take. The option I favored was that Jed would go down to intercept them and explain that they weren't welcome on the beach, but he didn't want to do that. Although he was sure he'd be able to make them leave, he was also sure that they'd go straight back to Koh Phangan and tell everyone what they'd found. Instead Jed wanted to rely on the island's natural barriers. There was the swim, they had to get past the dope fields, find the lagoon, and then find a way of getting down to it. Jed was confident that this obstacle course would put them off, apparently unconcerned that it had failed to deter me, Etienne, Françoise, the Swedes, and himself.

It was during one of our endless plan B discussions that I discovered Jed had once watched me in exactly the same way as we were now watching Zeph and Sammy. He'd seen the spiv drop us off and when we made the swim he'd told Sal—which was why she, Bugs, and Cassie had been ready to greet us when we reached the camp. This was the main function of his detail, as a lookout, and the dope collecting had been more of a sideline. He went on to tell me that since his arrival, there had been three groups that had tried to find the lagoon. Two had given up at one or another of the obstacles. The ones to get through had been the Swedes.

Knowing this made me feel marginally less guilty about having given out a copy of the map, because people were managing to find us anyway. Jed explained that they'd heard about the beach as the Eden rumor Zeph had described. Jed himself had heard it from a guy in Vientiane, and "with nothing better to do," he'd decided to follow the rumor up. He'd had to check out six other islands in the Marine Park before finding the right one. The Swedes had gone on more concrete information. They'd overheard Sal talking with Jean on a Chaweng Rice Run.

It came as a surprise to me to hear that acting as a lookout was the primary function of my new detail. I couldn't understand why the job needed to be clouded in so much mystery, and Jed, in turn, was a little surprised to hear that the mystery existed. He admitted that Sal didn't want it talked about, as she felt it would be bad for the morale, but as far as he was concerned, the main reason he didn't talk about it was because nobody ever asked him.

This had led to the most interesting revelation about Jed, connected to Daffy's reaction to his uninvited arrival on the beach. I remembered Keaty telling me that the camp had listened outside the longhouse while Daffy shouted and Sal tried to calm him down. What I didn't know was that Daffy had refused to speak to Jed from that day on. For thirteen months, until Daffy left the island, he and Jed had never exchanged a single word. It had been the original reason for the creation of Jed's detail: to keep him away from the rest of the camp for most of the day.

I felt a great deal of pity for Jed when he told me this. It explained why he'd always seemed so distant from the rest of us. His apparent aloofness was only because he felt he ought to keep out of people's way, even now that a year and a half had passed. It also explained why he so conspicuously accepted unpopular tasks, such as the Rice Run.

But Jed didn't appear to feel any pity for himself. When I suggested to him that it must have been hard to face such a cold reaction, he shrugged and said he could understand it.

"Something's bothering me," I said, putting down Jed's binoculars.

Jed frowned. "You and me both."

"I'm afraid they'll find my rucksack."

". . . Your rucksack?"

"I hid my rucksack there, and so did Etienne and Françoise. We couldn't swim with them . . . and if they find our bags they'll know they're on the right track."

"How well did you hide them?"

"Pretty well. The thing is, I'm starting to think I might have copied the map down wrong. I drew it in a real hurry and there were a lot of islands to fill in. I remember there were differences between Daffy's map and the map in Etienne's guidebook too. I easily could have missed out an island between Koh Angthong and here."

Jed nodded. "It's possible."

"So if they reckon they're on the right island, that explains why they haven't moved for the last nine days. They're checking the place out, looking for the beach . . . which they won't find, but they might find the rucksacks."

"It's possible," Jed repeated. "But they might also have spent the last nine days wondering how the fuck they're going to get back to Koh Phangan."

"And wondering how they could have been so stupid as to believe in a map that someone slid under their door."

"That would make them about as stupid as you then."

"Stupid as me . . . Yeah."

Jed scowled and ran his hands over his face. "What I want to know is what they're doing for food and water."

"Magi-Noodles and chocolate. That's what we did."

"And water? They'd have needed to take a barrel of the stuff to've lasted this long."

"Maybe there's a source on the island. It's high enough."

"Must be . . . I'll tell you what, though, you're wrong about that map. Look at them. They sit in that one spot all fucking day. It faces us, right? So they *know* this is the right island. They're sitting there and trying to work out how to reach us . . ."

I sighed. "You know what we should do?"

"No."

"We should take the boat and head round to them. Then we get them on board, set a course for the open sea, and make them walk the plank. Problem solved."

Jed tilted his head at the sky. "Okay, Richard, let's do it."

"Okay. Let's."

"Okay."

"Okay."

We looked at each other briefly, then I went back to staring through the binoculars.

white lies

We'd stay on our lookout post until the bottom curve of the sun was just about to hit the horizon line, then we'd head back. There wasn't much point in spying if it was too dark to see, and anyway, Jed said it wasn't safe to be up on the island after nightfall. You didn't know what or who you might walk into. Back at camp, Jed would go and talk to Sal, filling her in on the day's nonevents, and I'd get some dinner. Then, carrying my bowl of leftovers, I'd look for my old fishing detail. Usually I'd find them near the kitchen hut, having a smoke before bedtime.

Lying to Sal and Bugs was easy, but I hated lying to my old detail, and I hated lying to Keaty even more. The truth was that I didn't have a choice. Until we knew whether Zeph and Sammy would make it to the beach, there was no sense in stirring. The best I could do was to satisfy Keaty's curiosity about the exact nature of Jed's work, and when I told him, he wasn't as surprised as I'd expected him to be.

"It's a good idea," he said, matter of factly. "Since the Swedes, people have been worried about who might turn up."

"What about since me?"

"Daffy told you. It's different."

"Were people angry about the Swedes then?"

". . . Daffy mainly."

"Jed said Daffy didn't like him much, either."

Keaty started cleaning his Game Boy screen against his shorts. "He didn't make it very easy for any of them, but once they were here . . . you know . . . what could he do?"

"Is that why he left the beach?"

My question hung in the air while Keaty carefully inspected the tiny glass panel.

I asked him again.

"Basically," he said eventually. "Yeah." He pushed in the Mario cart and switched on the machine. "You completed this yet?"

"About twenty times."

"I was wondering where the batteries were going . . ." He gazed at the Nintendo but didn't begin playing. "So what do you do if you find someone coming?" he asked casually.

". . . Just watch them, I guess."

Keaty grinned. "You mean you take them out, right? Terminate with extreme prejudice."

"I'll tell you when it happens," I replied, laughing uncomfortably, and was spared any further questions by the arrival of Jesse, looking for some rizlas.

After that conversation I'd more or less managed to avoid the subject of my detail. It wasn't difficult. Keaty had taken to his work in a big way and it only needed a small nudge to get him talking about it. To my relief, the same applied with my other ex-colleagues, so I could always steer the conversation toward fishing. From their point of view, I suppose they were trying to emphasize my inclusion in the group by sticking to topics of shared experience. From my point of view, I was happy to talk about anything that upheld a sense of normality.

For the first few days, during my panicky stage, this was a bit of an effort. Given the way I was feeling, a calm exterior required constant concentration. When I let my guard drop I would drift off into my own anxious thoughts while people were talking to me. I could only use the excuse of being stoned or tired up to a point.

But there was a helpful side to the constant concentration: I never had time to feel jealous of the ease with which Keaty had replaced me, or sad that the secrets I was keeping were creating unexpected barriers between me and my friends. Unexpected because I'd been worried that the detail would distance me from them, but soon I understood that it actually distanced them from me. I was still involved in their lives. I knew what was going on. I knew when they'd caught a strange fish, and that Jean was trying to lure Keaty back to the garden, and that Cassie was trying to arrange a move from carpentry so she could work with Jesse, and that Bugs wasn't having any of it.

I no longer had to struggle to maintain a calm appearance. In theory, perhaps then I should have started to feel jealous of Keaty and sad about the lies. But I didn't. I realized that I had been given one less problem to worry about, because if I was the one creating the distance, then I had equal power to remove it. And if Zeph and Sammy failed in their attempt to reach us, I would be able to bring my friends closer without any effort. It would simply be a matter of not lying to them anymore, which would be easy, as there'd be nothing to lie about. Obviously, this was only a comfort if Zeph and Sammy failed to reach us, but if they didn't fail, then Sal would certainly get to hear about the map, and I'd be fucked anyway.

It was in this frame of mind—alert but calm or something close—that the second aspect of my new detail emerged. I think I first noticed it on the fifth day, when I woke half an hour before Jed and impatiently counted the minutes until it was time to go. Or maybe it was the sixth day, when the figures were missing from their beach and we scanned the sea for three silent hours, coolly professional, nothing to be said, until they reappeared. Most accurately, Keaty noticed it first, although he didn't realize it at the time. "I bet you're secretly looking forward to prowling around up there," he'd joked when I told him about the switch in details, but my mood had been too sour to see that he was right.

There was nothing strange about it. Jed and I were on a covert mission. We had binoculars, jungle, a quarry, a threat, the hidden presence of AK-47s and slanted eyes. The only missing element was a Doors soundtrack.

Too familiar to be strange, and too exciting to dread. Before long, impossible not to enjoy.

ol' blue

At the end of the tenth day we were, as usual, hurrying to get back to the lagoon before nightfall. The sun was already below the western curve of the seaward cliffs and the orange light of early evening was turning blue. Whenever we were on the move we wouldn't talk, so all our communication was made by way of hand signals. A clenched fist meant stop and stay still, a flat palm held horizontally to the ground meant hide, a pointing gesture with all fingers together meant move forward cautiously. We'd never discussed the meanings of these signs; neither had we discussed the new words we'd started using. We'd say, "I'll take point," instead of, "I'll walk first," and we described distances in terms of Klicks. I don't actually remember how or when these things had been adopted. I think they'd simply felt like the most appropriate vocabulary for the circumstance.

That evening, Jed had taken point. He always did if the light was failing, because he knew the island so much better than I did. I was having a little difficulty keeping up with him, unable to find his easy compromise between speed and stealth, and when he gave the clenched fist signal I missed it and walked straight into his back. The fact that he didn't frown or swear made me aware that something serious was up. I eased myself away from him and stood still.

Just ahead of us the jungle became patchy and broke into a wide area of grasses and shrubs, so at first I assumed that Jed had seen someone in the clearing. Then I noticed that his gaze was pointed almost directly at his feet. For a couple of moments we both remained motionless. I still couldn't tell what the problem was because his body was obscuring my view. After a long minute of silence, I cautiously reached out and tapped him on the shoulder. He didn't react and it suddenly struck me that there could be a poisonous snake on the ground in front of him. I glanced around for a stick but I couldn't see one; then I inched to the side in order to get a better view.

I would have gasped if my jaw and chest muscles hadn't seized up. Lying less than a meter from Jed's feet was a Thai. He was flat on his back, eyes closed, and he had an automatic rifle lightly resting in the crook of his arm. Jed slowly moved his head to face me, as if he was afraid that by disturbing the air he might wake the man up. "What now?" he mouthed. I jabbed a finger in the direction we'd come, but he shook his head. I nodded vigorously, and Jed shook his head again, glowering. Then he pointed at his foot. He was standing on the barrel of the rifle. The pressure had lifted the butt several inches above the Thai's bare arm. As soon as he moved his foot away, the butt would drop.

"Shit," I mouthed, and Jed rolled his eyes desperately.

I thought for a minute. Then I started to creep backward along the track. Jed stared at me, as if to say, "Where the fuck are you going?" but I raised a hand to tell him not to worry. I knew what to do because I'd seen it done on *Tour of Duty.*

I can never remember the names on *Tour of Duty*. That's partly because the series is so terrible, but it's also because the characters come from the same school as *NYPD Blue* (black lieutenant, unorthodox cops who get results). So in *Tour of Duty* you have the tough sergeant who knows all the tricks, the green lieutenant who learns all the tricks, the simple southern hick who learns to make friends with the sassy blacks, the Hispanic whom you can rely on in a firefight, and the East Coaster who wears glasses and probably reads books. The names really aren't important.

The main thing is the scenes that these characters play out. These would include tending for the orphan who's been wounded by shrapnel, stopping a rival platoon from doing a Zippo raid, leaping from helicopters into a whirlpool of flattened grass, hugging comrades as they cough and die, and dealing with mines.

The platoon is walking through the jungle when suddenly there is a barely audible click. Everyone hits the dirt except one man, an FNG, who stands rigid with fear. "I don't wanna die, Sarge!" he blurts, and starts to recite the Lord's Prayer. Sarge crawls over on his belly. "You hang on in there, soldier,'' he mutters. He knows what to do. He had the same thing happen in Korea, '53.

Bizarrely, Sarge starts to tell the soldier about an apparently unrelated incident that happened when he was a kid, working on his daddy's farm. Sarge had a hound dog that he loved dearly, name of Ol' Blue, and the soldier listens, distracted by the clever ploy. Meanwhile, Sarge is easing his knife under the soldier's boot and sweat is cutting a line through the dirt on his brow.

Ol' Blue was caught in a rabbit snare, Sarge explains, and every time he struggled the snare grew tighter. The soldier nods, still not grasping the connection. ''What happened to Ol' Blue?'' the soldier asks. ''Did ya get him out, Sarge?'' ''Sure we did, soldier,'' Sarge replies. Then he tells the soldier to lift his foot, nice and easy now. The soldier is confused, frightened, but he trusts Sarge. He does as he is told, and Sarge slips a rock on to the knife blade, maintaining the pressure on the mine. Sarge chuckles. ''Son, all Ol' Blue had to do was relax.''

I wasn't going to start blathering on to Jed about Ol' Blue. As I gently laid the stone on the rifle barrel, even the noise of rock scraping against metal sounded like someone hammering on a petrol drum. When the stone was positioned I looked up at Jed. He shrugged calmly and motioned for me to get up. I suppose he wanted me to be ready to start running if the gun dropped.

Inch by inch, Jed eased up his foot. The butt shifted downward a fraction and I heard him draw in a quick breath, but it didn't contact the Thai's arm. We exchanged a glance, stepped gingerly over the man's legs, and continued quietly down the island.

It took us another forty-five minutes to reach the top of

the waterfall, and I grinned continuously every step of the way. I was grinning so much my jaws were aching, and if we hadn't needed to keep silent I would have been laughing out loud.

credit

I dove off the waterfall that day, much to Jed's surprise, and much to my surprise too. I hadn't been planning on it. We were standing on the cliff edge looking at the sunset, which was cloudless and very beautiful and deserved a moment's reflection. Sometimes, with these cloudless evenings, the light played a strange trick. Instead of beams of brightness radiating out from the horizon, there were beams of darkness—in other words, the polarized image of a traditional sunset. At first glance you accepted the image, only vaguely aware that something about it was wrong. Then, as with Escher's endless staircase, you suddenly realized it made no logical sense at all. Each time I saw this effect it intrigued me and I could always pass twenty quiet minutes pleasantly confounded.

Jed had no better answers for the phenomenon than I did, but he always gave it a try. "Shadows, cast by clouds hidden behind the horizon line," he was arguing that night, when I tapped him on the arm and said, "Watch this." Then I toppled forward. The next instant I was watching the cliff face rushing past me and feeling a distant sense of alarm that my legs were bent. Their displaced weight was turning me in the air, and I was in danger of landing on my back. I tried to straighten them and a moment later I hit the pool, where I spun through several violent underwater revolutions, lost all the air from my lungs, and drifted back to the surface.

Up on the cliff top I could see Jed watching me with his hands on his hips. He didn't say anything but I knew he disapproved. A little while later he snapped at me as we made our way from the waterfall pool to the camp, although it may also have had something to do with the song I was singing.

It was: "I saw a mouse! Where? There on the stair. Where on the stair? Right there! A little mouse with clogs on, well I declare, going *clip-clippity-clop* on the stair, *right there*!"

"Jesus, Richard!" he said as I looped the tune and began the chorus again. "What's got into you?"

"I'm singing," I replied breezily.

"I know you are. Cut it out."

"You don't know that song?"

"No."

"You must know it. It's famous."

"It's the stupidest song I ever heard."

I shrugged. I couldn't deny it was a stupid song.

We walked in silence for a few minutes, me turning the tune over in my head and humming under my breath; then Jed said, "You know, you want to watch yourself, Richard." I didn't know what he meant so I kept quiet, and a couple of seconds later he added, "You're high."

". . . High?"

"Dope. High."

"I haven't smoked a joint since last night."

"Exactly," he said with emphasis.

". . . You're saying I should cut down on smoking dope?"

"I'm saying dope's got nothing to do with it." A branch was blocking our path and he held it aside until I passed him, then let the branch snap back. "That's why you should watch yourself."

I snorted dismissively. The way he was talking reminded

me of his obscure references to blame on Koh Phangan. Sometimes Jed could be willfully cryptic, and uncharitably I decided that his attitude had probably led to his alienated position in the beach life just as much as the awkward circumstances of his arrival. That, in turn, made me think of my own budding alienation.

"Jed," I said, after a pause. "Do you think it would be okay if I told people about our run-in with the dope guard? It doesn't involve Zeph and Sammy . . ."

"Mmm."

". . . See, I'm constantly being coy about what we're doing up on the island. I sort of feel like this would be a chance for me to—"

"Tell them," he interrupted. "No harm. It's probably a good idea."

"Uh-huh?"

"We don't want it to seem like we're hiding stuff from people."

"Great," I said, and started to whistle the first bars of the mouse song before catching myself.

It was pitch-black back at the camp. What color remained in the sky was entirely blocked by the canopy ceiling. The only light came from candles through the open door of the longhouse and spatterings of red cigarette and joint butts, glowing in clusters around the clearing.

Although I was looking forward to telling my ex-detail about the sleeping guard, my first thought was food, so I aimed straight for the kitchen hut. Every day Unhygienix wrapped a couple of portions in banana leaf for me and Jed, and made sure we got some of the choicest bits of fish. It was cold by the time we'd get to it, but I was usually too hungry to mind. That night I noticed Unhygienix had added papaya to the stew, which irritated me slightly as it meant Bugs had succeeded in tracking down my orchard.

After getting my dinner portion I walked around the clearing, joining the dots between the clusters of smokers, looking for my friends. Unusually, they were nowhere to be found, and nobody seemed to know where they were. Confused, I checked Keaty's tent and then the longhouse, where I found Unhygienix, Cassie, and Ella playing blackjack, and, further up, Jesse writing in his diary.

"Ah!" said Unhygienix when he saw me, and pointed to my food. "What do you think?"

"Of the stew?"

"Yes. You notice the fruit? A good taste?"

"Sure. Sweet and savory. Very Thai."

Unhygienix beamed. "You know what I did? I made some papaya juice and stewed it with the fish, but I only put in the flesh in the last two minutes, or it falls apart in the heat. So this way you have the taste and the texture."

"Ah."

"And Richard, we can have this again, because Jean will plant the seeds and we will grow papaya in the garden. I am very pleased with this dish."

"You should be. It tastes really good. Well done."

Unhygienix shook his head modestly. "You should be thanking Bugs."

". . . Why is that?" I said suspiciously.

"He discovered these papayas in the jungle."

I choked on a fish bone. "Bugs did what?"

"In the jungle, he found a whole orchard of papayas and monkeys."

"No he didn't!"

"Yes. Yesterday, he found this orchard."

"I found the fucking orchard! I found it a couple of weeks ago!"

". . . Really?"

"Was Bugs saying he found it?"

". . . Uh . . ."

Cassie smiled. "Yes, he was."

"That *prick*!" In my temper I squeezed the banana leaf and some of the stew spilled onto the ground.

"Careful," said Ella.

I frowned, suddenly aware that I was making a scene. "Well, anyway . . . he's lying."

"Don't worry," Cassie chuckled, laying down a long run from threes to picture cards. "We don't doubt it."

"Good."

They went back to their game and I continued up the longhouse toward Jesse.

"I heard," he said dryly, as I approached. "Congratulations on finding the papayas."

"Yes, well, it isn't a big thing. It just . . ."

"Got on your nerves," he finished for me, and lowered his diary. "Course it did. Understood. Are you looking for Keaty?"

"Yeah." I nodded morosely. As a consequence of the papayas my mood had gone bad. "And the others. I can't find them. I think they've all gone off together somewhere."

"Right. He left me a message to give you."

"Oh," I said, perking up a bit. "Let's hear it."

"It was a note. I put it on your bed."

I thanked him and jogged the rest of the way up the longhouse, keen to find out what was going on.

The note was folded on my pillow, and beside it was a rolled joint. It read: "Smoke this quick! Phosphorescence! Keaty!"

I frowned. "Hey, Jesse," I called. "What does the note mean?"

I waited while he completed his sentence; then he looked up. "Dunno, mate. Didn't read it. What's it say?"

"Phosphorescence. And it's got a joint."

"Ah." Jesse waggled his pencil at me. "Phosphorescence!"

"What is it?"

"You don't know?"

". . . No."

He smiled. "Go down to the beach. You'll see. And make sure you smoke that joint on the way."

phosphorescence

I walked along the path to the beach as fast as I could, which wasn't that fast because I didn't want to bump into any tree trunks or stub my foot on a root. At the same time, I smoked the joint, practically hit-and-running it even though I was alone, because I felt like getting wasted and because Keaty had told me to smoke it quick.

Meanwhile I seethed about the papayas, and pretty soon I was very stoned and deeply involved in a fantasy about beating up Bugs. In its earliest form the fantasy started off as just me and him, but soon I decided I needed an audience to bear witness to his humiliation. I added Françoise, then Jed and Keaty, then Etienne and Greg, and eventually the whole camp.

It was a Sunday. It had to be a Sunday, because that was the only time you got the whole camp in one place. Most people were kicking a ball around, a few were swimming, and a few were playing Frisbee. I was standing with Françoise. We were sharing a joke when Bugs appeared from the treeline with Sal, and three big papayas cradled in his arms.

"Got some more papayas," he called. "Enough for everyone."

"Excuse me," I said quietly to Françoise. "Won't be a moment."

He caught my eye as I strode toward him and did a double take, recognizing the purposeful nature of my step and the grim set of my mouth. First he looked alarmed, then arrogant. He was going to bluff it out, I realized.

"Yes," he said loudly, holding up the fruit for all to see, still watching me from the corner of his eye. "Here are some more papayas that *I found.*"

I stopped a meter away from him. "Papayas that *you* found, Bugs?"

"That's what I said."

"Uh-huh. Then how about we take a walk down to the orchard . . . right now."

His eyebrows flicked upward. ". . . Now?"

"Now. And I'll show you the joint butt I left . . . when I found the orchard less than *two weeks ago!*"

Everyone gasped, including Sal. A crowd had formed a circle around us and Françoise had come running over to stand by my side. "Is this true?" she demanded angrily.

Bugs scoffed. "Of course not! He's lying! I found the orchard!"

"So how about that walk?"

"I don't have to prove myself to you!"

"I think you do."

"Up yours. I found the orchard. End of story."

I smiled. "You know what, Bugs?" The silence was deathly, aside from the gentle lapping of the waves on the shore. "You're kinda *buggin'* me!"

The crowd laughed and Bugs's face twisted with rage. "Is that right?" he sneered. "Well, take this!" A papaya hurtled toward my head but I ducked and it flew past me into the crowd.

"Hey!" someone yelled. "Watch it!"

Bugs swore and made like he was about to throw another, but quick as a flash I grabbed the Frisbee from Cassie, who was standing beside me, and hurled it with lethal accuracy. The papaya exploded at the impact. The remaining chunks slithered from his hand and fell to the sand, harmless.

"Why you . . ." he started to say, but I was already on him. I faked with a left and floored him with a right. He dropped like a sack of potatoes.

"I'm thorry," he yelped, holding a hand up to cup the blood splashing from his busted lips. "It'th true! I didn't find the papayath! Richard did!"

Slowly I bent down and picked the Frisbee up again, pausing to wipe away a few shreds of pulped papaya flesh. "Too late for that, Bugs," I muttered softly, almost kindly. "Too late . . ."

The Frisbee shot down and connected squarely with the bridge of his nose, shattering the bone. Then he rolled onto his side and scrabbled weakly at the sand, trying to crawl away. I kicked him on the back of the head and gave him four hard punches in the kidney.

He whimpered. "Pleathe," he said. "Don't."

A bad choice of words. My temper rose. Looking around me, I spotted a fishing spear.

"Rewind," I said, taking the last drag from the joint. "Can't do that."

I sucked until the tips of my fingers burned, then threw away the roach and rewound back to my first punch.

I faked with a left and floored him with a right. He dropped like a sack of potatoes.

"I'm thorry," he yelped. "It'th true! I didn't find the papayath!"

"Say that again!" I shouted, looming over him with the Frisbee poised.

"I didn't find them! You did! I'm thorry!"

"Louder!"

"You found the papayath!"

I nodded curtly, and turned to Françoise. "Just wanted to set the record straight."

She glanced down at Bugs's twitching figure. "Of course," she said briefly.

"You want to swim out to the coral garden?"

"Yes, Richard," she breathed, interlocking her arm with mine. "I would love to."

The fantasy might have happily continued from there, but the dead leaves and dirt under my feet had become sand. I'd reached the beach.

It took me ages to find Keaty and the others. Even with the moonlight I couldn't see them, and their laughter seemed to come from everywhere, spread evenly over the water and faintly echoing off the cliffs. But after twenty minutes of stoned wandering along the shore I finally pinned them down to a group of small boulders, one hundred meters out.

As I couldn't see them and they couldn't see me, I decided there wasn't much sense in calling out, so I slipped off my T-shirt and began swimming toward them. Gradually their figures became discernible in the darkness. They were all standing and bending over to look downward into the water. Then—at roughly the moment I must have become visible to them—their laughter abruptly ceased, and as I got closer I saw that they had all turned to face in my direction. "Hey!" I said, finding their watchful silence a little eerie. "What's up?" They didn't answer. I continued swimming and repeated the question, irrationally thinking they might not have heard me. When they didn't answer again, I stopped, treading water ten feet from the boulder. "Why aren't you answering me?" I asked, puzzled.

"Look down," Keaty replied after a moment or two.

I paused, then did so. The water was as black as ink, except for where the moonlight caught the ripples. ". . . What's to see?"

"He is too close," I heard Etienne say.

"No," said Keaty. "Richard, move your hands, just under the surface."

I did as he said. From the boulder I heard Françoise sigh, but I still couldn't see anything past the blackness. "I don't get it. . . . What's this about?"

"Too close," Etienne repeated.

Keaty's silhouette scratched its head. "Yeah, you're right. . . . Come up onto the boulder, Richard. Watch me dive. We'll show you . . ."

At first I could see nothing but the disturbed water and reflected moonlight from where Keaty had vanished. Then, as the water settled, I began to see light below the surface. A milky glow at first that separated into a thousand tiny stars, next becoming a slowly moving meteor trail behind the brightest cluster. The cluster rose and turned back on itself, and turned again to form a glittering figure eight. Then it sank downward, disappearing for several seconds.

"What . . . ?" I said, baffled and astonished and unable to think of anything better to say.

Françoise put her hand on my arm. "Wait," she whispered. "Look now."

Deep in the blackness the glow returned, but this time it quickly divided into seven or eight clusters, brighter than before. They flickered and darted, dissolving and shedding light, but somehow replenishing themselves and becoming more intense. I took an instinctive step backward, suddenly aware that the miniature fireballs were traveling up toward me at an increasing speed. The next instant the surface broke into a flurry of bubbles and Keaty appeared, gasping for air.

"What did you think," he spluttered between lungfuls. "Did you ever see anything like it?"

"No . . ." I replied, still stupidly dazed. "Never."

"Phosphorescence. Minute creatures or algae or something. They glow when you make a movement." He hauled himself onto the boulder. "Phew! What an effort! We've been practicing that all night. Trying to get the best display."

"It looked incredible. . . . But . . . where do the creatures come from?"

"Daffy would say they come from the corals," said Gregorio. "It only happens on some nights. Not often. But now it is here, it will stay for the next few days. Maybe three or four."

I shook my head. "Amazing . . . Just amazing . . ."

"Ah-ha!" Etienne slapped me on the back and pushed Gregorio's diving mask into my hands. "But there is still the best to see!"

"Underwater?"

"Yes! Put this on and follow me! I will show you something you could never imagine!"

"It'll blow your mind," Keaty agreed. "It's indescribable."

the dmz

I returned Jed's binoculars to him and lay on my back. My head was still bleary from all the dope I'd smoked the night before, despite the brisk morning trek up the island, and I couldn't seem to focus on the tiny figures. "Basically,"

I said, folding my hands behind my head, "it was like being in space. Floating with loads of stars and comets around you. One of the most amazing things was disturbing a shoal of fish . . ."

Jed readjusted the binoculars to suit him. "I've seen phosphorescence before."

"But not underwater."

"No. Underwater sounds good."

"Yeah. Really good . . ." I sighed. "Did I tell you about Bugs and the papayas?"

"Nope."

"I found a papaya orchard a couple of weeks ago, and now Bugs is making out like he found it. Granted, I couldn't remember the orchard's exact location, but it was me that found it first." I sat up to see how Jed was reacting. He didn't appear to be reacting at all. "I suppose it isn't that big a deal. What do you think?"

"Mmm," Jed replied absently.

"Mmm, it is a big deal, or mmm, it isn't?"

"Oh . . . probably . . ."

I gave up. This was, after all, the precise problem with Bugs. Unless you were tuned into the subtleties of his character, you couldn't appreciate how irritating he was. I lay back down again and looked up at the clouds, feeling frustrated.

Actually, I'd been feeling frustrated for quite some time. It had started when we'd arrived at our lookout post two hours earlier to find, yet again, that Zeph and Sammy were still on their same patch of beach. I was aware that this should have been cause for relief, but instead it had gotten on my nerves, and as the morning passed I'd thought carefully about this paradox. My first guess was that it was connected to the uncertainty of the situation. I'd become tired of the waiting and I wanted some kind of resolution to occur. Even if it was the worst-case scenario and they set off toward us, at least the situation would become tangible. It would be something that was in our power to affect.

But it didn't take long for me to realize that my first guess was wrong. In the process of working through the worst-case scenario, I inevitably worked through the best-case. I imagined Zeph and Sammy disappearing, going back to Koh Phangan or Angthong; and never seeing them again. It was at that point I realized my mistake, because what I registered, while entertaining this optimistic thought, was disappointment. The strange truth was that I didn't want them to leave. Neither, as the root of my frustration, did I want them to stay put. And that left only one possibility; the worst-case scenario was the best-case scenario. I wanted them to come.

"Bored," I murmured carelessly, and Jed laughed.

"Bored is good, Richard," he said. "Bored is safe."

I paused. I hadn't mentioned my thoughts about Zeph and Sammy yet, assuming that Jed wouldn't take them too well. But I wasn't sure. It was possible that he felt the same way. I knew he took pleasure from evading the dope guards, part of which had to be a danger buzz, and I hadn't forgotten the way Keaty used to talk about him. I decided to obliquely test the water.

"Jed," I said, yawning to reinforce the casual nature of the question. "You remember the Gulf War?"

"Course."

"I was just wondering . . . You remember the buildup? When we were saying get out of Kuwait or we cream you, and Saddam was saying whatever he was saying."

"He was saying no, wasn't he?"

"Right." I leaned on my elbows. "So I was just wondering, how were you feeling at the time?"

"Feeling?"

"About the buildup to the Gulf War."

Jed lowered the binoculars and rubbed his beard. "I was

feeling that it was all a load of hypocritical bullshit, if I remember correctly."

"No, I meant about the possibility of there being a war. Did it bother you much?"

"Uh . . . not really."

"You weren't sort of . . . looking forward to it?"

"Looking forward to it?"

"Yeah. . . . Speaking personally"—I took a deep breath—"I was kind of hoping Saddam wouldn't back down. You know, just to see what would happen."

Jed narrowed his eyes. "Now, Richard," he said dryly. "I can't imagine why you've suddenly brought this up."

I felt my cheeks flush. "I can't either. It popped into my head for some reason."

"Uh-huh. Well, I suppose I was looking forward to the Gulf War in a way. It was all dramatic and exciting, and like you said, I wanted to see what would happen. But when I saw the pictures of the Basra road and that civilian shelter that got hit, I felt pretty bad. I felt like I'd missed the point, and only got it too late. Does that answer your question?"

"Oh yes," I said quickly. "Absolutely."

"Good." Jed chuckled. "So, Richard, you're bored."

"Not bored . . ."

"Listless."

"Maybe."

"Whatever. You want some excitement. Fine. Perhaps we should go and nick some grass."

"We?" I said, stammering slightly because I was both eager and surprised. Since I'd begun working with Jed he'd only gone dope collecting once, and he'd left me behind on our lookout spot. "You mean both of us?"

"Sure. We've got plenty of time to come back here later, and we can risk them not doing anything while we're away. Anyway, I noticed camp supplies are getting low."

"I think it's a great idea!"

"Okay." He stood up. "Come on then."

The pass between the island's two peaks was the one position from which you could clearly make out the location of the dope fields, although the fields themselves were obscured behind trees. The only thing you could see were sudden dips in the canopy where one terrace dropped down to another. From higher up, the terraces seemed to merge into a single slope with natural-looking breaks in the canopy, an illusion caused by the elevated angle. I guess it prevented them from getting spotted from the air.

Once we reached the pass, Jed made the closed-fingers-pointing gesture and we began our descent into the DMZ—as I'd decided to call it. While we walked, I watched Jed's feet closely. I'd noticed he was able to walk much more quietly than me, even though we were both treading on the same mixture of dead leaves and twigs, and I was determined to discover how he did it. One thing was that he used the flat of his foot instead of the ball. I'd been doing the opposite, simply because of my instinct to walk on tiptoe when trying to move without noise. But after watching him, I realized that my way lacked common sense. By spreading the pressure across his whole foot he put less weight on twigs and flattened an area of leaves instead of just one or two. When I switched to his method, I heard the change immediately. The other thing he did was to lift his feet quite high, so that they weren't skimming just above the surface of the ground and catching loose material.

In order to press these lessons home, I played a private game as we crept through the DMZ. If I snapped a twig, then I'd triggered a land mine, and if I rustled a leaf above a particular volume—a rustle that couldn't pass as a regular jungle sound—then I'd been shot by a sniper. I also decided that the spiderweb strands which occasionally stretched across the path were Claymores, and took care to step over them if they hadn't already been broken by Jed. In deference to video games I gave myself three lives, allowing an extra life if I saw any animal larger than a beetle before it saw me. The only flaw to the game was that there was no punishment if I lost all my lives—as I did several times. But the shame was punishment enough, and that one flaw aside, the game proved to be excellent.

I was enjoying myself so much that I was a bit pissed off when we reached a dope field. At the edge we crouched in silence for several minutes, checking that the coast was clear. Then Jed turned to me. "Okay," he mouthed, pointing at me. "You go."

I raised my eyebrows and touched my chest, and he nodded. I grinned and gave him the thumbs-up. Then I hunched down as low as I could go without being on all fours and scuttled forward.

Between the trees and the start of the dope field was a space of at least three meters, well beaten down where the guards made their patrol. Once clear of the trees, I looked both ways and sped across the gap. I was mindful that a guard might appear on my perimeter at any moment, so I wasted no time in trying to pull off a few good-sized branches. But I immediately ran into difficulty. The stems of the marijuana were remarkably tough. I twisted and ripped, as quietly as I could, but was completely unable to get them free of the main stalk. Worse, my hands were sweating like mad and infuriatingly slippery, and I couldn't get a proper grip. I looked back at Jed, who had a hand clamped to his head in despair.

"What do I do?" I mouthed.

He held up his knife, waving the point sarcastically. I realized I'd scuttled off before he'd had a chance to give it to me. Cursing my haste, I cupped my hands, indicating that he should throw it. The knife came sailing through the air and finally I was able to sever the troublesome stems. In order to compensate for the fuckup I hung around a minute longer than I had to, so I could return with a particularly daring-sized bunch.

"What's the matter, Richard?" said Jed when we'd got back to the safety of our lookout position. "I thought you'd be happy after all that excitement." He patted me affectionately on the back. "I thought you'd be singing that ridiculous mouse song."

I shook my head and laid out my bushel. "I'm fine, Jed."

"It wasn't that thing with the knife, was it? That was my fault, you know, not yours. I told you to go before I'd given it to you."

"No, no. The knife thing didn't bother me . . . not much anyway . . . and it wasn't your fault. I should have stopped to think. But I'm fine, really."

Jed seemed unconvinced. "I know what it is. You wanted to spot some of the guards, right?"

"Well . . ." I shrugged. "It would have been interesting."

"I don't know, Richard. You get disappointed by all the wrong things. Listen, take it from me, you're glad we didn't run into anyone."

"Sure . . ." I thought for a moment, idly plucking at a couple of buds. "Out of curiosity, what do you think would happen if they were to find us?"

"Mmm . . . don't know. Rather not find out."

"Do you think they'd kill us?"

"It's possible. In a way I doubt it though, because there'd be no sense to it. They know we're here and vice versa, and neither of us want our secrets to get discovered, so . . ."

"I heard that Daffy once talked to them."

Jed looked surprised. "Who told you that?"

"Uh . . . Greg I think."

"I think maybe Greg has that wrong. Sal would have told me if there'd been any contact with them, and she never has."

"So what if they caught Zeph and Sammy? That would be different, because they're not connected to us."

"Yeah. They might kill Zeph and Sammy."

"That would solve our problem at least," I suggested cautiously, waiting for Jed to say something disapproving, but he didn't. He just nodded.

"Yep," he said bluntly. "It would."

zombie fish eaters

It was dark by the time we got our act together. We had to jump into pitch blackness, unable to see the edges of the pool or even the white foam where the waterfall landed. Then we had to find our way through the forest, something I'd have found difficult without Jed to guide me.

My plan was to eat some food quickly and spend the rest of the evening swimming in the phosphorescence. I also wanted to tell my friends about the sleeping dope guard, which had slipped my mind in the excitement of the previous night. But when I got to the kitchen hut, I discovered that our banana-leaf food parcels were missing. All I found was a cold pile of boiled rice. Next, I hunted for the big cooking pot, assuming that Unhygienix had just forgotten to lay the fish and vegetables out, but the pot was empty too. That was strange because usually the cooks kept some dregs for the next morning's breakfast. Pensively, I patted my empty stomach and looked around me. Then I noticed something else even stranger. Apart from Jed, who was sitting a few meters away, the clearing seemed to be completely empty. I couldn't see any joint butts glowing in the darkness, or flashlights inside the tents.

I walked over to Jed. "You notice anything weird?" I said.

He shrugged. "Only that I can't see my food."

"Well . . . exactly. There isn't any food. And there aren't any people, either."

"People?" Jed shone his Maglite around him.

"See what I mean?"

". . . Yeah." He stood up. "That is weird . . ."

We gazed about us for a few seconds, following the yellow beam. Then, from somewhere close by, there was a loud moan, clearly the sound of someone in pain.

"Jesus!" Jed whispered, and switched off the light. "Did you hear that?"

"Of course I did!"

"Who was it?"

"How should I know?"

We paused, listening carefully. Then we heard the moan again and the hairs on the back of my neck stood up.

"Christ, Jed! Put the torch back on! This is making me nervous!"

"If you're nervous, why are you smiling?"

". . . How did you know I was smiling?"

"I could hear it in your voice."

"Just put the bloody light back on!"

"No," he hissed, "we don't know what's going on yet."

We listened some more. I remembered my first morning on the beach, waking up after my fever to an empty clearing. I'd found it pretty freaky in broad daylight. There was something unsettling about an empty place that you knew should be full of people. In the blackness with the eerie moans it was ten times as bad.

"This is like a zombie film," I muttered darkly, and giggled. *"Zombie Flesh Eaters."* Jed didn't reply.

The next time we heard the moan we were able to place it. It was coming from our left, around where most of the tents were pitched.

"Okay," said Jed. "We'll investigate. You take point."

"Me? You've got the torch!"

"I need to hold it so you've got both your hands free."

"Free for what?"

"Fighting off the zombies."

Jed put the beam on and illuminated Unhygienix's tent, so I mumbled a swearword and began slowly walking toward it.

I'd only gone a few feet when the flap opened and Ella's head poked out. "Jed?" she said, squinting against the glare.

"Richard."

"And Jed. What's going on, Ella?"

She shook her head. "Come inside. It's a disaster."

"It was Keaty," Ella explained, mopping at Unhygienix's forehead. It had been Unhygienix who was moaning, and he continued to do so while we were talking. His eyes were closed and he was clutching his great brown belly in both hands. I don't think he was even aware we were in the tent. "That idiot."

I raised my eyebrows. "Why? What did he do?"

"He put a squid in one of the fishing buckets, and we chopped it up and chucked it in with everything else."

"So?"

"The squid was already dead when he speared it."

Jed sucked in his breath sharply.

"Most of the camp is sick. The bathroom hut is clogged with vomit and you don't want to go near the Khyber Pass."

"What about you?" I asked. "You seem okay."

"Five or six of us are all right. I've got a few pains, but it looks like I've been lucky."

"And why did Keaty spear a dead squid?"

Ella narrowed her eyes. "I'd like to ask him that myself. We'd all like to ask him that."

"Yeah . . . Where is he? In his tent?"

"Maybe."

"Okay. Well, I'll go and see him . . ."

I chose the right moment to leave, because as I was backing out, Unhygienix sat bolt upright and vomited everywhere. I vanished quickly into the darkness with Ella's exasperated cries ringing in my ears.

It took me ages to find Keaty. He wasn't in his tent and there was no response in the clearing when I called his name. Eventually I decided to check the beach, where I spotted him, sitting in a patch of moonlight a little way down the shore.

When he saw me coming toward him he made a movement, as if he was half considering running away. Then he relaxed and his shoulders slumped. "Hi," he said in a low voice.

I nodded and sat beside him.

"I'm not flavor of the month, Rich."

". . . Neither is squid."

He didn't laugh.

"So what happened?"

"Don't you know? I poisoned the camp."

"Yeah, but—"

"I was using Greg's mask, I saw this squid, we've eaten squid a hundred times before, so I speared it and chucked it in the bucket. How was I supposed to know it was already dead?"

"Because it wasn't moving."

He glared at me. "Well, I know that now! But I thought . . . I thought squid were like jellyfish. They just floated around and . . . and its arms looked like they were moving . . ."

"So it was a mistake. It wasn't your fault."

"Yes, Rich. That's right. It was Jean's fault." He paused to punch the sand between his legs. "Of course it was my fucking fault! *Jesus!*"

"Okay . . . it was your fault, but you shouldn't—"

"Rich," he interrupted. "Please."

I shrugged and looked away. Across the lagoon, the moonlight was catching the jagged fissure that ran down the cliffs to the coral garden. "Kapow," I said quietly.

Keaty leaned forward. "What?"

"Kapow."

". . . Why?"

"Just because that's the sound lightning makes." I pointed at the fissure. "See?"

bedlam

I only stayed with Keaty a short while because I wanted to check on Etienne and Françoise. He wouldn't come with me because he said he wasn't ready to face people yet, the poor guy. It was rough to have fought for so long to get into the fishing detail and then to be responsible for such a fuckup. He felt especially guilty that he'd been one of the few unaffected by the squid. I tried to tell him not to be so daft, because he could hardly blame himself for having a good immune system, but it didn't do any good.

When I saw what was happening at the longhouse, I was glad Keaty had decided to stay behind. The scene inside would only have made him feel worse. I'd had no idea that the effects of the food poisoning had been so severe, and actually I doubted that Keaty had realized it either or he'd have been back at the camp helping.

Running all the way down the center of the room were candles, placed there, I guessed, to keep them from being kicked over by the writhing figures on the beds. Through the burning wax fumes was the sour smell of vomit. Everybody was moaning—probably not constantly, but there were enough moans to overlap and keep the noise at a steady level. And everybody seemed to have reverted to their own language. Picking out recognizable words in the meaningless babble made it all the more surreal. People needed water or wanted sick to be wiped off their chests. When I passed Jesse he lunged for my foot and asked me to carry him to the bathroom hut. "I've got shit all over my fucking legs!" he gasped incredulously. "All over! Look!"

I spotted Cassie and Moshe darting between the beds, hopelessly trying to attend to all the different requests. When Cassie saw me she made a despairing motion with her arms and said, "Are they dying?"

I shook my head.

"How do you know, Richard?"

"They're not dying."

"How do you *know?*"

"I don't." I shook my head again. "Jesse's calling for you."

Cassie ran to check on her boyfriend and I continued down the longhouse toward Françoise and Etienne.

Françoise was the worse off, I think. Etienne was asleep, so I suppose he might have been unconscious, but he was breathing steadily and his forehead didn't feel too hot. Françoise, however, was awake and in a great deal of pain. The cramps seemed to come in regular waves about sixty seconds apart. She didn't cry out like everybody else, but she bit her bottom lip and all over her stomach were marks from where she'd been digging in her fingernails.

"Stop doing that," I said firmly, after she'd nearly drawn blood from biting so hard.

She looked at me through dull eyes. "Richard?"

"Yes. You're chewing your mouth to pieces . . . You shouldn't."

"It hurts."

"I can see, but . . . Here." I reached into my pocket and pulled out my cigarettes. Then I ripped off the top of the box and pressed it flat. "You can bite on that instead."

"It still hurts."

I smoothed her damp hair away from her face. "I know it does, but this way you get to keep your lips."

"Oh." She managed to look faintly amused. She might even have managed a smile if another pain wave hadn't followed.

"What is happening, Richard?" she asked when her muscles had relaxed.

"You've got food poisoning."

"I mean, what is happening now?"

"Well . . ." I looked down the longhouse. I wasn't sure how to answer. I didn't want to frighten her. "People are chucking up, and . . . Moshe and Cassie are here helping . . ."

"Do you think this is serious for us?"

"No, no," I replied, laughing encouragingly. "You'll all be much better tomorrow. You'll all be fine."

"Richard . . ."

"Uh-huh?"

"When Etienne and I were in Sumatra, someone died from eating bad shellfish."

I nodded slowly. "Yes, but they probably ate the whole thing. You would have only had a tiny little bit, so you'll be okay."

"Really?"

"Sure."

She sighed. "Good . . . Richard, I need some water . . . Please will you bring me some?"

"Of course. I'll be back in two minutes."

As I stood up her cramps came back again. I watched her for a moment, uncertain of whether I should go or wait with her until the pain had passed; then I jogged down the longhouse, ignoring the pleas I passed on the way.

incubus

Unexpectedly, I found Jed sitting outside the kitchen hut, eating plain rice with his Maglite upended in front of him like an electric candle. He held out his bowl as I approached, and mumbled, "You should eat."

"I'm not hungry. Have you seen inside the longhouse?"

He swallowed. "Stuck my head round the door, saw enough not to go in. Got plenty to deal with in the tents."

"What's happening in the tents?"

"Same as the longhouse. The Swedes seem okay, but the others are fucked."

"Are you worried?"

"Are you?"

"I'm not sure. Françoise said people can die from this stuff."

"Mmm. They can." He took another mouthful and chewed carefully. "We need to keep them tanked up with loads of water. Can't let them get dehydrated. And we need to keep ourselves fit so we can look after them. That's why you should eat some food. You haven't eaten since this morning."

"Later," I said, thinking of Françoise, and scooped a pitcher into the drinking water barrel. "And if the Swedes are okay, then tell them to come and help."

Jed nodded, his cheeks too puffed up to speak, and I set off back across the clearing.

Back inside the longhouse, Bugs was metaphorically and literally losing his shit. He was squatting alongside the line of candles, eyes bulging like cue balls, while a pool of feces collected around his feet. Moshe was standing a few feet away, gagging, and when he saw me he hurriedly moved away, as if having seen Bugs, I'd been tagged with the responsibility of dealing with him.

Bugs groaned. A string of drool looped out of his mouth and swung crazily from his chin. "Richard," he spluttered. "Get me outside."

I looked around. Cassie was several beds away and Moshe was bent over one of the Yugoslavian girls. "I'm in a hurry," I replied, covering my nose and mouth with the crook of my arm.

"What?"

"I'm in a hurry. I've got to get this water to Françoise."

"I've got to get outside! She can wait!"

I shook my head, then grimaced. The smell was so bad it was making me feel giddy. "She already *has* waited," I said.

His face contorted as though he was going to yell at me. I looked at him impassively while he held the expression, then he gurgled and another stream of shit splashed onto the ground. "No!" he wailed, then his legs buckled and he slipped backward.

I took a step sideways to keep clear of the spreading dark puddle. "Jesus, Bugs. Can't you hold on?"

Bugs whimpered and doubled up into the fetus position, tried to straighten, and doubled up again.

I continued watching him, still breathing into my elbow though it did nothing to block the stench. The giddy feeling was getting stronger, mixing with intense rushes of irritation. It seemed to me, through the pulse that had developed behind my eyes, that there was something self-indulgent about his debasement. How could he not have had the strength to drag himself to the door? He'd distracted me from bringing the water to Françoise, and he was making a terrible mess that someone else would have to clean up. I remembered his stoicism when he'd bashed his leg, and the memory nearly made me laugh out loud.

"I've got to get this water to Françoise," I said coldly, but didn't move. "I said I'd only be two minutes. I've already been longer." Bugs opened his mouth, maybe to reply, and a slimy bubble of spit popped over his lips. This time I did laugh. "Look at yourself," I heard myself say. "Who the fuck do you think's going to clean that mess up?"

Suddenly a hand grabbed my shoulder.

"My God, Richard! What's the matter with you? Why aren't you helping him?"

I turned and saw Cassie staring at me. She looked very angry, but when our eyes met the anger quickly changed to something else. Something like concern, I noted vacantly, or alarm.

"Richard?"

"Yes?"

"Are you okay?"

"I'm fine."

"You . . ." She paused. "Come on. We've got to get him outside at once."

"I need to take this water to—"

"You need to get Bugs outside."

I rubbed my eyes and wished they would stop throbbing.

"Now, Richard."

"Yes . . . Right." I put the pitcher down, a safe distance from the puddle, and went to help her lift Bugs.

He was heavy, being so broad, and he made no effort to walk, so we practically had to drag him along the ground. Luckily one of the Swedes, Sten, arrived before we'd got halfway to the door. With his assistance we got Bugs outside and over to one of the diverted streams, where we dropped him so the current could wash him down.

Sten agreed to stay with Bugs—probably a relief after seeing what was going on in the longhouse—and Cassie and I headed back. I wanted to jog but she made me stop so she could feel my forehead.

"What's the matter?" I asked testily.

". . . I thought you might have a temperature."

"Do I?"

"You're a little hot . . . but no, thank God. We can't have anyone else getting ill." She gave my hand a squeeze. "We've got to be strong."

"Uh-huh."

"We've got to keep calm."

"Sure, Cassie. I know."

"Okay . . ."

"I've got to get the water to Françoise."

"Yes," she said, and I thought she might be frowning, but in the darkness it was impossible to tell. We started walking again. "Of course."

During the time I'd been away, Françoise's condition had gotten worse. She was still talking but she'd deteriorated into a dreamy, feverish state, and her cheeks were burning up. I had to prop her up against my lap so I could feed the water into her mouth without her choking, and even then she lost most of the liquid down her chest.

"Sorry I took so long," I said as I dried her down with one of her T-shirts. "Bugs was all over the place. Had to deal with him."

"Richard," she whispered, then said something in French that I couldn't understand.

I made a guess at the meaning. ". . . I'm fine. I missed out on the squid."

"Etienne . . ."

"He's here, right next to you . . . sleeping it off."

Her head twitched to the side. "I love you," she muttered drowsily.

I blinked, thinking for the slightest second that she might be talking to me. Then I caught myself, seeing the direction that her head had pointed, and realized her words were for Etienne. But in a way it didn't matter. It felt nice just to have heard her say them. I smiled and stroked her hair, and her hand reached up and closed weakly around mine.

For the next five minutes I stayed as still as I could, supporting her shoulders on my crossed legs. Then, when her breathing had become slower and heavier, I eased myself backward and gently lowered her onto the sheets. They were a little damp from where the water had spilled, but it couldn't be helped.

It isn't something I feel I ought to justify, but I'll justify it anyway. I was thinking about the time I'd had a fever. Françoise had given me a kiss, so I gave her one too, in exactly the same affectionate spirit. And I wouldn't have called it a kiss that was open to interpretation. It was straightforward; on the cheek, not the lips, unambiguous.

Technically, if you can get technical about such things, maybe I did hold it for a couple of seconds too long. I do remember noticing how soft and smooth her skin was. In the middle of that hellish night, with all the vomiting and groaning and flickering candle flames, I wasn't expecting to find sweetness. It took me by surprise, the little oasis. I dropped my guard and closed my eyes, drifting a few moments, just for the chance to block the bad stuff out.

But when I pulled back from the kiss and saw the way Etienne was staring at me, I knew he hadn't seen it the same way.

There was a short silence, as you might imagine, then he said, "What were you doing?"

". . . Nothing."

"You were kissing Françoise."

I shrugged. "So?"

"What do you mean, so?"

"I mean, so?" If I sounded irritable, it was nothing more than exhaustion, and maybe a hangover from the business with Bugs. "I gave her a kiss on the cheek. You've seen me do that before, and you've seen her kiss me too."

"She has never kissed you like that."

"On the cheek?"

"For so long."

"You've got this wrong."

He sat up in bed. "So what should I think?"

I sighed. The pulsing behind my eyes was starting again, turning into a sharp ache. "I'm very tired," I said. "You're very ill. It's affecting you."

"What should I think?" he repeated.

"I don't know. Anything. I kissed her because I was worried, and because I care about her . . . Just the same as I'm worried about you."

He didn't say anything.

I tried a joke. "If I give you a kiss, will that even things up?"

Etienne paused a bit longer, and finally nodded. "I am sorry, Richard," he said, but his voice was flat and I knew he didn't mean it. "You are right. I am ill and it is affecting me. But I can look after her now. Maybe some others can use your help."

"Yeah. I'm sure they can." I stood up. "If you need anything, give me a shout."

"Yes."

I glanced back at Françoise, who, thankfully, was still fast asleep. Then I began walking back down the longhouse, keeping to the side so I didn't get roped into helping Moshe as he shoveled away Bugs's shit.

good morning

I slept in the clearing. I would have slept there even if I hadn't thought it best to stay away from Etienne. I'd lost my sense of smell and become selective about which moans I chose to hear, but I couldn't stand the candles. Their accumulated heat was so strong that the ceiling was wet with condensation. The drips fell like a light rain through clouds of waxy fumes, and by midnight there wasn't a dry square inch in the longhouse. That aside, Gregorio was in my bed. I'd moved him there so he could get away from Jesse, who'd had the same incontinence problem as Bugs.

The last thing I remember before falling asleep was Sal's

voice. She'd recovered enough to walk around and was calling Keaty's name. I could have told her he was down on the beach, but I decided not to. There was something ominously controlled about her tone. It was the way a parent might call for a kid, trying to draw them out of their hiding place in order to tell them off. After a few minutes I felt her flashlight shining through my eyelids and she asked me if I knew where he was. I didn't move, and eventually she moved away.

The only other disruption that night was the sound of someone crying nearby. I tried to make myself get up and check on who it was, but it turned out I was too tired to care.

Jed woke me around six-thirty, with a bowl of rice and a boiled sweet, one of the last from Koh Phangan.

"Good morning," he said, violently shaking my shoulders. "Have you eaten yet?"

"No," I mumbled.

"What did I tell you last night?"

"Eat."

"So." He hauled me to a sitting position and put the bowl in my lap. The single sweet, a lurid chemical green, looked ridiculous perched on the mound of sticky grains. "Eat this now."

"I'm half asleep."

"Eat it, Richard."

I pressed a rice ball with my fingers and dutifully began to chew it, but my mouth was too dry to swallow. "Water," I croaked. Jed went to get me some, and I poured it straight into the bowl. Actually it didn't taste so bad, if only because it didn't taste of anything.

While I ate Jed talked, but I didn't listen to him. I was looking at the bone-white rice and thinking about the dead freak on Koh Phangan. I was sure the ants would have stripped him down by now. They work fast, ants. He probably never even got to the rotting stage. I pictured the freak on his back, a clean skeleton grinning through his loose covering of leaves, dappled in a few pinpricks of sunlight. In fact I'd left him on his front, lying on his arms, but there wasn't much sense in picturing the back of his head, so I revised the image to make it more aesthetic. The dappled effect was another revision. As I remember his shallow grave, no light filtered past the thick foliage above him. I just liked the idea that it did.

"Pretty," I said, putting the sweet in my mouth. "Maybe a monkey exploring the rib cage."

Jed looked at me. "Huh?"

"Or maybe a monkey would be too . . . kitsch . . ."

"Kitsch?"

"Monkeys."

"Have you listened to a word I've been saying?"

"No." I crunched the sweet and my tongue tingled with the sudden flood of lime. "I've been thinking about the freak on Koh Phangan."

"The dead guy you hid?"

"Yeah. Do you think he's been found yet?"

"Well . . ." Jed started to say, looking perplexed. "I suppose he might have been found if the girl was . . ." Then he slapped his head. "Jesus Christ! What the fuck am I talking about? Who cares about the dead freak? You should have left him where he was, and we've got much more important stuff to deal with right here!"

"I was only interested. And he's bound to get found one of these days."

"Shut up! Now listen! One of us has to get up to the island to check on Zeph and Sammy!"

"Oh, okay . . . Why not both of us?"

Jed made an exasperated sobbing sound. "Why do you think, you dozy fool? Someone has to stay here to look after the sick people, and almost all the fishing detail is out of action. Only the Swedes and Keaty are healthy, and Keaty's still missing."

I nodded. "I guess that means me."

"No. It means me. I need to stay here because I know some stuff about first aid, so you'll be going up to the island alone. Are you up to that?"

"You bet!" I said brightly. "No sweat at all!"

"Good. Now before you go I want you to find Keaty. There's about fifteen who are well enough to eat, so we need food. But I won't have time to go fishing, so he'll have to do it."

"Okay. And what should I do if Zeph and Sammy are on their way?"

"They won't be."

"But what if they are?"

Jed paused. "I'm trying not to think about it, but if they are, then get back here as fast as you can and tell me."

"And if there's no time?"

"Plan B."

". . . Which one?"

"You wait and see what happens. I'm positive they'll turn back at the dope fields, but if they don't, then follow them to the waterfall. Then, if they get down, intercept them and make fucking sure they know not to start talking about your map."

Across the clearing, Jesse appeared out of the longhouse. He wobbled toward the bathroom hut, got about a quarter of the way there, and threw up.

"Right," I said, suddenly feeling immensely cheerful. After last night I hadn't expected the next day to start so well. "I'd better find Keaty then."

———

There was only one bad note to the morning. On the way to the beach I passed Sal sitting outside the longhouse and she called me over. It turned out that Bugs—who was sitting next to her and giving me the evil eye—had told her what I'd done to him. Sal wanted an explanation.

I was slick. I said that I'd been exhausted and was only catching my breath before I gave him a hand outside, and if Bugs remembered it differently I was truly sorry but maybe his sickness had warped his memory of the incident. Then I suggested we shake on it, and that pleased Sal a lot. She was so hassled, what with everything else she had to deal with, that she was more than ready to get the distraction out of the way.

Bugs wasn't though. When I set off again for the beach he hobbled after me and called me a bastard. He was really angry, poking his finger in my chest and saying what he'd do to me if only he was well enough. I waited until he'd finished, then told him to fuck off. I wasn't going to let him spoil my good mood.

epitaph

Keaty was sleeping in the same spot I'd left him. High tide was well on its way and it wasn't going to be long before the wash reached his feet, so rather than wake him I decided to smoke a cigarette. I assumed he'd had a rough night and could do with the extra fifteen minutes. I was just getting down to the filter when the Swedes appeared. I put my finger to my lips, pointing at Keaty, and we walked out of earshot.

Karl, Sten, Christo. Considering that two of them ended up dead and the other ended up nuts, I feel bad that their names mean so little to me.

Like Jed, the Swedes had arrived at the beach uninvited, and although they'd probably found it easier to get accepted—having arrived second—it partly explained why they chose to fish outside the lagoon. They'd never been as involved in beach life as everyone else. They were around but they kept mainly to themselves, all sharing a single tent and often eating away from the crowd. The only times I ever saw them participate socially was on Sundays. They were good soccer players and everyone wanted them for their team.

If they had found integration difficult, it couldn't have helped that only one of them, Sten, could speak fluent English. Christo could just about muddle along but Karl was hopeless. As far as I knew, his vocabulary was limited to a few words based around fishing, like "fish" and "spear," and a couple of pleasantries. He would greet me with an uncertain "Hulloo Ruchard," and would bid me good morning even if he was just about to go to bed.

"So," I said when we were a safe distance from Keaty. "You've got your work cut out for you today."

Sten nodded. "But there is only half the camp to fish for, no? We only need to catch fifteen fishes. Not so difficult, I think . . . Would you like to fish with us?"

"No. I'll be staying here."

"You are sure? There is room for four in the boat, and you may be lonely working alone."

I smiled. "Thanks, but Keaty will wake up soon."

"Ah yes, Keaty. Is he sick?"

"No, he's fine. A bit down, but he didn't get food poisoning."

"That is good. Well, we should be going. We will see you later, Richard."

"Okay."

Sten said something to the other two in Swedish. Then they walked down to the shore and began swimming for the caves.

It was a short, bland conversation. Not the sort of conversation you'd want to be remembered by. I've tried to think of ways to jazz it up a bit, to make it more poignant or more of an epitaph, but the best I could think of was some kind of pun based around Sten saying, "See you later." Something along the lines of, I didn't see him later but I did see him late. Dead late. Late/dead. "I saw him later, though not in the way I expected . . . I saw him late!" It doesn't even make sense.

I also looked for extra information to provide about their characters, aside from their similarities with Jed and soccer skills, but our relationship had revolved entirely around a vague rivalry based on fish sizes. I barely knew them. If two of them hadn't died I doubt I'd have given them a second thought.

So, if I'm going to be honest, I suppose their epitaph must be this: If you've ever sat down with an old school friend and tried to remember all the kids that used to be in your class, the Swedes were the kids you remembered last.

The only thing I'd tag on the end was that they seemed like decent guys, and they shouldn't have had to die that way. Especially Sten.

Eventually I got bored with waiting for the tide to reach Keaty's feet, so I scooped some water in my hands and poured it on his head.

"Hi," I said after he'd recovered from the shock. "Did you sleep all right?"

He shook his head.

"Me neither." I squatted beside him. "I got about four hours."

". . . Are things bad in the camp?"

"They were last night. It's better now, but people are still pretty sick."

Keaty sat up and rubbed the sand off his legs and arms. "I should get back. Got to help."

"Then don't go back. You'll only have to come back here. They want you to do some fishing."

"They want *me* to go fishing?"

"That's what Jed said. All the fishers are ill except for the Swedes and Moshe, and Moshe's busy looking after people in the longhouse. That leaves you."

"It leaves you, too."

"Uh, yeah . . . but . . ." I thought for a moment. "I really need some sleep. I mean, when I said I got four hours, it was more like three. Or two and a half. I'm going to collapse if I don't get some rest." Keaty still didn't look convinced, so I added, "Also, if you turn up with food instead of empty-handed, it might calm Sal down a bit. She's pretty pissed off that you haven't been around to help."

"Yeah, I heard her calling for me last night. That's why I didn't go back to my tent." He shrugged wearily. "But I've got to go back sometime, and . . . I don't know if it's such a good idea, me going fishing. I mean, that's what caused all this."

"I haven't talked to anyone who sees it that way."

"I could help at the camp."

I shrugged. "The camp needs fish."

"You really think I should do the fishing?"

"Uh-huh. I was specifically told to find you and give that message."

Keaty frowned and twirled his fingers in his hair. He hadn't shaved it for so long that he was getting tiny dreads. ". . . All right then. If you're sure."

"Great." I patted his shoulder. "So I'll catch some sleep in the trees."

"Should I come and find you before I head back?"

I didn't answer. I was looking across the lagoon at the circle of cliffs, wondering how I'd swim over without him seeing.

Keaty repeated the question.

"Uh . . . No . . ."

If Keaty chose the main boulder to fish from, I could just manage an underwater leapfrog between the smaller boulders, hiding behind them when I needed air.

"What if you oversleep? Then Sal will get pissed off with you, too."

"I won't oversleep. I only need a few hours."

"Okay. And how many fish should I catch?"

"Ten or so. The Swedes will be fishing too, and most people won't be eating." I started toward the trees. "I'll see you back at the camp."

"Back at the camp. Sure."

I could feel his eyes on my back, so I dropped my shoulders and dragged my feet to show how tired I was. As I reached the grasses he called after me, "Hey, Rich, I'm sorry you got kept awake. I feel like it's my—"

I waved a hand. "No trouble," I called back. Then I slipped into the bushes.

It was easy to hide from Keaty as I swam across the lagoon, but it was infuriatingly slow. It took over twenty-five minutes just to make it to the caves, and it shouldn't have taken half that. The slowness gave me a nasty feeling inside. It was like

I wanted to take a deep breath, but however hard I sucked I could never fill the bottom of my lungs. I didn't shake the feeling until I'd climbed the chimney and worked my way around the cliff tops to the mainland.

the vc, the dmz, and me

I paused for a few minutes at the pass, looking down at the DMZ. There was no need, I knew, for me to descend the terraced slope, but at the same time I knew I would. I might never be alone on the island again and the opportunity was too big to miss. But I also had to check on Zeph and Sammy, so I continued upward toward our lookout point.

"Delta-One-Niner," I murmured as I located the figures. I could see two of them, one in the normal spot and the other about thirty meters to the right, standing down by the shore. The other three were obviously exploring, or busy doing whatever it was they did behind the treeline. "This is Alpha patrol. We confirm we have a positive ID, repeat, positive ID. Request further orders." In the back of my head I heard the fuzz of radio static. "Orders acknowledged. Will continue re-con as advised."

I dropped the binoculars and sighed, feeling the familiar frustration well up in me again. Their apparent inactivity no longer held any interest for me and had started to seem like a complicated insult. Part of me wanted to yell at them to get a fucking move on. If I'd thought it would work I'd have probably done it.

In that frame of mind, the time went slowly. I felt duty-bound to stick around for at least two hours, even though I was sure that nothing would happen. So every ten minutes I checked to see if they were up to anything new, and when I saw that they weren't—occasionally another would appear or two would disappear—I went back to daydreaming about what I'd do in the DMZ.

I had only one goal, because there was no sense in getting more grass. All I wanted to do was to see one of the dope guards. Not napping on a jungle path but active and armed and patrolling. That alone would satisfy me. It would be a proper engagement, a fair fight on equal terms. Him looking out for trespassers, and me trespassing.

The more I daydreamed, the harder it became to stay at my lookout post. Over the last half hour of my two-hour tour of duty, I counted the minutes like a kid waiting for Christmas morning. When the minute finally came—12:17—I made one last check on Zeph and Sammy. Typically, for the first time that day, none of the figures were visible, but I only hesitated for an instant. I made a quick check of the sea to make sure they hadn't started swimming, then said, "Fuck it" out loud and set off down the hill.

My daydream came true not far from the field that Jed and I had visited the previous day. I'd chosen to go there because it seemed logical that the best place to find a dope guard would be at a dope field, and also because it meant I was traveling on a route I'd taken before, if only once.

The contact came about three hundred meters above the terrace. I'd been just about to step around a thick copse of bamboo when I saw a flash of brown through the leaves, too golden to be anything but Southeast Asian skin. I froze, of course, holding the awkward position of three quarters of the way through a step. Then the brown vanished, and I heard the sound of rustling footsteps heading away from me.

I debated my options swiftly. To follow the guard was a serious risk, but a glimpsed impression was not what I'd had in mind, and the longer I delayed the less chance I'd have of seeing him again. Also, I knew that if I didn't follow him at once I'd probably lose my nerve and have to head back. This, I suppose, was what clinched it. I didn't even wait for the footsteps to get out of earshot before creeping around the thicket in pursuit.

The next ten minutes are vague in my memory. I was listening and looking so intently that, as when I made my original descent down to the waterfall, I was incapable of storing anything past the immediate. My memory returned when I heard his footsteps stop—making me stop too—and I spotted him less than fifteen feet away, taking a breather between two tall trees.

Gradually I crouched down and eased my head around a branch to get a better view. The first thing I registered was his markings: a black-blue dragon tattoo crawling up a densely muscled back, with a claw on one shoulder blade and flames on the other. Then I saw that he was the same guard I'd seen with Etienne and Françoise, the guy with the kick-boxer build. Recognizing him, I had to concentrate hard to control my breathing. At first it was from an adrenaline rush and a throwback to the fear I'd had on the plateau, but then it became awe.

The man was facing away from me in three-quarter angle, with one arm resting on his rifle and the other on his hips. Across his tattoo, running from his neck to the left side of his rib cage, was a deep, pale scar. Another scar cut a white line across the cropped hair on his head. A crumpled packet of

Krong Thip was tied to his upper arm with a filthy blue bandanna. He held his AK as casually as a snake charmer holding a cobra. He was perfect.

I knew he'd probably be gone in a minute or less, and my mind was frantic trying to record each aspect of his form. It was all I could do to stop myself from crawling nearer. If only I could have frozen him I'd have circled him like a statue in a museum, taking my time, noting his posture and listing the items he carried, studying his eyes to read what was happening behind them.

Just before he walked away he turned to face in my direction. Maybe he'd sensed someone watching him. He opened his mouth as he turned and I saw he had his top two front teeth missing. It was the final touch, a dangerous complement to the broken butt of his AK and the torn pouches on his baggy green combat trousers. At that moment, if I'd tried to slip further into the bushes he would have seen me. I could tell from his expression that he wasn't looking hard, just absently scanning, but he'd have noticed a movement. I stayed still. I was hypnotized. Even if he had seen me I doubt I'd have tried to run.

I didn't move for quite some time after the guard had gone. I realized that to leave at once would be the wrong thing to do, not so much because he might be near and out of sight, but because I needed a moment to collect my thoughts. I was dimly thinking of road accidents, of the drivers who crash soon after a narrow escape.

Hours later, on the way home after spending the afternoon at the lookout point, I paused for a second time at the pass. This time, the sight of the terraces and steamy evening jungle made me clench my fists. I was shaken by a powerful surge of jealousy toward Jed. He'd had the DMZ for over a year, all to himself. I couldn't begin to imagine what it would feel like, such extended private access, and the briefness of my own encounter only seemed to make it worse. I felt like I'd been damned by a glimpse of paradise.

split

The clearing was empty apart from Ella, who was gutting fish outside the kitchen hut, and Jed, who was chatting to her. Jed stood as I approached and I answered his inquisitive look with a subtle nod. He returned it, then excused himself and set off for the tents.

"Haven't you brought any fish?" Ella asked briskly. "I was hoping you'd be bringing some more."

"Oh . . ." I glanced at her bucket, which held less than ten small milk-fish. "No, Ella. Sorry, I haven't. . . . Is that all there is?"

"Yes. It's pathetic. I can't see how I'm supposed to make this stretch to half the camp. Was this the best you and Keaty could do?"

"Uh, yeah . . . but it's my fault. Last night caught up on me and I had to get some sleep. Keaty was working alone really. . . . But what about the Swedes? Haven't they brought any?"

"No," she replied irritably, gouging out a handful of guts and tossing them into the dirt. "They bloody well haven't. The only person who's brought me anything is Keaty. What time is it, anyway?"

"Six-thirty."

"Six-thirty! I've waited over two hours for them to show up. But most people are feeling much better than yesterday and that means they're getting hungry, so I can't wait any longer."

"I wonder what could be taking them so long."

"I haven't a clue. It's so stupid of them. Of all the possible days they might have gotten delayed, I can't believe they decided to pick this one."

I frowned. "Come on, Ella. That's ridiculous. I'm sure they didn't choose to get delayed. They know what's going on. . . . Maybe their engine broke down or they ran out of petrol."

Ella clucked her tongue as she sank her knife into the belly of the last fish. "Maybe," she said, with an expert snap of her wrist. "Maybe you're right. . . . But if you stop to think about it, they could have swum back by now."

I brooded on this last comment of Ella's as I walked toward the longhouse, because she was absolutely right. The Swedes could easily have swum back in two hours, even dragging the boat behind them. I knew from previous conversations that they never fished more than two hundred meters out to sea, a safety precaution in case they spotted another boat and had to get to cover in a hurry.

In a way then, I was already aware that something serious had happened. Logically, it was the only explanation. But I didn't act on my sense of foreboding, probably for the same reasons that no one else had. There were too many problems at hand to start worrying about new ones. For the others, perhaps it was a call for water that distracted them, or a need for sleep, or a puddle of sick that had to be cleaned up. For me, it was the prospect of seeing Etienne again. I'd been having second thoughts about the kiss. I still didn't think I'd been at fault, but I could see why Etienne had thought I was, and I was sure that our next meeting would be awkward. So as I pushed open the longhouse, I also pushed thoughts of the Swedes to the back of my head, with no more consideration than a vague decision to worry about it later.

My immediate impression inside the longhouse was that some kind of division had occurred while I was away. A tense silence greeted my arrival, shortly followed by a low buzz of noise. At the near end was my old fishing detail, along with Jesse, Cassie, and Leah, another member of the gardening detail. At the far end, in the area of my bed, were Sal, Bugs, and the remainder of the gardening and carpentry details. Moshe and the two Yugoslavian girls were sitting between the two groups, apparently neutral.

I assessed the situation. Then I shrugged. If a division had occurred, choosing sides wasn't going to be an issue. I closed the door behind me and went over to my old detail.

Nobody spoke for a couple of seconds after I sat down—which gave me a brief scare, since I automatically assumed that the split was related to me. A chain of events quickly began to form in my mind, connected to the kiss. Perhaps Etienne had told Françoise, and Françoise was furious, and everyone had heard, and the tension was nothing to do with divisions in the camp but an embarrassed reaction to my arrival. Fortunately, I was way off track, as was shown when Françoise leaned forward and took my hand. "There has been trouble," she said in a hushed voice.

"Trouble?" I withdrew my hand slightly clumsily, glancing at Etienne, who was watching me with a completely unreadable expression. "What kind of trouble?"

Keaty coughed and pointed to his left eye. It was badly puffed up. "Bugs hit me," he said simply.

"Bugs *hit* you?"

"Uh-huh."

I was too shocked to speak, so Keaty continued.

"I turned up with the fish around four and hung around with Jed in the tents. Then I came to the longhouse about half an hour ago, and as soon as Bugs saw me he jumped up and threw a punch."

"What happened then?" I eventually said.

"Jean pulled him off, and then there was a massive argument between that lot"—he gestured to the group at the far end—"and this lot. Personally, I stayed out of it. I was trying to stop my nosebleed."

"He hit you because of the squid?"

"He said it was because I wasn't around to help last night."

"No!" I shook my head angrily. "I know why he hit you. It had nothing to do with being missing last night. It was because he shat himself."

Keaty smiled without humor. "That makes a lot of sense, Rich."

I struggled to keep my voice steady. My tongue felt thick and I was suddenly in such a rage that I could actually see blackness around the edge of my vision. "It makes sense to *me*, Keaty," I said tightly. "I know the way his head works. It was the knock to his pride, slipping around in his own shit. That's why he hit you."

I stood up, and Gregorio caught my arm.

"Richard, what are you doing?"

"I'm going to kick his head in."

"At *last*," Jesse said, rising. "That's *exactly* what I've been saying we should do. I'll help."

"No!"

I looked around. Françoise had also stood up.

"This is too stupid! Both of you sit down now!"

At that moment there was a jeer from the far end of the longhouse. Bugs was calling to us. "Oh, let me guess! The cavalry's arrived!"

"I'm going to stick a spear in your fucking *neck!*" I yelled back.

"I'm worried!"

Jesse howled. "You'd better be fuckin' worried! You'd better be very fuckin' worried!"

"Is that right, you kiwi cunt?"

"You've got no fuckin' idea how right it is!"

Then Sal was standing too. *"That's enough!"* she screamed. *"Both of you! All of you! Enough!"*

Silence.

The two groups stared at each other for a long thirty seconds. Then Françoise stabbed a finger at the ground.

"Sit!" she hissed. So we sat.

Ten minutes later I was crawling up the walls. I wanted a cigarette so severely I thought my chest was going to cave in, but my supply was at the other end of the longhouse and there was no way I could get them. In an effort to help, Cassie rolled a joint, but it didn't do much good. It was nicotine I needed. The dope only made the craving worse.

Not long after, Ella brought in the food she'd cooked, but she'd burned the rice and without Unhygienix's magic touch the fish stew tasted like seawater. Plus she had to hand it round in the most uncomfortable atmosphere imaginable, which baffled her and made her think it was her cooking. No one bothered to explain, so she left the longhouse nearly in tears.

Jed stuck his head through the door at eight-fifteen, gazed around curiously, then disappeared.

So that's how the time passed, a succession of tense episodes, all serving to distract us from the fact that the Swedes still hadn't returned from fishing.

At a quarter to nine the longhouse door banged open.

"Oh there you are . . ." Keaty started to say, but the words dried up in his throat.

Karl was half bent over, barely illuminated by the candles.

It was the expression on his face that instantly informed us there was something badly wrong, but I think it was his arms that had choked Keaty. They seemed to be absurdly dislocated, jutting out from the top of his shoulders. And there was what looked like a tear in his right hand. Between his thumb and forefinger the split continued down to his wrist, so that the two halves hung like a limp lobster claw.

"Jesus Christ," said Jesse loudly, and all over the longhouse I heard movement as people rose to get a better look.

Karl took a single heavy step toward us, moving into the brighter candlelight. That was when we realized that the mutilated arms belonged to the person he was carrying on his back—Sten. Abruptly Karl collapsed, toppling forward without making any effort to break his fall. Sten slipped off him, balancing for a moment on his side, then rolling over. There was a ragged semicircle of flesh as large as a basketball missing from his side, and the remainder of his stomach area had been flattened to no more than four inches thick.

Etienne was the first to move. He barged past me, almost knocking me to the ground.

When I looked up he was bending over Sten, trying to give him mouth-to-mouth resuscitation. Then I heard Sal call behind me, "What's happened?" and at once Karl began yelling at the top of his lungs. For a minute he yelled nonstop, filling the longhouse with a high, frantic sound that made some people cover their ears or yell equally loudly, for no apparent reason other than to block him out. It was only after Keaty had grabbed him, shouting at him to shut up, that he managed to form an intelligible word. "Shark."

the third man

The stunned quiet after Karl said "shark" only lasted a heartbeat. Then we all started jabbering again as abruptly as we'd all shut up. A circle quickly formed around Karl and Sten—the same kind of circle you get in a schoolyard fight, jostling for position while keeping a safe distance—and suggestions started flying thick and fast. It was a crisis after all. Whatever else a crisis causes, it causes a buzz, so everyone wanted to be in on the act. Etienne and Keaty, tending to Sten and Karl, respectively, were instructed, "He needs water!" and, "Put him in the recovery position!" and, "Hold his nose!"

"Hold his nose" was directed at Etienne by one of the Yugo girls, because you have to hold a victim's nose when giving mouth-to-mouth to stop the air from escaping. I thought it was a stupid thing to say. You could see the air bubbling out of the hole in Sten's side, so his lungs were obviously fucked, and anyway, you couldn't imagine anyone looking more dead. His eyes were open but showing the whites, he was as limp as rags, and there was no blood coming out of his wounds. In fact, just about all the advice was stupid. Karl could hardly be put in the recovery position while he was jerking around and screaming, and I didn't have a clue what use he'd have for water. Morphine yes, water no. The only person talking sense was Sal, who was yelling at everyone to get back and shut up. No one took any notice though. Her role as leader had been temporarily suspended, so her good suggestions were about as useful as the bad ones.

The whole scene left me feeling flustered. I was telling myself, "Alert but calm," and waiting for my head to come up with the kind of suggestion that was needed. Something that would cut through the chaos, creating a stern efficiency that was appropriate to the gravity of the situation. Specifically, something like the way Etienne had acted on the plateau. With that in mind, I considered pushing my way through to Sten and saying, "Leave him, Etienne. He's dead." But I couldn't shake the idea that it would sound like a line from a bad movie, and I wanted a line from a good movie. Instead I pushed my way backward through the crowd, which was easy as most people were trying to get closer.

As soon as I was out of the circle I began thinking a great deal more objectively. Two realizations hit me at once. Number one was that I now had a chance to get my cigarettes. Number two was Christo. Nobody had even mentioned the third Swede, who might have been on the beach, wounded and waiting for help to arrive. Possibly even dead like Sten.

I dithered for a couple of moments like a cartoon character, first looking one way, next the other. Then I made my decision and ran down the longhouse, passing the few squid-sufferers who were still too sick to see what was going on. I lit up on the run back, taking two matches to catch the flare of the phosphorus. Just before I ducked out of the longhouse door, I shouted, "Christo!" but I didn't wait to see if anyone had heard me.

Through the jungle, I cursed myself for not having also grabbed a torch. I couldn't see much apart from the red glow of my cigarette, occasionally brightening as it burned through a spider's web. But having recently walked the path in darkness, en route to seeing the phosphorescence a couple of nights before, I didn't have too much trouble. My only mishap was walking straight into a bamboo thicket which had been recently cut for spears. My tough feet were okay. It was my shins and calves that got cut, which bothered me because I knew they'd sting if I had to go into the salt water.

On the beach, however, there was enough moonlight to see clearly. Across the sand were deep tracks where Karl had dragged Sten. He seemed to have reached the beach about twenty meters from the path to the clearing, come down, missed the entrance to the path, and doubled back. Christo, I noted as I dropped the butt, couldn't have made it as far as the shore. In the light from the moon, the sand was silver. The odd coconut husks and fallen palm branches were black. If he'd been there, I'd have seen him.

I took a deep breath and sat down a few feet from the water, juggling options and ideas. Christo wasn't on the beach and I hadn't passed him on the path—unless I'd walked over him unawares—so he was either in the lagoon, in the open sea, at the cave that led to the sea. If he was in the open sea, he was probably dead. If he was in the lagoon, he was either on a boulder or floating facedown. If he was at the cave, he had to be at one of its two entrances, maybe too tired to swim the lagoon or too injured to get through the underwater passage.

That was the Christo angle. The shark angle was more straightforward. It, or they, could be anywhere. I had no way of knowing any more than that, short of spotting a silhouette fin weaving across the lagoon, so I figured I'd be better off if I ignored the shark angle altogether.

"I bet he's in the caves," I said, and lit another cigarette to help me think. Then I heard a noise behind me, a padding footstep on the sand.

"Christo?" I called, and heard myself in stereo. The other person had called Christo at the exact same moment.

"No," we both answered together.

A pause.

I waited a few seconds, looking in all directions, unable to spot the figure. "Who then?"

No answer.

"Who then?" I repeated, standing. ". . . Is that . . . Is that you, Mister Duck?"

Still no answer.

A swell swept up the sand and tugged at my feet. I had to take a quick step forward to keep my balance. The following swell was just as strong and I had to take another step. The next thing I knew, the water was up to my knees and my cuts were smarting at the salt. The second cigarette, which I'd forgotten about, fizzled out as my hand hit the water.

I tried to swim along the route Christo would most likely have taken between the cave and the beach, pausing every so often to climb a boulder and scan around me. By the time I'd crossed three quarters of the lagoon, I could see flashlights on the beach. The others had arrived, but I didn't call to them. I hadn't decided whether their distant presence was a reassurance or a drag.

shadowed

Christo's name was being called. Low-pitched and high-pitched, boys' voices and girls' voices, floating across the lagoon. I didn't like the sound. From my position, resting on a boulder by the entrance to the cave, the call was always answered by an echo. It gave me the creeps, so I swam into the cave to cut the sound out. Then, once started, I didn't stop. I swam straight ahead until I bumped blindly against the rock face where the passage ducked below the water level, took a lungful, and dived.

It was very exciting underwater. The rock walls, never warmed by sunlight, cooled and deadened the water. I felt as if I'd dared to enter a forbidden area; the zone I'd shied away from with Etienne and Françoise, diving for sand on Koh Samui. Braver now, I thought dreamily, relaxing my legs and slowing my arm strokes. I wasn't hurried. Christo and the shark seemed rather distant concerns. I was almost enjoying myself, and I knew my lungs were practiced enough to keep me under for over a minute and a half without serious discomfort.

Every few feet I stopped and groped around to make sure I wasn't accidentally heading down the side passage to the air pocket. In the process, I discovered that the central passage was far wider than I'd previously imagined. At full arms' length I couldn't touch either of its sides, only the barnacle-covered ceiling and floor. I realized, with a reproachful grimace, that to have ended up in the air pocket I must have strayed quite a way off course.

I grimaced harder when I came up on the seaward side of the cliffs. A strong night swell gave me a harsh reality check, pulling me out of my otherworldly stupor by knocking me against the rocks. I had to clamber awkwardly out of the water, slipping on algae and cutting my legs yet again. When I'd found my balance I looked around for Christo and yelled his name, without a lot of hope because the moonlight was bright enough for me to see he wasn't there. I could, however, see the boat. It was floating freely in the small cove that served as its port and hiding place, untied. I made my way over and scooped the rope out of the sea, securing the boat with as many granny knots as the rope's length would allow, not very nautical but the best I knew how. Then I perched on a small rock shelf and wondered what I should do next.

The problem was, I could easily have missed Christo on

several stages of my search, the boulders particularly. It was possible that he'd already been found and was back at camp. But I also had a powerful sense that I hadn't missed him. The untied boat told me that the Swedes had gotten as far as the entrance to the cave. If Christo hadn't been injured, he'd have made the swim with Karl. If he had been injured, however, Karl would have left him where I was sitting, intending to come back for him later.

"Unless . . ." I muttered, clicking my fingers and shivering in the sea breeze.

Unless he'd been killed outright at sea, in which case it was a safe bet he'd never be found.

"Or . . ."

Or he'd only been injured a little. He'd been fit enough to make the swim through the underwater passage. He'd swum under with Karl, helping him with Sten, but something had happened. Swimming three men wide. Slightly hurt. Had to be scared and confused.

"That's it," I said firmly.

Karl wouldn't have realized Christo had gone until he came up in the lagoon. With Sten to deal with, maybe still alive, he couldn't go back. Maybe he waited for as long as a man could last without breathing. One or two desperate minutes extra to be sure. Maybe then he gave up.

"That's it. Christo's in the air pocket."

I stood up, filled my lungs, and dived back into the water. I found the side passage to the air pocket on my third attempt.

I surfaced, incredibly, into stars. I wondered if I'd missed the turning a fourth time, got disorientated, come up in the open sea or the lagoon. But the stars were beside and ahead of me. The stars were everywhere, unnaturally dense, within reaching distance and a thousand miles away.

Lack of oxygen, I thought, and took a tentative breath.

The air tasted better than the last time in the air pocket, maybe freshened by an extra-low tide, but the stars didn't go away. I took another breath, shut my eyes, waited, opened them again. The stars remained, twinkling away, even a little brighter. "Impossible," I whispered. "This makes no—"

A murmur cut me off, coming from somewhere in the thick constellation. I paused, treading water slowly.

"Here . . ." said a quiet voice.

I pushed my hands out and felt a rock ledge, then I ran my hands along and felt skin. "Christo! Thank God! I've been—"

"Richard?"

"Yes."

"Help me."

"Yes. I'm here to help."

I continued feeling along the skin, working out which part of the body I was touching. It was surprisingly difficult to tell. What I first took to be an arm turned out to be a leg, and what I took to be a mouth turned out to be a wound.

Christo groaned loudly.

I shook my head. "I'm sorry . . . Are you badly hurt?"

". . . I have . . . some injury . . ."

"Okay. Do you think you're able to swim?"

"I do not know . . ."

"Because you have to swim. We have to get out of here."

"Out?"

"We've got to get out of the air pocket."

"Air . . . pocket . . . ?" he repeated, forming the sounds uncertainly.

"Air pocket. Uh . . . this little cave. We need to get out of this cave."

"But sky," he muttered. "Stars."

I frowned, surprised that he could see the stars, too. "No. They aren't stars. They're . . ." I hesitated. Then I reached up and my hand sank into cold strands of hanging seaweed. "Not stars," I finished, managing a short laugh, and pulled down a glittering strand.

"Not stars?" He sounded upset.

"Phosphorescence."

There was a small space left on the ledge, so I hauled myself out of the water and sat beside him. "Listen, Christo, I'm afraid we're going to have to try for this swim. There's no choice."

No reply.

"Hey, did you get that?"

". . . Yes."

"So what we'll do is, I'll swim ahead using my arms, and you'll have to hold on to my legs and try to kick. Are your legs injured?"

". . . Not legs. It is my . . . my . . ." He felt for my hand and put it someplace on his torso.

"So you can kick. We'll be fine. No sweat."

"Yes."

His voice sounded like it was getting fainter, so I talked my plans out loud to keep him awake. "Now our only problem is going to be finding the right passage out of here. If I remember right, there are four passages to choose from, and we don't want to get the wrong one. You understand?"

". . . I understand."

"Good. Let's do it, then." I leaned forward to drop back into the water, but stopped myself just as I was about to slip off the ledge.

"What?" asked Christo feebly, sensing that something had happened.

I didn't answer. I was transfixed by a chilling and beautiful sight, a slender comet cruising through the blackness beneath my feet.

"What happens, Richard?"

"Nothing . . . There's just . . . uh . . . something down there."

"The shark?" Christo's voice instantly rose to a frightened sob. "Is it this shark?"

"No, no. Definitely not. Don't worry." I watched the comet carefully. Actually, when I'd first seen it I had thought it was the shark, which is why I'd hesitated before answering Christo. But now I was sure it wasn't. Something about the way it moved wasn't right; it wasn't gliding and it was too jerky. It was more like a person.

"It's probably me," I said with a drunken smile.

"You?"

"My wake . . ." I giggled. "My shadow."

"What? I do not . . ."

I patted Christo's leg gently. "It's probably a shoal of fish."

The comet continued on its leisurely path and then, curiously, began to shorten. It took me a moment to realize it was passing into one of the passageways leading out.

"Okay, Christo," I said, putting a cautious hand on the back of my head. I'd suddenly felt as if part of my skull had fallen away and its contents were streaming out or expanding like vapor. Relieved to find hard bone and wet, matted hair, I allowed myself to slip into the water. "I think I know which direction to take."

Within a few strokes I understood that the passage was not the one leading back to the original cave. It twisted almost immediately to the right, whereas the other passage was virtually straight. But I was also confident, so I didn't attempt to turn back. Ten or so meters along we found a second air pocket, and ten meters further we found another. At the last air pocket we came up into fresh air. Ahead was the exit, circled by darkness. Through it I could see real stars and the real sky, just bright enough to pick out the faint black shapes of palm trees. Claws on pencil arms, running along the cliff top as it curved around to the mainland.

I laid the exhausted Christo out on the flat shelf beneath the lightning-bolt fissure and walked forward a couple of steps so I was looking over the coral gardens.

"Mister Duck?" I hissed softly. "Daffy? It was you, wasn't it? You're here."

"Yeah," Mister Duck replied, from so nearby it made me jump. "I'm here."

incoming

politics

"Damn," I said, spotting Cassie. She was standing near the kitchen hut, talking to Ella. It meant I had no choice but to pass her. My only other options were to walk directly across the center of the clearing or to skirt around and come from behind the longhouse. In other words, passing Bugs or passing Sal. Not really options at all.

I sighed. Getting from one side of the clearing to the other had become like an eye-contact obstacle course. It was true that the shark attack had diverted attention away from the flare-up in the longhouse, but although an unspoken truce had been agreed, the tensions behind the incident were still there. Tactically, I had to hand it to Bugs. His group—basically the carpenters and gardeners minus Cassie and Jesse—had taken over the center of the clearing. Starting from the first afternoon after the shark attack, I'd come back from the island to find them all sitting there in a loose circle, smoking dope and chatting quietly. So as well as the commanding vantage point they had over the camp, there was a psychological aspect. It was like they represented the establishment, making the rest of us feel like dissenters.

Our dissenters' role was accentuated by the fact that, unlike the Bugs group, we had no sense of unity. In effect we were several subgroups. There was my old fishing detail and Keaty, which I included myself in, but there was also Jed, and I included myself with him as well. Then there was Moshe's detail, who seemed uncertain of where their affiliations lay, and there were the cooks. The cooks, as a result of Ella, partly included Jesse and Cassie. But you could also partly include

Jesse and Cassie with my old fishing detail, because of their friendship with Keaty.

Finally, there were Sal and Karl. Karl was a law unto himself, drifting somewhere in outer space, and Sal was trying extremely hard to appear neutral—though we all knew where her loyalties would lie if push came to shove.

If it sounds complicated, that's because it was.

This, then, was the politics involved in crossing the clearing, and we all had to deal with it to the same degree. Except me, that is, who had an extra burden to deal with in the form of Cassie. Ever since the incident where Bugs had shat himself, she'd been treating me like I was mentally unstable, talking slowly, carefully enunciating each word, using an evenly modulated tone, as if she thought a sudden noise would scare me. It was really getting on my nerves. But I'd have shinned up a rocket ship tree to avoid passing Bugs, and Sal would make me give her a troublesome report on our guests on the neighboring island, so Cassie it had to be. Biting my lip and looking intently at the ground, I moved out from behind the foliage and set off in her direction. Out of the corner of my eye I could see that she was deep in conversation with Ella. I'm going to make it, I thought optimistically, but I was wrong.

"Richard," she said, just as I was about to move out of her range.

I looked up with a studiously blank expression.

"How are you?"

"Fine," I replied quickly. "On my way to see the patient."

She smiled. "No, Richard. I mean, how *are* you?"

"Fine," I repeated.

"I think this has been harder for you than anyone."

"Oh, well, not really."

"Finding Christo . . ."

"It wasn't so bad . . ."

"And now you have to work up on the island without company, without . . . support."

I shrugged helplessly. It would have been quite impossible to explain that from my point of view, the three days since Sten's death had been great. Jed's knowledge of first aid meant he was spending all his time looking after Christo, and that meant I got to spend my days alone in the DMZ.

Alone in a manner of speaking, anyway.

"But maybe being without company is a good thing, Cassie. It gives me time to think and come to terms with what's happened." From similar encounters, I knew this was the right thing to say.

Cassie widened her eyes as if she hadn't considered this, but now that she had, yes, it was a good idea and she was impressed I'd thought of it. "That's a *positive* attitude," she said warmly. "Well done."

I felt that this exchange was enough for me to disappear without appearing rude, so I made my excuses and continued on my way.

I was aiming for the hospital tent. More accurately, the Swedes' tent, but seeing as Sten was dead and Karl had started living on the beach, I'd begun calling it the hospital tent. Disappointingly, no one else did. Even though I'd made a point of using the new name at every opportunity, it had stubbornly refused to catch on.

"Back early today," said Jed when I climbed in. "It's still light." He sounded very tired and was sweating like a pig. It was baking under the canvas, even with the flap pegged open.

"Got hungry, needed a fag. Nothing much going on."

"No developments then."

I looked at Christo.

"He's asleep. It's okay."

"Oh . . . well yeah, no developments," I lied. There had

been a very particular development, but not one I could go into. "Just the same as always."

"So we're lucky again. I wonder how long it will last."

"Mmm . . . I got some more grass, by the way."

"More? Richard, you . . ." Jed shook his head. "We've got grass coming out of our ears. Every day you've brought some back."

"People are smoking a lot at the moment."

"We'd need all the hippies in Goa to smoke through your supplies, and if you take too much the guards might notice."

I nodded. The same thought had crossed my mind, though with a different slant. I'd been hoping that my regular expeditions would get the guards on their toes. They were so pathetically easy to avoid that it made you wonder why they were there in the first place.

"So what about Christo?" I asked, changing the subject. "Any developments with him?"

Jed rubbed his eyes. "Yes. He's getting worse."

"Delirious?"

"No, just in pain. If he's awake. He spends most of the time unconscious and he's running a bad fever. Without a thermometer it's hard to tell, but I'm sure it's higher than yesterday . . . To tell you the truth"—Jed lowered his voice—"I'm getting seriously worried about him."

I frowned. Christo looked okay to me. When I'd seen him in the daylight the morning after rescuing him, I'd felt slightly let down by the undramatic nature of his injuries. Apart from a single cut on his arm—the cut I'd mistaken for a mouth—his only wound was a large bruise on his stomach from where the shark had rammed him. The injuries were so superficial that he'd walked around on the first day, trying to find Karl. He'd only collapsed on the second day, which we'd thought was a result of stress or possibly a relapse of the food poisoning.

"I mean," Jed continued, "the bruise should be going down, shouldn't it?"

"You're the doctor, Jed."

"I'm not a fucking doctor. That's the point."

I leaned over to take a look. "Well, it's blacker than it was. Not so purple. I think that means it's healing."

"Do you know that for a fact?"

"Not for a fact, no." I paused. "I'm sure it'll just be the food poisoning that's keeping him low. Jesse is still getting gripes."

"Uh-huh."

"And so is Bugs . . . unfortunately!" I added, with a mischievous wink that Jed either missed or ignored. "Well, I'm going to get some food and catch up with Françoise and the others."

"Okay. Leave a cigarette, will you? And come back later. Nobody comes in to check on me apart from you and Unhygienix. I think they're avoiding having to see Christo . . . Pretending it hasn't happened maybe."

"Pretty hard," I said, chucking him the packet. "Sten's still lying in that sleeping bag around the back of the longhouse. It's right on the other side from where I sleep, and I can smell him through the walls."

Jed glanced at me. There was obviously something he wanted to say, so I nodded, to say, "Go on," but he only sighed. "Tomorrow morning," he said sadly. "Sal said she's given up on trying to persuade Karl to be there, so he'll be buried by the waterfall tomorrow morning."

dissent

Sal had been sitting in her usual spot outside the longhouse entrance, which, if one wanted to get to the beach, was unavoidable without an exhaustingly roundabout route via the Khyber Pass. But to my relief she'd moved by the time I left the hospital tent. I assumed she'd gone to the center of the clearing to talk to Bugs; something I could have confirmed with a simple turn of the head, but I didn't want to look in the enemy's direction so I took it on faith. My mistake. I should have confirmed. Just like with Cassie, I was sprung as I thought I was leaving the danger zone—in this case past the longhouse, about to join the path from the clearing to the beach.

"Richard," said a stern voice.

Sal was standing chest-deep in the shrubs beside the track. She'd clearly been hiding there in order to ambush me. "You were hiding," I blurted, surprised into speaking the truth.

"Yes, Richard. I was." She stepped forward, delicately parting the ferns with a pudgy hand. "I didn't want to force you into one of your ludicrously transparent evasion exercises."

"Evasion? I haven't been evad—"

"You have."

"No, really."

"Save it, Richard."

This was the third time she'd used my name, so I knew she meant business. I gave up the pretense with a feeble grin.

"Wipe that smirk off your face," she said immediately. "Have you got any idea what trouble you've been causing me?"

"Sorry, Sal."

"Sorry doesn't cut it. You're a pain in the ass. How simple were your instructions?"

"Very simple, Sal."

"*Very* simple. But you've forgotten them already."

"No, I—"

"Repeat them."

". . . The instructions?"

"Yes."

I had to make an effort to keep a schoolboy's insolence out of my voice. "While Jed is looking after Christo, it's my responsibility to keep you up to date on . . ." I stammered and a cold flush pricked my neck. I'd nearly said Zeph's and Sammy's names.

"On?" Sal demanded.

". . . on our potential new arrivals."

"Exactly. Now perhaps you can tell me why you're finding that one little task so difficult."

"There was nothing to tell today. No developments, same as always."

"Wrong." Sal shook a finger at me. I watched the little hammocks of fat under her upper arm wobble indignantly. "Wrong, wrong, wrong. If there's nothing to tell, I want to hear it. Otherwise I worry, and I've got a *lot* to worry about at the moment, so I don't need you making things worse. Get it?"

"Yes."

"Good." She lowered her finger and took a breath to compose herself. "I don't mean to be tough on you, but I just can't deal with extra hassles at the moment. Morale is . . . well, morale is bad."

"We'll pull through."

"I know we will, Richard," she said curtly. "I have no doubt of it. But to make certain, I want you to pass on a message to all your friends."

". . . Sure."

"Yes. I want you to tell them that for the past three days, for obvious reasons, I've been tolerating this absurd rift that has blown up in the camp."

I made a rather foolish attempt at appearing innocent. "Rift?"

"Rift! As in half the camp not talking to the other half! As in people threatening to stick spears in other people's necks!"

I reddened.

"Now you may or may not know that tomorrow morning we're going to be burying Sten. I want that burial to mark the end of the tension so that some good can come out of this appalling tragedy. I also want you to know that I'm giving the same message to Bugs. I don't want you guys thinking he's getting preferential treatment because he's my man. Okay?"

"Okay."

Sal nodded. Then she put the base of her palm flat on her forehead, and held it there silently for several seconds.

Poor Sal, I thought. I hadn't been very understanding of the stress she was under, and I made a resolution to be a good deal more understanding in the future. I wasn't even sure why I'd been avoiding her. My problem was with Bugs. I'd unfairly allowed my dislike of him to spill over to her.

"So," she said eventually, "where were you going before I nabbed you?"

"To the beach. Looking for Françoise . . . and checking up on Karl."

"Karl . . ." Sal muttered something indistinct and looked up at the canopy. When she looked down she seemed surprised to find me still with her. "Go on then," she said, ushering me away. "What are you waiting for? Get lost."

It was getting close to six o'clock when I reached the beach, cool enough to walk slowly on the dry sand if I'd wanted to. But I didn't. I was playing one of my games, and it required walking in the damp sand by the shore.

The aim was to leave the perfect footprint, and it was a lot harder and more preoccupying than it might sound. If the sand was the dry side of damp, the footprint crumbled; the moist side and it melted as the squeezed-out water seeped back in. Then there was the application of pressure. The toes sank too deeply with a normal step and flawed the imprint. The alternative, taking an artificial step with even pressure, created a good imprint at the cost of ethics. This was the compromise I wrestled with.

In this way I made my way along the beach, hopping, pausing, groaning, mashing up bad prints in frustration. My eyes were always pointed downward, so I didn't realize that I'd reached my friends until I was within a couple of meters of them.

"Are you going insane, Rich?" I heard Keaty say. "If you are, tell us. It might mean you'll have better luck getting through to Karl."

"I'm trying to make the perfect footprint," I replied without raising my head. "It's really difficult."

Keaty laughed in a way that told me he was stoned. "The perfect footprint, huh? Yeah, that's getting pretty close to insane. And more original than trying to draw the perfect circle."

"Circle?"

"It's what mad people do."

"Oh." I stamped out my last effort and trudged over, disappointed to see that Françoise wasn't with them. "Is that what Karl is doing?"

"Nope. He's too mad even for circles."

"Actually," Etienne interrupted, not about to join in with Keaty's flippant appraisal, "Karl is not mad. He is *dans un état de choque*."

Keaty arched his eyebrows. "Uh-huh. Just what I figured . . . Now maybe you could tell us what it means."

"I do not know the correct English. It is why I said it in French."

"That's helpful."

"If you had been interested to help, you would be taking Karl to Koh Phangan," said Etienne stiffly, and stood up. "And I am tired of arguing this with you. Excuse me, Richard. I am going back to camp. You will tell Françoise when she returns?"

"Okay," I replied uncomfortably. I'd obviously turned up in the middle of something, and I wasn't at all happy with the idea that my friends had been arguing. We had to stick together, even if Sal was going to be calling for a truce tomorrow.

Etienne began walking away. A couple of seconds later, Keaty turned to Gregorio and hissed, "Why the fuck weren't you backing me up?"

Gregorio looked at his hands pensively. "I do not know . . . I thought perhaps he was right."

"He isn't right. How can he be right?"

"Hold on," I said, first checking behind me to make sure that Etienne was out of earshot. "Was Etienne being serious about Koh Phangan?"

Keaty nodded. His tiny dreadlocks were still short enough to stand bolt upright and they seemed to accentuate his expression of incredulity. "Dead serious. He's been saying it all day. Says he's going to bring it up with Sal."

"But he *must* know we can't take him to Koh Phangan. What would we say? 'Here's a friend of ours who's been attacked by a shark and had a nervous breakdown on our secret beach. Well, we'll be off then. See you . . .' "

"He thinks we could take him there and drop him off near Hadrin."

"That's ridiculous. Even if he didn't give everything away, how would we know he got looked after? There's a million fucked-up freaks over there. If someone saw him wasting away on the sand, they'd just ignore him." I shook my head. "No way. The best thing for Karl is for him to be here."

"I've been telling that to Etienne all day. But wait, it gets worse. He wants to drop Sten off on Koh Phangan as well."

"Sten?"

"Yep."

"But he's dead! What would be the point of . . ."

"His family. Etienne thinks we have to let them know what's happened to their son. See, if we left them both on the beach, then Karl would definitely be noticed and Sten's family would be contacted."

I smiled in disbelief. "Yeah, and meanwhile we'd definitely get discovered. We'd be finished. It's the worst idea I ever heard."

"Tell me about it," said Keaty. "And while you're at it," he added, pointing at Gregorio, "tell him."

Gregorio lay on his back to avoid our accusing stares. "I only think we should think about what Etienne says. If Karl is not talking to any people here, maybe he will not talk to any people on Koh Phangan."

"No," said Keaty. "He'll talk, eventually. And when he does, I'd rather he did it to us. Not some fucking Thai cop or Swedish shrink."

I couldn't have put it better myself.

whoosh, boom, 333

After all the discussion about Karl, I decided I ought to go and see him myself. Or that's what I told Keaty and Gregorio. Really I was just interested in catching up with Françoise, whom I'd barely seen over the past few days. The main reasons were our different work details and the hectic circumstances, though I hadn't been very active in seeking her out. Following the misunderstood kiss, I'd been slightly wary of giving Etienne any reasons to be suspicious.

I found Françoise by Karl's hole, about four hundred meters further on from Keaty and Gregorio. Karl had dug the hole when he'd decamped to the beach. It wasn't much of a hole: thigh-high if he stood up, chest-deep if he sat down. More impressive was the shelter which Etienne and Keaty had rigged up. Because Karl refused to budge from his hole all through the day, they'd been worried about him getting sunstroke. They'd found three long palm branches and tied them against each other like a teepee. The gaps in the fronds wouldn't have stopped rain but they kept him in the shade.

I was expecting Françoise to be in a bad mood, as everyone else seemed to be, so I was happily surprised when she ran over and gave me a hug.

"Richard!" she said. "Thank you! I have not thanked you yet! So, thank you!"

I paused. "What for?"

"For helping me when I was sick. Really, you were so kind. I wanted to tell you before, but there was never a good chance. Always so much to do. We have to catch all the extra fish now and then I stay with Karl, and often you are not back until late."

"Françoise, don't give it another thought. It was nothing. Anyway, you did the same for me once."

"Yes, with your fever." She smiled, then looked at me straight in the eyes, and suddenly the smile turned into a sly chuckle. "You kissed me!"

My eyes flicked away. "I thought you were sleeping . . ."

"I was. Etienne told me the next day."

"Oh," I said, mentally unleashing a stream of curses at Etienne's big mouth. "Well . . . I hope you don't mind . . . It was sort of complicated . . ."

"Of course I do not mind! You know, when you were ill I also kissed you."

"I was never completely sure if I dreamed that or not."

"You did not dream it. And remember the next morning! You were so worried!"

I nodded, remembering my awkwardness and Françoise's Exocet-style questions extremely clearly.

"So tell me," she said. "Why do you say it was complicated?"

"Well . . . complicated is probably the wrong, uh . . . It wasn't like the kiss was . . . The kiss wasn't . . ." I stopped myself and started again. "I'm not sure what Etienne told you, but he took the kiss the wrong way. I was kissing you because you were so sick, and there was so much other sickness around that once I'd started . . . it was kind of hard to stop."

"How was Etienne taking it?"

Whoosh, I thought. Boom.

". . . Well, I guess he thought it was . . . you know . . ."

"A sexy kiss."

"Mmm."

Françoise laughed again. Then she leaned over and planted a little kiss on my cheek.

"Was that a sexy kiss?"

"No," I replied; only a small fib. "Of course not."

"So there is no problem. Not complicated."

"I'm glad you understand."

"Always," she said. "I always understand."

For a moment we held each other's gaze, just long enough for it to acquire a mild resonance. It reminded me of other moments from months back, loaded exchanges on Koh Samui, our midnight conversation about the parallel worlds in the Milky Way. Then the moment was over, broken by Françoise as she turned to look at Karl.

"He does not push down the shelter anymore," she said a few seconds later.

"Yeah. I saw it was up. Maybe it's a good sign. An improvement or something."

She sighed. "No. It means nothing. We discovered he only pushed the shelter down because of the leaves . . . He could not see the caves. He likes to watch them. When we left a space for him to watch through, he left the shelter alone."

"Ah . . ."

"But maybe he is improving . . . He eats the food I give him now."

"That's something, I guess. Not much though."

Françoise nodded. "Yes . . . Poor Karl . . . Not much."

Sal cornered me a final time that day. I'd stayed with Françoise until long after the sun went down, and Sal got me just as I was about to enter the longhouse on my way to bed.

"Did you pass on my message?" she asked.

I slapped my forehead. "Shit, Sal, it totally slipped my mind. I'm really sorry. I got distracted because people were talking about Karl and then . . ."

Sal shook her head dismissively. "Okay, okay. I know what happened because I've had a chat with Etienne this evening. It seems like there'll be a lot of ground to cover at the funeral tomorrow morning and . . . Please don't tell me you've forgotten about the funeral."

"Sal!" I said, probably overdoing the outrage. "Of course not!"

"Well, it's hard to tell with you . . . Anyway, following the talk with Etienne, I've had a slight change of plan. I've decided to be a bit blunter with the camp than I'd originally planned to be. Desperate times and desperate measures, or something like it . . ." She hesitated. "Funerals have a way of drawing people together, don't you think, Richard?"

"They can," I said doubtfully.

"They can, yes. . . . So the point is, don't lose any sleep over not passing on the message."

I nodded. "I won't."

"Good. I'll see you tomorrow then."

"Sure. Tomorrow."

Moshe was the last to bed, so he blew out the last candle. The Jim-Bob game, obviously, was out of the question, but it crossed my mind to try it. I was interested to know what would happen. Probably we'd have labored through it, only calling out the names of our friends until some poor sap was stuck and had to pass it over to the Bugs side. Probably via the Yugo girls, I imagined, or maybe Sal.

I moved on to thinking about Françoise, a train of thought that, once started, could occupy me almost indefinitely. Indefinitely turned out to be at least an hour. That was how long I'd been lying awake before I realized that everyone else in the longhouse was lying awake too. It was a revelation I found annoying. As there was no light in the longhouse for one's eyes to become accustomed to, normally one felt snugly cocooned by the insulating wall of blackness. Paradoxically, it was the snores and sounds of others sleeping that reinforced this cocoon, the sleepers distanced by their unconsciousness.

Once I was alerted to the lack of heavy breathing, the cocoon illusion was ruined. Ruined and, worst of all, replaced by a nagging puzzle. I was awake because I had Françoise to mull over, but why was everyone else awake? It took me another half hour to deduce that it had to be because they were fretting about Sten's funeral.

Five minutes later, the puzzle solved, I fell fast asleep.

ashes to dust

Despite the stench of rotten Sten (a sudden hot blast erupted when his feet slipped out of his sleeping bag), the funeral had some dignity. We all circled the grave that Jean had dug the day before, close enough to the waterfall to make a pleasant spot, far enough to stop our drinking water from being spoiled. Then Sal said a few words, talking of his unfailing commitment to the camp and the extent to which we'd all miss him. Unhygienix, as head cook, said a few more. He talked about how Sten always caught big fish, which weren't necessarily tastier than the smaller ones from the lagoon, but went further in terms of keeping people's stomachs full. He also pointed out that although Sten hadn't played the most active social role in the camp, he was always ready to join in if a Sunday soccer game was organized and had never been known to foul. This last point drew a couple of murmurs of agreement from the crowd.

No one was visibly upset until we started filling in the grave. Then several of the girls started crying. Ella particularly—like all the cooks, she'd had more contact with him than the rest of us had. Anyway, I could understand the tears because there was something poignant about watching the sleeping bag shroud become slowly covered with earth. It brought home how absolute Sten's absence from the world had become.

Finally, Bugs planted a wooden headstone. To his credit, he'd made a real effort with the carving, putting little flourishes around Sten's name and the date. If I had to niggle, I'd mention that the headstone was missing Sten's second name and date of birth. The trouble was, Christo wasn't able to answer questions about Sten, and Karl wasn't willing, so there was nothing that anyone could do about it. But perhaps it was more appropriate that way. Second names felt connected to the world, maybe because they were a link to family and home, so they were never used or asked. It's a funny thought that if today—for some inexplicable reason—I wanted to track down any of the people I once knew on the beach, I'd have no better clue to work from than a nationality and a fading memory of a face.

Throughout the proceedings, I was wondering at which point Sal would address us about the tensions in the camp. I'd assumed it would be when she spoke at graveside, and I think she'd assumed the same thing, but the smell had probably changed her mind. It was distracting. Although we all listened attentively to her and Unhygienix, I think there was a quiet sense of relief when the earth sealed the head hole of Sten's sleeping bag.

Sal eventually made her move when we thought it was over. Jed turned to head off back to camp—he was in a hurry because he didn't want to leave Christo unattended for too long—but Sal stopped him.

"Hold on, Jed," she called over our heads, standing on tiptoe. "I don't want anyone leaving yet. There's something important I want to say, and I want everyone around to hear it."

Jed frowned but stayed put. Among the others I noticed several more puzzled frowns. I also noticed some expectant expressions among Bugs's crew, and to my dismay, something in those expressions which appeared worryingly close to smugness. More worrying was that Bugs had maneuvered himself so that he was standing right by Sal's side. This wouldn't have been surprising in normal circumstances, but when Sal had called to Jed she'd taken a couple of steps forward. Bugs had matched these steps to remain with her, nudging Cassie aside in the process. I kicked myself for having forgotten to pass on Sal's message. "Forewarned," I muttered to myself, "is forearmed," which made Keaty glance at me.

"Okay!" Sal clapped her hands. "I'd like to start by asking everyone to sit down so you can all see me . . . and so I can be reassured that there are still a few things, funerals excluded, that we can all do together."

With a good many exchanged looks we arranged ourselves on the grass, Bugs, predictably, remaining standing longer than everyone else.

Sal surveyed us until we were settled, then nodded. "In case anyone hasn't realized or heard," she began, "I'm going to talk about the atmosphere in the camp. I'm going to talk about it because I have no choice. I'm going to talk about it because no one else seems willing to do so, except in painfully indiscreet huddles."

Here, to my astonishment, she stared directly at Bugs. But my astonishment was nothing to his, and a broad grin leapt to my face as I saw his cheeks flush. She'd kept her word about being evenhanded, I thought approvingly, and suddenly wondered if there were unknown strains in their relationship. Delighted, I imagined the nosedive his position in the camp would take if Sal chucked him. The grin vanished, however, when she directed her next comment straight at me.

"I'll add that matters have not been helped by certain individuals who have hardly tried to patch things up. In fact, I might say they've deliberately made things worse. And yes, Richard, before you even dream of denying it, I mean you. I don't want to repeat anything that was said in the longhouse a few nights ago, but I will say that if anything like it ever happens again, the one who'll be chucking spears is me. Clear?"

She didn't wait for an answer.

"Not that Richard should be singled out. As far as I'm concerned, with *very* few exceptions, everybody here is guilty of having acted like a fucking idiot over this whole mess. Between the two sides of the split, I haven't seen anyone making an effort to cool things down, so I don't see Richard's behavior as any worse than the ones who sit around in sullen gangs."

By now the exchanged glances had stopped and we were all picking at loose threads on our shorts or looking rather intently at the leaves above us. Anywhere but at Sal.

"So the way I see things is like this. We've had two severe disasters over the past week. First there was the food poisoning and then we had the unspeakable tragedy that has collected us here now. For these reasons, the atmosphere in the camp has been understandably bad. If we weren't all in a state of shock with tempers fraying, we wouldn't be human. . . . *But*"—Sal punched a fist in her palm—"it ends *here!* It ends with the burial of a friend, so that something positive will come of his otherwise senseless death.

"Now, dates don't mean much on the beach, but I keep a calendar. And it may interest you to know that the date is September the eleventh."

As a matter of fact, it interested me a lot to hear that the date was September 11, because it meant it was close to five months since I'd left England. But I was surprised that it interested everyone else to the extent that it did. There was a ripple of exclamations around me and someone whistled.

"For the sake of our newest arrivals, it means that the Tet festival is in three days' time. The Tet festival, named by another absent friend, Daffy, is our yearly birthday. It was the date we first spent a night on the beach, and we celebrate it accordingly.''

As she said this, the fire dropped from Sal's eyes and she looked rather sad. ''To be honest, I haven't been much looking forward to this year's Tet. Without Daffy, I don't mind telling you, it will feel very strange. But after the trouble we've been through, particularly losing Sten, I now feel that the festival is exactly what we need. It will remind us what we are and why we're here. As it marks our birthday, it will mark a fresh start.''

Sal paused for a moment, clearly lost in thought. Then her face hardened and she snapped back into business mode. ''Obviously, this means a trip to Koh Phangan to get party supplies. Normally I'd ask for volunteers, but this time I won't. Bugs and Keaty, as you two were the catalyst for the split, I want you to make the trip together.''

I instantly checked to see how Keaty was taking this bit of news, and he looked completely appalled. Bugs I couldn't see anymore because he'd slumped over slightly, but I was pretty sure he would have known about Sal's decision already. I doubted he'd have been happy with it, but he wouldn't have been as shocked as Keaty.

''You can see it as a symbolic gesture if you like. I see it as practical. . . . And Etienne,'' she said as an afterthought, ''I've been thinking about your suggestion to take Karl to Koh Phangan, but for the reasons we discussed I simply don't think it's possible.''

Suddenly I felt a finger jab into my ribs. I turned around and saw Jed leaning toward me. ''Hey,'' he whispered. ''I didn't know Etienne wanted to take Karl to Koh Phangan.''

I nodded. ''Yeah. He went to see Sal about it yesterday. Why?''

Jed's eyes flicked down. ''Just interested,'' he muttered.

I shrugged and looked back at Sal, but while I'd been

turned away she'd obviously made a gesture to show that her sermon was over. People were stirring and starting to rise.

"Okay," she said. "So that's it. I hope you all listened hard. For today, details as normal. Tomorrow Keaty and Bugs leave for Koh Phangan."

I tried to catch Jed as we all filed out of the waterfall clearing, but he'd run on ahead to get back to Christo. Instead I walked with Keaty and Gregorio.

The conversation, as we made our way through the jungle, was amusingly surreal. It was blindingly obvious that we were all dying to swap opinions about Sal's speech, but we had to limit ourselves to small talk for fear of our insights being overheard. So ahead of me I had Jean conferring with Ella about whether the tomatoes were ready for the pot, and behind me I had Cassie saying that her machete needed sharpening.

But this facade of geniality aside, it was also apparent that Sal's speech had had its desired effect. The mood was curiously upbeat, our walking pace fast. Already the funeral seemed as if it had been consigned to the past. If it hadn't been for Jed hurrying off to look after Christo, I could almost have forgotten that the Swedes had been the main reason for the meeting by the waterfall.

Neither did the mood change when we reached camp. I was half expecting us to fall back into our factional huddles and begin the analysis of the morning's events. But within a few minutes the different details had separated out and the clearing was empty. Apart from me, that is, and Sal.

"Was I fair?" she said, walking over.

"Fair . . ." I scratched my head and dropped the cigarette I was smoking, stubbing it out with my toe. "Yeah, you were fair. I think it all worked out pretty well. I was even surprised you let me off so light . . . seeing as Bugs is your boyfriend and all."

"Favoritism isn't my scene, Richard. I'd have hoped you knew that by now. Anyway, I think you redeemed yourself when you rescued Christo. That was a brave thing you did . . . not to mention dumb."

I smiled. "Thanks."

"Well." She smiled back. "So shouldn't you be going? Our neighbors might be up to something, and I'm looking forward to my evening report."

"Right."

I started to walk toward the path to the beach, then, on instinct, I stopped and glanced around. Sal was still looking at me.

"You like me, don't you, Sal?" I said.

She was just close enough for me to see her eyebrows rise. "Excuse me, Richard?"

"You like me. I mean . . . you tell me off when I do something wrong, but you never stay angry for long."

". . . I don't hold mistakes against anyone."

"And you trusted me with the Rice Run and the Jed detail. You could have easily refused his request, especially with me being one of the newest arrivals. And you chose me to pass on the message about your meeting, even though you knew I couldn't be relied on."

"Good Lord, Richard. You do say the strangest things."

"But I'm right, aren't I?"

Sal sighed. "I suppose you are. But that isn't to say . . ."

"I know. Favoritism isn't your scene." I paused. "Shall I tell you why you like me?"

"Go on then."

"It's because I remind you of Daffy, isn't it?"

". . . Yes. But how could you . . ." She shook her head. "Yes, you do remind me of Daffy. Very much."

"I thought that was it," I said. Then I continued on my way.

my lost shit

Mister Duck was waiting for me at the lookout post, as he had done every morning since the shark attack.

I'd had a shock the first time I found him up there, and we'd promptly had an argument. I felt it had been reasonable for him to appear while I was helping Christo in the caves. With or without the phosphorescence, the caves had the qualities of a nightmare—exactly where you'd imagine Mister Duck might show up. But to see him in crisp sunshine, sitting with an unlit joint clamped between his teeth like a cowboy's cheroot, was hard to take.

For as long as the initial bewilderment gripped me, I'd stood gaping while he grinned and tilted his head from side to side. Then I said, "It's *broad daylight,* Mister Duck!"

I said it angrily because I felt obscurely insulted by the brazen nature of his apparition.

"Broad daylight," he'd replied evenly, "is what it is."

I paused. ". . . I'm not dreaming."

"True."

"Then I'm going insane."

"Do you want an honest answer?"

"Yes."

He shrugged. "I'd only query the tense. But I'm not a professional, so, you know, seek out a second opinion."

I threw up my arms, threw them down again, and sat heavily on the ground. Then I reached out and touched his shoulder. It was as dry and warm and solid as my own.

Mister Duck frowned when I shuddered. "You have a problem?"

I shook my head. "Yes, I have a problem. I'm mad."

"So? Are you complaining?"

"Complaining?"

"Is that what you're doing? Complaining?"

"I'm—"

He cut me off. "If you're complaining, buddy, I'm going to tell you right now, I don't want to hear it."

"I'm just—"

"I'm just, I'm just," he mimicked. "You're just what?"

"I'm very fucking shocked! Seeing you and . . . being mad!"

Mister Duck's face screwed up in disgust. "Where's the shock in being mad?"

"Everywhere!" I said furiously. "I don't want to be mad!"

"You don't *want* to be mad? Well, well. Mind if I pick you up on that?"

I pulled out a cigarette with slightly shaking hands, then put it back, remembering I couldn't smoke on the island. "Yes. I mind. I want you to go away."

"Tough. Answer this. Where are you?"

"Leave me alone!"

"Where are you?" he repeated.

I covered my face with my hands. "I'm in Thailand."

"Where?"

"Thaila—"

"Where?"

Through the cracks between my fingers, I stole a glance down to the DMZ. My shoulders slumped as I got the gist. "Vietnam."

"Vietnam!" A great crowing grin spread across his features. "You said it! You *wanted* it! And now these are the breaks! In country, losing your shit comes with the territory!" He whooped and slapped his thigh. "Fuck it, man, you should be welcoming me! I'm the proof you made it! Rich, I *am* your lost shit! Viet-fuckin'-*nam!*"

By the end of that day, I was already feeling pretty comfortable with Mister Duck's presence. And by the end of the second, I realized I was quite pleased about it. He was good company, in his way, and he knew how to make me laugh. Also, as we were spending hours with each other, a lot of our conversation was about commonplace stuff, like places we'd both been to or films we'd both seen. It was hard to stay shocked by someone while you were talking about *Star Wars*.

After the burial I was very keen to get to the lookout post. I had lots of questions for Mister Duck about Tet and I wanted to tell him about Sal's speech to the camp, so I jogged almost all the way up to the pass.

I found him with Jed's binoculars clamped to his eyes.

"I've got loads to tell you," I panted as I sat down beside him, breathless from my haste. "We buried Sten, and Sal made a long speech to the camp. She talked about Tet. You haven't told me about Tet. And she talked about you, too."

An odd look passed over Mister Duck's face. "Sal talked about me? What did she say?"

"She said Tet would be different this year because you were gone."

". . . Is that all she said?"

"That's all she said about you. But she also talked about Tet and camp morale."

Mister Duck nodded. "Very nice," he muttered disinterestedly.

"Don't you want to hear about it? It was really impressive the way she spoke. I think she had a real effect on—"

"No," he interrupted. "I don't."

"You don't want to hear about it?"

"Nope."

"Oh . . . Why not?"

"Because, Rich . . . Because . . ."

He seemed to drift off for a moment, lowering the binoculars, raising them to have another look, and then lowering them again.

"Because I want to talk about Airfix models."

to those who wait

"Airfix models."

"Or Matchbox models. Either."

"Any particular reason?"

"Curiosity."

"Mister Duck, we just buried Sten today. Sal made an amazing speech. There's some celebration called Tet coming up, which you've never mentioned, and—"

"Spitfires," he said patiently, sliding himself round to face me. "Messerschmitts. Did you ever make them?"

I looked at him. "Yes."

"Hurricanes?"

"Hurricanes too."

"Lancaster bombers? Lysander bombers? Mosquitoes?"

". . . I think I made a Lysander once."

"Hmm. Any jets?"

I resigned myself to the unlikely topic. "No. I never liked making jets."

"Me neither. How about that? No jets . . . Or boats, tanks, trucks . . ."

"Or helicopters. They were such a pain, which was a shame because I loved the way they looked."

"Naturally."

"It was the rotor blades . . ."

"Those bloody rotor blades. They'd keep falling off before the glue was dry."

I didn't reply for a moment. A gentle tickling had alerted me to an ant that had found its way onto my stomach. After a couple of seconds I found it, trapped in the line of hair that ran from my belly button. I picked it up by licking my finger so the ant stuck to the spit. "Very difficult," I finally said, and blew the ant away.

Mister Duck's eyes gleamed mischievously. "So you weren't very good at making models then."

"I didn't say that."

"Well, were you any good?"

"Uh . . ." I hesitated. "I was okay."

"You didn't used to mess them up? Too much polyester cement, the pieces not fitting together properly, annoying gaps where the wings met the body, or where the two halves of the undercarriage met. Be honest now."

"Oh, well . . . Yeah. That used to happen all the time."

"Same. It used to drive me nuts. I'd start the model with the best intentions, trying so hard to do a perfect job, but it would almost never work out." Mister Duck chuckled. "And at the end, I always got left with the same problem."

"Which was?"

"What to do with the messed-up model once it was finished. I knew a guy who made perfect models and he'd hang them from his ceiling with bits of thread. But I didn't want to do that with the planes I made. Not with their gluey fingerprints all over the place. It would have been embarrassing."

"I know what you mean."

"I thought you would."

Mister Duck lay back on the grass contentedly, using his folded arms as a pillow. As he did so a butterfly passed near him. A big one, with long strips on each wing that ended in a bright blue circle, like tiny peacock feathers. He reached up a finger, hoping for the butterfly to land, but it ignored him and fluttered off down the slope toward the DMZ.

"So, Rich," he said lazily. "Tell me what you used to do with the messed-up models."

I smiled. "Oh, I used to have the best laugh with them."

"Yeah? It didn't drive you nuts then."

"Sure. At first I'd be kicking chairs around and swearing. But then I'd go out and buy some lighter fuel and I'd drop them out of windows. And also I'd cut holes in the bodies and slide in a firecracker to blow them up."

"Good fun."

"Great fun."

"Burning the bad models."

"So you used to do the same thing?"

"Sort of." Mister Duck closed his eyes against the hot sun. "I burned the good ones, too."

It must have gone midday before I checked on Zeph and Sammy. Our chat had distracted me from the job at hand, which may have been its intent. I'd sunbathed and dozed for a couple of hours, remembering melting Focke-Wulfs and plastic burns from being careless. I might have forgotten about them altogether if Mister Duck, with careful timing, hadn't reminded me.

"Sal's not going to be happy," he said.

I sat up. "Huh?"

"Sal's not going to be happy. In fact, she's going to be seriously pissed off. She'll do her funny little frown . . . You ever notice her funny little frown?"

"No. But how come she isn't going to be happy?"

"I can't believe you've never noticed her frown. I always used to think she looked so pretty when she was pissed off. Her eyes would glow and . . . Do you think Sal's pretty?"

"Uh . . ."

"I think she is."

I looked at him for a couple of moments, then burst out laughing. "Well, well! You had a crush on her, didn't you?"

"A crush?" He went red. "I wouldn't call it a crush. We were very close, that's all."

"You mean she didn't fancy you."

"I just told you, we were very close."

I laughed harder. "Nothing ever happened, did it?"

Mister Duck shot me an annoyed look. Then he said, "Nothing physical happened. But some relationships, *close* relationships, don't need a physical connection. A spiritual bond can be more than enough."

"Unrequited love," I groaned, wiping tears from my eyes. "Now I understand why you put up with Bugs all that time."

"Well, you'd be the expert on unrequited love."

"Excuse me?"

"Does the name Françoise ring a bell?"

I stopped laughing.

"Ding dong!" Mister Duck chimed. "How's that for a fucking bell?"

"Do me a favor. It's completely different. For a start, Françoise actually does fancy me. And whereas Bugs is a prick, Etienne is a great guy. Which, I should point out, is the only reason nothing happens. Neither of us wants to hurt his feelings."

"Mmm."

I glowered at him. "Anyway. Do you think we could get back to the point?"

"What point?"

"You said Sal was going to be seriously pissed off about something."

"Oh . . . Yeah." Mister Duck chucked me the binoculars. "Because of the raft."

". . . *Raft?*" I scrambled over to the edge of the lookout point and slammed the binoculars to my face. Quickly I scanned along their beach. It was empty. "I don't see anything," I said. "What are you talking about?"

"Where are you looking?" Mister Duck replied languidly.

"Their beach!"

"Find the split palm."

". . . Got it."

"Okay. Now go to six o'clock. Six or seven."

I eased the binoculars downward, leaving the sand behind, moving into the blue water.

"There yet?"

"*Where* yet? I still can't see anythi—" I gulped. "Oh fuck."

"Impressive, huh? They may have taken their time, but they sure put it to good use." He sighed while I hyperventilated. "Tell the truth, Rich. No bullshit. Do you think Sal ever thinks about me?"

fine, thanks

Discovering that Zeph and Sammy were on their way left me a lot more anxious and a lot less excited than I'd expected. I found this confusing, and was still trying to make sense of my reaction when I arrived back at camp. Whereupon, immediately, I became even more confused.

There was nothing in the clearing to suggest we'd buried Sten that morning. The atmosphere was more like a Sunday than a wake. A few people were kicking a soccer ball beside the longhouse, Jesse and Cassie were whistling as they laid out some washing to dry, Unhygienix was playing the Game

Boy with Keaty watching over his shoulder. Françoise was the biggest surprise. She was sitting with Etienne and Gregorio in the spot occupied by the Bugs faction until only yesterday. I'd expected her to be keeping an eye on Karl until sundown, as she had every day since the attack. In fact, a quick look around didn't show up any missing faces, so I guessed Karl had been left alone.

In a way, it was reassuring to learn that whatever my own state of mind, I was sane enough to recognize this as abnormal behavior. And to make sure that my companions' behavior was as inappropriate as it appeared, when I passed Cassie I asked her how she was feeling. I chose her partly because she was on my route, but also because this was the question she'd nagged me with in the days following the food poisoning. "Um," she said, not pausing from hanging up the washing. "I've been worse."

". . . You aren't feeling sad?"

"About Sten? Oh yes, I am, of course. But I believe the burial helped. It puts it in the past, I think. In perspective, wouldn't you say?"

". . . Sure."

"It was so difficult to find perspective while his body was lying around." She laughed, looking puzzled. "What an awful thing to say."

"But it's true."

"Yes. I think the burial was the release we needed. Just look how it relieved the tension around here. . . . Shorts, Jesse."

Jesse handed her a pair of shorts.

"And Sal's speech was a great help too. We needed her to bring us together. We've been talking a lot about Sal's speech. We thought it was very good, didn't we?"

Jesse's face was hidden by the heap of damp T-shirts he held in his arms, but I saw his scalp nod.

"Yes," Cassie continued, in her vague and cheerful

monologue. "She's good at that kind of thing. . . . Charisma and . . . And what about you, Richard? How are you feeling?"

"I'm feeling fine."

"Mmm," she said absently. "Of course. You always are, aren't you?"

I left Cassie and Jesse a few minutes later, after some small talk that wouldn't bear mentioning if it wasn't that the small talk was another reason why everything felt so strange. The only time I got close to unsettling Cassie was when I asked after Karl and Christo. She dropped the T-shirt she was holding at the time—not the dramatic response it might seem but an inconsequential slip of the hand. Less inconsequential was her reaction. "Fuck it!" she snapped, which was unusual in itself because Cassie rarely swore, and her face darkened with a sudden flush. Then she held the shirt up, glowering at where the dirt had stuck to the damp material, and threw it back at the ground. "Fuck it!" she said again. A strand of spit that had been linking her lips broke with the force of the words, and the top half swung upward and clung to her cheek. I didn't bother to repeat the question.

cabin fever

On my way across the clearing, I briefly debated who I should tell first about the raft, Jed or Sal. Going by the book, it should have been Sal. But we didn't have a book, so I went with my instincts and told Jed.

I noticed the bad smell as soon as I climbed into the hospital tent. It was sweet and sour, vomit for the sour and something less distinct for the sweet.

"You get used to it," Jed said quickly. He hadn't even turned round, so he couldn't have seen me wince. Maybe he'd heard me cut my breathing. "In a couple of minutes you won't smell a thing. Don't go."

I pulled up the neck of my T-shirt to cover my nose and mouth. "I wasn't going to go."

"Not one person has come in all day. Can you believe it? Not one person." Now he did turn to look at me, and I frowned with concern when I saw his face. Spending almost all his time in the tent had taken a toll. Although his tan was still deep—it would have needed more than five days to wash that out—it seemed underlaid by gray, as if his blood had lost its color. "I've been listening to them out there since two," he muttered. "They came back at two. Even the carpenters. They've been playing soccer."

"I saw."

"Playing soccer! None of them thinking to check up on Christo!"

"Well, I think after Sal's speech everyone's trying to get back to—"

"Even before Sal's speech they were staying away . . . But if it was Sal in here . . . if it was anyone else . . . apart from me . . ." He hesitated, looking blankly at Christo, then laughed. "I don't know. Maybe I'm being paranoid . . . It's just that it's so weird. Hearing them outside, wondering why they don't come to check up . . ."

I nodded, although actually I was only half listening. His confinement with Christo was obviously getting to him and he clearly wanted to talk about it, but I had to bring up the subject of the raft. Sammy and Zeph would have covered the sea between the two islands before nightfall—a conservative estimate I'd worked out with Mister Duck by halving the time it had taken us to make the swim. At the earliest, that meant they could start the journey across the island tomorrow morning, and could conceivably reach the beach by tomorrow afternoon.

Christo stirred, distracting us both. For a second his eyes opened, clearly not focusing on anything, and a line of dark bile ran out of the corner of his mouth. Then his chest heaved and he appeared to slip back into unconsciousness.

Jed wiped away the line with Christo's sheet. "I try to keep him on his side but he always rolls back . . . It's impossible. I can't tell what I should be doing."

"How long will he be like this?"

"Two days at best . . . It might coincide with Tet."

"Well, that's perfect. It'll be the perfect birthday present for the camp, and maybe it will help Karl snap out of his—"

"Help Karl?" Jed looked at me curiously.

"Sure. I think half the problem is that no one can talk to him in his language. I think if Christo was talking to him, then—"

Jed shook his head. "No," he said quietly. "You don't understand. Christo's not getting better."

"You just said, in two days—"

"In two days Christo will be dead."

I paused. "He's dying?"

"Yes."

"But . . . How do you know?"

Jed reached out and took hold of my hand. Confused, I thought he was trying to console me or something, which got on my nerves and I pulled my hand back. "How do you know, Jed?"

"Keep your voice down. Sal doesn't want people to find out yet." He reached out again to take hold of my hand, and this time he held it tightly, drawing it toward Christo's stomach.

"What the fuck are you doing?" I exclaimed.

"Shh. I want you to see."

Jed pulled back the sheet. The entire area of Christo's stomach was almost jet-black, as black as Keaty's.

"Feel there."

I stared at the skin. "Why?"

"Just feel."

"I don't want to," I protested, but at the same time I felt my arm relax. Outside I heard the soccer ball bouncing near the entrance of the tent, a regular thumping that rose and faded like passing rotor blades. Someone cheered, or screamed, and someone else chuckled. Through the canvas, short bursts of conversation sounded singsong and foreign.

Gently Jed guided my hand until it rested on Christo's torso.

"What can you feel?" he asked.

"It's hard . . ." I muttered. "It's like rock."

"He's been bleeding inside. Bleeding badly. I couldn't be sure until last night. Or I knew . . . I think I knew, but—"

"That thing . . . it's a hemorrhage?"

"Uh-huh."

I nodded respectfully. I'd never seen a hemorrhage before. "Who else knows?"

"Just you and Sal . . . and Bugs too, probably. I talked to Sal today. She said nobody can find out. Not after we've started to get things back to normal. I think she's mainly worried about Etienne hearing."

"Because he wanted to take Karl to Hadrin."

"Yes. And she's right to worry. Etienne would insist we take Christo to Koh Phangan, and it would be for nothing."

"You know that for sure?"

"If we'd taken him the day after the attack, maybe two days after, he might have been okay. And I'd have taken that chance, even if it meant losing the beach. I think Sal would have too . . . But now . . . what would be the point?"

"No point . . ."

Jed sighed and stroked Christo's shoulder before pulling back the sheet. "No point at all."

We sat in silence for a minute or two, watching Christo's shallow and irregular breathing. It was strange that, once explained, it was obvious to me he was dying. The smell I'd noticed on entering the tent was the smell of encroaching death, and the waxy appearance of Jed's flesh was from living in death's proximity.

This thought jolted me and I broke the silence bluntly. "Zeph and Sammy built a raft. It was what they were doing behind the treeline. They're on their way."

Jed didn't even blink. "If they make it to the beach," he said, "they'll see Christo die. Everything here will fall apart." And that was all.

secrets

I walked close to the longhouse entrance, past where Sal sat talking with Bugs and Jean, and continued along to the beach path. At the first corner I stopped, leaning against the fin of a rocket ship tree, and lit up. Sal appeared when I was about an inch from the filter.

"Something is up," she said immediately. "What is it?"

I raised my eyebrows.

"By the way you walked, by the look in your eye. How do you think I know? So spit it out, Richard. Tell me what's happened."

I opened my mouth to reply but she beat me to it.

"They're on their way, aren't they?"

"... Yes."

"Fuck." Sal stared into middle distance for a few seconds. Then she snapped back into sharp focus mode. "What's their ETA?"

"Sometime tomorrow afternoon, if they don't get scared off by the dope guards."

"Or the waterfall."

"Or the waterfall. Yeah."

"Their timing is unbelievable," Sal muttered. "Absolutely unbelievable."

"It turns out they were building a raft."

"Building a raft. Of course they were. They had to be doing something ..." She clutched her forehead. "I'm taking it for granted you know about Christo."

I thought for a moment, then nodded. I didn't want to get Jed in trouble, but when Sal was in this mood it was dangerous to lie. "You don't mind me knowing?" I said nervously.

"No. The thing about secrets is, you can't keep them unless you tell at least one other person. It's too much pressure. So I knew he had to tell someone, and I was fairly sure it would be you ..." She shrugged. "Seeing as you have your own secrets to keep, I figured that this way we'd keep all the secrets together in one little bunch."

"Oh."

"Yes. It is clever, isn't it? Unless ..."

I waited.

"Unless the person you told about our guests wasn't Jed. After all, Jed already knew, so it was hardly telling him a secret ..."

"... Hardly relieving the pressure."

"Quite," she said casually, but watching me pretty close. "So did you tell anyone apart from Jed? Keaty maybe ... or Françoise? I certainly hope it wasn't Françoise, Richard. I'll be extremely upset if you told Françoise."

I shook my head. "I didn't tell a living soul," I said firmly, thereby excluding Mister Duck.

"Good." Sal looked away, satisfied. "To tell the truth, I was worried you might have told Françoise. She'd tell Etienne, you see . . . And you haven't told Françoise about Christo, either?"

"I only found out about Christo twenty minutes ago."

"If Etienne finds out about Christo . . ."

"I know. Don't worry. I won't tell anyone."

"Fine." Her gaze lapsed back into middle distance. "Okay, Richard . . . It looks like we have a slight problem with these rafters . . . But you don't think they can possibly get here until tomorrow?"

"No way."

"Absolutely sure?"

"Yes."

"Then I'm going to sleep on this. I need time to think. I'll give you my decision on what we do about them in the morning."

"Right . . ."

I hung around, unsure as to whether I'd been dismissed or not. But a full minute later, Sal was still gazing into nothingness, so I slipped away.

black cloud

I felt I could use some time to think myself, so instead of going back to the clearing I headed down to the beach. I had complicated thoughts about the way things had developed over the course of the day, and I wanted to clear them up in my head.

The way I saw it, there was something that both Sal and Jed hadn't picked up on. Whether the rafters reached the beach or not, there was still the question of Karl.

I'll put it another way. Sal and Jed were stuck on the worst-case scenario. They were thinking in terms of what would happen if the rafters reached us. Zeph and Sammy would arrive, probably during Tet. Everyone would go crazy and freak out about the secrecy of the beach being compromised, and unless I got to Zeph and Sammy first, I'd be in a lot of trouble too. The morale that had been revived by Sal's stirring speech would be completely destroyed. Not only that, there'd be the difficulty of explaining to outsiders why we had one insane and one dying Swede with us. It would be a catastrophe.

I, however, was thinking in terms of the rafters not reaching us. In the back of my mind, the reason I'd been half looking forward to Zeph and Sammy's arrival was the challenge of stopping them. And, I was fairly confident, the challenge would somehow be met. The point was that it *had* to be met. The consequences of them succeeding were far too serious. I didn't know how we'd manage it, but with Sal on the case my instincts were that we wouldn't fail.

So this left not a worst-case scenario to consider, but a medium-case one.

The rafters never reach us. The beach is never aware they

even tried. The Tet celebration gives us a fresh start for the new year, and we cope with Christo's death the same way we coped with Sten's. But what about Karl? Karl wasn't about to die. He was going to stick around indefinitely, a constant reminder of our troubles, an albatross around our necks.

This bothered me a great deal.

I bent over, peering at Karl's yellow face through the palm tree fronds of his shelter. He was painfully thin. Even though he'd accepted food recently, flesh had fallen off him over the past week. Already his collarbone stuck out so far it looked like a suitcase handle, as if you could pick him up by it. He'd probably have been light enough if I'd wanted to try.

Lying by the gap in his shelter—the one that gave him a clear view over the lagoon to the caves—was a coconut shell, half full of water, and a banana-leaf parcel of rice. What was left of the rice, I noticed, was browning. From this I guessed it was the parcel Françoise had left him yesterday, dried out from a day in the sun. It suggested that Françoise hadn't replenished the supply. I contemplated the possibility that this was a new therapy tactic—ignoring him so he'd be goaded into signs of life—but I doubted it. It was more likely that, gripped by the camp's sudden upbeat brand of madness, Françoise had simply forgotten. I remembered my conversation with her the day before. She'd seemed concerned about him then. It was interesting how quickly Sten's funeral had turned everything around.

"Karl," I said.

Maybe it was hearing his name, or maybe I was tricked by a breeze disturbing the palm fronds and playing the shadow slits across his head, but I thought I saw him move. I chose to take this as a reaction.

"Karl, you're a fucking albatross."

I wasn't much bothered that he couldn't understand me. In a way, for Karl's sake, it was probably a good thing.

"You're a black cloud."

This time Karl did move. No doubt about it. He made a little jerky movement forward, like he was stiff from having sat still so long. Then slowly he reached out of the shelter and picked up the coconut shell.

"Hey," I said. "Drinking. That's good." I rubbed my stomach. "Mmm."

He took a tiny sip—it couldn't have done more than wet his mouth—and put the shell back in its place. I glanced over. There was still a gulp of water left in the bottom.

"You left some. Aren't you going to finish it up?" I rubbed my stomach again. "Mmm-mm. Very delicious. Aren't you going to have a little more?"

He didn't move. I watched him for a short while before shaking my head.

"No, Karl. You aren't. And that's my point. You're going to keep going like this for days. You'll get so thin and weak that you won't be able to drink even if you want to. Then we'll have to force-feed you or something and this shark business will end up hanging over us for weeks. . . . Maybe more!"

I sighed and, as an afterthought, kicked down his shelter.

"Get sane, Karl. Do it in a hurry. Because Christo's going to be dead soon."

shh

To confirm my fears about the black cloud, when I did return to the clearing I found it causing trouble. Françoise, Etienne, and Keaty were sitting in a circle, and Etienne and Keaty were repeating the argument I'd heard them have before.

"What's the big deal?" Keaty was saying, at the same time as he played his Game Boy. "He's taking water. That's good, isn't it?"

"Good?" Etienne scoffed. "Why is it good for him to take a little water? Nothing is *good* about his condition. Karl should not be here. This is obvious to me, and I cannot believe it is not obvious for everybody else."

"Give it a fucking rest, Etienne. We've been over this a hundred ti— Oops." He paused, frowning in intense concentration. Then his body slumped and he let the Nintendo drop to his lap. "One-five-three lines. I was going fine until you distracted me."

Etienne spat in the dust. "So sorry. How could I distract you from a computer game because our friend is in need of help?"

"Wasn't my friend. Hardly spoke to him."

"Does that mean you do not care about his problems?"

"Sure I do. I just care about the beach more. And you should too. Okay. Now this time I'm going for the record, so I don't want any more of these bullshit distractions."

Etienne got to his feet. "What would be a real distraction for you, Keaty? Please tell me. Then I will pray I never have to see it."

The question went unanswered.

"Sit down, Etienne," I said in an attempt to lower the

temperature. "Remember what Sal was saying at the funeral. We've got to get over all the difficulties we've had."

"Difficulties," he echoed coldly.

"Everyone else is making an effort."

"Really? I am surprised to hear that you find it an effort."

"What's that supposed to mean?"

"It means maybe I do not know you anymore, Richard. I recognize your face when you walk toward me, but when you are close I recognize nothing in your eyes."

I took this as some French saying he'd translated. "Come on, Etienne. This is stupid. Remember Sal's—"

"Sal," he interrupted, "can fuck herself." Then he marched away in the direction of the waterfall path.

"Actually," Keaty muttered thoughtfully, not looking up from the tiny monochrome screen, "I doubt even Sal could manage that."

A couple of minutes later Françoise also left. She seemed annoyed, so I guessed she didn't feel the same way as Etienne.

When Keaty had finished his Tetris high-score attempt, I finally got the chance to ask him how he felt about doing the Rice Run with Bugs. He said he was pretty relaxed about it. He also said it had been a bit of a shock at first, but he'd come round to the idea if it was for the benefit of the camp. Aside from its being a decent conciliatory gesture, he wanted to make sure we had some good stuff brought in for the Tet festival.

I wanted to talk more about Tet, but Sal wanted the Rice Run over in one day, so they were getting a very early start and he needed to turn in. I sat alone for twenty minutes or so, polishing off a bedtime joint, then I decided to turn in too. With Zeph and Sammy on their way, Keaty wasn't the only one with a heavy day ahead.

I stuck my head into the hospital tent on the way back to

the longhouse, thinking Jed would appreciate another look in. But as soon as I saw inside, I wished I'd stayed away.

Jed was fast asleep, lying next to Christo. Christo, however, was semi-awake. He even recognized me.

"Richard," he whispered, then muttered something in Swedish and made a gurgling noise.

I hesitated a moment, unsure of whether I should be talking to him.

"Richard."

"Yes," I whispered back. "How are you feeling?"

"I feel very bad, Richard. I feel very bad."

"I know. But you'll be better soon."

"Stars . . ."

"You see them?"

"Phos . . . phos . . ."

". . . phorescence," I finished. "You can see it?"

"I feel very bad."

"You need some sleep."

"Sten . . ."

"You'll see him in the morning."

"My chest . . ."

"Close your eyes."

". . . hurts . . ."

"I know. Close your eyes."

". . . very bad . . ."

"Shh now."

Beside him, Jed stirred, and Christo turned his head a fraction. "Karl?"

"Right there next to you. Don't move or you'll wake him."

He nodded and at last his eyes shut.

"Have good dreams," I said, maybe too quietly for him to hear.

I pegged the tent flap open behind me as I left. I wanted to keep Jed from breathing too much of that dying air.

fnq, kia

fuckin' a

Bugs and Keaty left just after five-thirty. Sal gave me my instructions at a quarter to six.

I liked being up while everyone else was asleep. I almost always was, since I'd started working up on the island, but usually there were a few signs of stirring: a spot of movement in one of the tents or someone padding their way across the clearing to the Khyber Pass. That morning the camp was as still and quiet and cool as it could ever be. It made everything more exciting. While I talked with Sal and Jed outside the hospital tent, I was so keyed up for the day ahead that I had to keep hopping from one foot to the other. I could tell it was pissing Sal off, but I couldn't stop myself. If I hadn't channeled my energy somewhere, I'd have started shouting or running around in little circles.

Sal and Jed were arguing. They both agreed that I should head into the DMZ and track Zeph and Sammy's progress across the island. The disagreement was over the interception point. Sal said not until they reached the top of the waterfall, putting some faith in the obstacle course. Jed said earlier, as early as possible, although he seemed reluctant to explain why. Personally, I was siding with Sal, although I kept my mouth shut.

Interception point aside, they both agreed on what to do next. I was to tell the rafters that they weren't welcome and that they should leave at once. That failing, I was to keep them from descending the waterfall. Any way I saw fit to delay them was acceptable, in Sal's words. If necessary I would stay up there with them, missing Tet. It could be explained to the rest of the beach later. Nothing was more important than making sure they didn't arrive at camp until Christo was dead. After that, we would work out whether to let them down or keep them out.

By the way Sal was talking, I was sure she had a fallback plan that she wasn't telling us. I knew the way her head worked, and she wasn't the type to say, "We'll cross that bridge when we come to it." Especially with something so important. The thing I particularly didn't understand was the idea of turning Zeph and Sammy's group back. If we got to the point where I was forced to intercept them, turning them back seemed as problematic as letting them stay. You could as good as guarantee they would talk back on Koh Phangan or Koh Samui, about what they'd found, and we'd have lost our secret status.

If it had been anyone else but Sal, I'd have pointed this out, but with her I didn't feel it was worth bothering. I felt sure that if I'd been able to think of it, she would have too. I don't think I remember her asking my opinion about anything, unless it was to lead me into something by making it seem like my idea. Come to think of it, I don't remember her asking anyone's opinion. Not even Bugs's.

If it needs saying, the argument about the interception point was eventually won by Sal. A big surprise. I honestly don't know why Jed even tried.

Mister Duck was waiting for me at the pass. He was dressed in full combat fatigues with an M16 over his shoulder and his face all painted up with green and black camouflage stripes.

"What's with the gun?" I said when I saw him.

"Just making sure I fit the bill," he replied flatly.

"Does it work?"

"Works for me."

"Guess that's a yes . . ." I walked past him so I could see down the pass to the DMZ. "So how you feeling? Nervous?"

"I feel good. I feel ready."

"Ready for the recon?"

"Well . . ." He smiled. "Just ready, that's all."

"Just ready," I muttered. I always felt suspicious of his lopsided grin. "Daffy, there'd better not be something going on here that I don't know about."

"Mmm."

"Mmm what?"

"Mmm let's get going."

"I'm serious. Don't start any of your shit. Not today."

"Time is ticking, Rich. We've got an RV to keep."

I hesitated, then nodded. "Okay . . . If you're all set."

"All set."

"Then let's do it."

"Fuckin' A."

their big mistake

By setting off so early, I was hoping that Zeph and Sammy would still be with their raft. Finding them would be a lot harder if they'd already entered the jungle. I was also trusting that they'd have landed on the same stretch of beach where Etienne, Françoise, and I had first come ashore. I was fairly confident they would have, but you never knew. They might have tried to circle the island, not realizing they'd passed the only open stretch of sand. Either way, the more time I gave myself to play with, the better.

At least dodging the guards wasn't a problem. They were dozy enough at the best of times, but at seven a.m. they'd definitely still be sleeping off their dope hangovers. In a way, my biggest problem was Mister Duck. He was badly out of shape, wheezing like an old coal miner, frequently pausing to lean against trees and catch his breath. I tried to tell myself that his ghostly status made it unlikely that anyone else could hear him, but all the same, each time he barked a swearword my heart would miss a beat. I'd turn and glare at him, and he'd raise his hands apologetically. "Sorry," he muttered after a stream of abuse at a razor-leaf thicket. "I'm not as good at jungle warfare as I'd imagined." A few minutes later he tripped and fell on his gun, letting off a round into the bushes. He didn't have his safety catch on, the idiot, and he'd been walking with his finger on the trigger. After that we decided the gun was more trouble than it was worth—seeing as it couldn't kill anything real—and we left it hidden in the undergrowth.

About thirty meters before the treeline along the beach, I made him wait behind. Even though I was sure that no one else could see or hear him, he distracted me. If I wanted to get close to the rafting group, I couldn't afford to be compromised.

Unexpectedly—though clearly hurt—he took it in good grace.

"I understand, Richie," he said gamely. "You hate me."

"I don't hate you," I sighed. "But like I said, this is serious."

"I know, I know. You go ahead. Anyway . . ." His eyes became slits and flicked to the side. "In my experience these types of jobs are one-man affairs."

"Exactly."

I left him under a coconut tree, using a serrated bowie knife to pick the dirt from under his nails.

The early-morning effort paid off. The rafters were still on the beach.

Even though I'd been watching them for months, it was a shock to see the group close up. It confirmed that it actually *was* Zeph and Sammy we'd been watching; that our assumption had been correct and that the blame for their presence could only come down to me. It was also curious because I'd been anticipating this moment for what seemed like ages, but the reality of their presence left me feeling cold. I'd anticipated something more dramatic than the bedraggled figures who sat huddled around their raft. Something a lot more sinister, considering that—as outsiders—they represented a threat to the secrecy of the camp and a threat to me. I still hadn't worked out what I was going to say to Sal about the map. I didn't have the nerve to countermand her orders, so I just had to rely on the island's obstacle course. That failing, my only hope was that I could explain the situation to Zeph and Sammy while I kept them delayed above the waterfall.

From my spy point—about twenty meters from where they sat, lying flat under the shelter of some ferns—I could see only four of them. The fifth was obscured behind their raft. Of the two visible Germans, one was a boy and one was a girl. With some satisfaction, I saw that the girl was pretty but not as pretty as Françoise. No one on the beach was as pretty as Françoise and I didn't want her usurped by a stranger. The girl would have been prettier if it wasn't for her nose, which was tiny and turned up so she looked like a tanned skull. The guy, however, was a different matter. Even though he was clearly exhausted, weakly hauling his (pink pastel) backpack off the raft, he had the same build and appearance as Bugs. They could have been brothers, even down to the long hair, which he kept having to flick out of his eyes. I took a comfortably instant dislike to him.

Eventually the fifth popped up to finish off the team. Another girl, and, annoyingly, I was unable to find anything to hold against her. She was short and curvy, and she had an attractive quiet laugh that rolled cleanly across the sand to where I lay. She also had very long brown hair that at one point, for a reason I couldn't fathom, she wrapped around her neck like a scarf. It was a surreal sight and it made me smile, until I remembered I should be scowling.

I was mildly put out that the rafters didn't make the same mistake as I had with Etienne and Françoise—walking to each end of the arrival beach before realizing that the only way to get around the island was to go across it. But this was more than compensated by another, far more serious mistake they made.

Actually, I knew they were about to make the mistake even before it happened. Firstly, they hadn't properly hidden their raft—only dragging it up beyond the high-tide mark—and secondly, they chatted loudly as they walked. In German, I noticed with grudging respect. (Grudging respect for Zeph and Sammy rather than the Germans, obviously.) To me, this clearly suggested one thing: they were entirely unaware of any need for caution. Mister Duck, who had rejoined me when the group turned inland, noticed it too.

"Not very perceptive," he said, just under an hour into the trek.

I nodded, putting a warning finger to my lips. I didn't want to talk because we were following them so closely. Not closely enough to see them through the thick foliage, but always close enough to hear.

"If they carry on like that they'll get caught," he continued, undeterred.

I nodded.

"Maybe you should do something, don't you think?"

"No," I whispered. "Now shut up."

I was a bit perplexed by Mister Duck's concern, but no more than that. The next time he opened his mouth I put the warning finger to his lips instead of mine, and he got the message.

So anyway. That was the rafters' big mistake: not being very perceptive. When they came to the first plateau, not one of them realized they were in a field.

i know abou' tha'

Sammy whooped, just as he'd whooped six months ago, running through the rain on Koh Samui. And he shouted, "This is way outa fuckin' line, man! I've never seen so much fuckin' weed! This is more weed than I've ever fuckin' seen!" Then he started ripping up big handfuls of leaves and throwing them in the air, and the other four started whooping and throwing leaves in the air too. They looked like million-dollar bank robbers throwing their loot around. Completely out of control. Completely dead meat. It was ten a.m. The guards would have been patrolling for two hours at least and if they hadn't heard them crashing through the jungle, they'd heard them now.

By a twist of fate, nothing intentional about it, Mister Duck and I were hiding in the same bush that I'd hidden in with Etienne and Françoise. It certainly gave the scene an extra edge. Watching Zeph and Sammy was like watching myself—what could have come to pass six months ago if not for Etienne's cool head—and I felt a peculiarly vivid blast of empathy for Scrooge. Perhaps Mister Duck is my Ghost of Christmas Future, I remember thinking as my stomach knotted with the memories of my fear. But I was also buzzing. It looked like the problem with our uninvited guests was about to be solved, and as if that wasn't enough, I was also going to find out what happened when the dope guards caught someone. Better than that, I was actually going to see it.

Not that I'd want anyone thinking I was without pity for them. I didn't want Zeph and Sammy on the island and I knew it would be convenient if they were to disappear, but it didn't have to be this way. Ideal scenario: They arrived, I had a couple of days tracking them as they found their way across the island, then they gave up at the waterfall and went back home. I would have had my fun and there'd have been no spilt tears and no spilt blood.

Zeph bled like a stuck pig. When the guards had appeared, he'd begun walking straight over toward them like they were old friends. To my mind an inexplicable thing to do, but that's what he did. He *still* didn't seem to realize what was going on, even though the guards all had their guns off their shoulders and were jabbering in Thai. Maybe he thought they were part of the Eden community, or maybe he was so shocked that it just didn't click how much trouble he was in. Either way, as soon as he got close, one of the guards smashed him in the face with the butt of his rifle. I wasn't surprised. The guard looked very nervous, and just as confused by Zeph's strange behavior as I was.

After that there were a few seconds of silent staring across the heads of the dope plants, Zeph taking little backward steps while he cupped the blood spilling out of his nose. It seemed as if each of the two groups was as bewildered as the other. The rafters were having to make a considerable mental adjustment, Eden to hell in the space of a few seconds. The dope guards seemed stunned that anyone could be so stupid as to walk into their plantation and start ripping it to pieces.

It occurred to me—during this brief interlude—that most of the guards were more like country boys than experienced mercenaries, with scars from sharp corals rather than from knife fights. A bit like the real VC. But I'm sure these observations would have been of small interest to Zeph and Sammy, and in this case I think it made the guards more dangerous than they might otherwise have been. Maybe someone more experienced wouldn't have panicked and smashed Zeph's face in. Isn't there a saying that the only thing more dangerous than a man with a gun is a nervous man with a gun? If there isn't, there should be. Once the short period of staring was over, the guards flipped. I read it as a panicky reaction to the situation. They just waded in and began beating the shit out of what were now their uninvited guests, and not mine.

I suppose the rafters might have been battered to death right there and then, but just as I was beginning to feel that the scene was getting too unpleasant to watch, another bunch of guards arrived, and this lot appeared to have a boss. I'd never seen him before. He was older than the others and had no automatic rifle; only a pistol, still in its holster. Traditionally a mark of power among gunmen. One word from him and the beating stopped.

Beside me, Mister Duck reached over and clutched my arm. "Rich, I think they're going to be killed."

I frowned at him and mouthed, "Quiet."

"No, listen," he persisted. "I don't want them killed."

This time I shut him up not just with my finger but my whole hand. The guards' boss had started talking.

He spoke in English. Not flawlessly by any means. Not like a Nazi POW camp commandant who appreciates English poetry and says to his prisoners, "You know, we are much alike, you and I." But good enough.

"Who are you?" he said, very loud and clear.

A deceptively tricky question. What do you say? Do you formally introduce yourself, do you say, "No one," do you beg for your life? I thought Sammy handled it very well, considering he'd just had his front teeth knocked out.

"We're travelers from Koh Phangan," he replied between tight gasps for air, involuntarily dribbling as he spoke. "We were looking for some other travelers. We made a mistake. We didn't know this was your island."

The boss nodded, not unkindly. "Ve'y big mistake."

"Please, we're very . . ." Gasp. "Sorry."

"You alone now? Any frien' here now?"

"We're alone. We were looking for a friend. We thought he was here, and we know we made a mis—"

"Why you look for frien' here?"

"Our friend gave us a map."

The boss cocked his head to the side. "Wha' map?"

"I can sh—"

"You can show me tha' map. La'er."

"Please. We're very sorry."

"Yes. I know abou' you bein' sorry."

"We'd like to go. We could leave your island now and we wouldn't tell anyone about anything."

"Yes. You tell no one. I know abou' tha'."

Sammy tried to smile. All his remaining teeth were bright red. "Will you let us go? Please?"

"Ah." The boss smiled back. "You can go."

". . . We can go?"

"Yes."

"Thank you." With an effort, Sammy raised himself onto his knees. "Sir, thank you. I promise you, we won't tell any—"

"You can go wit' us."

". . . With you?"

"You go wit' us now."

"No," Sammy began to protest. "Please, wait, we made a mistake! We're *very* sorry! We won't tell *anyone*!"

One of the German guys started to get up, holding his arms in the air. "We will not speak!" he blurted. "We will not speak!"

The boss gazed at the German impassively, then spoke quickly to the guards. Three of them moved forward and tried to lift Zeph by the arms. He began to struggle. Another guard stepped forward and jabbed the barrel of his rifle into Zeph's stomach.

"Richard," said Mister Duck, who had squirmed from under my grip. "Listen to me. They're definitely going to be killed."

I took no notice.

"Do something, Richard."

Again I didn't respond, and this time he poked me hard in the ribs with his finger. Luckily, my yelp was drowned out by the sounds of the rafters screaming.

"Jesus fucking Christ!" I whispered incredulously. "What's your problem?"

"Do something to help them!"

"Like what?"

"Like . . ." He considered this question while over in the field the guards piled onto the German girl. She'd tried to run away and had been brought down after only a couple of stumbling meters. "I don't know!"

"Well neither do I, so belt up! You'll get me killed too!"

"But—"

Resisting the urge to shout at him, I grabbed him by the lapels of his combat jacket and put my mouth right up against his ear. *"For the last time, shut the fuck up!"*

Mister Duck covered his face with his hands and the guards began dragging their terrified captives away.

cheap shots

The cries and howls were gradually replaced by jungle noises. Commonplace sounds I'd never normally have registered, but which now seemed unnatural. Worse, obscurely facetious: twittering birdsong like twittering bad jokes, jangling my nerves and my temper. I stood up without a word to Mister Duck and set off on my way back up to the pass. It wasn't an easy trek. My head ached with a fading adrenaline rush, my legs felt unsteady, and I was giving far too little thought to stealth. Twice I tripped and more than twice I pushed through a thicket without pausing to see who might be on the other side.

Looking back, it seems obvious that I was shaken by what I'd seen and in a hurry to leave an area which still felt heavy with screams. But that wasn't how I saw it at the time. I only thought about the importance of getting back to camp and filling in Sal about the morning's developments. I was also furious with Mister Duck. From the moment we'd started tracking the rafters, his wires seemed to have gotten severely crossed. Not only had he asked me to intercept Zeph and Sammy before the plateau, his blathering had put me in jeopardy. As far as I was concerned, that was a serious offense. The DMZ was way too dangerous a place if you couldn't rely on your company.

I think Mister Duck sensed this anger, because, rarely for him, he made no attempt at conversation. Until we reached the pass. Then he stopped me with a firm shove and said, "We need to talk."

"Fuck you," I replied, shoving him back. "You could have got me killed."

"The rafters probably *are* being killed!"

"You don't know that. And I didn't want that beating shit to happen any more than you, so don't get on some fucking moral high horse. We *knew* they might be caught. That was understood when we made the decision to make no contact with them unless they got to the waterfall, so what do you want from me?"

"Decisions? I didn't make any decisions! I wanted you to help them!"

"Steaming in like Rambo, waving an M16 that doesn't even exist?"

"You could have done something!"

"Like what? You live in a dream world! There was *nothing* I could have done!"

"You could have warned them before they got to the plateau!"

"I had clear orders *not* to warn them!"

"You could have broken the orders!"

"I didn't want to fucking break them!"

"You . . . didn't?"

"Not for one second!"

Mister Duck frowned and opened his mouth to reply, then appeared to check himself.

"What?" I snapped.

He shook his head, his features calming. When he eventually spoke I knew he wasn't saying what was on his mind. "That was a cheap shot, Richard," he said quietly. "About me living in a dream world."

"You could have got me killed, but I hurt your feelings. God forgive me. I'm a monster."

"It's your world I live in."

"That must be a comfort, considering you were the one who pointed out that I'm—"

I cut myself off. While I'd been talking, I'd heard a sharp crack from somewhere in the DMZ.

"Did you hear that?"

Mister Duck hesitated, his eyes narrowing, and suddenly he looked extremely worried. "Yes. I heard something."

"You sure?"

"Definite."

We both waited.

Within five or six seconds the silence was exploded by a burst of gunfire. It was entirely unambiguous, somehow managing to ripple through the trees like a quick breeze and tear through them with shocking loudness. A single burst, but a long one. Long enough for me to blink and hunch my shoulders, and then be aware that the shooting was still going on.

When it finally did stop, the next thing I heard was Mister Duck taking a deep breath and exhaling slowly.

"Jesus . . ." I muttered. "Jesus Christ . . . It's happened. They've actually . . ."

"Been shot," he finished vacantly.

To my surprise, I nearly threw up. Out of nowhere, my stomach knotted and my throat tensed up. An image jumped into my head: the rafters' bodies, their shirts scattered with spreading stains, limbs twisted. Swallowing hard, I turned to the DMZ. I suppose I was looking for a corroborating sign, maybe a vague blue smoke in the distance. But there was nothing.

"Been shot," I heard once more, and then, very faintly, "Damn."

A moment later I turned back to Mister Duck. He was gone.

mama-san

It had all gone wrong or it had all gone right. I couldn't decide which.

On the one hand, just like on the plateau, when it came down to it I'd lost my nerve. I hadn't been alert but calm; I'd been alert but queasy. But on the other hand, maybe that was how it should be. Right to panic on the plateau, right to feel sick when I heard the gunshots. I've read about it enough times, seen it in enough films: the first day on your first tour, you're supposed to lose your shit in a contact. Later, more experienced, jaded, you are caught unawares one day that death still has the capacity to appall you. It is something you dwell on, and through it you gain strength.

I ran this second interpretation over and over as I made my way down to the waterfall. I also tried to look on other bright sides. Mainly that our problem with the new arrivals was over, and my part in compromising the beach's secrecy was irreversibly closed. But they didn't make a dent in the way I was feeling. Still battling with my contracting stomach, struggling to focus on the terrain ahead of me, trying to work through my urge to yell. I wanted to yell a lot. Not an Iron John, exorcising kind of yell. More this kind: running down a road at top speed to catch a bus, and bashing your knee straight into a concrete bollard. Just like you'd done it deliberately, as hard as you possibly could. It isn't a yell born from pain, because at that moment nothing hurts. It's a yell that comes from a brain on overload, refusing to concede what has just happened, and refusing to try.

Sal was waiting for me beneath the waterfall. "What the hell happened?" she said, more angry than anxious, before I'd even finished swimming to the shore. "Why did I hear gunshots?"

I didn't answer until I'd reached the shallows and was wading toward her. "The rafters," I puffed. The impact on hitting the water always knocked the air out of me, and this time it had been worse than usual.

"They've been killed?"

"Yes. I saw them get caught by the guards and then later I heard the firing."

"You didn't see it?"

"No."

"What happened when they were caught?"

"They were beaten."

"Badly?"

"Yes."

"Badly enough to scare them? Maybe just a message?"

"Worse."

"Then?"

"They got taken away somewhere. Dragged."

"Dragged . . . You didn't follow."

"No."

"What next?"

"The shooting . . . when I reached the pass."

"I see . . ." Sal's eyes bored holes into my head. "Badly beaten, you say . . ."

"Very badly."

"You feel responsible for their deaths."

I thought about this before replying, not wanting to give away my connection to Zeph and Sammy at this late stage. "It was their decision to come here," I said eventually, shifting my weight from my left foot to my right. I was still standing knee-deep in the pool and my feet were sinking slightly into the mud. "They made a lot of noise in the jungle. It was their fault."

Sal nodded. "Others may have heard the shooting. What will you tell them?"

"Nothing."

"I think Etienne might know about Christo. He's being difficult again—"

"I won't tell Etienne," I interrupted. "I won't tell Françoise or Keaty or anyone . . . Except Jed . . . You know I'll tell Jed."

"Of course I do, Richard," she said crisply. "But it's nice of you to ask permission." Then she spun on her heel and began walking away. She didn't even wait for me to climb out of the pool, or to hear me whisper, "I wasn't asking your fucking permission."

reanimator

I didn't follow Sal back to camp because I didn't want to see everyone yet. In fact, I didn't want to do anything much. Except maybe sleep. It was the idea of oblivion that appealed; nothing to do with tiredness. I wanted to get away from the brain that was still making me want to yell. The problem was, of the various benefits sleep might provide, oblivion wasn't in the cards. If I slept I'd dream and I knew dreams were not the place to avoid these things.

I ended up talking to myself. Walking around the pool, treating my mind as if it were a separate but reasonable entity,

I asked it to leave me alone for a while. Or at least turn down the volume.

This wasn't the deranged caricature it might sound, full of expressive gestures and wild looks. It was an earnest attempt for some peace and quiet that happened not to work. My mind deflected reason like Superman deflecting bullets, chest puffed out, completely unfazed. So I tried a few different tacks, like attempting to get interested in a pretty flower or the bark patterns on the carved tree. But all these techniques failed equally. If they achieved anything, it was that my failure compounded my frustration and made me feel worse.

My last attempt was to dive back into the pool. Underwater had always had the qualities of a refuge for me. Calming, blinding, deafening; a perfect escape. It worked too, enveloping me in anonymous coolness, but in an unavoidably temporary way. Without gills I had to keep surfacing, and as soon as I surfaced my mind resumed its circular debates.

No place to avoid these things. I realized this eventually, hammered into breathless submission. I climbed out of the pool and headed straight into the jungle. I didn't follow the gardeners' path. I followed the network of carpentry paths, which I could use to reach the beach without crossing the clearing.

I'll keep this brief. Absolutely limited to what I remember, with no filling in the blanks. Not that I've been filling in the blanks up until now; it just so happens that my memory of the next few minutes is patchy. No doubt a result of the traumatic morning and the previously described frame of mind.

"The rafters are dead," I said. "Christo will be dead within forty-eight hours. All our problems are over except you. It's time you got sane."

Karl looked at me through his waxy eyes. Or he looked

through me, or he wasn't looking at anything at all. Whatever. I didn't really care. I took a step toward him, and as I did so he lashed out viciously at my legs. Maybe revenge for having kicked down his shelter. The blow hurt, so I hit him back.

I sat on his chest, my knees against his upper arms, trying to push a handful of rice into his mouth. His skin reminded me a lot of the dead freak on Koh Phangan, slack to the touch, moving loosely over the muscle. Touching it wasn't a pleasant sensation at all. Especially when he began to writhe.

He made sounds, probably words. "That's the boy!" I shouted. "Guess I'm curing you now!" His fingers clawed at my neck. I pushed them away. I think I may have lost the rice in the struggle. I think I may have been holding sand.

I assume I closed my eyes. Instead of Karl's face with bugging eyes, I have a mental picture of a reddish-brown blanket. Nothingness, so closed eyes seem like a logical explanation. They would also explain the next image I have in my memory slide show: a blue blanket, reopening my eyes for a split second as I fell backward and glimpsed a cloudless sky. And the next image, returning to the red-brown blanket again.

I sat up. Karl was twenty or more meters down the beach, running like crazy. Amazed that he could still have so much strength after days of virtual starvation, I leapt to my feet and sprinted after him.

reasonable doubt

Down the beach, through the treeline, up the path, into the clearing. I'd nearly caught him. I was just about to get a hand to his hair. Then I tripped over a guyline on one of the tents and went flying, and Karl made a beeline for the Khyber Pass.

I scrambled up. Several people were standing directly in his way. "Catch him!" I shouted. "Jesse, Greg, for fuck's sake! Bring him down!" But they were too shocked to react and Karl whizzed by. "You idiots! He's getting away!" A few seconds later he'd reached the pass. In the baffled quiet that followed we listened to him crashing through the undergrowth, and then the silence was complete.

"Fuck!" I shouted, sinking to my knees, and started banging my fist on the ground.

A light hand touched my shoulder. I looked round to see Françoise leaning over me, and behind her a semicircle of curious people. "Richard?" she said anxiously.

Another hand, Jesse's, reached under my arms and hauled me up. "You okay, mate?"

"Yes . . ." I began, and then stopped, trying to remember what had happened. ". . . I think Karl's out of his coma thing."

"So I saw. What happened?"

". . . He attacked me," I said doubtfully, and everyone gasped.

"You are hurt?" said Françoise, peering at my face to check for damage.

". . . I managed to fight him off. I'm fine . . ."

"Why did he do it?"

"I . . . I really don't know . . ." I shook my head in desperation. I didn't feel at all ready to cope with these questions. "Maybe . . . Maybe he thought I was a fish. He was a fisher and . . . he's mad . . ."

Sal saved me from this shit I was coming out with. The crowd parted and she came striding through.

"Karl attacked you, Richard?"

"Just now. On the beach."

The second confirmation of Karl's assault brought a second gasp from the crowd and they all started to talk at once.

"It should have been me to catch him!" said Unhygienix furiously. "He ran so close!"

"I saw the look in his eye!" added Cassie. "He looked right at me! It was terrifying!"

"And the foam in his mouth!" said someone else. "Like rabies! We should catch him and tie him up!"

Only one voice went against the flow: Etienne's. "This is impossible," he shouted above the racket. "I do not believe Karl would attack Richard! I do not believe it! I was with him this morning!"

The din began to die down.

"This morning I was with him for one hour! One hour, and he ate rice with me! He was getting better! I know he would not attack anyone!"

I got myself together enough to frown in disbelief. "Are you saying I'm a liar?"

Etienne hesitated, then turned away from me, addressing the others. "For one hour I was with him! He said my *name!* For the first time in a week he talked! I *know* he was getting better!"

Quickly I began to backtrack, not caring about this argument, just wanting to get away. "Yes, Etienne's right. It may have been my fault. I could have frightened him—"

"No!" Sal interrupted sharply. "I'm afraid that Karl has become dangerous. This morning I also went to see him, and he made a lunge at me, too."

Startled but not about to contradict her, I studied her expression hard and wished I had her capacity for sniffing out a lie. She was acting like she was telling the truth, but I knew that meant fuck-all.

"Luckily Bugs was there to pull him off. We were down on the beach, just before he left for Koh Phangan with Keaty. I should have warned you all already, but I was trying to work out the best way to deal with him . . ." She sighed with apparent and entirely uncharacteristic regret. "I was stupid. I didn't want to bring down the Tet celebration with more bad news. It was irresponsible, but things had been going so well . . . I didn't want to ruin morale."

Jesse shook his head. "Tet's all very well, Sal, but we can't have someone that dangerous just roaming around."

Everyone nodded, and for some strange reason, I felt they were all nodding at me.

"Richard, I hope you can accept my apologies. You shouldn't have been put in that situation."

"No need for that, Sal," I replied immediately. Even in the context of a lie—and by now I was sure she was lying—I felt extremely uncomfortable having her apologize to me. "I understand."

"But I do not!" said Etienne desperately. "Please! Please, everybody *must* listen! Karl is not dangerous! He needs help! I think maybe we could take him to Koh Pha—"

This time it was Françoise who cut him off, by doing nothing more than walking away. His voice failed him as he watched her march across the clearing. Then he started after her, still not able to speak, holding his arms ahead of him, paralyzed in midplea.

upended

Almost as soon as Etienne and Françoise walked off, the rest of us began to wander across the clearing. There was no further discussion about Karl. As far as the others were concerned, I think they were all aware that the calm since Sten's funeral was in jeopardy, and that a huge exercise in denial was under way. Instant, informal, an intuitive consensus, so that talking about anything remotely contentious was out of bounds. No problem for me. It meant that no one asked me to elaborate on Karl or brought up the topic of the gunshots. The only downside was having to labor through a few contrived conversations, which seemed a fair trade-off.

The strangest of these exchanges was with Jean, not least because he almost never spoke to me. He came over with a shy smile and asked the kind of stupid question that can only come from uneasiness. "You are working, Richard?" he said.

At the time I was having a smoke outside the kitchen hut, trying to reconstruct my splintered nerves. "No, Jean," I managed to reply, relatively steadily. "Not at this exact moment. I'm smoking a cigarette."

"Ah."

"Would you like one?"

"Oh no!" he said hurriedly, looking quite alarmed. "I do not want to take your cigarette."

"Go ahead. Keaty's bringing me some back from Hadrin."

"No, no. I can smoke grass."

". . . Okay." I returned his smile, willing him to fuck off with all my heart.

But he didn't. He scratched his head and shuffled his feet a bit. I had the impression that if he'd owned a cap he'd have been holding it in his hands. "You know, Richard, I was thinking."

"Mmm?"

"Perhaps you would like to see the garden one day. Sometimes you would come to see Keaty, but now it has changed. After Keaty was fishing, I made the garden even larger. Now it has seven areas."

"Seven?" I said tightly. "Great."

"So one day you will come to see it?"

"It's a date."

"A date! Yes!" He let out a roar of laughter, so theatrical that for a few seconds I thought he was taking the piss. "A date! Then we will see a film!"

I nodded.

"A date," he repeated. "See you on our date, Richard!"

"See you then," I replied, and mercifully he backed away.

I avoided visiting Jed until darkness was beginning to set in. I didn't want to be seen entering the hospital tent. I knew that this would be a tacit acknowledgment of Christo's existence—which, under our consensus, was perhaps the most important of the Things to Ignore.

If possible, conditions were even worse inside the tent than they had been before. Stenchwise it was the same deal, but the trapped heat inside seemed more intense and there were puddles of dried and drying black liquid everywhere. Blood from Christo's stomach, soaking in the sheets, collecting in the folds of the canvas floor, and smeared across Jed's arms and chest.

"Jesus Christ," I said, feeling sweat begin to prickle my back. "What the fuck's been going on in here?"

Jed turned toward me. He was lit from below by his upended Maglite. It made the stray hairs of his beard glow like light bulb filaments and hid his eyes in absolute darkness. "Do you have good news for me?'' he murmured. ''I'm tired of bad news now. I only want to hear good news.''

I paused, squinting at the shadows in his eye sockets, looking to see some form inside them. Something about his manner was threatening and his demonic glow made me wonder if I was having a hallucination. So much so that I felt I should confirm his realness if I was going to stick around. Eventually I reached for the Maglite and shone it directly at his face. His hand flicked up to shield the glare, but I saw enough flesh to reassure me.

I rested the torch back on the floor. ''I've got news. Zeph and Sammy are dead.''

''Dead,'' Jed said without emotion.

''Shot by the dope guards.''

''You saw it?''

''No.''

He cocked his head to the side. ''Disappointed?''

''No. I saw them get beaten and . . .''

''That was enough for you.''

''. . . it made me feel sick,'' I finished. ''I didn't expect it to, but it did.''

''Oh.'' The bright filaments of Jed's beard twitched as some invisible expression passed across his features.

''. . . Aren't you pleased? Not pleased, I mean relieved . . . In a way.''

''I'm not relieved at all.''

''. . . You aren't?''

''No.''

''But it means the beach is safe. Tet and morale . . . and our secrecy . . .''

''I don't care about the beach anymore, Richard.''

''You . . . You don't care about the beach?''

''Would you like to hear my news?''

I shifted my weight to disguise my unease. ''. . . Okay.''

''Today's news is that there isn't any.''

". . . No visitors."

"That's right, Richard. No visitors. Again." He cleared his throat. "I haven't seen a single soul, except his and maybe mine . . . Can't stop thinking about why that might be . . . Why do you think it is, Richard? Me and Christo, waiting here all day long, with no visitors . . ."

"Jed . . . We've been over this before."

"Are you in a hurry?"

". . . No."

"So we can go over it again."

". . . Okay. It's just like you said, people are trying to get back to normal. They don't want to be reminded."

"And it would be the same if it was Sal in here."

"It might be different if it was Sal. She's the boss. But I don't think—"

"What if it was you?" he interrupted.

"In here?"

"In here dying. What if it was you?"

"Some people would come, I guess. Françoise and Etienne. Keaty . . ."

"Me?"

"Yeah. You'd come." I laughed weakly. "I hope."

Jed let the laughter hang in the air, making it sound unpleasant and alien. Then he shook his head. "No, Richard. I meant what if it was me in here."

". . . You?"

"Me."

"Well . . . people would come to see you."

"Would they?"

"Of course."

"Would they?"

". . . Yes."

"But I *am* in here, Richard." He leaned toward me, blocking the Maglite, throwing the whole of his upper body into shadow. I pulled back at once, unsure of how close he was.

When he spoke, hissed, he couldn't have been more than five or six inches away. "I'm in here all fucking day and all fucking night. And nobody comes to visit."

"I come to visit."

"But no one else."

"I . . . I'm sorry."

"Yes. I'm sorry too . . ."

"But . . ."

"Sure."

A couple of seconds later he sat back, and we watched each other across Christo's stained body. Then his head dropped and he absently began rubbing flakes of dried blood off his forearms.

"Jed," I said quietly. "Do me a favor."

"Mmm."

"Get out of the tent for a while. I'll stay here with Christo and . . ."

He waved a hand dismissively. "I think you miss the point."

"You really should . . ."

"I don't want to see those fuckers outside."

"You wouldn't have to. You could go down to the beach."

"Why?" he said, suddenly sounding very clear and definite. "To clear my head? To get me thinking straight and keep me sane?"

". . . If you like."

"As sane as everyone else?"

"It would help you get some perspective."

"It would help nothing. It doesn't matter where I am. I'm still in this tent. I've been in this tent since the day I got here, just like Christo. Just like Karl and Sten. The tent, the open sea, the DMZ. Out of sight and out of . . ."

Just for the briefest moment I heard a thickness in his voice. I held my breath, oddly panicked by the prospect of him in tears, but he appeared to regain control and continued.

"When the Swedes arrived and Daffy freaked . . . Daffy vanished . . . I really thought it would change . . . With him gone, I thought it would change . . . But he was so sly . . . He came back . . . so sly . . ."

Jed's voice faded to an indistinct whisper. Then he rocked forward and touched his temples with his fingertips.

"Jed," I said, after a pause. "What do you mean, he came back?"

"Killed himself," he replied. ". . . Came back."

I frowned, dislodging the buildup of sweat in my eyebrows. It ran down my face and stung the corners of my mouth. "You've seen him?"

"Seen him . . . yes . . ."

"When?"

"Koh Phangan, first . . . Should have seen him earlier . . ."

"You saw Daffy on Koh Phangan?"

"With your friends. Your dead friends . . ."

"With Zeph and Sammy?"

"He gave them the map."

I hesitated. "Jed, I gave them the map."

"No . . ."

"I'm telling you, I gave them the map. I remember doing it clearly."

"No, Richard." He shook his head. "Daffy gave them the map."

"You mean . . . they had the map before I gave it to them?"

"I mean he gave them the map when he gave it to you." Jed sat upright again. The movement drew the canvas floor tight and unbalanced the upended Maglite. As it fell it briefly dazzled me, then rolled to rest as a single beam. "He gave the map to Etienne," he said, carefully replacing the torch. "And to Françoise, and Zeph, and Sammy, and the Germans, and all the others . . ."

"The others?"

"The ones we haven't seen yet. The ones that will arrive next month, or week, and the ones that will arrive after them."

I sighed. "Then . . . you see Daffy when you see me."

"Not so much before . . . But now, yes." Jed nodded sadly. "Every time I see you . . . Every time . . ."

same-same, but different

As I got into bed, the first into the longhouse that night, I heard the sound of Bugs and Keaty returning with the Tet supplies. There was a lot of excited chatter when people saw what they had brought for the celebration, and later I heard Keaty calling my name. Later still, Françoise joined him. I didn't answer either of them. I was lying on my back with a T-shirt draped over my head, waiting for sleep. Surprisingly I didn't have to wait too long.

The clearing had always been a clearing. It had almost doubled in size as the camp grew, but had existed in some form since the rocket ship trees were saplings. Two hundred years ago? Maybe more. The only way I know how to date a tree is to cut it down, but it wasn't hard to imagine those rocket ship trees having seen a few centuries through.

"A Herculean task," said Mister Duck thoughtfully. He

was standing in the spot where the longhouse now stood, thigh-deep in ferns. "Diverting the stream. We only attempted it in the second year, when there were fourteen of us living here. Couldn't have done it without Jean, of course. Not just the know-how. He worked like an ox . . . kept us going . . . I wish you could have been with us, Rich. I wish you could have been with us from the very beginning. Me, Sal, and Bugs . . . The mood, you can't imagine . . ."

I pushed carefully through the shrubs, pacing out the distance from the longhouse door to where I estimated my bed must be. It was curious to be in the position where I knew, at that moment, I was also sleeping. "I can imagine the mood," I said, stepping sideways, disconcerted by the idea that I was standing on my head. "I can imagine it easily."

Mister Duck waggled a finger at me. "If I didn't know you better, Rich, I'd take offense at that. There's no way you can imagine the way we felt. Apart from anything, you're too young. On and off, I'd been traveling with Sal and Bugs for over eleven years. Eleven years, Rich! How can you imagine what it's like, living with cancer for eleven years?"

". . . Cancer?"

"Sure, cancer. Or AIDS. What do you want to call it?"

"Call what?"

"Living with death. Time limits on everything you enjoy. Sitting on a beautiful beach, waiting for a fucking time limit to come up. Affecting the way you look at the sand and the sunsets and the way you taste the rice. Then moving on and waiting for it to happen all over again. For eleven years!" Mister Duck shivered. ". . . Then to have that cancer lifted. To think you've found a cure . . . That's what you can't imagine, Rich."

The waterfall and its pool, at least, were exactly the same. A few shrubs different, I suppose, and doubtless a few invisible branches had broken in the trees, but not enough differences to warrant a double take.

One major difference perhaps, but one that would have taken me a while to notice. The carved tree hadn't been carved, and as soon as we arrived by the pool, Mister Duck produced a pocketknife and set about cutting in the names.

I watched him for a while, interested by the concentration on his usually restless face. Then, as he began to write the zero calendar, I asked, "Why me?"

He smiled. "I liked the way you talked when I threw the joint at you. You were so indignant and funny. But mainly, I chose you because you were a traveler. Any traveler would have done the job. Spreading the news is in our nature."

"Our?"

"I'm no better than you. I'm just the same."

"Maybe worse . . ."

Mister Duck completed the last zero with a twist of his wrist, and an oval of bark dropped cleanly onto his lap. "Hey," he said happily. "I'd forgotten I did that. How amazing."

"Maybe worse," I repeated. "If I had a part in destroying the beach, I did it unwittingly. You did it on purpose."

"Who says I destroyed this place? Not me, pal. Not from where I'm standing." He glanced at his crossed legs. "Sitting."

"Who was it then?"

Mister Duck shrugged. "No one. Stop looking for some big crime, Rich. You have to see, with these places, with all these places, you can't protect them. We thought you could, but we were wrong. I realized it when Jed arrived. The word was out, somehow out, and after that it was just a matter of time . . . Not that I acted on it at first. I waited, hoping he was a one-off, I guess. But then the Swedes arrived and I knew for sure. Cancer back, no cure, malignant as fuck . . ." He stood up, dusted the earth off his legs, and flicked his bark zero into the waterfall pool. "Terminal."

I punched him as hard as I could, square on his solar plexus. Then, when he doubled up, I pushed him on the floor and kicked him in the face.

He took it all without any attempt to fight back. He let me lay into him until my knuckles were cut and my ankle was twisted. Then, when I'd run out of breath and had collapsed on the grass beside him, he uncurled, pulled himself up, and started to laugh.

"Shut the fuck up!" I panted. "Shut your fucking mouth!"

"Cripes," he chuckled, spitting out a broken tooth. "What's got into you?"

"You tricked me!"

"How? What did I ever offer you? What did I ever say I'd provide?"

"You . . ."

"I never offered you anything but Vietnam, and only because you asked for it. It so happens you wanted the beach, too. But if you could have had Vietnam and kept the beach, it wouldn't have been Vietnam."

"I didn't know that! You never told me!"

"Exactly." Mister Duck beamed. "That was the beauty of it. You not knowing was Vietnam too. Not knowing what was going on, not knowing when to give up, stuck in a struggle that was lost before it started. It's incredible really. It all works out."

"But I didn't want that Vietnam!" I began. "I didn't want that kind! I wan—" Then I stopped. "All? . . . Wait, you're saying it *all* works out?"

"All. Right to the bitter end." He rubbed his hands together. "You know, Rich, I always thought euthanasia was a kindness. But I never dreamed it could be so much fun."

beaucoup bad shit

spud bashing

I watched Sal from just inside the longhouse door. Everyone was standing in a big circle and she was in the middle, glowing, marching round, dishing out orders like they were birthday presents. For Greg's and Moshe's teams, special fish quotas to achieve; for Bugs and the carpenters, an eating area to construct; for Unhygienix and the gardeners, a feast to prepare; for Ella, seven whole chickens to pluck.

"Meat!" I heard one of the Yugoslavian girls say. "I have not eaten meat since . . . since . . ."

Since the last Tet celebration, it was generally agreed. Nine or ten months ago, a few had eaten a monkey that Jean had killed. Monkey, which tasted more like lamb than chicken, Jesse reported. Something Sammy might have found interesting, as an exception to his rule of exotic food.

Watching Sal's skillful organizing, I wondered how she'd react if I explained that our respite with the rafters was temporary in the extreme, and that all our efforts to protect the beach would come to nothing. I wondered if this news would frighten her as much as it frightened me.

When everyone had woken that morning and the longhouse had begun to buzz, I'd pretended to be asleep. Difficult, when Françoise tried to rouse me, but Sal soon called her off.

"Leave him be," she'd said, doubtless realizing I was faking. "Richard had a tough day yesterday, collecting all the dope for tonight."

Thankfully it didn't take long for the longhouse to empty

and I was able to remove the sheets from over my head, light a candle, and light a cigarette. I'd actually been awake for a good two hours before the others, itching for nicotine all that time. I should have crept out when I had the chance. It would have meant I wasn't trapped in the longhouse. But at five a.m. I knew it would still be dark outside, and darkness was something I didn't feel ready for. I didn't know what it might be hiding. So instead I had two hours of my imagination running riot, trying to second-guess Mister Duck.

The only thing I could be sure of was that if Vietnam was heading for a bitter end, I was too. Past that, I couldn't be sure of anything. Working through the possibilities, the areas in which the end might come were as good as infinite. As an infantryman, all it might take was an ill-advised command from my CO. One that pushed my luck in the DMZ, one I accepted against my better instincts. Equally it might come from random bad luck. The same luck that jammed a soldier's M16 at the wrong time could make me slip as I jumped from the waterfall.

But knowing Mister Duck the way I did, I realized that these were not the threats that scared me the most. They were real enough, but they didn't have his nightmare hallmark. When he spoke about the bitter end, deep down I knew he only meant one thing. The VC. The fall of Saigon.

I was fortunate that, in her attempt to wake me, Françoise hadn't tried to pull the sheets from my head. If she had done, she'd have discovered that they were soaking wet and cold with sweat.

By eight, all the camp had been given their duties for the day's preparations and were busy working around the clearing. Worried about being seen and asked to join in, I went back to sit on my bed. It was a waste of time, knowing that someone would come to find me sooner or later, but I wanted to put it off as long as possible.

It was past eight-thirty when a plump silhouette appeared in the longhouse doorframe. "You're being missed," Sal said, walking through the shadows until she was caught in the light from my candle. "Greg's asked if you can work on his detail today. Keaty wants to swap notes on Koh Phangan." She smiled. "And Françoise, I know you'll be glad to hear, has asked me to make certain you join them as soon as you wake up."

"What about Jed?" I asked quickly.

"Jed?" Sal frowned as she settled into a lotus position beside my bed. "I haven't seen him yet. But I'm sure he'd like to see you too."

". . . I'll go to see him later."

"Fine." She nodded. "Actually, just a thought, but maybe leave it for a while. There's quite a few people near the tent at the moment, and I have a feeling that things are getting extremely delicate with Christo. Jed might prefer not to be disturbed, and I think we should respect that."

"But he might prefer me to—"

"I'll check on him myself in a little while if it's worrying you. And anyway . . ." The barest suggestion of apprehension appeared on Sal's face. So slight that if I'd looked away as it happened, I'd never have noticed a change. "There was something else I was hoping you might do."

I tried to keep my expression as steady as hers.

"You see, Richard, I know it may feel like with our rafters gone, our troubles are as good as over. But I'm afraid that isn't quite the case. We still have the problem of the Swedes, and having gotten this far, I'm extremely reluctant to risk anything else going wrong. Now . . ." She paused to tuck a stray curl of hair back over her ears. "If Christo dies during Tet, no one has to know. People aren't exactly begging for news, so I can hold it back until the time feels right. No, our real problem, to my mind, is . . ."

"Karl . . ."

". . . Karl. That's right. And I'm afraid the responsibility for him must lie with you."

Unconsciously I squeezed the sheets with my fists. "With me?"

"Yes, you're quite right to look so guilty."

"Guilty?"

"If you hadn't disturbed him, he'd have stayed in his hole all through today and tonight, and maybe through the next week as well. Of course, we'd have had to deal with him at some point, but I was planning to leave that matter until after Tet . . . thanks to you, a luxury that has gone." She gestured vaguely in the direction of the longhouse door. "Take a look out there. You can see how important Tet is to everyone here. It's vital we make sure it goes smoothly. I can't really stress that enough . . ."

With a jolt, I realized the direction she was taking. She might have been a long way from delivering the bottom line, but I suddenly understood exactly what it would be.

"So," she said, and now I could clearly hear the controlled tension in her voice. "Let me spell the problem out. With Karl running around like a headless chicken, who's to say he won't suddenly appear during—"

"Sal," I interrupted. "I won't do it."

There was a short silence.

Although her composure remained fixed, I could sense the level of calculation at which Sal's mind was working. With a chess player's vacant gaze she was running through lists of responses, possible responses to the responses, and beyond. Four or five moves in advance, the variables becoming more complex at each step.

Eventually she crossed her arms. "You won't do what, Richard?"

"I won't, Sal. I won't do it."

"Do what?"

"Don't ask me, please . . ."

"Don't ask you to . . ."

I looked at her carefully, wondering if it was possible I'd read the signals wrong. But as my eyes moved to her face, hers dipped, and I knew for certain I was right.

And Sal saw this too. Immediately the pretense dropped, and with a slight shrug she said, "I'm afraid I *am* asking you, Richard."

I shook my head. "Sal, please . . ."

"I'm going to leave the longhouse now. In half an hour I'll come back and you will be gone. By tonight, all of our troubles will be behind us. The last month will be concluded. We'll never have to even think about it ever again."

She stood up to go, drawing in a deep breath as she rose.

"The beach is my life, Richard, but it's yours, too. Don't forget that. You can't afford to let me down."

I nodded miserably.

"Good." She returned the nod, turned around, and walked away.

Outside, everyone apart from the fishing details was busy in the clearing. Most were outside the kitchen hut, helping to peel an enormous mound of vegetables, at least four times our usual ration. Unhygienix had stuck some of the chicken feathers in his hair. The carpenters were in the middle, marking out the dimension of the seating area. Bugs and Cassie had started to lay down palm leaves, loosely meshed together, as a carpet.

All engrossed in their work and laughter. I easily ducked around the jungle side of the longhouse without being seen.

is it safe?

I thought of the caves after I'd checked around the waterfall and the far end of the Khyber Pass. If I'd been thinking more clearly, I would have checked the caves first. Not that it would have made much difference. The boat had probably been gone since sunup.

These days I can find comfort in the idea that, weirdly, my deranged assault had cured Karl after all. I often picture him, trying to guess what he's doing at this moment or that. All the images revolve around him having a normal life, and a loose impression of what a normal life might be in Sweden. Skiing, eating, working in an office, drinking with friends in a bar. An oak-paneled bar with moose heads and hunting trophies on the walls, for some reason. The more mundane the picture, the more comfort it gives me.

But at the time, my reaction wasn't so straightforward. Part of me was relieved that killing Karl was now an impossibility. I doubt I'd have killed him if he had been in the caves, despite the inflexibility of Sal's order, but I'm glad I never had the chance to find out. Most of me, however, was numb with shock. For the first few minutes after seeing the empty cove, I didn't even have the will to climb out of the water. All I could manage was to hang on to the rocks, and let myself be scraped up and down by the swell. I couldn't begin to imagine how Sal would react to this development. Karl turning up during Tet was of almost zero consequence compared to losing the boat, let alone the possible consequences of his arrival on Koh Phangan.

Eventually one of the larger swells as good as threw me onto the shelf where the gasoline can was usually tied down. Once there I dragged myself a little further in and didn't move again until, a short while later, I saw someone surface near the underwater passage.

Instinctively I ducked down, not recognizing the dark bobbing head at first. An instant paranoid scenario had formed: since I was someone who knew too much, Sal had sent Bugs after me in the same way that I'd been sent after Karl. Maybe this was what she'd meant by saying I couldn't afford to let her down.

"Richard?" the head called over the sound of the waves. It was Etienne. He was treading water, looking around, apparently having spotted neither me nor the missing boat. "Are you here, Richard?"

Of all the people I might fear on the beach, Etienne was the least likely candidate. Warily I stood up and waved him over.

I only noticed how cold he was when he'd swum over to the shelf and hauled himself up. I could hear his teeth chattering. The sun was still too low in the sky to reach inside the cave entrance, and the sea wind chilled the spray. "I followed you," he said, rubbing goose bumps off his arms. "I wanted to talk."

I paused, wondering why he hadn't noticed that the boat was gone. Then it dawned on me that there was a good chance he'd never been on this side of the caves. In which case he'd also never been through the underwater passage before. Very brave, I commented to myself. Or just as crazy as everyone else.

"I know there has been some difficulty between us," he continued. "Some difficulty between us, yes?"

I shrugged.

"Please, Richard. I would be very happy if we could talk about this. We should not be this way. Not at this time . . ."

"What time is that?"

"Before . . ." Etienne swallowed awkwardly. "Before Tet. Sal wants all difficulties to be over for Tet. A new start for the new year . . . Everybody else in the camp has forgotten their arguments. Keaty and Bugs even. So . . . I thought we should talk about our problem and make friends again . . . I thought we should talk about when you kissed Françoise. . . ."

It was funny. My world was falling to pieces, everything in my life revolved around threat, and my nerves were shot to shit. But hearing that Etienne was still worried about the kiss with Françoise made me feel like laughing out loud.

"That is the problem, no? It is because of my reaction. My stupid reaction. Really, it was all my fault. I am very sorry that—"

"Etienne, what the hell are you talking about?"

". . . The kiss."

"The kiss." I glanced up at the sky. "Fuck the kiss. And fuck all that crap about Tet and Sal too. I know how much you care about Tet."

"I care about Tet!" he exclaimed, very alarmed. "Of course, I care very much! I am working very hard to make sure tha—"

"Bullshit," I interrupted.

Etienne stood up, making as if he was going to dive back into the water. "I have to get back to the fishing detail now. I only wanted to apologize so that now we can be friends and—"

I caught his elbow and dragged him back down. "Jesus! What's the matter with you?"

"Nothing! Richard, I only wanted to apologize! Please, now I must get back to—"

"Etienne, will you cut it out? You're acting like I'm the fucking Gestapo!"

He went very silent.

"What?" I shouted. "What is it?"

He still wouldn't reply, but looked extremely worried.

"Say something!"

After at least half a minute, Etienne cleared his throat. "Richard, I want to speak to you, but . . . I do not know . . ."

"You don't know what?"

He took a deep breath. "I do not know if it is . . . safe."

"Safe?"

"I . . . I understand Sal has not been happy with me . . ."

I dropped my head into my hands. "Christ," I muttered. "You do think I'm the Gestapo."

"I think you . . . do things. You do things for Sal. Everybody knows . . ."

"Everybody knows?"

"Today, you were looking for Karl . . ."

"What does everybody know?"

"Where is Karl, Richard? Did you catch him?"

I closed my eyes against a wave of nausea.

"Is he dead now?"

Everyone knew I did things for Sal. Everyone talked about it. They just didn't talk about it in front of me.

Etienne might have continued speaking, asking about what I'd done with Karl, but I can't be sure because I wasn't really listening. My head was filling up. I was remembering the way Cassie had looked at me when I'd let Bugs slip and slide in his shit. And the way a consensus of silence could drop as fast as an Asian rainstorm, and Jean nervously asking me on a date, and unmentioned gunshots. Unnoticed Christo dying in the death tent, Sten's funeral forgotten in half a day, Karl forgotten on a beach.

Except now, suddenly, not forgotten on a beach after all. Deliberately avoided to provide me with a discreet window of opportunity. A space for me to do the things I did for Sal.

God knows what those days since the food poisoning had

been like for Etienne. It's impossible for me to put myself in his shoes, working through how he must have interpreted the events around him. I know because I've tried. The nearest I got was while I was sitting with him in the empty cove, and I've never been close since.

Ultimately, I've only got one reliable touchstone to his experience. The scene that followed Karl running through the clearing with me on his tail. The moment when Françoise strode away from Etienne, distancing herself from the liability that he'd become, ignoring his outstretched arms. I'd give a lot to know what she'd said to him later. But obviously it was enough for him to realize that once Karl was out of the way, he might be next.

"Etienne," I said, hearing my voice from far away. "Would you like to go home?"

He didn't seem to reply for a long time. "You mean . . . the camp?"

"I mean home."

". . . Not the camp?"

"Not the camp."

"Not . . ."

"Leaving the beach. France for you and Françoise, England for me."

I turned to face him, and was immediately hit by a second rush of sickness. It was the expression on his face, hiding his hope so badly. "It's all right," I murmured, and reached out, intending to pat his shoulder for reassurance. But as soon as I moved, he recoiled.

"Don't worry," I said. "Everything will be okay. We're going to leave tonight."

efforts

I was a fool. I was kidding myself. As the idea of leaving had come into my head, another idea had sneaked inside with it. That maybe this was the way it could all end up. Not in some VC dope guard attack and a panic-stricken evacuation from the clearing, but with a simple demobilization of forces. After all, this was the way Vietnam ended for a lot of American soldiers. Most American soldiers. Statistics were on my side, I'd have played by Mister Duck's rules, and I'd be out in one piece.

I could not have been more wrong, but that was the way I was thinking. Full of hasty schemes and plans, and the fucked-up optimism that comes from desperation.

I wasn't bothered by the practicalities of leaving. It would have been easier if Karl hadn't taken the boat, but we still had the raft. If that was gone, we'd swim. We were all much fitter than we had been and I had no doubt we could do it again. So with transportation out of the way, the only other complication was food and water. But water could be solved with water bottles, and catching fish was our specialty. All in all, the practicalities weren't worth more than passing consideration. I had much more serious things on my mind, like who we'd take with us.

Françoise was the first to sort out. She was standing two boulders over from mine, one hand loosely resting on her thigh and the other pressed to her lips. Etienne stood in front of her, talking rapidly, too quiet for the sound to carry.

Their conversation became increasingly animated. Intense enough for me to start worrying that Gregorio would notice there was some kind of problem. He was in the water, closer to me than to them, diving with Keaty. But just as I began to contemplate ways I might distract Greg's attention, the exchange abruptly ended. Françoise looked over at me with wide eyes. Etienne said something urgent and she quickly turned back. Then Etienne threw a quick nod in my direction, and that was that. I knew she'd agreed to leave.

It was a big relief. I'd been completely unable to predict how she'd react, and, worryingly, so had Etienne. He'd said that it would all depend on whether she put the beach above her love for him. A close call, judging by the way things had been going, and we both knew it.

But however close the Françoise call was, it was a lot more straightforward than the other two names on our list: Jed and Keaty. Or my list, I should say, because Etienne didn't want to take either of them. I could see his point—if we only had to take Françoise, we could almost have left at once. We could have been above the cliffs and on our way to the raft within sixty minutes. But over the months of my beach life, I'd done enough to keep me in nightmares for the next twenty years. I didn't want to add to my sentence now. Jed and Keaty had been my best two friends on the beach, and even if it was risky—particularly with Keaty—I couldn't disappear without offering them the chance to come too.

The nightmares I couldn't avoid were Gregorio, Ella, Unhygienix, Jesse, and Cassie. Even if they agreed to come—which they wouldn't—and we managed to keep it secret from Sal—which would be impossible—we'd never all fit on the raft. So they had to be left behind. And I accepted that without any internal debate. It was irrelevant how it made me feel.

Soon after Etienne had finished talking to Françoise, she swam over to where I sat and pulled herself halfway out of the water. I waited for her to say something, but she kept quiet. She didn't even look at me.

"Is there a problem?" I whispered, keeping one eye over her shoulder. Gregorio and Keaty were still diving nearby. ". . . You understand why we have to go?"

"Maybe," she replied after a pause. "I understand that Etienne wants to leave because he is frightened of Sal."

"He's right to be frightened of her."

"Is he?"

"Yes."

"But I do not think that is why you are leaving . . . For you, there is something else."

". . . Something else?"

"You would not leave if it was only because Etienne is frightened of Sal."

"I would. I am."

"No." She shook her head. "Will you tell me why you want to leave?"

"It's just like Etienne told you . . ."

"Richard. I am asking you. Please tell me why."

"There's nothing to tell. I think if we stay Etienne may be in danger."

"You do not think it can get better after Tet? Everyone says life will be better after Tet. You do not think maybe we should stay? We can wait for a few more days, and then, if you are still afraid . . ."

"Tet will change nothing, Françoise. Life will only get worse."

"Worse . . . Worse than we have had."

"Yes."

"But you will not tell me why."

". . . I don't know how I could."

"But you are sure."

"Yes. I'm sure."

She slipped back into the water. "We will never be able

to come back," she said just before her head submerged, and sighed. "So sad . . ."

"Perhaps," I replied to the stream of bubbles she left behind her on the surface. "If there was anything to come back to."

Ten minutes later, Gregorio held up his fishing spear. A milkfish flapped on its point, sliding itself further down the shaft with its efforts to get free, the last fish needed for the extra quota.

Françoise, Etienne, and Gregorio began to make their way back toward the beach, jumping between the boulders where possible, swimming where necessary. Keaty and I stayed back.

"Hang on," I said when the others had set off. "I want to show you something."

He frowned. "We've got to get the catch back."

"It can wait. Twenty minutes. Twenty-five. It's important."

"Well," he said, and shrugged. "If it's important . . ."

show, don't tell

I had imagined that, of the three, Keaty would be the hardest to persuade. He'd lived on the beach longer than the rest of us, he didn't have Françoise's attachment to Etienne, or Jed's bleak disillusionment. But it turned out he was the easiest. All I had to do was to show him where the boat had been and he virtually came up with the idea himself.

"It can't be gone," Keaty said, and leaned over, trailing his arms in the water as if hoping to find its sunken prow. "It just can't be. It's not possible."

"But it is."

"It *can't* be."

"You can see for yourself."

"Don't tell me what I can see!"

". . . I don't know what Sal's going to say . . ."

"I do! She's going to fucking flip! She's going to lose her mind! She's going to—" He rose up with a jerk and clapped both hands to his head. "Oh my God, Rich . . ."

I frowned with what I imagine looked like innocent concern. ". . . What is it?"

"I was the one who tied it up . . . I was the one who . . . Jesus C*hrist*!"

"What? Tell me!"

"I'm dead!" he almost screamed. "I'm a fucking dead man!"

". . . Dead? Why?"

"The food poisoning! And now losing the boat! *Shit! Fuck!* Of all things, losing the . . . Don't you get it? She'll do for me like she did for . . . for . . . Oh no!" He leapt to his feet and started quickly backing away. "This is why you got me here, isn't it? She already knows! *She already fucking knows!*"

I stood up too.

"You stay where you are!"

"Keaty . . ."

He drew back a fist. *"Stay where you are!"*

"Keaty . . ."

"I swear, if you make one fucking move I'll . . ."

"Keaty!" I yelled, suddenly feeling angry myself. "Shut the fuck up! I'm not going to attack you, for Christ's sake!"

"Back off!"

"Okay, okay!" I took several steps away from him. "I'm backing off!"

"Further! Get right back against the rock!"

I did I as was told. "There! Satisfied?"

He stayed frozen with his fist raised. "If you make one move . . ."

"You'll pulverize me. I know."

"I will do it! I'm not Karl! I'm telling you, you won't have a fucking prayer!"

"I *know*. I'll be creamed. But you've *got* to believe me, I've got no intention of attacking you. I can't even believe you think I would! You're one of my best friends!"

His fist lowered, but no more than an inch.

"Does Sal know about the boat?"

"No."

"You *promise?*"

"On my life. The whole reason I brought you here is so you could find out before she did. And think about it, Keaty. How could she know? You only got back last night, so when could she have had a chance to find out?"

He thought about this a few seconds, then lowered his fist completely. "Yes," he murmured blankly. "That's true . . . She couldn't know . . ."

"Right."

"But . . . she'll find out soon . . . She'll have to . . ."

"She'll find out very soon."

"Fuck!" he blurted, his panic rising again. "And then what will I do? I won't be able to sleep at nights! I won't be able to go anywhere alone! I'll have to . . ."

"Leave?"

"I'll have to leave! Yes! Jesus! I should leave right now! I'll take the—" He whirled around and stared at the cove. "Oh God," he whispered. "But I can't. I'm trapped here . . . trapped . . ."

"No," I replied, raising a hand to my temples as if formulating a rapid and brilliant scheme. "There just might be another option."

spiked

Now I was on a roll. Getting on top of things. The two hardest converts were converted and all I had to do was get to Jed, fill him in, and wait for our chance to slip away. I was feeling so good that I started humming my mouse song as Keaty and I reentered the clearing. The only problem was, Keaty joined in too. Joined in with manic gusto, hitting the wrong notes, turning heads. "What are you doing?" I hissed. "You sound like a swarm of bees."

"I can't help it," he hissed back through a rigid ventriloquist's smile. "I'm freaking out. I feel like everybody's watching us."

"You've got to act normal."

"I don't know if I'll be able to handle this, Rich."

"The Game Boy. Go and play the Game Boy. And if Sal asks you to join in with the preparations, just try to be calm."

"Got it," he whispered, and walked off to his tent, arms stiffly swinging by his sides.

Etienne and Françoise were coping a lot more successfully, but they did have each other for support. They sat close to the kitchen hut, apparently chatting idly, busy helping to gut the enormous catch of fish.

Sal, meanwhile, was nowhere to be seen. I wanted to locate her before I tried to get to the hospital tent—remembering that she'd told me to stay away from Jed—so I moved to the center of the clearing, expecting to spot her with Bugs and the carpenters.

The seating area had progressed swiftly over the time I'd been away. Our bedsheets and one or two unzipped sleeping bags had been suspended between bamboo poles, making a flat marquee about twenty-five feet in diameter. Bugs had Cassie on his shoulders, who was giggling and laying palm leaves above the sheets. I guessed the canopy needed to be thick enough to block out the glow from our candles and barbecue, in case any planes happened to pass over us tonight.

But Sal wasn't with the carpenters, either. Which meant there was a strong possibility she was in the hospital tent with Jed.

"Shit," I said.

"Not impressed?" said a crisp voice, directly behind me.

I delayed for a second in order to compose myself and do some rapid thinking, then turned around. ". . . Impressed, Sal?"

"With our construction."

"Oh, I'm very impressed with that. *Very* impressed. It's amazing. No, I was thinking about something else."

"Mmm?"

"My cigarettes. I left half a packet on the beach."

"Oh."

"No big deal. I've just got a feeling they were at the low-tide mark, and the water's coming in. Stupid of me."

"Doesn't seem too serious."

"No, no." I shook my head. "Not at all serious."

"Good . . . I'm glad to see you've cheered up since this morning."

"I feel much better."

"I assume that means I shouldn't worry about any unexpected problems tonight."

". . . That's right. No problems. You can . . . forget about him."

"Forget?" Sal said, not missing a beat. "Forget about who?"

". . . Karl."

She gave me an odd look. "Who?"

"Karl."

"Who's Karl?"

"Karl's . . ." I began, then the penny dropped. "Nobody."

"I thought you were talking about someone here."

"No."

"Fine." Sal nodded fractionally. "Well, I'd better get back to work. Still lots to do."

"Sure."

"If you get stuck for a chore, let me know. We'll soon find something."

"Right."

"Lovely."

A few moments later Sal was standing under the marquee and pointing out gaps in the sheets to Bugs, although he didn't appear to be paying attention. He still had Cassie on his broad shoulders, and he kept breaking into a little jog to make her squeal.

It was past four o'clock before I had a chance to get to the hospital tent, and a chance to do something else as well. A piece of inspired opportunism, I thought at the time.

At four, all of the preparations for the evening were as good as finished. The marquee was complete, the stews were bubbling, the chickens were ready to barbecue, and the vegetable peelings, feathers, and fish guts had been taken down the Khyber Pass and thrown away. So Sal, sensing a lull, suggested a huge game of soccer down on the beach. "Let's work up an appetite!" she'd called out. "A serious appetite!"

This was excellent news. As Keaty and I never joined in the soccer, we had an excuse to remain behind. Plus we could offer to tend the cooking pots, meaning Unhygienix could leave with the others. By ten past, the clearing was empty.

"He's going to notice," said Keaty nervously, watching me

sprinkle huge handfuls of grass into the stew. "It's going to taste really strange."

"If he notices I'll just admit it was me. I'll say it was for the atmosphere."

"He hates people fucking with his food."

"Yeah, well, if we don't do something the party will go on all night." I paused, picking up roughly half an ounce, and chucked it into the biggest pot. Then I chucked in another half. "Anyway, after an hour he'll be too messed up to give a shit."

"He'll be tripping. Everyone will."

"Whatever. Just make sure you don't eat any of this. Stick to the chicken and rice. And make sure Etienne and Françoise get the same message."

"It won't be easy to avoid eating the stew."

"We'll manage." I dusted my hands off and surveyed my handiwork. After a couple of turns with a stick there was no evidence of the new ingredient. "You reckon we should chuck in some magic mushrooms or something?"

"No."

"Okay. So how much do you reckon is in there now?"

"In total? All the pots?"

"In total."

"A lot. Way too much. You're a fucking lunatic."

"A lunatic!" I laughed. "Hold the front page."

don't mean nothing

The atmosphere in the hospital tent was the kind where you feel uncomfortable if you cough or make a hurried movement—contemplative, detached. I felt like I was in a temple. Even more so because I was praying.

"Die," went the prayer. "Make this breath the last one."

But every time, Christo would breathe again. Despite all the odds, despite the achingly long gaps, his chest would suddenly inflate and deflate. He'd still be alive, and the waiting would start all over again.

For much of the time, I studied Jed. He looked strange because his hair and beard were completely slick, flattened down with blood and sweat. I could see the shape of his head in a way I never had before. It was more angular than I'd imagined. Smaller and, where his scalp showed between the wet curls, shockingly white.

He didn't look at me once; neither had he acknowledged my presence when I climbed in. His eyes were set on Christo's calm face, and weren't going to budge until they were good and ready. Christo's face, I noticed, was just about the only clean thing in the tent. Under his chin you could see the dark smear marks where Jed had wiped him down, and by the time you reached his neck you couldn't see past the dirt to his skin.

Another thing that caught my attention was that a little bag—which had been sitting just to the right of Jed until yesterday—was now gone. Karl's bag. I'd known it was his because peeking out of its top flap had been the Nike swim shorts he sometimes wore. Although the missing bag was my only evidence, and remains my only evidence, I felt sure that Karl must have visited Christo before he left. I liked that idea.

Visiting his friend, taking his bag, stealing the boat. Cured, all right.

Time passed much faster than I estimated. When I looked at my watch I was expecting it to read four-thirty, but instead it read ten after five. I'd been in there for a whole hour. But watching Christo was absorbing. It set my mind thinking about stuff like the afterlife, because there was something about the way Christo was dying that made an afterlife seem particularly unlikely. It's hard to explain what the something was. His eyes maybe, which were slightly open even though he was obviously unconscious. The two glittering slits made him look so nonfunctional. Just a machine that, for whatever reason, happened to be packing in.

When I saw my watch, I realized I had to go. The rest of the camp would be returning soon, so I decided that I had no choice but to break the temple atmosphere.

"Jed," I said in a soothing, priestly manner. "There's something we should talk about."

"You're leaving," he said bluntly.

". . . Yes."

"When?"

"Tonight . . . Tonight, when everyone's crashed out after Tet. Will you come?"

"If Christo is dead."

". . . And if he isn't."

"I'll stay."

I bit the inside of my lip. "You understand that unless you come tonight, there'll be no way off the island."

"Mmm."

"You'll be stuck here with whatever's coming. And the problem isn't going to be more travelers turning up. Karl's taken the boat. If he contacts his family or Sten's and Christo's families . . ."

"It isn't the Thai police that are coming."

"And when Sal finds out we're gone tomorrow, the shit's going to—"

"It's already hit."

"I won't be able to wait for you."

"I don't expect you to."

"I want you to come."

"I know."

"And do you know that it makes zero difference to Christo if you're here or not? Do you know that, too? With the amount of oxygen he's taking in, most of his brain has already shut down."

"He isn't dead until he stops breathing."

"Okay . . ." I thought hard for a couple of seconds. "So what if we stop him breathing? We could cover up his mouth. It would only take five minutes."

"No."

"You don't have to do it. I'll do it for you. You could hold his hand or something. It would be a nice way for him to go. It would be very tranquil and—"

"Fuck it, Richard!" Jed snapped, spinning his head round and looking at me for the first time. But as soon as he did so, his expression softened. I was biting my lip again. I didn't like Jed shouting at me.

"Look," he said. "Christo should be dead by tonight, so I should be able to come with you."

"But . . ."

"Now why don't you go? I don't think Sal would like it if you were in here."

"No, but . . ."

"You'll check on me before you leave."

I sighed. Jed turned back to Christo. I stuck around for a minute or so, then backed out of the tent.

Outside, I saw Keaty scurrying off toward the Khyber Pass with an armful of something soggy and unrecognizable. When he came back I asked him what he was doing.

"I took the dope out of the cooking pots," he explained, drying his sticky chest with a T-shirt. He smelled of lemongrass and his hands were shaking.

"What?"

"I had to. It kept floating to the surface. Unhygienix would have seen it immediately. But it was in there for an hour so . . ."

"Your shorts," I said.

"Shorts?"

"They're covered in stew. Go and change them."

His eyes flicked down. "Shit!"

"Just go and change them. It's no big deal."

"Change them. Right."

Before he'd returned, the rest of the camp began pouring into the clearing. Singing, laughing, arm in arm. Tet was about to kick off.

potchentong

Take a green coconut, still up in the tree, and cut a small incision in its base. Under the incision, hang a flask to catch the dripping milk. Then leave it for a few hours. When you come back, you'll find that the milk has fermented and that if you drink it you'll get pissed. A neat trick. It tastes okay; a bit sugary but okay. I was surprised I'd never seen it done before.

Thanks to the gardeners, we all had coconut-shell cups

filled with the moonshine beer. "Down in one!" Bugs was shouting. "Down the hatch!" And people had fizzy juice running over their chins and chests. Françoise was eyeing Keaty, and Etienne was eyeing me, and we had more running over our chins than anyone else.

Bugs finished his cup first and kicked it into the jungle like it was a soccer ball. It must have fucking hurt, like kicking a lump of wood. But the idea caught on and just about everyone had a crack, and soon the clearing was filled with people hopping around, clutching a foot, giggling like crazy. "Hopping mad," I said to Keaty, but he didn't get the joke.

"Sal keeps staring at me," he whispered. "She *knows* something. Should I kick the coconut? What if I break my foot? Would you leave me behi—" He interrupted himself by dropping the shell and punting it. His face screwed up with the pain and he let out a yell louder than all the others. "Did it," he gasped. "Is she still looking?" I shook my head. She never had been looking anyway.

When Jean began to produce a second round of drinks, I maneuvered myself around to where Françoise and Etienne were standing. I did it partly to get away from Keaty, whose jumpiness didn't seem helped by my presence. I think it reminded him of what was going on.

Françoise was giving a great performance. If she was feeling the tension, I'd never have guessed it. Externally, she seemed to be in the party spirit one hundred percent. When I walked up she gave me a flamboyant hug and a kiss on each cheek, and loudly said, "This is all so wonderful!"

I mentally congratulated her. She was even taking the performance through to slightly slurring her words, and not overdoing it either. Getting it exactly right.

"Can I have a kiss too?" said Jesse, nudging one of the carpenters.

"No," Françoise replied with a dizzy smile. "You are too ugly."

Jesse clasped one hand to his heart and the other to his forehead. "I'm too ugly! I'm too ugly for a kiss!"

"That's right," said Cassie. "You are." She gave him her beer. "Here. You'd better drown your sorrows."

"I think I should!" Tipping his head back, he drained the liquid in one slurp and tossed the empty vessel behind him. "But you still love me, don't you, Caz?"

"Not when you call me Caz, Jez."

"Caz!" he howled. "Caz! Jez! Caz!" Then he scooped her up in his arms and began staggering off toward the longhouse.

A couple of minutes later, Etienne was called over to help carry the food to the eating area, and Françoise and I were left alone. She said something to me, but I didn't catch it because I was concentrating on something else. By the kitchen hut I'd seen Unhygienix tasting some of the stew with a puzzled frown.

"You are not listening to me," Françoise said.

Unhygienix shrugged and began organizing the cooking pot carriers.

"You never listen to me anymore. Before, if I was talking to you, you would always listen. But now you have no time to even talk to me."

"Yeah . . . Has Keaty told you not to eat the stew?"

"Richard!"

I frowned. "What?"

"You are not listening to me!"

". . . Oh. Well I'm sorry. I've got a lot on my mind."

"Not me."

"Huh?"

"I am not on your mind."

"Uh . . . Of course you are."

"I am not." She poked me in the ribs. "I think you do not love me anymore."

I looked at her in astonishment. ". . . Are you serious?"

"Very serious," she said petulantly.

"You can't be."

"I am! For so many weeks you have not even talked to me. Not even *looked* at me. In fact, I think you are only interested in Sal."

"Sal?"

"Yes! You remember how it was with us before? Always, we were . . ." Françoise hesitated. ". . . You *know* how we were."

"Yes. I mean, no. But . . . Jesus! Do we have to talk about this right now? Of all times, does it have to be *right* now?"

"Of course, it must be now. Etienne is not here, and maybe soon I will never see you again!"

"Françoise!" I hissed. "Keep it down!"

"Maybe I should keep it down, but maybe I should not. In the dope field, when I would not be quiet, you pushed me to the ground and held me tightly." She giggled. "It was very exciting."

With a quick look around, I linked my arm in her elbow and began propelling her away toward the edge of the clearing. Once we were out of sight of the others I turned her round, held her head between my hands, and looked carefully at her pupils. They were all over the place. "Oh my God," I said furiously. "You're drunk."

"Yes," she admitted. "I am. It was this potchentong."

"Potchentong? What the fuck are you talking about?"

"Jean calls the drink potchentong. It is not the real potchentong, but—"

"How much have you had?"

"Three cups."

"Three? When?"

"With the football. The game."

"You *idiot*!"

"I had no choice! They were passing around the shell, and

you had to drink it all. They were watching and clapping, so what could I do?"

"Christ! Did Etienne drink some too?"

"Yes. Three cups."

I closed my eyes and counted to 10. Or meant to. That stuff never works. I stopped when I was on about 4.

"Right," I said. "Come with me."

"Where are we going?"

"Over here."

Françoise gasped as I pulled her behind a tree.

"Open your mouth," I instructed.

"Are you going to kiss me?"

The infuriating thing is, I'm sure that if I had tried to kiss her, she'd have let me. She was that drunk. But I had to shake my head.

"No, Françoise," I replied. "Not exactly."

She bit my fingers really hard when I stuck them down her throat. And she struggled and squirmed like a snake. But I was holding her with a vise grip around her neck, and once the fingers were in, there wasn't a lot she could do about it.

After she'd finished throwing up, she slapped me in the face, which I accepted. Then she said, "I could have done that myself."

I shrugged. "I didn't have time for an argument. Are you feeling more sober now?"

She spat. ". . . Yes."

"Good. Now go and wash yourself down in the waterfall stream and then discreetly make your way back to the clearing. And don't touch a drop of potchentong." I paused. "Or the stew."

When I returned to the party, Etienne had finished helping carry the food and was standing alone, probably looking for Françoise. I walked straight up to him. "Hi," I said. "Are you drunk?"

He nodded unhappily. "The potchentong . . . They made me drink it and—"

"I heard," I said, and tutted with sympathy. "Strong stuff, huh?"

"Very strong."

"Well, no worries. Just come with me."

a loose end

The layout was simple. Concentric circles under the marquee, the first a ring of candles, the second our banana leaf plates, the third our seated selves, and the fourth a final ring of candles. It looked spectacular and terrifying. Orange faces, flickering light, diffused through clouds of dope smoke. And such a level of noise. People weren't talking, they were shouting. Sometimes screaming. Nothing more than jokes or requests to pass the rice pot, but it sounded like screaming.

I'd made us all sit together. Keeping us together made it easier all round. We were able to get rid of our stew more easily and it kept Keaty and Françoise contained between me and Etienne. It also meant that our relative temperance was less likely to be noticed, something that was fast turning into a problem. Keaty had picked up on it first, a little under an hour after we'd started to eat.

"I told you they'd trip," he said. With the racket as a

backdrop, he didn't even have to whisper. "You put way too much in."

"You think they're actually tripping?"

"Maybe not seeing stuff, but . . ."

I looked over at Sal, who was directly opposite me in the circle. Strangely, despite the din, she looked like someone in an old silent movie. Sepia-toned, flickering, twisted lips with no discernible sounds coming out. Frozen lips. Arched eyebrows. She must have been laughing.

"But yeah, they're tripping," Keaty finished. "Either that or I am."

Unhygienix appeared behind us. "More stew!" he shouted.

I raised a hand. "So full! Can't eat more!"

"Yes! Eat more!" He reached over and ladled a huge dollop in front of me. It poured over the edges of my banana leaf like a lava flow, smothering rice grains, taking them with it. Little people in the lava, I thought, and suddenly felt like I was tripping too. I gave Unhygienix the thumbs-up, and he continued on his rounds.

A half hour later, around a quarter to nine, I excused myself on the pretext of a piss. I did need a piss as it happened, but mainly I wanted to check up on Jed. With the way things were going, I couldn't see the manic level being sustained later than midnight, so I wanted to know if our problem was resolved yet.

I relieved myself outside the hospital tent. Bad form in normal circumstances, but civic responsibility wasn't high on my list of priorities anymore. Then I stuck my head inside the flaps. To my amazement, Jed was asleep. He was in the same spot he'd been in earlier that day, but keeled over on his side. He'd probably been awake all the previous night.

Even more amazing was that Christo was still alive, doing

his pitiful inflate-deflate thing. So slight I'd be hard put to call it a genuine breath.

"Jed," I said, and he didn't stir. I said it louder, again with no response. Next a huge cheer came from the marquee. It lasted for a pretty long time, and when Jed still hadn't stirred I knew I had a golden opportunity in front of me.

I reached Christo's head by sliding around the left-hand side of the tent. Then, just as I'd suggested earlier, I pinched his nose and covered his mouth. There was no twitching, no resistance. A few minutes later I took my hands away, counted to 120, and slid back to the cool outdoors. And that was it. It really was that simple.

As I returned across the clearing, clicking my fingers in time with my footsteps, I saw the reason for the cheering I'd heard. Both the Yugoslavian girls were in the central circle of candles, heads resting on each other's shoulders, slow-dancing to the buzz of noise.

something happening
here

By the time I'd retaken my seat, the Yugoslavian girls had inspired some of the others. Sal and Bugs started dancing too, then Unhygienix and Ella, then Jesse and Cassie.

I may have had a few screws loose, but I was able to recognize this as a nice moment. Watching the four couples revolving around each other reminded me of the way things used to be on the beach. Even Sal seemed at peace, all her plans and manipulations pushed aside for the time being, aware of nothing more than straightforward affection for her lover. In fact, Sal looked like a completely different person. None of her confidence was apparent in her dancing. Her steps were tentative and slow, and she clung to Bugs with both arms, head pressed flat against his chest.

"You do not recognize her," Gregorio said to me, having followed the direction of my gaze. While I'd been killing Christo, he'd taken my place so he could chat with Keaty. "You have never seen her like this."

"No . . . I haven't."

"You know why?"

"No."

"Because tonight it is Tet, and Sal will only smoke or drink on Tet. The rest of the year, her mind is always clear, all hours in the day. We get high, but she keeps her mind clear for us."

"She cares very much about the beach."

"Very much," Greg echoed. "Of course." He smiled and stood up. "I will get us more coconut beer. You would like some?"

Both Keaty and I said no.

"Just for me then?"

"Just for you."

He ambled off toward the fishing buckets, which held the last of Jean's moonshine.

Ten o'clock. The dancing had stopped. Moshe was standing where the dancers had been, holding a candle up in one hand, the other hand touching the side of his face. I didn't know if anyone else was taking an interest in him, but I was. "This flame," he said as hot wax ran onto his wrist and down the length of his arm, forming a slim stalactite on his elbow. "Look."

"Look," said Etienne, gesturing to Cassie. She was also studying the candle flames, crouched over with an expression of rapt pleasure. Jesse was next to her, muttering something in her ear that made her jaw drop. Behind them, Jean sat with his back to one of the bamboo poles, covering his eyes with his fingers, removing them and blinking like a baby kitten.

"Night, Jim-Bob," called one of the Australian carpenters.

Six or seven people provided names, all at once. A ripple of laughter spread beneath the marquee. "Night, Sal," Ella called, above the competing voices. "Night Sal, night Sal, night Sal."

Soon Ella's cue became a soft chant that lasted as long as the cigarette I was smoking. Then Sal replied, "Thank you, children," and the ripple of laughter spread again.

A few minutes later the carpenter that had called out Jim-Bob said, "Is anyone else seeing shit?" When no one answered he added, "I'm seeing all kinds of shit over here."

"Potchentong," sang Jean like a tolling bell.

Moshe dropped the candle.

"Seriously, guys, I'm seeing all kinds of shit."

"Potchentong."

"Did you put mushrooms in the potchentong?"

"This flame," said Moshe. "This flame burned me." He began pulling the line of wax from his arm.

"Moshe's losing his fucking skin . . ."

"I am losing my skin?"

"Losing his skin!"

"Potchen-fucking-tong . . ."

I leaned over to Keaty. "This *can't* be just the dope," I whispered. "Even eating it, dope wouldn't do this, would it?"

He wiped beads of sweat off the back of his neck. "They're all crazy. It's worse being straight. It's doing my fucking head in just watching them."

"Yes," said Etienne. "Really, I do not like this. When can we go?"

I checked my watch for the fifteenth time in as many minutes. To the extent that I'd thought it out, I'd imagined leaving at around two or three a.m., when there'd be a bit of light creeping into the sky. But Etienne was right. I didn't like the way things were either, and at a pinch, we could probably set off while it was still dark.

"Give it an hour," I said. "I think we might be able to leave in an hour."

what it is ain't exactly clear

But an hour was no good. At ten-thirty, things started to go wrong.

Up until then I'd felt I was in control of the situation. Perhaps I even *was* in control of the situation. A number of difficulties—Françoise drunk, Christo breathing—had been solved; we'd gotten through the meal without anyone noticing that we were throwing our stew away; aside from Jed, there were no further loose ends to be tied; Tet was winding down. All we had to do was to bide our time and then make our move.

But at ten-thirty Mister Duck appeared in the marquee, and I knew I had a problem.

He appeared out of the shadows, stepping over the outer

ring of candles. Then he walked over to Sal and Bugs and, after acknowledging me with a vague grin, sat down beside them.

"Where are you going?" said Françoise as I stood up. It was the first thing she'd said in a while. Since the dancing she'd been lying with her head in Etienne's lap, staring intently at the sheets on the marquee. From her color I'd assumed she was feeling the effects of her afternoon boozing, but when she spoke I realized that she was also scared. Obviously, considering the circumstances, but I wasn't in a very empathic frame of mind. Neither was I in the right frame of mind to reassure anyone.

"We could be fucked," I said, stupidly speaking my thoughts out loud.

Etienne began looking around. "What? What is it?"

". . . I've got to check something out. The three of you don't move from this spot. Clear?"

"Not fucking clear." Keaty caught me by the leg. "What's going on, Richard?"

"I've got to do something."

"You're going nowhere unless you tell me what's going on."

"Let go of my leg. Greg is watching us."

Keaty squeezed tighter. "I don't care. You tell us what the fuck—"

I bent down and clamped my fingers on the soft underside of Keaty's wrist, blocking the blood. A couple of seconds later his hand fell away.

"Hi," I said to Sal.

"Richard," she replied happily. "Richard, my right-hand man. How are you, right-hand man?"

"Left-handed. I've started seeing fucked-up stuff." The

last words were directed at Mister Duck, who seemed amused.

"Sit down with us."

"I need to get some cigarettes from the longhouse."

"If you were sitting with us . . ." Sal drifted off briefly, then picked up the thread. "I'd know that you and Bugs were friends again."

"We are friends."

Mister Duck guffawed, but Bugs nodded, full of dreamy goodwill. "Yeah, man," he said. "All friends here."

"It was . . . This was the last thing I was worried about . . . I needed you two to be friends . . ."

I patted Sal's shoulder. "There's nothing more for you to worry about. Things are back to normal, just how you wanted."

"Yes . . . We did it, Richard."

"You did it."

"I'm sorry for shouting at you, Richard. All those times . . . I'm sorry." I smiled. "I need to get the cigarettes. We'll talk later."

"And you'll sit with us."

"Sure."

When Mister Duck walked through the longhouse door, I grabbed him by the neck and slammed him against the inside wall. "Right," I said. "Tell me what you're doing here."

He stared with a slightly baffled, innocent expression, then chuckled. "Are you here to stop us?"

No answer.

"Tell me why you're here!"

"The horror," he said.

". . . What?"

"The horror."

"What horror?"

"*The* horror!"

"*What horror?*"

He sighed, and with a quick movement, twisted out of my grip. "The horror," he said a final time, ducked through the doorway, and was gone.

For a few seconds I stayed where I was, my arms still pointlessly raised in the position where they'd been holding Mister Duck. Then I came to my senses and started jogging back to the marquee, making only the most cursory attempt at casualness in my haste.

"Okay," I whispered when I reached Keaty and the other two. "Get ready. We're going."

"Right now?"

"Yes."

"But . . . it's still pitch black out there!"

"We'll manage. I'll go first so I can get Jed and pick up the water bottles, then Etienne and Françoise, you leave five minutes later, then Keaty. We'll meet by the beach path in . . ."

that sound

At the exact moment I said "path," Bugs jumped to his feet. His dreamy goodwill was out the window. His eyes were wide and his teeth were bared. "What the *fuck* was that noise?" he hissed.

Everyone turned to look at him.

"What was that fucking *noise?*"

Unhygienix laughed sleepily. "Can you hear noises, Bugs?"

"It was . . . a branch being pushed. It was somebody pushing through branches."

Sal pulled herself out of the lotus position to sit on her knees. ". . . Are we all here?" she said, scanning around the sprawled figures.

"I'm not really *here,*" drawled Jesse. "I'm not really anywhere."

Bugs took a step away from the blackness outside the marquee. "Somebody is definitely out there."

"Maybe it's Karl . . ." someone offered.

Several heads turned to me.

"It isn't Karl."

"Jed?"

"Jed's in the hospital tent."

"Well, if it isn't Karl or Jed . . ."

"Wait!" Cassie was standing too. "I heard something! . . . There!"

We all strained our ears.

"It's nothing," Jesse began to say. "Will you all relax? It's just this strange trip—"

"This is no fucking trip," Bugs interrupted. "Everyone, get your heads together. I'm telling you there's people coming."

"People?"

And suddenly we were all rising to our feet, because we could all hear the noise. It was unmistakable. People, pushing through branches, walking on leaves, coming our way from the waterfall path.

"Run!" Sal shouted. "Everyone run! Now!"

Too late.

A figure materialized within four meters of us, picked out by the oily flames around the marquee. Within seconds, more appeared by his side. They all had their guns up, leveled straight at us. None seemed wet, so they couldn't have jumped from the waterfall. Maybe they knew a secret route into the lagoon or had used ropes to abseil the cliffs, or maybe they had simply floated down. The way they hovered in the darkness, it didn't seem unlikely.

I turned to look at my companions. Apart from Etienne and Françoise, I doubt any of them had seen the VC before and I was interested to see their reaction. It was suitably awed. Moshe and one of the gardeners had dropped to their knees, and the others were frozen in a perfect tableau of fright. Slack jaws, tensed jaws, arms bunched up to chests. I almost envied them. For a first encounter, it took some beating.

apocalypse

Escape was not an option. We were all about to get killed. I accepted the realization without bitterness. There wasn't anything I could do to stop it from happening and I felt I'd be dying with a clear conscience. Although I'd known that Vietnam might end this way, I hadn't run. I'd selflessly stuck around until I was sure that my friends would be able to run with me. For once, I'd done the right thing.

And this is why I was furious that the VC weren't doing the right thing. They weren't doing the right thing at all, and I was outraged.

As I turned back from looking at my companions, I saw the dope guard boss jab a finger at me. The next moment, one of his men dragged me out of the marquee and forced me to the ground. Appalled, it dawned on me that I was going to get shot first.

First! If I had to get shot, then tenth, eleventh, twelfth would be fine. But *first.* I couldn't believe it. I'd miss out on everything.

The guard rested the muzzle of his AK against my forehead. "You're making a big mistake," I said angrily. "You're *really* screwing up." I tilted my head at Moshe. "Why don't you do him instead? What difference does it make to you? Do him."

His sleek face gazed down at me indifferently.

"Him, for Christ's sake! That ape!"

". . . Aape."

"Ape, you fucking slope! You dink motherfucker! That gorilla! *Him* over there!"

I pointed at Moshe, who moaned feebly. Then the guard behind kicked me in the back.

"Oh shit," I gasped as red pain burned into my kidneys.

Unable to stop myself, I rolled over onto my side. The tableau didn't seem to have shifted, apart from Etienne, who had covered his eyes.

"Okay." With an effort, I got back onto my knees. "At least let me choose who does it."

I didn't make the mistake of pointing again. Instead I swiveled around so that it was the kick-boxer's gun that was aiming at my head.

"I want this guy. Fair enough, right? Get him to do it."

Kick-boxer frowned, then glanced over at the boss. The boss shrugged.

"Yes, you. You with the dragon tattoo." I paused, then had a look at his mouth. It was closed, pouting slightly with his puzzled expression. "Guess what? I know you don't have any front teeth!" I showed him mine and gave them a tap. "Missing, huh?"

He lifted a wary finger and touched between his lips.

"That's right!" I yelled. "You don't have any front teeth! And I already knew that!"

The kick-boxer kept his finger in his mouth a few moments, exploring his gums. Then he said something to the boss in Thai.

"Ah." The boss nodded. "You the boy always come to see us . . . Every day, ha? You li' to come see us."

I glared at him. Then, to my surprise, he squatted beside me and ruffled my hair.

"Funny boy in trees, every day. We li' you too. Take some Mary Jane, ha? Okay Mary Jane. Some Mary Jane, for you frien's."

"Hurry up and kill me," I said bravely.

"Kill you? Ah, funny boy . . . I no' kill you now." He ruffled my hair again and rose. "I no' kill anyone now," he said to the huddled figures under the marquee. "I give you warning. You people here, tha' okay for me. One year, two year, three year, no problem, ha?"

If he was waiting for a reply, none came. This seemed to piss him off. He took a slow lungful of air, then flew into a hysteria of rage. *"Bu' now, you makin' problem! You makin' bad fucking problem!"*

There was complete silence as he reached into his pockets and pulled out a piece of paper. Even the cicadas seemed to have got the message. *"You making maps!"* he screamed. Half the next sentence was lost on me, drowned out by a pounding in my ears. *". . . Bu' why you wan' do tha'? Maps bring new people! New people here! New people are danger for me! Tha' is bad fucking danger for you!"*

He hesitated, and with the same bewildering abruptness, became calm again. "Okeydokey," he muttered. Then he dropped the map on the dirt, unholstered his pistol, and fired a shot into it. The shot missed but was close enough to send the paper fluttering into the air. For the second time I was deafened. The muzzle had only been a foot away from my head.

When my hearing began to return, the boss was chatting away in an eerily conversational tone of voice. "So, my frien's. I li' you all ve'y much. Ve'y good. One year, two years, no problem. So you lis'en to my warning. Nex' time I will kill you all."

This final remark didn't have time to sink in, because for a third time my senses were put out of action. The boss punctuated his sentence by whipping his gun on the top of my head. Out of shock, I tried to stand up, and he hit me again. I dropped straight back down to my knees. The next thing I knew, he was holding on to the back of my T-shirt, keeping me steady.

"Wait," I said thickly. My bravado was entirely gone. I was afraid. Having had a little taste of what it might be like, I was absolutely certain I didn't want to be beaten to death. "Wait a moment please."

No use. The boss hit me incredibly hard. For a few seconds I was conscious, staring at his shoes. Reeboks, like the Koh Samui spiv. Then I blacked out.

I didn't know what was going on. A few things registered: footsteps, rustling, some hushed Thai voices, a couple of kicks that rolled me over. But none of these things felt connected to any of the others. They were arbitrary and baffling.

When I was finally able to get up and stay up, which must have been at least ten minutes later, the VC had gone. I began crawling back to the marquee, where I could still see the blurred shapes of my companions, and while I crawled I abstractly wondered why I'd been chosen as the punching bag. In fact, why have a punching bag at all? If they hadn't been planning on shooting us, it seemed unfair to have put me through all that pain.

now

There was another question that I should have been asking myself, but wasn't. In my now considerable experience, it's part of the strange way the brain works when reeling from a severe knock. You get hung up on the inconsequential mysteries and not the important ones.

The question I should have been asking was, why wasn't anyone coming to help me? If I'd been out for ten minutes, as I suspected I had, then they'd have had plenty of time to get their act together. But there they were, cowering behind the circle of candles, as much use as a bunch of waxworks.

"Help me," I slurred. "What's the matter with you?"

I tried to scowl at them, which was extremely difficult. Apart from being out of focus, I was seeing double, so I wasn't sure where the scowl should be directed.

"Keaty . . . help."

Hearing his name seemed to spur him into life. He took a few steps toward me, but even through my fucked-up eyes I could tell there was something weird about the way he was moving. It was as if he was scared of something over my shoulder.

My elbows gave way and my chin hit the ground. I dribbled to get the dust off my mouth. "Hurry, Keaty."

Then he was next to me, with someone else. Françoise, by the smell. They picked me up and pulled me back to the marquee, only strong enough to raise my arms and shoulders. When I passed over the candles, they were extinguished by my stomach. It was an extra bit of pain I really didn't need, but at least it startled me into thinking a bit more clearly. And a gulp of coconut beer was a boost too. It goes to vinegar pretty fast, and the stuff I gulped down was already on the turn. Sharp enough to make me wince and shut my eyes, and when I reopened them, my sight was back to normal.

At last I was able to see why everyone had turned into statues. Using Etienne and one of the bamboo poles that supported the canopy of sheets, I hauled myself up to a standing position. The VC hadn't felt that beating me up was a severe enough warning. They'd left us with a reminder, just to ram the point home.

Bullets had done nasty things to the rafters. Big holes, smashed skulls. All the bodies were naked, suggesting they'd been stripped before they were killed. Rigor mortis had given them strange positions. Sammy was lying on his back, but he must have been on his front when the stiffness set in, so he looked as if he were pushing upward against the weight of the sky. The German girl with the pretty laugh and long hair was on her side. She looked as if she were asking for a hug.

I don't see any need to describe them further than that. I've only described them as far as I have because it's relevant to what happened next.

To be confronted with such a sight would have been bad at the best of times. Directly following the scene with the dope guards would have made it worse. But to have been through all that while you were tripping—it would make anyone crazy.

"Right," Sal said, coming out of her trance, and she began to walk toward the heap of bodies. "I think we should get this cleaned up. It won't take long if we all . . ."

She paused. Her shoulders twitched as if she were slipping off a jacket, and she sat down with a thump.

"It won't take long. Come on, everyone. Let's get this mess cleaned up."

She stood up again.

"This mess. Such a mess."

The German guy was trapped beneath Zeph's chest, and his rigid arms were hooking the two of them together. Sal couldn't make him budge. We all watched in silence as she yanked uselessly at the German's legs.

"What a mess," Sal panted, and gave another hard tug.

Her grip slipped.

She fell backward, twisting as she fell, and landed on Sammy's corpse.

"Clumsy," she exclaimed brightly.

Then she started screaming and clawing at her cheeks. Sal's and Sammy's faces had made contact as she rolled off him, and Sammy had no lower jaw.

She screamed the way some people cry. People who never normally cry, so you know that the tears are coming from somewhere unthinkably deep inside. It was a sound that made my skin crawl, but for Bugs, it seemed to blow his mind.

I've thought a lot about what he did, and I've got two explanations. One is that he was angry with Sammy for having kissed Sal. The other is that he saw Sammy as the cause of Sal's misery, and he wanted to make the misery stop. Both explanations rely on Bugs being insane, but that's okay. He was.

He called Sal's name. Then he sobbed, only once, not loudly. Then he went over to the seating area and picked up one of Unhygienix's stubby cooking knives. Then he went over to Sammy and attacked him.

It began with kicking, which quickly became stabbing. In the chest, the groin, the arms, everywhere. Next he straddled the corpse and began tugging at the neck. Or that's what I thought he was doing. It wasn't completely clear through the shadows, and most of the view was blocked by Bugs's broad back. I only saw when he rose up. He'd cut Sammy's head off. Cut it off, and was swinging it by the hair.

And suddenly Jean had a knife and was cutting at the thin

German girl, slicing into her belly and pulling out her insides. Then Cassie joined them, hunched over Zeph, working on his thighs. Etienne vomited, and within seconds the corpses were swarmed.

Looking back, I know that we could have left at that moment. There were still people under the marquee—all the cooks, Jesse, Gregorio, and a few of the gardeners—but they wouldn't have tried to stop us. And I was physically able to leave. The scene in front of me had sent so much adrenaline pumping through my system that my battering was forgotten. I could have run a marathon if necessary, let alone crept into the darkness.

But we stayed put. We were transfixed by the dissection of the rafters. Every severed limb seemed to root me further to the spot.

friendly fire

I don't know how long the frenzy lasted. It could have been as long as half an hour. The cutters had to fret and struggle with some of the joints, twisting arms around until tendons gave way. But at some point, I noticed that the crowd had dispersed, sitting exhausted beside their handiwork or milling in the darkness. Only Moshe remained. He was concentrating on something small, a finger perhaps. It was while I was watching Moshe that I heard Sal's voice.

"Wait on Chaweng for three days," she read with numbing coldness. "If we haven't come back by then it means we made it to the beach. See you there? Richard."

The words took time for me to comprehend. Several seconds passed in which they meant nothing beyond random noises. But then, with a flash of understanding so tangible I almost saw it, their relevance became clear.

I turned. Sal was standing beside me, holding the piece of paper that the VC boss had left behind. It had passed me by, that piece of paper. Deafened, pistol-whipped, I had missed its importance.

". . . See you there," she repeated flatly. ". . . Richard."

Outside the marquee, the surgeons stirred. Some appeared, nudging past Keaty, who was staring at me with a peculiarly blank expression.

"Richard?" one of them whispered. "Richard brought the people here?" It was a girl, but she was so stained with red and black that I couldn't place her.

More arrived, quietly surrounding me, shutting off Keaty and Françoise. Desperately I began to search for a face I knew. I wanted to appeal to someone, plead a case. But the more cutters that arrived, the more anonymous they became. Under their shifting feet, candles were kicked over. Darkness spread, features melted. When Etienne vanished, I was alone with strangers.

"Jean!" I shouted.

The strangers laughed.

"Moshe! Cassie! I know you're here! . . . Sal! *Sal!*"

But even she had gone. Where she'd been, a squat creature hissed at me. "After Tet, life will be back to normal."

"Sal, *please,*" I said, and a needle jabbed into my leg. I looked down. I'd been stabbed. Not deeply, but somehow that scared me more. I cried out and was stabbed again. The same pressure. Half an inch into the skin, this time my arm, the next time my chest.

For a moment I was too shocked to do anything but stupidly wipe at the blood running down my stomach. Then terror bubbled up in me, and when it reached my throat I started screaming. I also tried to fight. I threw a punch at the nearest face but it landed poorly and glanced harmlessly off the person's cheekbone. The next punch I threw was blocked, and my wrists were held.

I pleaded, "Don't," and began spinning. Fear gave me strength and I managed to wrench myself free of the hold. But every time I spun away from the knives, I was simply cut from behind. I could feel by the impact of the blows that the stabs were getting worse. No longer piercing but slicing. A different pain, less acute. Infinitely more alien and alarming.

"Not like that," I sobbed.

Something slippery was wrapped around my neck. Intestines. Mine, I thought, my brain convulsing with fright, and tore them off. The strangers laughed and more objects were thrust at me. A ragged hand that pawed my chest. An ear clamped to the side of my head.

Feeling my knees about to buckle, I bunched up my arms. A last time, I looked up at the howling figures and their knives. I called for Sal again. I asked her to make them stop. I told her that I was very sorry for whatever I'd done, but I didn't know what it was anymore. I only knew that I'd never wanted to do anything bad.

Finally I called out for Daffy Duck.

Suddenly, in the whirling faces, I saw one I recognized.

but nothing

The stabbing continued, but no longer hurt. The faces continued whirling, but the face I knew remained constant. I could talk to it calmly, and it could talk back.

"Daffy," I said. "This is fucked."

"Yeah, GI." He smiled. "Beaucoup bad shit."

"Fragged by my own side."

"Happens all the time."

A blade punctured my top lip. "It doesn't mean anything, right?"

"Doesn't mean much."

"Never should have been here. That's all." I sighed as my legs collapsed and I fell down to the palm-leaf carpet. "Jesus, this is a nasty way to die. At least it's ending."

"Ending?" Daffy shook his head. "It can't end now."

"Can't?"

"Come on, Rich. Think. Think how it ought to end."

"Ought to . . ."

"A flat roof, a panicking crowd, not enough room on the . . ."

". . . Last chopper out."

"That's the boy."

"Evacuation."

"Every time."

Daffy was gone. The knives had stopped. One of the cutters had started twisting, fumbling at her belly, and another was toppling sideways, flailing out with his arms.

I looked around and saw Jed standing beside me. And beside him, Keaty, Etienne, and Françoise. The four of them carried fishing spears, points fanning outward. On the ground, Bugs sat with his arms crossed, fresh blood streaming into his lap. Moshe leaned against one of the bamboo posts, also bleeding, sucking air through clenched teeth, and clutching his ribs.

"You all keep back!" Jed yelled. He reached down, lifted my arm over his shoulders, and dragged me up. *"Keep back!"*

Bugs closed his eyes and slumped forward.

"But," said Sal. "But . . ." She took a step in our direction and Jed pushed his spear deep into her stomach. Immediately he pulled it back. Sal remained standing, swaying as the point exited.

"Back!" Jed yelled again. *"All of you keep back!"*

And amazingly, they all did. Though we were outnumbered and they could have easily prevented us if they'd wanted to, they let us go. I don't think it was because of Sal, who had closed her eyes and couldn't seem to catch her breath. It was because they were tired. Their slack arms and glazed eyes told me as much. Tired of everything. Beaucoup bad shit, too beaucoup.

game over

strange but true

I feel I should provide an account of how we all got back home. But it's going to be a brief account because the story is over. This is just an epilogue.

We talked a lot. That's what I remember most about the journey; the talking. It's stuck in my memory because it seems so unexpected. You'd imagine silence, all of us withdrawn into our private horrors. And the first part of the journey, the nighttime trek to the raft, *was* silent. But it was only because we were afraid of being heard by the guards. As soon as we'd pushed off and were on our way, we opened our mouths and never shut them. The funny thing is, I can't really remember what we talked about. Maybe because we talked about everything, maybe because we talked about nothing.

Because of my condition, I wasn't much help, but the others took a paddling-and-swimming rotation in pairs. I kept getting shivering attacks. When they hit, all I could do was curl up and shake. They'd only last a couple of minutes, but Jed thought it better to keep me out of the sea in case I drowned. I'd already nearly drowned once, when we were swimming across the lagoon on the way to the caves and the chimney. In any case, the salt water was murder on my stab wounds, superficial as they were.

We didn't have to paddle for long. A few hours after dawn broke, a fishing boat came to check us out. And after a bit of banter, they towed us back to Koh Samui. It was extraordinary. They didn't seem more than cheerfully curious about who we were and what we were doing on a raft in the Gulf of Thailand. The only thing that raised an eyebrow was me and my cuts. By which I mean, a raised eyebrow was the full extent of their reaction. We were just another bunch of weird *falang,* doing the weird kind of things that *falang* do.

On Koh Samui, we ran into a couple of problems because we had no money. But we were travelers, so it wasn't that big a deal. Keaty and I sold our watches. Then, to everyone's surprise, Etienne stole a wallet. Bit of a dark horse, Etienne. Some dickhead had left his room key under his T-shirt while he went for a dip. We stole a long-sleeved shirt and a pair of trousers, which I needed to hide my cuts. The cash was enough to get us all back to the mainland, eat, *and* buy Keaty's watch back.

From Koh Samui to Surat Thani, and the bus ride to Bangkok, for which Keaty had to resell his watch. And still we were talking, irritating our fellow passengers, keeping them awake.

Back in the city, the only thing left to do was to call home. We all took turns in an air-con phone booth on the Koh Sanh Road. The last thing I want to do is lapse into sentimentality at this late stage, but we were all crying by the time we'd hung up. We must have made a pretty stupid sight, me in my blood-flecked new shirt, and the others in their rags, all in floods of tears.

Seventy-two hours later we had airline tickets and replacement passports from our respective embassies. I had my last shivering attack getting cigarettes in the Bangkok duty-free. As soon as we boarded the plane, I felt okay.

At this exact moment, I'm sitting in front of a word processor. At this exact moment, I'm typing this sentence. At this exact moment, it's a year and a month since I flew out of Thailand.

I never saw Etienne and Françoise again. One day I will. It's going to be by chance but I know it's going to happen, because the world is a small place, and Europe is even smaller.

I see Keaty and Jed all the time. Like the talking, it's another thing you wouldn't expect. By rights we should have drifted apart, unable to deal with our shared history. But we didn't. We're good friends.

So I see Keaty and Jed all the time, and they see each other even more. This is strange but true: they both work at the same place. Different firms, same building. Stranger still, they got the jobs without knowing the other was there. And even stranger still, it sort of ties in with the way they stayed at the same Indonesian guest house all those years ago; the one that Keaty burned down. They haven't burned down their office yet, which would be the icing on the cake.

Actually Keaty hates the job (admin shit), so it might actually happen. I won't mention the name of the firm in case it does.

What else.

About three months ago, maybe four, I was flicking through Ceefax when I read, "Briton caught smuggling in Malaysia." A few nights later, I saw Cassie on the news. She was sitting in the back of an Isuzu van, flanked by policemen in khaki uniforms. The van was outside a crummy-looking courthouse. She'd been busted at Kuala Lumpur airport with over a pound of heroin, and the word is, she's going to be the first Western smuggler to be executed in *six years*. The BBC reporter managed to get a microphone to her before she was driven away, and she said, "Tell my parents I'm sorry I haven't written in a while."

Poor Cassie. She was probably trying to fund her flight home. Her mum and dad, who look like decent types, are appealing for clemency and appearing on TV. But they're wasting their time. She's dead meat. Or toast.

But the point is that Cassie got off the island, so at least some of the others must have too. I'm curious to know which ones. I like to think that Gregorio and Jesse made it, and Unhygienix and Ella. I'm sure they did. I'm also sure that Bugs died, and I'd like to think Sal died with him. Not out of maliciousness. I just can't stand the idea that she might turn up on my doorstep someday.

As for me . . .

I'm fine. I have bad dreams, but I never saw Mister Duck again. I play video games. I smoke a little dope. I got my thousand-yard stare. I carry a lot of scars.

I like the way that sounds.

I carry a *lot* of scars.

Alex Garland is the author of *The Tesseract*. He lives in London.

Praise for *The Tesseract*
also by Alex Garland

"Remarkable . . . Garland is a master at capturing that elastic moment before tragedy rips through the surface of ordinary life. Even in moments of explosion, he catches every contradictory thought of terror and compassion."
—*The Christian Science Monitor*

"Alex Garland works words the way a spider spins webs. Interweaving disparate story lines, he builds suspenseful narrative tapestries out of seemingly unrelated events. An expertly hewn page-turner . . . gripping."
—*Time Out New York*

"As thoroughly assured a performance as *The Beach* . . . Mr. Garland not only does a completely convincing job of sketching in these characters' lives in a series of quick, deftly drawn strokes, but he also fluently cuts back and forth between their stories, building suspense the way a film editor does, even as he is tying his disparate heroes' tales together with dozens of overlapping motifs. All those small details . . . come together to give the reader a mosaiclike view of Manila. Mr. Garland is a natural at orchestrating violent set pieces with deadpan panache, but he also proves in this novel that he can create odd, oddly sympathetic people with unexpected inner lives. [*The Tesseract*] reconfirms his prodigious and diverse talents."
—Michiko Kakutani, *The New York Times*

"Inventive and compelling . . . [Garland's] brain beats with the energy of ideas and the courage to bridge the big questions." —*Los Angeles Times*

"Complex and intriguing . . . This subtle fiction has nothing to do with the higher maths and a lot to do with good old-fashioned storytelling about big, old-fashioned themes—the mysteries of love and violence and death, the strange workings of fate. Mr. Garland tells a good, straightforward story, and he writes with great polish and superior control; so much control, in fact, that, like his characters, you don't really realize what's going on until it's too late. *The Tesseract* marks a significant departure from, and growth since, *The Beach.* Like a tesseract, it is composed of three dimensions that, in the end, inevitably imply a larger and more significant fourth . . . each story is delicately observed and ingeniously linked to the others . . . "
—*New York Observer*

"The tales converge in a climax that will leave you . . . impressed with the author's skill . . . a steam engine of a narrative."
—*Newsweek*

"A novel that bristles with suspense . . . Garland's skill at creating tension keeps the novel driving forward with the force of a thriller . . . mature, intelligent, and rewarding."
—*People*